ABOUT BEING A SHERLOCKIAN

60 ESSAYS CELEBRATING
THE SHERLOCK HOLMES COMMUNITY

ABOUT BEING A SHERLOCKIAN

60 ESSAYS CELEBRATING THE SHERLOCK HOLMES COMMUNITY

EDITED BY
CHRISTOPHER REDMOND

WILDSIDE PRESS

CONTENTS

His Latest Bows

The Book-Case of Sherlock Holmes

INTRODUCTION

CHRISTOPHER REDMOND

Most of my correspondence these days is electronic (and all of the essays in this volume, save two, came to me electronically) and I often find myself dictating messages using the voice recognition software provided in my iPhone. Often it works well, but there are a few less common words that it seems utterly unable to learn, including, wouldn't you know, "Sherlockian".

Probably most iPhone users don't need it regularly, but "Sherlockian" is a genuine word, beyond doubt. Noun and adjective, it's been in the *Oxford English Dictionary*'s database for decades, with the earliest citation dating from 1903. At the beginning it simply meant something like "characteristic of Sherlock Holmes", so that one could speak of an investigator's "Sherlockian methods", but as time went on, and the original tales were joined on the bookshelves by the works of Starrett, Baring-Gould, and the rest, it came into broader use. "Sherlockian" as an adjective now means "about Sherlock Holmes", and as a noun, we can provisionally say, "someone who likes Sherlock Holmes".

It may be dangerous to go further. If we do, we may have to define "Sherlock Holmes", and while that name, too, is listed in the *OED*, its meaning may have changed over time, as dictionary words do change. Everybody acknowledges that Sherlock Holmes was created by Arthur Conan Doyle (1859-1930) in four novels and 56 short stories published between 1887 and 1927; everybody accepts the literary figure from those pages as the, or at least a, genuine or "canonical" Holmes. A now long-gone generation of fans accepted actor-playwright William Gillette as the genuine article when he trod the stage (up to the remarkable age of 79) in a melodrama loosely based on a few of Doyle's stories. Connoisseurs also tend to see the genuine Sherlock Holmes in later actors: Eille Norwood, Douglas Wilmer, even Jeremy Brett in 41 television episodes from the 1980s, carefully crafted and for the most part faithful to the Doyle originals. But what about that sharp-nosed fellow in the fedora, calling himself Sherlock Holmes and pursuing Nazi spies in several black-and-white B films in the 1940s? What about the young man with the Belstaff coat, the cellphone and the shock of black hair, proclaiming himself a high-functioning sociopath and making a manic speech at his friend Watson's wedding? Are those characters Sherlock Holmes too, and are their admirers Sherlockians?

We have to say yes, or we shall incur the charge of "gatekeeping", which is metaphorically used nowadays to mean an assumed right to decide who is, and who isn't, a member of a cultural group, including a fandom. (Is the Sherlock Holmes community a fandom? More definitions; let's not go there.) "Gatekeeper" is one of the worst names someone can be called in a fandom context.

For that reason alone, it is safest not to exclude anyone from the cachet of being a Sherlockian. Besides, why on earth would somebody want to exclude an enthusiast, even an enthusiast with what seems like odd preferences? If the proponents of Tunalock (Holmes and Watson are fishes) or Farmlock (cows), the fans who post pictures of Martin Freeman on Tumblr and the devotees of crossover fanfic, want to claim the name of Sherlockians, they are welcome to it. To be sure, there might be demographic and cultural differences between them and the average member of the Baker Street Irregulars—but, as several of the authors in this book testify, many such differences melt away in the presence of a common passion for Sherlock Holmes.

Unsurprisingly, the authors here are unanimously enthusiastic about the Sherlockian life. It's not the sort of activity one would carry on for long without enjoying it. Still, there must be negatives at times, not least because of those potential differences in age, background and cultural attitude, and one or two of the essays do hint at some teething troubles when a stranger first appeared in the midst of a Sherlockian crowd. It goes mostly unremarked here that Sherlockians tend to be erudite and sensitive people, with perhaps a greater tendency to depression and social anxiety than the population at large. It would have done no harm to shed a little gentle light on those difficulties, and I did hope to include an essay in this volume by a *former* Sherlockian who left out of unhappiness, but that attempt failed.

There are no demographic statistics about our diverse tribe, not only for lack of a definition but also because no membership registration is required. "If one calls oneself a Sherlockian, one is," one veteran of the community told me recently. Another well-connected participant suggested that the criterion is "passion for the character or era" (presumably the Victorian and Edwardian period in which the original stories are set). A third defined the word as "someone who likes Sherlock Holmes and engages with other people who like the same". In the past, being "a Sherlockian" often involved being a member of a local Sherlock Holmes society, but in the internet era, even that affiliation is optional.

The Baker Street Babes, a highly influential ginger group in the Sherlockian world over the past decade, proclaim on their website and elsewhere that "All Holmes is good Holmes." The group's founder, Kristina Manente, says the motto was originally "All Holmes, all the time," and isn't too sure how it changed, but both would seem to apply.

The present volume, then, takes a fairly wide view of who is a Sherlockian, and gives 60 self-identified Sherlockians an opportunity to say what they do and why they do it. Some of the essays are more personal than others, and none purport to give a complete view of the theory and practice of Sherlockiana. Indeed, the book as a whole, with all 60 fragments of the mosaic, still does not do that, because every Sherlockian is an individual, sometimes strikingly so. Some segments of the community (movement?) are regrettably unrepresented here: there is little about Sherlockian tourism or fanart, there is barely a mention of the booming Sherlockian culture of Japan, there is little about how much Sherlockian enthusiasm overlaps with such related fandoms as *Star Trek*, *Dr. Who*, or detective fiction at large.

Perhaps most surprisingly, the book pays only modest attention to the "Great Game" of pseudo-scholarship which was the central activity of organized Sherlockian culture for several decades. The idea here, dating back to founding fathers Msgr. Ronald Knox and Sir Sydney Roberts, is to take the canonical texts not as pleasant tales written by a master story-teller, but as historical documents, and see where the rigorous research leads. Some Sherlockians of earlier generations were masters of such work; I myself was captured at an early age by a 1963 essay by Edward F. Clark, Jr., "Study of an Untold Tale", and have not yet been altogether released from its spell. Such game-playing is not extinct, but there are so many other things for Sherlockians to do nowadays, and it has been partly pushed aside by a growing interest in seriously exploring the flavour and minutiae of British Victorian life, which many of the more scholarly Sherlockians love to expound.

The 60 essays that make up this collection mostly address the Sherlockian activity of the present day; this is not a book of history, though a few of the authors include their own memories of decades past. Its topics range from old-fashioned formal dinners, such as those of the Baker Street Irregulars, to the shenanigans that take place during weekend conventions ("cons"); from radio drama to rare-book collecting; from Yorkshire to Calcutta; from religion to sexuality (although that is not so long a trip as some people may think); from charity work to medical practice. And over and over again, the authors begin by reflecting on books, and end by expressing their gratitude for friendship, since the Sherlockian experience is inescapably about both.

I am very grateful to all 60 contributors (and doubly so to the few who took on this challenge on very short notice). I hope they have not been too deeply offended by my tinkering with their work, or by my editorial asperity as deadlines grew close. My thanks go, as well, to many well-wishers; to Carla Coupe and her colleagues at Wildside Press; and now to those who will read and, I hope, enjoy the essays in this book. Perhaps most of the readers will be those who are already Sherlockians, but if the book should fall into the hands of someone who is not, I think it will give a very appealing picture of the endless riches to be found in What It Is We Do.

No royalties from the sale of this volume will be paid to either the authors or the editor. Royalties earned will, with the cooperation of the publisher, be turned over in their entirety to the John H. Watson Fund, which subsidizes the expenses of travel to New York for the annual BSI weekend for those who would be unable to make the trip otherwise. For many, that January get-together is of the essence of being a Sherlockian. For others, of course, the fireside, or the library, or a pleasant pub is the location of choice. There are many ways of being a Sherlockian; here you may read about some of them.

Christopher Redmond is the author of *A Sherlock Holmes Handbook, In Bed with Sherlock Holmes*, and other books, and editor of the 2016 anthology *About Sixty*. He was founder of the website Sherlockian.net, and is a Baker Street Irregular and a member of the Bootmakers of Toronto.

THE ADVENT OF SHERLOCK HOLMES

THE ADVENTURE OF
THE ADULT DETECTIVE

TRACY J. REVELS

I met Sherlock Holmes one summer, when I was alone. Not technically alone, of course, as I was eleven years old and resided with my maternal grandparents and my mother. But as an only child, on a farm in the North Florida countryside, I might as well have been the sole kid on the planet. My nearest classmate lived ten miles away, and none of our hardworking parents had time for playdates. Cell phones and computers didn't exist, and the rotary phone was off limits. In the months between classes I glimpsed my peers only at church on Sunday. My family assumed that I would entertain myself. I was fast outgrowing Lincoln Logs, stuffed animals, and even Barbie dolls, so my solace was found, increasingly, in books.

I had always loved to read, and if my world was void of real-life playmates, it was filled with fictional companions. I'd worked my way through Dr. Seuss and the various childhood classics. Exploring my inclination toward mysteries, I devoured several volumes of Nancy Drew, the Hardy Boys, and Encyclopedia Brown. I found them all to be terrible drips. Call me a cynic, but even at eleven I doubted that anyone would allow teenagers—no matter how clever—the latitude to chase down crooks or give grownups a sharp comeuppance for their criminal foibles. I felt that I needed an adult detective, not a boy or girl wonder. I tried an Agatha Christie novel, but found it cold and lifeless, too much tea and talking. I wanted bloody murder and action. (I'll freely admit I was a weird kid.)

I can still see the late afternoon sunlight filtering through the lace curtains as I sat down in that well of warmth between the bed and the oak dresser, opening a book that my aunt, an English instructor, had passed along. It was a high school "reader," a collection of short stories presumably far above my comprehension level. I'd never won a foot race, and I was always picked last for any ball team, but I had already established a reputation as the middle school champion of the reading contest. I knew I could read as well as an eighth grader, and I was ready to tackle the next level. The very first story came with an odd picture: a silhouette of a woman on a bed, rising up, screaming, presumably fighting for her life. Above the illustration was the title "The Adventure of the Speckled Band."

Within a few pages, I decided I liked Mr. Holmes. Here was an adult detective who not only heard his client's case, but confronted a snarling stepfather, straightened a steel poker, and traipsed blithely over a gloomy country estate despite the baboon and cheetah lurking in the shadows. About the time Holmes and Watson settled in for the midnight watch in Miss Stoner's bedroom, it occurred to me that something might be able to come slithering down the bell-rope onto the pillow. *Could it be a snake?* I wondered. And then, just a few paragraphs later, I learned it was the "deadliest snake in India" that had killed Miss Stoner. I did a mental victory dance. I had solved the case with Holmes, like a silent, ghostly partner at his side. I had found my adult detective, and much to my delight the story ended with a note informing the reader that there were many more tales of Sherlock Holmes.

I had to find them.

I became obsessed with Sherlock Holmes. I tracked down a few more stories in other old collections that were moldy from long years on the shelves. Once school resumed, I checked out everything I could find in the library (which wasn't much). It was my personal mystery and quest: how many Sherlock Holmes stories were there, and how could I get my greedy hands on them? Keep in mind that these were the days before Google, and nobody at home or at school shared my enthusiasm. I was in high school before I understood the concept of the Canon. Even when I acquired my two-volume Baring-Gould, I was not satisfied. I had stumbled upon the idea of pastiches, thanks mainly to *The Seven-Per-Cent Solution*, which I picked up because of the artistic rendition of Holmes on the cover. Learning that other authors had continued the adventures made the game even more exciting. Every visit to Valdosta (a town some 30 miles away, the closest place one could purchase reading material beyond a newspaper or a copy of *TV Guide*) meant that I would beg and plead to go to the bookstore, no matter our errand. My time in the store was usually limited to five minutes, and I became a master at spotting a pipe or deerstalker on a dust jacket.

Thanks to being in the high school band—and thanks to the band frequently disembarking from buses at the nearest mall for dinner while travelling—my access to bookstores and my collection of pastiches grew. I also established a tradition when I was sixteen: Christmas had to include a Sherlock Holmes book. No substitute would be accepted. College in Tallahassee meant free time and the availability of several used bookstores, and once I was on my own, eBay and Amazon were there to tempt me with books that had long been beyond my reach.

My Sherlockian collection has grown substantially now that I am gainfully employed and no one has the right to demand "What on earth do you need that for?" One large bookshelf in my office is filled with books on Holmes, as are two more at my residence. Along with books are prints, mugs, dolls, magnets, DVDs, ornaments, and just about anything that can bear the distinctive profile of the great detective.

For many years I pursued my hobby in solitude. I learned of the Baker Street Irregulars, but the chance of ever coming to the notice of such an august body was nil. As I became more familiar with the internet, I began to wonder if a scion society might be located anywhere within driving distance. I happened upon Classic Specialties, a web-based purveyor of

Sherlockian materials, and wrote an inquiry to the owners (the kind and wonderful couple, Joel and Carolyn Senter). They, in turn, passed my information along to David Milner, of the Survivors of the Gloria Scott, who called me up with his best Sherlock Holmes impression and invited me to the next monthly meeting in Greenville, South Carolina. I was equally thrilled and terrified. What if they had an exam? What if there were requirements for membership, such as scholarly publications? Would they admit a 30-ish woman to their club, which sounded pretty much all-male? I almost chickened out.

I'm glad I didn't. There was a quiz (I aced it, whew!) and the mood was playful, not intimidating. The members, while all male, were diverse enough in education, employment, and life experiences to make for interesting conversations, and eventually more women joined the club. I began offering historical articles and silly stories for our newsletter, and radio plays for our yearly gala. In due course I was invested with the nom "The Daintiest Thing Under a Bonnet." The Survivors have (sadly) declined in number due to deaths and relocations, but our meeting at a Chinese restaurant remains a monthly treat.

Sherlock Holmes also became a part of my teaching. I am a professor of history at Wofford College, a small liberal arts school in Spartanburg, South Carolina. One of my courses is Humanities 101, a class in which we ask our students to read, think, and write. We are expected to find something that will engage our students in debates about big ideas. It occurred to me that the Canon is all about some very big ideas: logic, reason, the power of the mind, the conflict between good and evil, duty, courage, and, perhaps most importantly, the meaning of friendship. I began offering "The Game Is Afoot: Sherlock Holmes Humanities." Several years later, my work came to the attention of the Beacon Society, and in 2009 I received the Beacon Award for my efforts in introducing Sherlock Holmes to young people. I love this class, for not only does it give me a good excuse to re-read most of the Sacred Writings, it also allows me to share my love of Holmes with a generation that has been introduced to him in a very different way, via *Sherlock*, *Elementary*, and the Guy Ritchie films starring Robert Downey, Jr. and Jude Law. Last year, I added a new class to my repertoire, teaching an "Introduction to Sherlock Holmes" in the Lifetime Learning program at Wofford, which is designed for retirees. I would leave my Humanities class of 18-year-olds and head to my LL class for 70-year-olds. It was a wonderful journey.

Sherlock Holmes also led me somewhere unexpected. One summer, as part of a student-professor research program, I decided to try my luck at writing a pastiche novel. I'd been struck by how often clients called Holmes a "wizard." What if they were right? What if Sherlock Holmes did have some kind of magical birthright, one he had rejected because he valued logic and reason above any supernatural gifts? And what if the world Holmes had exited, the world of Shadows, now threatened our own? How would Holmes respond? One of the first short stories collections I'd acquired as a student was Isaac Asimov's edited volume *Sherlock Holmes Through Time and Space*, so I was comfortable with an alternative Holmes.

While it's certainly not everyone's cup of tea (and I respect that), I've always believed that the idea of Sherlock Holmes is more important than his physical existence in the realms of Baker Street. Be true to that idea and all else can bend.

So I spent a summer happily researching strange things like Spring-Heeled Jack, the ravens of the Tower of London, and Highgate Cemetery. My work became *Shadowfall*, and much to my astonishment, it was accepted for publication by MX Press. Two more volumes, *Shadowblood* and *Shadowwraith*, have followed. I've spent many delightful hours wandering around an even more dangerous and deadly London with my strange Holmes and Watson. The work allows me to unite a number of my passions: Holmes, history, and mankind's dark mythologies.

So why have I given so much of my life to Holmes? Why is this mild-mannered historian (whose academic works are all based in Florida history) so devoted to the most famous resident of 221B? Why do I design Sherlockian quilts and bags and even a beloved cloth bunny called Sherlock Hares? I can only suppose it is because Sherlock Holmes was there for me when I was lonesome and needy. In a moment when I felt like nothing on the vast shelves was interesting, when my mind had grown beyond my grade level, the master detective appeared. I solved "The Speckled Band," but I'll freely admit I never solved another case. I was content to follow along and marvel at Holmes's abilities, for my poor wits could never equal his.

And as I grew, I felt Sherlock Holmes was teaching me something very important about life. People who seemed to have it all—money, good looks, high status—had very little compared to an individual who wielded the power of the mind. The mind was what mattered. No matter how many times I was teased, or hurt, or rejected by my peers, I always could go back to the adventures of the one character who mattered not because he was handsome, powerful, or popular, but because he *thought* so hard! All his adventures were, in essence, the product of his brain. And while I possessed nothing even close to Holmes's powers of deduction, or his courage, his wit, or his way with a disguise, I did possess a brain that I could work with, challenge, and train. In Sherlock Holmes I found a lifelong mentor and friend. My life is so much richer for having known him since I was eleven and alone.

Tracy J. Revels (Spartanburg, South Carolina) is a professor of history at Wofford College. She is a member of the Survivors of the Gloria Scott of Greenville, South Carolina, and the author of a series of supernatural Sherlockian pastiches.

THE ADVENTURE OF
THE GREEK INTERPOLATOR

CONSTANTINE KAOUKAKIS

In January, on my way to New York to attend my first BSI weekend, a young man sitting beside me on the plane asked me what a Sherlockian was. How does one explain to the uninitiated what it means to be a Sherlockian? It's a strange concept and difficult to make clear.

Being a Sherlockian is a way of life and a philosophy. Some might even call it a religion since the tales of Sherlock Holmes are referred to as the Canon. Reading and studying these sacred writings alter one's perspective of the world and oneself. For many, just the utterance of the name Sherlock Holmes releases endorphins and brings a natural high—the great detective is a seven-per-cent solution, and we have withdrawal symptoms when we are denied our fix.

Who can become a Sherlockian? Anyone who reads, studies, and applies his teachings can achieve this feat. The great detective constantly reminds his friend Watson, "You know my methods. Apply them." However, being a Sherlockian is more than just applying the master's techniques. This is a journey of self-discovery, and for me, one that has been lifelong.

Holmes is part of our collective unconscious: every generation reinvents the great detective, from the Victorian period to our contemporary one. From William Gillette through Basil Rathbone and Jeremy Brett to today's Benedict Cumberbatch, each incarnation caters to the needs of an era. There is a Sherlock Holmes for everyone because he is interpreted by each person differently. We each take what we need from the detective. When William Gillette asked whether the script could see Holmes married, Arthur Conan Doyle replied, "You may marry him, murder him, or do what you like to him." As Sherlockians, we recreate Sherlock Holmes in our own image.

For me, Sherlock Holmes has been surrogate father, therapist, and friend. He influences all aspects of my life, whether personal or professional. I lost my father when I was still in high school. Becoming a Sherlockian gave me the courage to deal with this loss. It is no surprise that many Sherlockians dream of being the great detective. I remember, from a young age, dressing up and pretending to be Sherlock Holmes. In fact, I used his methods to solve mundane mysteries in my school and neighbourhood.

This enabled me to solve problems by using reasoning. Logic became my constant companion.

Being a Sherlockian is a code of conduct, a part of my identity. Sherlock Holmes has been a mentor in my life and has given me strength and hope. Whenever I had to face crises, being a Sherlockian has brought a sense of security. I apply the methods of the great detective to solve any problem I face. During my darkest days, my association with Sherlock Holmes enabled me to defeat my many Moriartys. For me, he represents my potential.

As a Sherlockian, I have been able to associate with unique and talented people who have inspired me. However, here is a paradox. One aspect of Sherlock Holmes that attracted me was his anti-social behaviour: he prefers to be alone. Many Sherlockians mimic this behaviour. Although most of us are introverts, we enjoy meeting each other and socializing in honour of the great detective. As my friend and fellow Sherlockian Charles Prepolec once told me, "Sherlockians are our tribe." Because of our shared interest in the great detective, we are connected hives. Each connection helps improve ourselves. It is difficult to explain to a non-Sherlockian what the relationships between Sherlockians mean. All we need to do is utter a famous phrase from the Canon, and we instantly communicate a multitude of things. Of course, our allusions are not limited to the Canon because we make references to movies, television shows, pastiches, and other media associated with Sherlock Holmes. The admiration for the great detective gives us a shared consciousness.

Sherlock Holmes is my safe place. He connects me to others and keeps me sane. Being a Sherlockian gives me courage to be who I am. The great detective radiates self-confidence. He is a good role model because he does not care what others think of him. In situations when everyone disagrees with him, he sticks to what he believes to be right. He feels comfortable with who he is. This unconventional figure has inspired me to be accepting of myself regardless of what others think of me. His eccentricities appeal to me because I am eccentric. This has allowed me to accept myself as the unique individual I am.

My childhood admiration for the detective has become a lifelong obsession. I first became fascinated with Sherlock Holmes from the age of twelve by watching television reruns of Ronald Howard's *Sherlock Holmes* series. The next step was the silver screen incarnation of Basil Rathbone. This prompted me to borrow *The Hound of the Baskervilles* from the school library. Having thoroughly enjoyed Arthur Conan Doyle's gothic treat, I had to purchase my own Sherlock Holmes novel, so I bought *The Sign of Four*. My obsession compelled me to read the novel countless times. Like most Sherlockians, I purchased a deerstalker: the ultimate symbol of the great detective. Then, one day, I heard that someone was forming a Sherlock Holmes society in Montréal, my home town; I was ecstatic and quickly joined.

When I moved to Edmonton, I searched for a Sherlock Holmes society. Much to my chagrin, I discovered that there wasn't an active society. Therefore, I took it upon myself to start one and founded The Wisteria

Lodgers, the Sherlock Holmes Society of Edmonton, in 2012. This has fostered enriching friendships with unique individuals. Every month, we meet at a coffee shop to discuss anything and everything Sherlockian. The singular bond that exists among the members of a Sherlockian group has allowed a group of introverts to socially interact. After every meeting, I feel invigorated and rejuvenated. As a Sherlockian, I have a sense of belonging.

Although I knew there were many societies and Sherlockians out there, I had not really interacted with any. I was contacted by the Bootmakers of Toronto, the largest Sherlockian group in Canada. This ultimately led to the Wisteria Lodgers becoming a scion of the Bootmakers. Once again, Sherlockians were making connections.

However, the most important Sherlockian society in the world is the Baker Street Irregulars in New York. Therefore, I had to make the pilgrimage and attend the famous BSI weekend, held in January corresponding to Sherlock Holmes's accepted birthday. The connections I made there were astounding. I had the privilege and honour of meeting the most incredibly talented and diverse set of characters in the world: from all walks of life, different ages, creeds, and races. I felt like a fanboy meeting his heroes, but instead of capes and tights, they wore deerstalkers.

In 2016, I took part in the International Sherlock Holmes Exhibition at Telus World of Science in Edmonton. I had the honour of portraying Sherlock Holmes at the exhibition, especially in a replica of 221B Baker Street. Once I donned the deerstalker and Inverness coat, and held the pipe and magnifying glass, I was transformed into the immortal detective. Visitors came from around the world to experience the world that Arthur Conan Doyle invented. Because of my stint as the great detective, I am recognized by people on the street as far away as Calgary. CBC radio even interviewed me at the opening of the exhibition, and I have an entry on the *No Place Like Holmes* website because of my impersonation. I cannot express the thrill of portraying one the most influential figures in my life. In a way, being a Sherlockian is role-playing because one is playing "the game".

As a teacher, I admire Sherlock Holmes's teacher-student relationship with Watson, his greatest student. I find that Sherlock Holmes has influenced my teaching. He continues to teach me new things about myself and the world around me. As he informs his student in "The Red Circle", "Education never ends, Watson. It is a series of lessons with the greatest for the last." This means using minute details to uncover the whole: "From a drop of water a logician could infer the possibility of an Atlantic or a Niagara without having seen or heard of one or the other" (A Study in Scarlet). I teach students to observe their world, not merely to see it. By doing so, "the facts slowly evolve before [their] own eyes, and the mystery clears gradually away as each new discovery furnishes a step which leads on to the complete truth" ("The Engineer's Thumb").

That is what being a Sherlockian means to me: finding the truth. As I am writing this, I am surrounded by a myriad of Sherlock Holmes collectibles: posters of illustrations from the Strand magazine, the "Abominable Bride" calendar, statues of Sherlock Holmes, a deerstalker, a meerschaum pipe, action figures, and other idols in my shrine to the great detective.

They reflect who I am. This strange hobby defines who I am. It allows me to see the world from different perspectives. Like the great detective, I am unorthodox and contemplative. Being a Sherlockian is knowing how to play the game well, because life is the ultimate game.

Constantine Kaoukakis (Edmonton, Alberta) has taught English literature, ESL, ancient, modern, and koine Greek, Latin, ancient Greek and Roman history at the university and high school levels. He is founder of The Wisteria Lodgers, and an editor of *OnSpec*, a magazine of science fiction, fantasy, and horror.

THE AFFAIR OF THE
RED-AND-BLACK VOLUMES

SUSAN SMITH-JOSEPHY

I'll always be a Sherlockian. Or, rather, a Sherlock Holmesian.

The first time I read the Sherlock Holmes stories I was ten years old, at home, bored, having read all my books many times, not to mention all my library books and my mother's library books. My parents suggested I read Sherlock Holmes and gave me the two volumes from one of our family bookshelves.

The physical heft of the books intimidated me a bit. I opened a red and black hardcover, with staid silver wording on the side. "*Sir Arthur Conan Doyle, The Complete Sherlock Holmes, 1, Doubleday,*" it said. It started with an introduction by Christopher Morley. No illustrations, I noted. Surely this would be terribly boring.

I couldn't have been more wrong.

Almost 50 years later, time has done little to diminish the physical quality of those two volumes. They are still in good shape, bindings all firm, pages clear and crisp. The good quality has held up well despite hundreds of readings and rough handling.

The content has held up, as well, of course. In fact, in my opinion the stories reveal more of their wit and brilliance each time I read them.

I became immediately transfixed by the stories and the characters. Transported by the words to London, I felt that I was going home again as we'd only immigrated to Canada from the United Kingdom four years earlier.

I always did like the logical aspect of Sherlock Holmes's deductions, but that wasn't the main appeal for me. Three things I loved about the books kept me coming back over and over.

The first thing I adored was the cozy aspect of 221B Baker Street. The sameness of the rooms gave a stability to the stories, no matter how mysterious or harrowing. I enjoyed hearing about Holmes's violin playing, and Mrs. Hudson, and the Persian slipper, and the various guests and clients who came through the doors. The roommates Sherlock Holmes and Watson seemed so congenial, even when they were getting on each other's nerves, just like real family members.

Second, the adventures seemed so real to me. I rode with Holmes and Watson as they dashed through the streets of London in a hansom cab on their way to a crime scene. The trains enchanted me, as did the buildings, homes, and exterior settings. Looking back, the writing drew me in so deeply it actually transported me to another time and place. The author is describing actual places in an actual time period. It's not historical writing. The writing is contemporary and immediate and is so good, it transports you like a time machine to right where you want to be.

The science fiction theme isn't far off, either. Holmes's influence goes far beyond 221B, well into the future and beyond to include Mr. Spock from *Star Trek*. There have been many comparisons between Spock and Holmes, most focusing on, once again, the logical component of their characters. For me, it was something completely different that made me like both Holmes and Spock. And this is the third thing I love about the original Holmes stories.

Holmes—like Spock—is a deeply moral and kind person. His surface is somewhat cool and predictable, but underneath he exhibits a caring for fellow men and women. He also seemed, to my ten-year-old mind, to be a bit of a sad, lonely, and isolated person, perhaps because he was so different from other people. The friendship and companionship of Watson, therefore, became so much more valuable for its uniqueness.

In a way, I liked Sherlock Holmes because he shared a lot of characteristics with my father. Both were interested in science and experimentation. My father was an engineer with a fully functional lab in our basement. We even had an oscilloscope. Both my dad and Sherlock Holmes seemed to have a unique scope of knowledge. While my father was well-read, he certainly had some peculiar ideas. Not as peculiar as Sherlock Holmes not caring about whether the earth revolved around the sun or vice versa, but peculiar nonetheless. Both had an attraction to the esoteric. Many a day we would come home to find various religious personalities who had knocked on our door, sharing a good argument with my father in our living room.

Other specific aspects of the stories obviously appealed to me, as after reading them I immediately worked with my father to set up a target range in the basement where we could shoot our BB gun. I remember how I enjoyed loading the little pellets with feathery backs into the gun. We started with targets and moved on to aluminum pie pans hanging from string, and I was allowed to shoot a series of pellets right into the wall to make two letters: VR. Victoria Regina. Queen Victoria. Holmes had done the same in honour of his Queen.

I became intrigued with Queen Victoria and wanted to know more about her. I was always a big reader, and belonged to our local library. The library was tiny, just one room really. On the left as you entered were the children's books, and on the right were the adult books. I felt I had outgrown the children's section, and also had learned about the Dewey Decimal System. So I went over to the card catalogue, looked up Queen Victoria and found a book I wanted. I didn't hesitate, but crossed the floor immediately to the adult section, found the book and took it to the check out. The librarian looked at me in puzzlement. "Are you sure you want this?" and she looked at my mother. "Yes, she wants it." I took it home and read it over the next few days and began to understand why Sherlock Holmes revered Queen Victoria so much.

This early introduction to history awakened an interest that stuck through my teen years and into university, where I got a degree in history. I focused on British History, and enjoyed especially reading about the 19th century. This helped when I re-read the Sherlock Holmes stories. Now I could put them in context.

University was a long time ago now, but my interest in history and in Sherlock Holmes has not waned. In fact, the more I read the stories, the more I appreciate them. I may have read them hundreds of times since then.

I've never been a big fan of what are now known as pastiches, though. I remember when *The Seven-Per-Cent Solution* came out. I also remember I physically recoiled with revulsion when I realized it focused on Sherlock Holmes's drug use. I preferred to focus on his other qualities. I don't mean to sound mean-spirited or controversial when I say I haven't really yet found a pastiche, or fan fiction, that comes close to the original. This doesn't stop me from reading them, though. I am much more interested in the minutiae and lacunae of the Canon.

I can't get enough books about Sir Arthur Conan Doyle, books and articles analyzing the 60 stories, and research into the influences of the original works. My love affair with the literary Holmes continues. I have a growing "to read" pile of Holmesian works, both fiction and non-fiction. Although I live too far away to participate in many organized activities, I take solace in the constant of the Canon, and the ever-growing list of books that feed my permanent hobby thanks to Sir Arthur Conan Doyle, Mr Sherlock Holmes, and Dr John Watson.

Susan Smith-Josephy (Quesnel, British Columbia) is a writer and researcher, and a former reporter, curator, and sailboat cleaner, who loves historical mysteries, both real and imagined. She has a BA in history from Simon Fraser University, and is currently writing her third book.

THE ADVENTURE OF
THE GOODNESS OF EXTRAS

JACQUELYNN MORRIS

"It is only goodness which gives extras." ("The Naval Treaty")

This is a chronology, of sorts, of what Sherlock Holmes has brought into my life. It is the testament of the "goodness" and the "extras" with which I have been blessed. Each part connects to the next, which connects to the next, and so on.

It was sometime in 1994 that I rediscovered Sherlock Holmes. I say "rediscovered" because of course I had read a great deal of the Canon as a young girl, along with Poe and Christie and Jules Verne and Bradbury—I was the quintessential bookworm, who dreamt of one day becoming a writer. I was not, however, a particular fan of the Rathbone/Bruce films. The Sherlock Holmes in my head was not Rathbone; the John Watson in my heart was not Bruce. I read the stories, grew up, and my life continued on, post-Canon and Holmes-free for many years. Then after I'd married and had children, a chance conversation with my brother introduced me to the portrayal of Holmes by the phenomenal Jeremy Brett. My brother and his wife had been recommending mystery novels to me as I began to fill unencumbered time by going back to my favorite genre of mystery fiction. He mentioned that they had been watching a show on PBS, *Sherlock Holmes*, that he thought I would enjoy. And so it began.

It may have been the Granada version of "The Red-Headed League" that I first watched, as I distinctly remember the now iconic sofa-jumping scene as being the moment I fell in love with Jeremy Brett and Sherlock Holmes. Though I later learned that some considered Brett's portrayal overly dramatic and flamboyant, I found his eccentric Holmes to breathe life into the character, matching the Holmes in my head. Reading the stories again after watching Brett was like meeting up with an old friend. I was hooked.

But I was not a part of the Sherlockian community. In fact, I had no idea of its existence. So when the last episode of *Sherlock Holmes* aired on PBS, and the final screen had a dedication to Jeremy Brett and noted his passing, I was shocked and stunned. What had happened? How could Sherlock Holmes die, and there be no "Empty House?" This was about a year before I first ventured into what was then called the World Wide Web;

there were no immediate answers. Even my local library and its extensive information system could provide none. I was left to grieve, alone and uninformed. And then something remarkable happened.

Within the span of about a year—it now being 1996—the "extras" of which Holmes spoke in "The Naval Treaty" miraculously came into my life. First, I met a woman (Debbie Clark, who would become a very dear friend) at a mystery fiction con, and she told me of the existence of Watson's Tin Box, a local Sherlockian scion society, and invited me to the next meeting. The second involved acquiring a computer and discovering AOL's Mystery Fiction Forum (after choosing the screen name "Sherlockia," which was meant to be "Sherlockian," but AOL only allowed ten characters) and its Sherlock Holmes Chat. I was finally able to do online searches, and one of my first searches on AltaVista (remember that?) was to learn about Jeremy Brett's—and my Sherlock Holmes's—tragic death.

Those of you who know me now know that every BSI weekend in New York I am nearly joined at the hip to another very dear friend, Regina Stinson. It was on the AOL Sherlock Holmes Chat that I first met Regina, and it was through her that I was made aware of the international community of Sherlock Holmes enthusiasts. What a remarkable discovery this was for me! There were others who enjoyed rereading the stories as I had come to do, and discussing them! In today's vernacular, I had found my "tribe," though I have since come to consider it my family. More on that later.

And it was a good thing to have that family, when in 1998, my nearly 20-year marriage disintegrated. It was a trying time for me and for my children, and it was a struggle for me to take care of the details, be present for my children, and find a little time to recharge myself for each day's challenges. The Sherlockian community gave me respite from the difficult moments and bolstered my damaged confidence by simply being a safe place to which I could turn for happy diversion. Few knew of my divorce, but if they had I know they would have been supportive. I didn't need a place to unload my sorrows; I needed a place that would be an escape, and involvement in the community did just that.

My first Watson's Tin Box meeting was a challenge for me. Not that I felt out of place; on the contrary, I was warmly welcomed by one and all. But being an introvert, and feeling damaged by the deeply unpleasant experience of a divorce, I struggled to be social when I really felt like running and hiding. The Tin Box was balm for my battered soul. I was welcomed and accepted and made to feel at home from the very start.

Between the AOL chat and the Tin Box, as well as support and encouragement from Regina and members of the Tin Box, I began to gingerly explore a world which I had never before realized was there. I went to my first Sherlockian symposium—the former Dayton Sherlock Holmes and Arthur Conan Doyle Symposium (reincarnated now as "Holmes, Doyle, & Friends"), where I met Roy Pilot and Al Rodin—Sherlockian luminaries, but unknown to me. My first "symp," as we came to call it, was where I first met Regina in person, and a lifelong friendship was born. We would meet there every springtime for years, with other AOL chat friends, David

Richardson and Mark Curtis. Within a short time I connected with other regulars, such as Steven Doyle, Don and Teresa Curtis (no relation to Mark), Bob and Joni Cairo, Marcy Mahle, Mel Hoffman and Pat Ward and other Illustrious Clients of Indianapolis and Agra Treasurers of Dayton. My world was expanding; my universe was taking me farther than I could have ever dreamed.

It was at that Dayton Symposium that I first presented a Sherlockian paper. For years Regina had been encouraging me to present; for years I had resisted, though the idea intrigued me. My previous forays into public speaking had been embarrassing disasters, and I had convinced myself that it was just going to be something I could never do. However, with the changes in my life, and the challenges I had to take on, I began to toy with the idea of putting myself out there once and for all to see if I could do it without "throwing up, passing out, or dying" (my challenge to myself). My first presentation was "Arsenic: It's What's for Dinner," where I explored Sherlock Holmes's comment, "The most winning woman I ever knew was hanged for poisoning three little children for their insurance-money" (*The Sign of the Four*). I delved into that enticing rabbit-hole of research, and more than a decade and a half later have yet to come up for air. I found that, having survived my first presentation, I was ready to take on the Sherlockian world.

My full understanding of that world has been a process, entirely due to my own ignorance. Tin Boxer Andy Solberg (one of my first, and most influential, mentors) would report back to the group after each BSI weekend, and though it sounded fun, it also seemed most intimidating to me. I heard of what was then called the Baskerville Bash, now known as the Gaslight Gala, and a group known as "ASH"; at some point I discovered it was actually the Adventuresses of Sherlock Holmes. I began to receive mailings from ASH and the annual Bash; in my ignorance, I discarded them. I learned of the Baker Street Irregulars, and looked upon the group as the gods and goddesses of Olympus. It was so remote an idea to even consider ever being among them that I went out of my way to convey an aura of indifference. Thankfully, as it turned out, no one noticed my efforts.

Over the next several years I branched out—to other events, other Sherlockian society meetings. My "family" grew, and I got this wacky idea about putting on a Sherlockian family reunion. In 2008 "A Scintillation of Scions" was born, initially as a way to gather together East Coast Sherlockians once a year. Because of the friends I had made from my travels, it soon became apparent that Scintillation was bringing together people from all over the U.S., and each time I looked around the room at a Scintillation my heart grew to see so many wonderful people—friends—in one place, for one purpose: to celebrate our love for Holmes. When the Robert Downey, Jr. films were released, and when BBC *Sherlock* and *Elementary* brought newer and younger Sherlockians into the fold, Scintillation was enhanced by their enthusiasm and yes, scholarship (though some may dispute this, and should go stand in the corner until they come to their senses). My "family" grew yet again. Scintillation recently celebrated its tenth annual gathering, and each one has brought me much joy.

In 2010 I became involved with the Undershaw Preservation Trust, an organization formed to bring awareness of the plight of Doyle's former home in Hindhead, Surrey. Undershaw became my passion, and I was given the title of U.S. Ambassador by the Trust. I was invited to speak in Washington, Dayton, and Chicago, to try to drum up support here for the crumbling and neglected historic home across the pond. Through our work with the Trust, I became friends with author Alistair Duncan and Baker Street Babes founder Kristina Manente. I visited Undershaw with them and others, touched the outside wall of Conan Doyle's study, and brought home a small piece of broken brick that had fallen to the ground as the house fell into disrepair. I worked long and hard on behalf of Undershaw; it was a labor of love, though it all did not work out quite as we had hoped. In 2014 Undershaw was purchased and developed, being saved as well as anyone could have hoped for—renovated, restored, added to, and turned into a school for children with disabilities.

In 2011 I was approached by Andy Solberg to write part of a chapter of a new BSI Manuscript Series book, *The Wrong Passage*, which would explore the story of "The Golden Pince-Nez." Remember that arsenic paper I wrote and presented years before in Dayton? That paper, over which I had agonized and struggled, became my open door to becoming published by the Baker Street Irregulars, no less! Since I had written about poisons, my task was to write about the poison Anna Coram used, and that piece, though short, may become my personal mini magnum opus. Never have I so much enjoyed—before or since—the research and the analysis and the writing of a Sherlockian essay or paper, and my hope is that someday the conclusion at which I arrived will cause people to read that story just a little differently.

In 2010 I was invited to become a member of ASH, an honor that I cherish deeply. I'd finally been attending some of the twice-yearly ASH meetings in New York and making more Sherlockian friends. A dear friend and long-established member of ASH, Susan Rice, took me aside at one of these gatherings, looked me square in the eye and said, nodding toward the group, "You do know how to become a part of this, don't you?" and proceeded to educate me on the traditions of investiture. In ASH one is allowed to choose their investiture name, and it is usually a story, a place, or a character. I, instead, chose a phrase. In "The Abbey Grange," Holmes says to Watson, "had we approached the case *de novo*...," meaning "to begin again" or "to begin anew." My life since rediscovering Sherlock Holmes had begun anew, and who I had become as a person over the years since was someone of whom I could be proud, with a circle of friends and kindred spirits unparalleled in my life up to that point of renewal. I truly was "*de novo*."

The "goodness" of my Sherlockian life has been that renewal, and with it, the "extras." As my childhood heart had longed for, I have become a published writer. I received my BSI investiture in 2014 as "The Lion's Mane," an honor that I had once deemed impossible. The following year I was asked to give a toast to Mycroft Holmes in front of the gathering of BSI dinner attendees, which included Mr. Kareem Abdul-Jabbar. I did not throw up, pass out, or die. I am part of an international community, with friends in Canada, Germany, the UK, Sweden, India, Korea, and more. My life is richer than I ever imagined it could be.

I am forever indebted to Sir Arthur Conan Doyle, for not only saving my life, but for giving me one as well.

Jacquelynn Morris (Laurel, Maryland) is a Baker Street Irregular and an Adventuress of Sherlock Holmes, was for ten years the organizer of the annual "Scintillation of Scions" symposium in the Baltimore area, and a long-time member and former Gasogene (twice) of Watson's Tin Box. She is also a member of The Sherlockians of Baltimore and a charter member of the John H. Watson Society.

THE ADVENTURE OF THE SITTING-ROOM DOOR

SCOTT BOND

December 8, 1942: on a quiet Tuesday evening, the latest addition to the human family made his appearance at Muhlenburg Hospital in Plainfield, New Jersey. The new arrival was quite ordinary in every way but one. His grandmother, one Jennie Robinson of Nova Scotia, was the sister of Boardman Robinson, a well-known art figure in the first half of the 20th century. Those at the birth of the young Scott Bond failed to notice the shadowy figure who was also present. This benign phantom, wearing a double-billed cap and smoking a pipe, apparently approved of what he saw; after all, his grandmother also had been the sister of a famous artist, a French painter by the name of Vernet. A sense of kinship was born that night, and although the babe—I—would not learn the spectre's name for some years to come, ultimately the two would become closely associated. I would accept the association with Sherlock Holmes as a badge of honor, becoming Scott Bond, Sherlockian, and eventually Scott Bond, Baker Street Irregular.

Fast forward to the early 1950s. The future Sherlockian, now living in his childhood home on West End Avenue in North Plainfield, discovered a new book on the living room coffee table. It had a textured dark green cover with silver lettering proclaiming itself to be a pictorial review of the first half of the century. Exploring the volume, I came to a spread devoted to the cinema of that classic Hollywood year, 1939. In a row of small black-and-white photos, one in particular caught my eye: a night-time outdoor scene with two gentlemen in period garb. The caption informed me that they were Basil Rathbone and Nigel Bruce, portraying a striking detective named Sherlock Holmes and his plump friend and companion, Dr. John H. Watson. The film was *The Hound of the Baskervilles*. Something about the title and the characters, especially Holmes, made an indelible impression, though no additional information was provided. I wouldn't see the film itself until the 1970s, but I would be on the lookout for Mr. Sherlock Holmes from then on—I wanted to know more.

In 1954, "more" arrived on our living room television set in the form of *The New Adventures of Sherlock Holmes*, a series of half-hour programs created by writer-producer Sheldon Reynolds and set in England and Paris. Holmes was portrayed by Ronald Howard, son of movie star Leslie

Howard, and Howard Marion Crawford was a befuddled but quite believable Watson. Howard, then in his early thirties, modelled his portrayal after the Holmes of the early canonical adventures. He was less the deductive superman of Basil Rathbone and more the earnest young man making his way through the early years of a career as a consulting detective. Even though something about the program seemed to lack the suspense of an adult mystery series, it was well produced for a youthful audience and is, when viewed today, a wonderful introduction to the Sherlock Holmes adventures.

A few years later I found myself in Mrs. Glaser's 8th grade English class. One afternoon I was delighted to find that we were going to be studying a Sherlock Holmes adventure, entitled "A Scandal in Bohemia." That became my literary introduction to Holmes, Watson, Baker Street, and fog-shrouded Victorian London. It turned out to be everything I could have wished for: a colorful, beautifully written tale featuring vivid characters, exciting action, and a brilliant central figure, the classic detective of mystery fiction.

Then the complete Sherlock Holmes Canon was issued in a series of inexpensive paperbacks. During my high school years, copies of the complete stories were hard to find, especially if you did most of your literary shopping at the newsstand or Woolworth's. I snatched up every new Ballantine release and devoured it with enthusiasm: slowly the four novels and 56 short stories revealed their pleasures and secrets. When I reached the last tale in *The Case-Book*, I realized with a heavy heart that the door to the 221B sitting-room had closed.

In 1961, after graduating from high school and being voted Class Artist and Class Actor, I entered Drew University, where unsurprisingly I took up art history. For the next four years Holmes and Watson would be distant figures, swamped by the demands of a liberal education. This would all change, however, when in 1966 I moved to Philadelphia to become a novice art director at Aitken-Kynett, a successful advertising agency.

Watching TV one evening after work, I chanced on a local interview program whose guests that day were a group of talkative Sherlock Holmes enthusiasts. All male, mostly middle-aged, they represented two local societies, the Sons of the Copper Beeches and the Master's Class. How amazing, I thought: people just like me! I immediately wanted to be a member of the Sons, but was disappointed to learn that you had to be sponsored into the group by an existing member. But then a colleague at A-K, a Yale-educated art director named Jim Scharnberg, became a member, and soon agreed to be my sponsor.

The Sons met twice a year at the Orpheus Club, a Civil-War-vintage building on South Van Pelt Street that served primarily as the headquarters of a male singing society by the same name. It was outfitted as a theatre with a small stage at the rear of the ground floor, and a meeting or dining room and library on the second. On the brisk October evening of my first meeting, I entered, hung up my coat, and was welcomed by Philadelphia Medical Examiner Dr. Marvin Aronson. I soon discovered that the group I was joining included many eminent gentlemen, including pioneering dermatologist Dr. Herman Beerman and artist and critic Ben Wolf. As that evening progressed, drinks were consumed, toasts were given, and the group proceeded up to the dining hall. Here I became acquainted with the Sherlockian scholarly essay, that traditional cornerstone of scion societies. To reach the Sons' highest rank, Master Copper-Beech-Smith, you had to write one, exploring some aspect of the Canon in the broadest sense. My own paper, a few years later, detailed the life of famed Victorian cracksman Charlie Peace, noted in "The Illustrious Client."

Soon after joining the Sons I was invited to become their Recorder of Pedigrees, or secretary. Up to that time the Sons' minutes had been tapped out on a manual typewriter with little attention to appearance. My idea was to add a decorative masthead at the top, and a bit of cartoon humor at the end. Each Sons meeting featured a hotly contested quiz based on the story of the evening, and that seemed a likely topic to parody. So began my decades-long career as a Sherlockian cartoonist. As a child of about three, I had fallen in love with *Walt Disney's Comics and Stories*, especially the work of the great Carl Barks, and I began to imitate him and the other popular cartoonists working during the golden age of comics. My early drawings for the Sons were small-scale efforts, but other opportunities would soon appear.

Around this time I got to attend my first meeting of the Master's Class. While the Sons had been modelled on the all-male Baker Street Irregulars, the Master's Class, a relatively recent creation, was Philadelphia's first co-ed scion. I happened to be dating a high school art teacher who had been consulted by a Master's Class member for some advice on creating a large banner to be displayed at each meeting. My teacher friend and I attended a meeting to admire the new banner. At that gathering I saw a presentation entitled "In the Footsteps of Sherlock Holmes" delivered, complete with slides, by a very nervous, but very attractive, female member of the group. This turned out to be the designer and creator of the banner, a single woman the same age as myself. Here, I realized, was the person destined to be The Woman in my life. This was in the spring of 1977, and by the following fall I had worked up enough nerve to ask her on a date. She accepted, and so began an intense courtship which culminated with our marriage on December 30, 1978. At this point the Sherlockian careers of Scott Bond and Sherry Rose-Bond went into high gear.

The Master's Class published a journal, *Holmeswork*, which was distributed at the society's annual dinner held in Philadelphia on the Sunday following the BSI's January dinner each year. The journal was a fairly primitive affair at the time, as were most scion publications. For the 1982 dinner I was asked to do a cover for the publication. I decided to show Professor Moriarty menacing Sherlock Holmes with a revolver—a scene inspired by a publicity photo from the Royal Shakespeare Company revival of the William Gillette "Sherlock Holmes" play. The cover proved a great success, and a couple of months later I heard from the then editor of the *Baker Street Journal*, Peter E. Blau, who had been present at the dinner. Apparently the *BSJ* had a longstanding problem filling the page opposite the editorial at the beginning of each issue. The editor offered me the opportunity to fill the troublesome spot, and I agreed to work up some samples.

I was immediately confronted with two problems: what style to employ, and where the gags were going to come from. At the time I was enamored of the style of British cartoonist Ronald Searle, noted for his popular depiction of Mr. Holmes in the Baker Street sitting-room. Something in that direction had much appeal—or I could choose a more modern style, akin to the political cartoons of the day. I decided on the former, and sent off three fairly rough samples to the *BSJ*. The editor, while encouraging, favored something more in the classic comics style of my *Holmeswork* cover, and so the matter was decided.

But the second problem remained: I could always come up with a drawing, but what about the writing? Fortunately, Sherlock Holmes and his milieu come with some well recognized clichés, such as "Elementary, my dear Watson," the three-pipe problem, the deerstalker, lens and Inverness, and so on. The three-pipe problem seemed a good bet for my debut effort, and was duly produced; it showed Holmes smoking three pipes at once, with Watson commenting to Mrs. Hudson, "It's part of his new efficiency kick." The drawing was accepted and appeared in the December 1982 issue of the *BSJ*. After laboring mightily for three years or so to create my earliest drawings (assisted by some clever suggestions from Sherry), I finally learned the trick, and regular production of the cartoons has become far easier. Soon after the launch of "Art in the Blood," as the series was titled, I was accepted into the ranks of the BSI, with the investiture of "The Copper Beeches."

The official keepsake of the January dinner in those days was a four-page program and menu with an original illustrated cover. Apparently, my artistic efforts found favor in the eyes of the BSI's new leader, or "Wiggins," Tom Stix, Jr. He invited me to take over production of the cover illustration and ultimately of the entire document. I was delighted to get this assignment, which gave me the opportunity to experiment with styles and themes. My maiden effort, for January 1988, was an homage to noted comics artist Richard Steranko and portrayed a night-time New York skyline, with an intense, calabash-smoking Holmes glaring up into a raging blizzard. It proved a great success, and in subsequent covers I paid tribute to Maxfield Parrish, Leonardo DaVinci, *Mad* magazine's Gerry Gersten and Jack Davis, *New Yorker* magazine's Barry Blitt, Boardman "Uncle Mike" Robinson, and Victorian cartoonists in general.

In 1984, Sherry and I and our friend Bob Katz founded a third Philadelphia society, the Clients of Sherlock Holmes. Along with a full schedule of scion activities, there were major events on the horizon, as 1987 was the centenary of the first Sherlock Holmes adventure, *A Study in Scarlet*. One afternoon our phone rang, and on the other end was an enterprising young chap by the name of Irv Walzer. He posed an intriguing question: if we were to go on a Sherlock Holmes themed trip, where would we go? We offered suggestions, and in the following weeks we discussed plans with him and with Costa Rodriguez, head of Geographics Travel and sponsor of what became known as The Final Problem Tour. To our amazement, the following spring, after much promotion, we and a merry band of Final Problem Tourists boarded an airliner heading across the Atlantic. For two weeks we explored Baker Street and other sites associated with the Master. We then crossed the Channel to France and trekked northward to Brussels and then to Switzerland. Settling into the Hotel Parc du Sauvage in Meiringen, we found ourselves standing in awe at the foot of the majestic Reichenbach Falls. When we departed for home we all agreed that it was a spectacular, unforgettable experience. Indeed so popular was it that the excursion was repeated two years later as The Return of Sherlock Holmes Tour, again to great acclaim.

Some months after the first tour, our phone rang again and we found ourselves recruited by the *Armchair Detective* magazine to write a regular Sherlockian column. This publication, covering all aspects of the mystery field, had finally decided it was time to devote some space to Sherlock Holmes, who was enjoying another massive surge in popularity, partly thanks to the Granada TV series starring Jeremy Brett. "Report from 221B Baker Street," as it was dubbed, made its debut in 1988 with coverage of our Final Problem Tour. We saw ourselves not as book reviewers but rather as purveyors of Sherlockiana to the broader mystery-reading public. We alternated writing the column, and by some trick of time and fate, I found myself writing the obituaries of some prominent figures, including Peter Cushing, Jeremy Brett, and Robert Stephens.

What, patient reader, is the bottom line of this unlikely saga of art, mystery, travel, romance, and Sherlockian scholarship? I am always struck by the remarkable scope of what I was able to both experience and contribute, and how I was able to employ virtually all my talents and interests at different times: cartooning, illustrating and design, writing and criticism, scion organizing, travelling and conducting Sherlockian tours and teaching Sherlock Holmes in adult classes with Sherry, guest speaking, acting, and of course participating in the many meetings and activities of my fellow Sherlockians. I even got to meet many of the incarnations of Mr. Holmes himself—Peter Cushing, Jeremy Brett, Douglas Wilmer, Patrick Horgan, Paxton Whitehead, Ron Moody, Keith Michell. I also had the peerless experience of walking the boards myself in the Master's shoes.

This is only a rough outline of decades in the service of Sherlock Holmes. And where, you may ask yourself, does this leave the aspiring Sherlockian? Veteran Baker Street Irregulars have long subscribed to the tradition that whatever your interests or talents may be, you can find a way to relate them to the great detective and his world of Victorian mystery and intrigue. Try it. And when you do, trust me: the sitting-room door will open wide.

Scott Bond (Columbus, Ohio) is a retired art director, writer, and cartoonist, a Baker Street Irregular and a member of other Sherlockian societies.

THE ADVENTURE OF THE UNEXPECTED PATHOLOGIST

ROBERT S. KATZ

I may be one of the few Sherlockians who can state without hesitation or equivocation that my choice of career, in particular, and with it so much of my life, in general, was due to my reading of the Canon. I started reading the Holmes stories when I was in my early teens, perhaps just before the start of high school. By the time I was ready to enter college, I had gone through the Doubleday edition, cover to cover, at least four or five times.

Throughout high school, my plan had been to attend college, major in history, and then continue with my studies through a PhD in history. I anticipated a career in historical research and teaching. During the summer following high school graduation, I spent most of my time going to the Museum of Modern Art in Manhattan, watching old film after old film in their screening room. One afternoon I sat in the cool darkness of the auditorium watching Robert Donat in *The Citadel*. I am not normally the type to become very emotional during film screenings. But when this movie ended, I found myself in tears and trembling. I left the museum and walked up Fifth Avenue to the old Brentano's bookstore and bought a paperback copy of Cronin's novel. By the time I got off the subway at my home stop, I felt an emotion that was both powerful and puzzling.

Later that night, I picked up the Canon and started on page one of *A Study in Scarlet*. A reading of the 60 stories always clarifies thought. On that first page, Watson talks about his earliest days as a physician. Suddenly my mind cleared and everything made sense. For years, I had been studying the Canon, exposed to the logical and deductive methods of Sherlock Holmes. Just as in the study of history, details count, and often count for everything. Observation overrides mere vision. The emotion of seeing that marvelous film forced me to reconsider my own goals and understand my own motivations.

I now realized that my fascination with history reflected my interest in using deduction to understand events of the past. After all, Dr. Joseph Bell heavily influenced the Literary Agent, and the stories are narrated through the eyes and the pen of a physician, John Watson. Holmes uses the same intellectual approach to solving crimes that a doctor uses in diagnosing and understanding disease. Not surprisingly, two of my favorite books from that period in my life were Altick's *The Scholar Adventurers* and

The Historian as Detective, by Winks. Both describe historians solving mysteries using Holmesian approaches. I knew I was not smart enough to be Sherlock Holmes (who is, after all?), but maybe I could be Watson-like and apply his methods in making a career in diagnosis.

Again, Sherlock Holmes soon appeared in my path. As summer ended, I matriculated at Haverford College, in the suburbs of Philadelphia. Only upon arrival did I realize that I was attending the alma mater of Christopher Morley, founder of the Baker Street Irregulars, and, perhaps more importantly at that time, the author of the wonderful introduction to the Doubleday edition of the Canon, which I had reread so often.

I stayed with my original plan of majoring in history, as I still found it fascinating. In addition, I took the requisite courses in chemistry, biology, and physics that were required for admission to medical school. Holmes was undoubtedly a better chemist than I was, but I did well enough to gain acceptance at the Albert Einstein College of Medicine, located in the scenic South Bronx of New York City. As I recounted in *Irregular Stain*, the BSI Manuscript Series book I co-edited with Andy Solberg, the Haverford College librarian let me see the "Second Stain" manuscript, which Morley had donated to the school, just before graduation day. One can't ask for a better send-off.

I spent the summer between college and medical school editing a paper I had written during my senior year for a class in the history of science and medicine. The paper dealt with the unusual distribution of deaths in the influenza epidemic of 1918-1919. The article was eventually published in a Johns Hopkins-sponsored medical journal. I titled the paper "A Study in Mortality." I think all Sherlockians will see this as my bit of homage to my own first exposure to the Canon and my early foray into publication.

Medical school was a whirlwind of reading and rounds. While rotating through vascular surgery, I did have to present a case of aortic aneurysm and created quite a stir by quoting Watson's description of Jefferson Hope's case. But then came the point when all medical students, on the verge of becoming doctors, must choose a specialty. I thought of the wise Sir James Saunders and considered dermatology. I did an elective at one of the hospitals and enjoyed the experience, but it just did not click for me. Then I remembered that Watson was introduced to Holmes in the pathology laboratory at Bart's. If a pathology laboratory was congenial to Sherlock, maybe I should think about it as well. I signed up for an elective in pathology at the hospital and, within an hour of arriving, was taken to the autopsy suite by one of the residents. I not only witnessed an autopsy but I was allowed to assist.

In the few short hours it took to complete the case, my life's path was determined. The chairman stopped by to review the case and pointed out to me that pathology was really the only specialty of medicine where the physician spends the entire day just making diagnoses. Holmes making deductions from bits of evidence was, to my thinking, like diagnosing disease from clues and data. It fit. All that had preceded coalesced and I finished the day knowing what I must do with my career.

Medical school allows for but little leisure time. I did manage, however, to make one trip from the Bronx to nearby White Plains, New York, for a meeting of the Three Garridebs, which I learned about through my newly acquired *Baker Street Journal* subscription. I met several people, including Peter Blau, who later became life-long friends. I was unable to attend another Sherlockian scion until a few years later, but I knew that I was with kindred spirits.

My time in the Bronx was fun, but I decided I needed a change of scenery. The pathology chairman told me that the hospital of the University of Pennsylvania had a fine residency program. I still had friends from Haverford in the area and always liked downtown Philly. I filled out the application and was summoned for an interview. There was a line on the application form that asked about hobbies and other interests. I just put the two words "Sherlock Holmes." When I got to the interview, the chairman at Penn, Dr. David Rowlands, started by asking me where I thought Watson had been wounded. It turned out that he was not only a Sherlockian but also a member of the Sons of the Copper Beeches, the venerable Philadelphia scion society. I like to think that my academic record was the major determining factor in the near-immediate acceptance that I received. Of course, Holmes and Watson might just have put in a word on my behalf.

When I started my training, Dr. Rowlands mentioned that Dr. Marvin Aronson was the Chief Medical Examiner for the City of Philadelphia. He was also a member of the Copper Beeches and a Baker Street Irregular. One day I had some spare time and I walked down the street to his offices. I told his secretary to say that I had come from Maiwand to meet him. Dr. Aronson bounded out of the office and greeted me warmly. During the course of my residency, I had the opportunity to observe and help a bit with forensic examinations. I suspect that I am the only Sherlockian who has performed an autopsy with another member of the Baker Street Irregulars.

As a resident, I had at least a small amount of free time and finally had a chance to actually join a scion society. The Copper Beeches had a long waiting list in those days, but the Master's Class was accepting new members. I had stationery with a rather primitive Sherlock Holmes letterhead and sent a request to Michael Kean for information about the group. Mike called me within a few days and warmly invited me to join. I got a follow-up call from Sherry Rose (not yet Bond) asking me to come to a private screening of the soon-to-be-released *Seven-Per-Cent Solution* film. I met Sherry, Mike, Steve Rothman, and Bev Wolov, amongst others. It was one of the most enjoyable of evenings and the direction of my social life was set.

As I continued my residency training (1976-1980), I became increasingly active in scion activities. I became a regular attendee at the Red Circle in Washington and enlarged my role in the Master's Class, eventually becoming one of the chairs and editing their publication, *Holmeswork*. In January of 1979, I attended, along with Chris Redmond, the first co-ed Adventuresses of Sherlock Holmes dinner in New York City.

Once I became a full-fledged pathologist, I moved to Baltimore and things got busier and busier. The Six Napoleons was the local scion and I eventually became its Gasogene. I helped co-found the Clients of Sherlock Holmes in Philadelphia, and also got off the waiting list and became a Master Copper-Beech-Smith of the SOCB. In 1981, I had the thrill of attending my first annual dinner of the Baker Street Irregulars, at the Regency Hotel.

But medicine continued to intertwine with Sherlock Holmes and his world. In 1983, Dr. Julian Wolff awarded me the Irregular Shilling with the investiture of "Dr Ainstree," who is mentioned in "The Dying Detective" as the greatest living authority on tropical disease. In addition to my teaching obligations at Johns Hopkins, I helped to supervise the clinical laboratories at Baltimore City Hospital (shades of Bart's!). The microbiology laboratory was part of the operation, and any time a new case of malaria was suspected, I had to review the blood smear and decide which species was causative. I assumed that Dr. Wolff took this interest in tropical medicine into account when choosing my investiture. A few years later, I figured out that Dr. Ainstree was the only physician name not already awarded in the BSI. Even though I suppose I drew the last straw, I still love the investiture.

In 1987, I moved from Baltimore to Morristown, New Jersey, where I practiced until my retirement in 2011. Throughout all the years of practice, however, the lessons of the Canon were always just over my shoulder. In pathology, every detail matters. In fact, what others pass off as trifles are often the defining factors in making a difficult diagnosis. I also learned never to theorize in the absence of facts or data. A snap judgment made in haste can have serious adverse consequences. I spent a great deal of my time looking at slides through the microscope. Over the years I realized that what might be absent can be as important as what is present. The diagnosis might have to be made through the absence of some otherwise expected findings, rather like the dog in the night-time. Perhaps most important, I learned that no matter how improbable, nothing is impossible in medicine.

And there were fun moments. Since I performed a great many autopsies, I frequently found myself presenting the findings at educational or mortality conferences. I must admit to taking particular glee at going through all the details of the case and then, with an inability to resist a touch of the dramatic, presenting a diagnosis that was both unexpected and startling. The reactions of the white-coated audience would have been music to the ears of the Master. After a few years, this became known in our hospital as "Dr. Katz pulling a Sherlock Holmes." I loved it!

With the advent of retirement, I avoided becoming a lounger and idler by turning even more attention to Holmes. I founded the Epilogues of Sherlock Holmes here in New Jersey in 1990 and, as one of the few scions with an all-discussion format, that group continues to this day. I was also able to return to writing and have co-edited books in the BSI Manuscript Series with Andrew Solberg and once with Steve Rothman. Andy and I recently put our collective health care experience to work in co-editing *Nerve and Knowledge*, which presents a series of articles on medicine and doctors in the Canon. Again, vocation and avocation intersected.

My family has been my greatest joy and honor. But my career in pathology and medicine and my Sherlockian activities have been hugely important, fulfilling, and cherished. The friendships continue to this day, and so many are like family to me. I practiced medicine with, hopefully, the attention to the most minor of details, as did Holmes when pursuing a case. Above all, the process of making a diagnosis is the process of assembling clues, collecting data, and only then drawing conclusions...or deductions, as I preferred to call them. None of this would have happened for me had I not had that early exposure to the Canon. Should he have desired it, Holmes could have had a great medical career. I hope, to some small degree, he would have approved of mine. I know he would have understood the choices I made. I daily thank him for that guidance.

Robert S. Katz (Morristown, New Jersey) is a retired pathologist and the co-editor of several volumes in the BSI Manuscript Series and the BSI Press volume *Nerve and Knowledge.* He is active in many scion societies in the northeastern United States and holds the office of Billy the Page in The Baker Street Irregulars.

THE ADVENTURE OF
THE OPENING DOORS

DAVID STUART DAVIES

The room is quiet. I take my seat in the semi-circle and give a silent nod to the others in the group and wait for my turn. When it comes, I stand up, holding a copy of the Canon in my right hand, and in a clear voice, I state: "My name is David Stuart Davies—and I am a Sherlockian."

Well, I have been a Sherlockian since the age of twelve, although I didn't know it by that term then. It was in my salad days that I fell in love with Sherlock Holmes after encountering him on the school library shelves. *The Hound of the Baskervilles* was the particular volume in question, and I devoured it with glee. Around the same time the local television station was screening the Basil Rathbone films. Those two happenstances sold me into Sherlockian slavery for life.

Eventually I read all the Holmes Canon, and also *The Exploits*, by John Dickson Carr and Adrian Conan Doyle. In those days that was more or less all the Holmes fiction one could read. And so I began to pen my own adventures. Although this juvenilia was corny, creaky and very amateurish, it helped to deepen my love of the character and his world.

When I went to university, I wanted to write my final dissertation on Arthur Conan Doyle, but I was told in no uncertain terms that he was not an important enough author for such a project. As an antidote to this dismissal of the great man, for my own amusement, I began writing an article on the films of Sherlock Holmes—a particular passion of mine. The piece just grew, and before I knew it I had a book-length manuscript. I sent it off to a publisher and, glory be, it was accepted. So the year I received my degree I also had my first book published, *Holmes of the Movies*. Peter Cushing agreed to write the introduction, and I had the thrill of meeting the great man and beginning a correspondence with him.

The publication of *Holmes of the Movies* helped to open the door to the Sherlockian world. I joined the Sherlock Holmes Society of London and began making friends with individuals who shared my Sherlockian passions. This network of friends has grown and grown over the years and spread around the world, particularly in the United States.

1987 was a pivotal year in my Sherlockian life. It was, of course, the centenary of the publication of the first Holmes novel, *A Study in Scarlet*. There were lots of events to celebrate this in London, but none in Yorkshire where I lived. Then a young woman in this neck of the woods advertised in the SHSL newsletter, *The District Messenger*, for any Sherlockians living in the north of England who would be interested in forming a society in this locale. I replied and, to cut a long story short, we formed the Northern Musgraves and ran the society for eleven glorious years. This young lady was Kathryn White, and we grew so close that there was nothing else to do but get married. Thank you, Dr Doyle and Mr Holmes, for bringing us together and providing us with nearly thirty years of love and affection.

The Northern Musgraves grew from a scant half-dozen members to more than 700, including a fair number overseas. We published two substantial newsletters, *The Ritual*, each year and a bumper journal, *The Musgrave Papers*. Also around this time I became editor of the *Sherlock Holmes Gazette*, a title I eventually changed to *Sherlock*. I interviewed Tom Stix, Jr (Wiggins of the Baker Street Irregulars at the time) for the magazine and we got on like a house on fire. The next thing we knew Kathryn and I were invited to the BSI annual dinner, and a year later we were invested. The Irregulars welcomed us with open arms.

There is something remarkable about the Sherlockian community which embraces individuals from all walks of life from postmen to presidents and students to sages. You feel at home immediately in their company, and although you may not have seen them for a long period of time, you pick up where you left off. The camaraderie is intoxicating and very difficult to explain to those outside the circle.

I was lucky enough to meet and interview Jeremy Brett when he was making the Granada series. He liked and trusted me, I think, because I knew my Doyle and the Holmes Canon and I was not just a journalistic hack wanting a story about the series. I even went to visit him in his apartment in London. He always impressed me in his determination to bring Doyle's Holmes to the screen. My time with Brett resulted in the Sherlock book of which I am most proud: *Bending the Willow*.

While editing *Sherlock*, I went to review a stage production of *The Hound*. The play was all right, but I thought that Roger Llewellyn, the actor playing Holmes, was very good. I interviewed him after the performance and he told me that he had enjoyed playing the Great Detective and would really like to do a one-man play featuring the character. I told him that I didn't think that was possible—you would have to have Watson involved at least.

But driving home, I had a eureka moment and saw how such a play could be done: Holmes returns from Watson's funeral and reminisces about their friendship, addresses the absent doctor as though he were there, and goes on to reveal things about his own history and character that he never told him while he was alive. This became *Sherlock Holmes: The Last Act*, which opened at Salisbury Playhouse. Roger performed the play in various venues in Britain and locations in Europe and America for ten years.

He even gave an off-Broadway performance for the Baker Street Irregulars. That was a night I will never forget. I was very nervous, wondering how this esteemed crew would view my dramatic take on Holmes. After the play started, I couldn't bear the tension and escaped the theatre and sat in a bar across the road. I needn't have worried: The Irregulars cheered and stamped and loved Roger's interpretation. Some years later, at Roger's request, I penned another one-man play for him, *Sherlock Holmes—the Life and Death*, which had a good five years' touring life. It is so wonderful to sit in the stalls and see your version of Sherlock Holmes come to life and engage an audience.

In recent years I have put together an hour-long show for myself—*The Game's Afoot*—which I have performed at various literary festivals and bookshops and at the Edinburgh Fringe. This entertainment, which tells the story of the career of both Holmes and his creator, gives me the opportunity to read extracts from the stories and play Holmes, Watson, Doyle, Lestrade, and even Oscar Wilde.

The deerstalkered one is a constant part of my life. I have written seven novels, the latest being *Sherlock Holmes & the Ripper Legacy*, and a further book about his film career, *Starring Sherlock Holmes*. I also meet regularly with friends in an informal group we call The Scandalous Bohemians to discuss the stories.

He has opened many doors for me, none more prestigious than being invited to join the Detection Club in 2015. This exclusive organisation of detective story writers was originally formed in 1930 by the likes of G.K. Chesterton and Dorothy L. Sayers. Conan Doyle was invited to be its first president but he was too ill to accept the offer. Being a member of this august body with a direct link to the creator of Holmes is the icing on my Sherlockian career.

I know my life would not have been as rich and exciting and entertaining if I had not discovered Conan Doyle's fabulous creation all those years ago when, as a scruffy short-trousered lad, I reached for that copy of *The Hound*. God bless you, Sir Arthur and Mr Holmes.

David Stuart Davies (Huddersfield, West Yorkshire) is a writer, editor, and occasional performer. He sits on the national committee of the Crime Writers Association and edits their monthly journal, *Red Herrings*. He is the editor on the Mystery and Supernatural series for Wordsworth Editions and is working on a new Holmes novel.

THE ADVENTURE OF THE FIXED POINT

RACHEL E. KELLOGG

Many people think of Sherlock Holmes as a dry reasoner, a caustic wit, a clever and theatrical personality. A case can be made for all those things, but I think of him first and foremost as a friend. He is a friend who has opened new worlds for me, and someone who is always there when I need him no matter how long it's been since we last saw each other. Most importantly, Sherlock Holmes is a friend who has grown along with me through every part of my life, from childhood to adulthood. His charm never fades, and his company is ever a delight (even when he's being kind of a jerk).

I first met him when I was ten. One night I was sick and feverish, lying on the living room couch at home, unable to sleep. My parents were watching TV and switched over to "Mystery!" on PBS, which I had never seen before. (I knew I liked mysteries, though, because I devoured Nancy Drew and Trixie Belden, balancing stacks of a dozen books in my arms as I walked home from the library.) I had heard of Sherlock Holmes through various pop culture references, such as cartoons, but I had never really paid attention to him before.

But as soon as the episode started, I was transfixed. From the beautiful violin theme to the authentic Victorian everything, I was fascinated. A complete world of story, costume, setting, and props—all were new to me. Here was something to satisfy a part of my dramatic little soul (I had decided the year before to become an actress) that I didn't know I needed.

That episode, the Granada series' "The Crooked Man," was rather trippy, even for someone who wasn't drifting in and out of consciousness. But I was hooked. I borrowed my mom's illustrated stories and started reading. I struggled a bit at first with the Victorian language but persisted—the illustrations were so evocative of the show I had seen; it was a delight to learn many years later that the Granada people had, indeed, used the Paget illustrations as models.

My fandom really took off when our family purchased a VCR. I was able to get the videocassettes from our local library or rent them from a specialty video store in town, and I started working my way through the available episodes and the corresponding stories. Victorian and Edwardian England came alive in my imagination.

One day, when I was casually looking through the library stacks at my high school, I chanced upon two collections I hadn't heard of—*The Case Book of Sherlock Holmes* and *His Last Bow*. What riches! "The Lion's Mane," with its unusual cause of death, made an impression on me, as did the foreshadowing of World War I in "His Last Bow." The combination of romance and tragedy in the final paragraph touched my adolescent heart:

"Good old Watson! You are the one fixed point in a changing age. There's an east wind coming all the same, such a wind as never blew on England yet. It will be cold and bitter, Watson, and a good many of us may wither before its blast. But it's God's own wind none the less, and a cleaner, better, stronger land will lie in the sunshine when the storm has cleared."

From the vantage point of the early 1990s, I knew that the hope in those words was not to come true, and that war would again descend on Europe only twenty years later. I marveled at the shifts of history, the difference between foresight and hindsight.

Also during high school, I developed a terrible crush on Jeremy Brett (as Sherlock Holmes, of course). The accent, the purring delivery, the perfectly tailored clothes—I was an easy mark. My family was both amused and supportive; my little brother made a doll version of Jeremy Brett out of a cardboard roll and some paper, because, he told me, he "tried to think of what I would want most for Christmas, and he figured it would be Jeremy Brett." The doll fell apart years ago, but the idea has survived for two decades as a family joke.

Several years later, when I was a sophomore in college, my mother called me with some bad news: Jeremy Brett had died. I hadn't even known he was sick, and this was just awful. He was too young! He hadn't finished all the stories! I cried and tried to explain it to my roommate, who was sympathetic, but I could tell she thought I was a little odd. I wore black for three days. Someone who I knew and loved, whom I associated with my enjoyment of the whole genre of "Sherlock," was gone. I still mark the date every year.

My junior year, I studied at Oxford for a month with a small group from my college. I was determined that, on one of our scheduled trips to London, I would make a pilgrimage to 221B Baker Street. Alone in the city for the first time, I managed to find Baker Street an hour before closing time (this was before the era of smartphone apps and GPS and it took a while to get there the old-fashioned way). The bored young woman dressed in a Victorian maid costume who was an "interpreter" of the Sherlock Holmes Museum was nice but clearly thought I was daft. I managed to see what I wanted to see and got her to take my picture with the deerstalker cap and meerschaum pipe provided for that purpose. On the one hand, I felt a little silly. On the other hand, I felt awesome. Despite none of the other students on the trip wanting to go with me, I had made it to 221B! I had achieved a lifelong dream.

Going to a museum alone was one thing, but making my way through London back to the bus station and finding the Oxford bus in the gathering gloom was a little more intimidating. However, I managed to do it, and realized later that I had gained an independence and confidence in my own ability. Truly, my passion for Sherlock Holmes led me to discover confidence I hadn't known I had.

A few years into my twenties, I had a romantic relationship go sour (tough at any age, but especially bitter in one's angsty youth). While it wouldn't take long for me to realize that losing that particular fellow was a blessing in disguise, at the time, it was an Epic Tragedy. I felt like I had been hit with a truck—mentally stunned, and with pain all over my body. I didn't know how I could keep going. Enter Sherlock Holmes, whom I hadn't "seen" in a while. I found a wonderful website called "The Brettish Empire" which I read while at work, and after work, I spent hours and hours watching Sherlock videos and rereading the stories to numb the pain. During this time, I rediscovered my love of Holmes, and started delving into Sherlockian scholarship, or the Great Game, which was fascinating. As a theatre geek, I was used to theatre fandom, which focused on actors or musicals. But the idea of doing that for stories that I cared about (as opposed to just doing it in literature classes) was new to me, and very exciting. Even more interesting was finding out that it had been going on for decades, and that other favorites of mine such as Dorothy L. Sayers had participated. It was like meeting a whole series of new friends who liked my old friend Sherlock as much as I did.

In the intervening years, I reread the Canon, bought the complete Granada Holmes DVD collection, read pastiches, and watched other Holmes movies. My intense interest and fan behaviors waxed and waned, and I always assumed Sherlock Holmes would be a part of my life.

And so he has proven to be. New avenues of Sherlockian communication, collection, and interpretation have opened with the internet age—so many new friends to be made! I am a creature of enthusiasms, and many obsessions have come and gone. Some have reappeared, some not. But Sherlock Holmes is a constant. Even when I am not paying attention to him, I know he's there, patiently waiting for the next time I want to knock on the door of 221B and call on the world's only private consulting detective. And I know we'll pick up right where we left off, no matter how much time has passed—just as good friends always do.

Rachel E. Kellogg (Fort Wayne, Indiana) has worked in higher education for several years, teaching English and working in student affairs.

THE ADVENTURE OF THE FIERCE FELLOWSHIP

KASHENA JADE KONECKI

I love talking about Sherlock Holmes. There is something wholly satisfying about having a single set of works—56 short stories and four novels—create an entire world we can add to, reference, reimagine, and repurpose. In addition to more than a hundred years of adaptation in radio, theatre, and film from the original source material, we are gifted with looser versions of Holmes and Watson in pastiche and popular culture.

There are books like Michael Chabon's *The Final Solution*, where an old retired detective—who isn't named as Sherlock Holmes, but keeps bees and a magnifying glass with an inscription from his "sole great friend"— takes on the case of a missing parrot, the only friend of a young Jewish refugee in 1944. Television shows like *House* and *Psych* play around with the professions of our heroes; *House* makes doctors of both main characters (House and Wilson), but House is preternaturally gifted in sussing out curious cases. *Psych* makes neither Shawn nor Gus professional detectives, but Shawn's exceptional observational skills makes him, much like Holmes, one of a kind: the world's only "psychic" detective. Gus, a pharmaceutical rep, is his best friend and conductor of light.

We can find where inspiration's been drawn and homage paid to Arthur Conan Doyle in multiple forms of art and entertainment, making "spot the reference" a delightful pastime with a real sense of accomplishment. The joy is slightly lessened, however, when you're the only one in the room spotting Easter eggs, so that's where the best part of loving Sherlock Holmes comes in: being with other Sherlockians.

Sherlockians easily bring out the best in one another with their kindness, encouragement, curiosity, and intellect. I have the honor and privilege to serve as Vice President of the Sound of the Baskervilles, a scion society in Seattle. When I ventured to my first meeting years ago, my knowledge of the Canon was somewhere between "feeble" and "variable" and I expected to come across eight or ten young people in deerstalkers talking excitedly about Benedict Cumberbatch, Jeremy Brett, Robert Downey, Jr., and Tumblr. I hesitantly approached the hostess station of the pub where the meeting was supposed to take place and asked the waitress if she knew the group that met about Sherlock Holmes.

"Oh," she said. "They're in there." She pointed to her left, to a room just off the main dining area. I peered past her, squinting to spot a small sea of deerstalkers. There were none.

As I ventured into the room, I found I was also dead wrong about the demographic. While there were a handful of younger people, the vast majority were over 40 and had obviously known each other for years. Had I done my research I would've known the group had formed in March 1980. The group was christened as they traveled from Seattle to Bainbridge, Washington, on a ferry over the dark waters of the Puget Sound, and so their name choice seemed obvious—an amalgamation of *The Hound* and the Sound.

Thirty-two years later, I was immediately welcomed and ushered to a seat in the pub. Beer in hand, I had one of the best afternoons in recent memory. Members talked about the new books they'd read, Sherlockian news, upcoming events, and the story they'd studied for that day. I can't remember which story it was, but I remember thinking that the whole thing felt like a church service. In the front of the room our president led the meeting, which included summarizing the story, the call and response of questions and answers, and the ultimate lesson we could take away from Holmes's deductions. In the back of the room, there were all the people who had come together initially under one purpose—to study Sherlock Holmes—and stayed because of the fierce friendship and fellowship. Encouraged by the warmth of this community in stark contrast of the alleged Seattle Freeze (a widespread belief that it is hard to make friends in the cold cliquishness of Seattle), I quickly joined.

It was easy to see that this intergenerational group was not drawn together simply because of an interest in Sherlock Holmes, the most portrayed literary character of all time. They were not drawn together only because they played the Great Game. They were drawn together because of the kind of person a Sherlockian is: curious, bright, and driven. As I spent more time with the Sound of the Baskervilles, I found that Sherlockians are rarely passionate about Sherlock Holmes alone. We have members who are also deeply interested in World War II, Shakespeare, puzzles, comics, classic cars, travel, museums, the *Titanic*, baking, fanfiction, and growing Victorian roses, among many other things. Their knowledge and enthusiasm is infectious, and I've never left a conversation knowing, or caring, less about a subject than when I entered it.

Recently, I ran a panel on "The Adventure of the Gloria Scott" for a meeting. This story rarely appears in anyone's Top 10 List for a variety of reasons: admittedly, the mystery is weak, it has an odd story structure, and poor Watson only has three lines. Its weaknesses and significant omissions, however, make space for rich character development and a lot of fodder for my favorite literary question: "Do you trust the narrator?" As I prepared for the panel, I armed myself with open-ended questions about language choice, the criteria for a "good" Sherlock Holmes story, and the story's place in popular culture.

Afterward, I realized how much I enjoyed diving into the nitty-gritty of a story, and the empowerment that came with the deep knowledge of a work. I wondered if that meant I was a true Sherlockian now, and not just someone who "loves to talk about Sherlock Holmes." While my knowledge of the Canon has finally moved past "variable" into "accurate, but unsystematic," I don't think quantifying canonical knowledge is what makes someone a Sherlockian. Instead, I believe myself to be a Sherlockian because Sherlockians smarter, kinder, and more interesting than me have encouraged me to speak up, share, and learn beside them. They have invited me to their homes, shared meals, and followed me on Twitter. Their continued inclusion is what has made me a better person, and I can only hope to be a good example for Sherlockians to come.

Kashena Jade Konecki lives in Seattle with her cat and her espresso machine. She has a degree in English from the University of Washington and is passionate about diversity and inclusion.

THE ADVENTURE OF
THE MULTIPLYING FRIENDS

BOB COGHILL

As a Sherlockian who often gives talks to a variety of audiences, I am frequently asked how I got introduced to Sherlock Holmes. It is an easy answer because I remember exactly and very clearly how it happened. And the story reminds me of the butterfly effect: The things that really change the world, according to Chaos theory, are the tiny things. A butterfly flaps its wings in the Amazonian jungle, and subsequently a storm ravages half of Europe. It was such a small thing, but it did change my world.

When I was a teenager, I worked in a book and stationery store. It was more for the love of stationery than of books at that time, because for some reason, I loved the pens and file cards and all the assorted things we sold. It is embarrassing to admit that I was pretty much a non-reader during high school. I certainly never or rarely read for pleasure. After high school, when I was looking for a full-time job, I was able to get one at the same store. It was there that I met Mary, the boss's niece, and it was Mary who became my butterfly wing.

One day, Mary showed up at the store beaming. I asked her why and she explained that the night before, she had attended a Tom Jones concert at the O'Keefe Centre in Toronto and that the singer had invited Mary to come on stage so that he could sing a song directly to her. She, of course, was thrilled. I remarked that she must have had a good seat. Mary explained that her mother had season tickets, front row center. My response was that if her mother ever had tickets for a show that she didn't want, she should let me know. I said I would love to have those seats for any event.

A few months later, Mary asked if I was serious about buying her mother's tickets. I said of course and then asked what the show was. It was a play. By William Gillette. Called "Sherlock Holmes".

In preparation for the play, I found a copy of the complete long stories of Sherlock Holmes and read each one. Then I saw the play and I wanted more. I found a copy of the Murray edition of the complete short stories, and that is when I really got hooked. My daily bus ride to the stationery store took about 40 minutes, and I found I could easily read one of the short stories in that time. I could also read one at lunchtime and a third on my way home. I was lost in the stories and when I reached the final one, I felt such a disappointment that it was over. I had no idea.

I was surprised and delighted to find a copy of *The Exploits of Sherlock Holmes*, by John Dickson Carr and Adrian Conan Doyle, and then the *Sherlock Holmes Scrapbook*, edited by Peter Haining. It was in the scrapbook that I read about the Baker Street Irregulars. At the time, I thought it was a bit bizarre that a group of adults could actually belong to such an organization. What I soon learned was that once my "ear was tuned to catch the distant view-halloo," I began to hear of Sherlock everywhere. I had, in fact, become a Sherlockian.

There is quite a difference between *becoming* a Sherlockian and *being* a Sherlockian. Becoming a Sherlockian is easy and happens entirely by accident in most cases. All it takes is a careful reading of the Sherlock Holmes stories. For me, it happened relatively quickly. Becoming a Sherlockian was a quick and solitary affair. But being a Sherlockian meant that a whole level of adventures was to continue for the rest of my life.

When I became a Sherlockian, I had no idea that it would introduce me to a world where I would meet such interesting people, some of them very celebrated. At my first Baker Street Irregulars dinner, for example, I sat between the prolific author Isaac Asimov and Dr. Charles Goodman, who among other things, had been Harry Truman's dentist. At my last dinner, I met basketball legend and author Kareem Abdul-Jabbar. Other luminaries I have met include Governor George Pataki, Nicholas Meyer, the amazing Neil Gaiman, and Pulitzer-Prize-winning book reviewer Michael Dirda. But it is not the celebrities who make the world of Sherlock Holmes so important in my life.

Being a Sherlockian is rarely solitary. It involves connecting with others and developing relationships, some of which have become among the closest and richest in my life. Being a Sherlockian is all about friendship. I was listening to the wonderful podcast *I Hear of Sherlock Everywhere* when hosts Scott Monty and Burt Wolder were interviewing prominent Sherlockians Al and Julie Rosenblatt. A line that stuck with me was when Julie remarked, "It began with Sherlock Holmes, but it ended in friendship."

There are two passages in the Sherlock Holmes Canon that people look to for examples of the friendship between Dr. Watson and Sherlock Holmes. The first, from "The Three Garridebs":

> In an instant he had whisked out a revolver from his breast and had fired two shots. I felt a sudden hot sear as if a red-hot iron had been pressed to my thigh. There was a crash as Holmes's pistol came down on the man's head. I had a vision of him sprawling upon the floor with blood running down his face while Holmes rummaged him for weapons. Then my friend's wiry arms were round me, and he was leading me to a chair.
>
> "You're not hurt, Watson? For God's sake, say that you are not hurt!"
>
> It was worth a wound—it was worth many wounds—to know the depth of loyalty and love which lay behind that cold mask. The clear, hard eyes were dimmed for a moment, and the firm lips were shaking. For the one and only time I caught a glimpse of a

great heart as well as of a great brain. All my years of humble but single-minded service culminated in that moment of revelation.

The second is from "The Final Problem" and captures Watson's feelings when he believes that Holmes has died:

Of their terrible chief few details came out during the proceedings, and if I have now been compelled to make a clear statement of his career it is due to those injudicious champions who have endeavored to clear his memory by attacks upon him whom I shall ever regard as the best and the wisest man whom I have ever known.

While these passages show the depth and quality of the friendship, they certainly are not the only references to friendship. In fact, when you look only at the beginnings of the stories, the phrase "my friend, Sherlock Holmes" or "my friend, Mr. Sherlock Holmes" or just "my friend," "my companion," "my long and intimate acquaintance," or, "my long and intimate friendship" appear regularly. In fact, 25 stories of the 60 contain the above expressions.

So it is fitting that Christopher Morley's 1944 collection of annotated stories was called *Sherlock Holmes and Dr. Watson: A Study in Friendship*. It is difficult to separate the concept of the doctor and the detective from the concept of friendship.

With this idea in mind, I asked a number of Sherlockians who were attending the annual festivities around the Baker Street Irregulars in January 2017 to finish the thought that began "Sherlockian friendship...." Here are the results.

- "runs deep and wide." Julie McKuras, Minneapolis
- "is the purest form of friendship and it is timeless." Dick Sveum, Minneapolis
- "is enhanced by affection, scholarship, and alcohol." Richard Olken, Boston
- "includes meeting someone who looks or at least thinks, like you do." Ben Vizoskie, Westchester County, New York (who when we first met, was told he looked just like me)
- "means you can get a free meal pretty much anywhere on Earth!" Cliff Goldfarb, Toronto
- "goes coast to coast and around the world." Marsha Pollak, San Jose
- "is a gateway to a world of erudition and fascination." Dana Richards, Virginia
- "a companion that can be trusted to solve complex situations and resolve uncertainty." Marino C. Alvarez, Nashville
- "is the *aqua vitae* of our hobby." Scott Monty, Michigan
- "enlarges the scope and scale of our lives with global friendships that endure." Mike McKuras, Minnesota
- "is worldwide and lifelong." Yuichi Hirayama, Japan
- "connects one to a global family that spans the ages from 1895 onward and blesses those so bonded with love, humor, support,

and camaraderie until we cross the Reichenbach to be with our fellows long past." Michael J. Quigley, Virginia
- "creates a community of kindred spirits, where everyone feels at home." Jacquelynn Morris, Maryland
- "means building relationships with people that you may have nothing else in common with and probably would never have met otherwise." Dan Andriacco, Cincinnati
- "is the lifeblood of scions all over the world—it is the lasting and continuance of relationships both complete and simple—it is a renewal of life on many levels and the ritual renews itself each year with added conviction—Sherlockian society is a wondrous thing!" Barbara Herbert, Indianapolis

This is just a taste of the thoughts based on a very small sample of the hundreds of attendees at some of the events at the gathering in New York. One gets a sense of the genuine warmth and feeling among those gathered.

It would not be hyperbole to say that while becoming a Sherlockian made me a better and more interesting person, being a Sherlockian quite literally changed my life. And it is primarily through the friendships that I developed along the way. It was my friend Betty Jane Kraemer, whom I met at my first Sherlockian event, the John Bennett Shaw workshop at the University of Notre Dame, who convinced me that I might be capable of university. I applied, got in, and did well. Betty Jane came to my graduation and we remained close friends until she died well into her 90s.

It was my good friends, well known Sherlockians Christopher Redmond and Kate Karlson, who introduced me to Chautauqua, an introduction that opened a whole new world to me and presented a new layer of rich friendships. When I retired, I started travelling and of course, along the way visited with many good friends I had met because of our mutual interest in Sherlock Holmes. I shared many meals and much hospitality wherever I went around the world, including across the United States and Canada and in New Zealand and Australia.

Although I now live a long way from the Bootmakers of Toronto, some of the best friendships I encountered were from that group. I remember fondly folks like Maureen Green, Cameron Hollyer, and Mary Campbell, all of whom enriched the lives of those they knew and were walking definitions of what it meant to be a friend. A move across the country and before I even got settled, I was invited to lunch by members of the Stormy Petrels of British Columbia, the Vancouver society, which I joined enthusiastically and which has now added a number of new friends to my life.

I never could have imagined when I sat down with my collection of the Sherlock Holmes short stories that I was about to begin an adventure that was to enrich my life so richly and in so many ways. As Julie Rosenblatt has said, "It began with Sherlock Holmes, but it ended in friendship."

Bob Coghill (Vancouver, British Columbia) is a retired teacher and archivist, a Baker Street Irregular, and a Master Bootmaker, renowned for introducing children to Sherlock Holmes. Since 2013 he has been travelling the world, meeting Sherlockians and adding friendships as he goes.

THE ADVENTURE OF
THE STULTIFIED HOUSEWIFE

LEAH GUINN

So, you've faced the truth. You're a Sherlockian. You don't just like Sherlock Holmes, the way everybody does. In fact, by now you've probably had at least one experience in which, believing you've found someone who shares your interest, you start discussing the finer points of Rathbone v. Brett, or whether or not "The Mazarin Stone" belongs in the Canon, only to come to yourself ten minutes later to see your companion's eyes glazed over. If she's still there at all.

That's okay. You're not alone. There are thousands out there, just like you—just like *us*, just like *me*, utterly obsessed with the Great Detective. It's been going on for 130 years, and it shows no signs of stopping any time soon, so...

Give yourself permission. First, for younger people...remember when you were a little kid and loved dinosaurs, or ponies, or superheroes, and life was awesome and no one cared? Now that you're probably over the age of ten, you may be wondering if your love for Holmes makes you "weird." No. It doesn't. It makes you lucky.

Everyone is different. People have different interests, abilities and goals. And for the most part, unless any of those involve committing actual crimes, they are all okay. You may look at the kids around you and imagine that they are all "normal," or "cookie-cutter," but I assure you, they are not. No one is. It's possible, however, that some of them have interests which are more common than yours, or that they may feel them less intensely. They really like baseball, whereas you have memorized the dialogue from "A Scandal in Belgravia." They read fashion magazines, while you pore over maps of 19th century London. They enjoy movies, but there are moments when you know, deep in your bones, that if you turn that corner, Holmes and Watson will be standing there.

Don't hide this. Own it. Wear that deerstalker. Throw out quotes no one notices. Use Canon references in your school papers. My guess is that, in most cases, the kids around you may not understand, but they'll be accepting. If you hide from yourself, however, you will be miserable, and life will seem cold and dull. Don't do that. What you have is magical. Embrace it.

And if you're an adult? The advice is the same. No matter how you handled your passions in your youth, it's very likely that now you're a bit embarrassed by them. You believe that they belong in the pile of "childish things" we all must put away. This view is particularly a problem for women. It's more acceptable, in our society, for men to have "toys" and "play." They can fish, golf, collect anything (everything), and pretty much pursue their hobbies to their hearts' content, but women often feel that we aren't allowed pursuits that don't fit the stereotypical notions of femininity. Do you like cooking? Working out? Great! Attending Star Trek cons? Hmm…

I came to the Sherlockian world late in life—as a 40-something mother of three. After ten years of trying to be what I thought a stay-at-home mom should be, I was bored, lonely, and not much fun to be around. Still, it took time to give myself permission to do more with Sherlock Holmes than simply reading the Canon at home. The fact is, most of us live regular lives, with dull routines and jobs that can exhaust or waste our abilities. Like that of our hero, our minds "rebel at stagnation." You'll find that being an active Sherlockian will enrich your life, both when you happen to be in Baker Street, and when you're not.

Get out there. Now that you've embraced your Inner Holmes, Watson, or Moriarty, what happens next? Well, for some people, that's enough. They're happy sitting by the fireside on foggy days reading one of the four novels or 56 stories. But most people—even the most introverted of us—typically want to share our enthusiasm with at least one other person. How do you find that person? Or a whole group of them?

Short answer: The internet. If you are on any form of social media, searching for "Sherlock Holmes" will give you the names of dozens of groups and people who not only share your interest, but may also enjoy your particular subspecialty. Rathbone devotees, Cumberfans, Doyleans, it really won't take you long to find at least a few kindred spirits.

And if you want more than online interaction? Then I suggest you check out a resource like Sherlockian.net for a list of BSI "scion societies." These are clubs, often with a regional basis, which are affiliated with the Baker Street Irregulars—the oldest, most prominent Sherlockian organization in the U.S. If you live within reasonable driving distance of such a group, I would highly recommend you attend a few meetings. You'll be welcomed and (don't worry) no one will give you a Canon quiz. Or if they do, it's for fun and just about everyone will fail. Promise. Worried that being introverted and just "not very social" will hold you back? Don't be. Join us—we'll be sitting on the outer edges of the room, just listening, and we're saving you a (quiet) seat.

Get educated. Even though knowledge isn't the price of admission to the Sherlockian world, it's really no fun without it. If you came to the fandom via a television show or movie, take the time to read the actual stories. Read pastiche. Explore fanfic. Check out late Victorian or Edwardian history. Cook your own brace of quails. I wouldn't recommend cocaine in any solution, or tobacco, but other than that, everything you can learn about Sherlock Holmes, his times, his portrayals, his methods, his literary agent, will only serve to bring you more enjoyment in our little world.

Stretch a bit. When you're a child, you have the illusion that you're good at everything. The fastest runner, the best artist…and you know that being a marine biologist/astronomer/concert violinist is entirely possible. Then reality hits, and at some point, you decide "this is Who I Am." In some ways, that's great—"Who I Am" doesn't stress too much about having a messy car or hating beets, for example—but "Who I Am" can also become stagnant, avoiding new or scary situations. As you get to know other Sherlockians, you'll find public speakers who used to run from the podium; writers who thought their dreams of publication had died in college; people who fly to conferences, white knuckles and all; painters, actors, cosplayers, podcasters, researchers—even people who start their own scion societies. Sherlock Holmes invented his own job, and he's been inspiring others to re-invent themselves ever since. What have you always wanted to do? Chances are, you'll find in Sherlockiana a supportive and inspiring community who will cheer you on.

Involve the family. One thing you might notice about Sherlockian gatherings is that, while there are many attendees who are older and younger, there can be a dearth of participants who are in the middle—the kind with kids at home. Let's face it: it's hard to nurture your own interests when you have younger children. Between school, activities, playing referee and, well, *being a parent*, it's no wonder that no one between the ages of 25 and 65 finishes a craft project.

It may be challenging, but seek chances to involve your family in your Sherlockian life. My husband goes with me to events. At first, he was my "crutch," because I was nervous and he is likeable. Now, scion meetings have become our date nights. Involving younger children is a little tricky, as many group events are geared towards adults. Still, at our house, we watch Sherlock Holmes videos (Granada was a favorite), I share my projects, and we celebrate special dates, such as Holmes's birthday (January 6), Arthur Conan Doyle's birthday (May 22), and Reichenbach Day (May 4). Now that the kids are teens, they attend some scion events, and have tagged along to conferences. They may never be Sherlockians themselves, but we have fun together, and they get to meet wonderful people doing wonderful things.

Have a budget. As hobbies go, Sherlocking doesn't fall in the realm of car-collecting, but neither is it as cheap as, say, saving bits of string. Of course, if your income allows you to collect actual Conan Doyle manuscripts and own your own London flat, then it's as expensive as you want it to be, but the truth is, most of us must budget. There are three main expenditures that many Sherlockians share: books, collecting (all sorts of things), and conferences. Never feel pressured to participate in any of these things, particularly if you cannot afford them. And even if you can do some things, set spending limits and stick to them. In the excitement of BSI weekend, or any dealer's room, it's easy to lose your head and can be so painful when the bill comes due. Remember, even Watson had to lock his cheque-book in Holmes's desk drawer.

It's all fine. After seven years in this hobby, I still believe that Sherlock-ians are some of the finest people on earth. But it's important to remember that we are all imperfect. After the newness wears off, many new Sherlock Holmes fans notice that there is, occasionally, trouble in Baker Street—what one Mrs. Hudson calls "domestics." These can be over something as minor as a show that some people love, and others love to hate. It can be a clash of personalities, each with their own supporters. Or it can be more serious, and involve questions of gender, age, race, or other issues which echo those of our larger society. No matter how it comes about, you'll eventually realize that even your greatest Sherlockian heroes can have feet of clay. In the age of social media, many of these conflicts play out in very public ways.

In my early days in fandom, I felt compelled to join in—to give my opinion, to take sides. As time has gone on, I've learned that, with a few exceptions, online fracases accomplish little; I advise against getting too deeply involved in most of them. Patience, tolerance, open-mindedness, and personal connections solve more problems than even the most elo-quent Facebook post, while becoming too entangled in the politics of any group can lead quickly to hurt, misconception, and disillusionment. We're celebrating a great author and his creation, not practicing a religion. In the end, adopting the BBC *Sherlock* motto, "It's all fine," covers a multitude of sins and keeps you sane.

It's the work. I'll confess, one of the reasons why I love Sherlockiana is that it provides opportunities for measurable progress. I worked for 15 years before leaving the workforce to become a stay-at-home mom, and one of the hardest adjustments I had to make was that I had no way to know, really, that I was doing a good job. No raises. No promotions. No "Diaper-Changer-of-the-Month." No paycheck. As a Sherlockian, I can use my talents (very few of which are applicable to housewifery) and get some recognition for them—writing a blog, publishing an article, and even writing a book. I've learned something fascinating from this, however.

When I held *A Curious Collection of Dates* in my hands, or saw my article in the *Baker Street Journal*, I felt much…calmer than I had antici-pated. It struck me that what I liked most about both of those endeavors—and anything else I've done—was the actual *doing* of them, and not the finished product, or even the achievement. It was then that I understood what Sherlock Holmes meant when he quoted Flaubert: "L'oeuvre, c'est tout." As a Sherlockian, you'll have times when you'll receive recognition, and times you won't. Times you'll get opportunities, and times when those will go to others. *Never compare.* Instead, find a niche you love, and go to town! No matter what happens after, you'll be busy and happy with your own adventures.

The Sussex Downs. When you're in the thick of things—making toasts at meetings, memorizing "221B," writing for *IHOSE* and running around with your friends at every possible conference—it's hard to believe that anything will ever change. But it can. One day, you're 27 in the lab at Bart's, and the next, you're 50 and Watson is married again. Some people stay in the Sherlockian world their entire lives, but it seems very common to fade in and out, and some drop out completely. Always remember, no matter which path you take, "It's all fine," but keep the best parts (and your friends) with you. Grow vegetable marrows, join that new fandom, take up parasailing, or keep bees—but no matter what you choose, if Watson shows up at your door in a Ford, jump in, for the game is ever afoot!

Leah Guinn (Fort Wayne, Indiana) is a member of the Illustrious Clients of Indianapolis and, with Jaime N. Mahoney, the author of *A Curious Collection of Dates: Through the Year With Sherlock Holmes*. In her spare time she has a husband and three children.

THE MEMBERS OF
SHERLOCK HOLMES

THE ADVENTURE OF THE MOST INTERESTING PEOPLE

THOMAS J. FRANCIS

My earliest recollection of Sherlock Holmes is the Ronald Howard TV series, which I watched faithfully. I recall my mother saying that when she was young, she saw Holmes in the movies, and that the films always ended with Holmes saying, "Quick, Watson! The needle!"

By high school, I had read all the stories. I had an English teacher who told us that many people were sure that Holmes and Watson were real—in such a way that I suspected he might be one of them himself. I thought he was a nut case. Still, by the time I turned 20 in 1963—the same year I got married—I had bought my first hardcover copy of *The Adventures*. After quickly acquiring the rest of the Canon, I began reading everything else Doyle had written, and made it my mission to get a copy of each of his books. Holmes became the principal literary interest in my life—one which my wife, Diana, fully supported. She made me a Persian slipper in which I could store my tobacco, and was always on the lookout for great stuff for me. Once she saw that there was a Sherlock Holmes play being performed in London, wrote to the company, and got me a Playbill.

In 1972, we made our first trip to England. Before we went to the Tower and all the other tourist places, we went to Baker Street. The site of 221B was occupied by the Midland Bank, but I went in anyway, and asked about Holmes. A bank employee gave me two postcards from the 1951 Festival of Britain, showing the reconstructed sitting-room, the same one which can now be found at the Sherlock Holmes Pub.

He also gave me a card directing me to the nearby Marylebone Library. There I met Heather Owen, who was in charge of the Holmes collection (the same collection that was the source of the *Strand Magazine* reprints). Heather had other duties and was supposed to spend no more than perhaps a half-hour per week on the Holmes material. She spent well over that with me!

When she asked to which societies I belonged, I told her none. She told me about the Sherlock Holmes Society of London's trip to Meiringen—in costume, including the air rifle belonging to "Colonel Moran" (Lord Gore-Booth in civilian life), which the pilot promptly confiscated. At Meiringen the group's luggage arrived in a covered cart that also brought an apparent corpse. The police were summoned and loaded everyone into vintage police vehicles, driving them all over town, thus providing a tour. When they got to the Town Hall, the Mayor of Meiringen berated them for being poor excuses for Sherlockians, as not one of them had observed that the "body" was their waitress.

When I left the library, Ms. Owen said I was the most knowledgeable person who had ever shown up there, and it was a shame that I did not belong to any Holmesian groups. She may well have said the same to everyone who came by, but I prefer to believe she was being honest. And after hearing her stories, I knew I needed to find a group.

It took me some time, however. When I first got home, I read an article about the Speckled Band of Boston which stated that they met at the Club of Odd Volumes. I wrote to them, in care of the Club, but I never heard back. Later, I learned that the Band had last used that venue in 1954. My search finally ended when Diana and I went to see the Shakespeare Company of Rhode Island's production of "The Hound of the Baskervilles," a very clever play which used only quotes from the book. The playbill contained information regarding the next dinner of the Cornish Horrors, the Rhode Island scion. It was at the Horrors that I first met many of the people who are still the core of my Sherlockian circle: Al Silverstein, Jan Prager, Burt Wolder, Bob Thomalen, and the late and truly great Charlie Adams.

The Horrors met in the middle of nowhere at the last exit in Rhode Island before you entered Connecticut. Dinner was always Cornish game hen. There was so little meat on those birds that I took to stopping for a snack on my drive down. Periodically, the meeting would be a joint one with Connecticut's The Men on the Tor and would be held at Gillette Castle, where we'd have the run of the place. It was at one of these that I first heard Bob Thomalen read his version of a Sherlock Holmes tale as a hard-boiled detective story.

As scions do, the Horrors had their own particular traditions, toasts, rituals, and presentations. First, there was the "scholarly paper" presented by Al Silverstein, loaded with the most outrageous statements, and constantly challenged (loudly) by the audience. Al's ability to have a comeback for every comment was a delight, and the repartee was breathtaking. The other item was a play that Burt Wolder would write, filled with outlandish puns. The play was "performed" by members of the audience, led by Bob Colonna—son of comedian Jerry Colonna, and producer of the "Hound" play that brought me to the Horrors in the first place.

Then, of course, there were the toasts. One particular year, Al had given every toast presenter plenty of lead time. There was never any coordination between the toasters; I was first and had written a bluesy one, with Charlie Adams playing harmonica in between my sung choruses. Charlie, as it happened, was next, and he gave a toast using a Gilbert and Sullivan melody. Scott Monty followed with a toast sung as Frank Sinatra. The poor woman who came next began to read her toast, and was assailed by the crowd for not singing it.

I still wondered about the Speckled Band of Boston, however. Although a few members of the Horrors told me the Band's gatherings were "stuffy and dull," when I finally got on the Band's mailing list I found they were no such thing; rather, they were Boston-proper and bound to tradition in a charming, Old World way. Dr. John Constable was the Keeper and, while I would prefer to avoid absolutes, the man who has become my best Sherlockian friend, Dan Posnansky, was the Cheetah. Decades later, Dan is now the Keeper, and I am the Cheetah.

At my first dinner with the Band, my quiz score tied with that of another man who was also there for the first time, Jim Duval. The tie was resolved by having the two of us stand in front of the entire group while, perched above us on the stage, Dr. Constable began reading random quotes from the Canon. After the first quote, I named the story, and Jim said he agreed. The second citation was read, Jim named the story, and I agreed. Constable then looked over our heads at the assembly and said, "How do I know they are not lying?" There was a consensus expressed that Sherlockians do not cheat, so he continued for several more quotes. Finally, Jim gave "Thor Bridge" as an answer, and I had to admit that I did not recognize the quote. Jim won. He laughed, and told me he only recognized it because of some remark I had made earlier in the evening.

I became friends with Jim, who ran a scion based in New Hampshire called Cox and Co. Jim was an amazing Sherlockian; every time I met him he had made another new convert. Cox and Co. met at a little library, and the main theme was the unwritten cases. One time, Jim scheduled a meeting in a restaurant in Manchester, where we had to dress as characters from the Canon. I went as Black Peter, devising what looked like the end of a harpoon to stick out of my chest. We caused quite a sensation walking through a crowded dining room to get to our area.

Many of the members were actually from Massachusetts, so we had several meetings at our house. Jim thought people would like to see my collection, which consists of about 5,000 books, half of which are Holmes or Doyle-related. One of the best moments of these home meetings came about because John McAleer, one of the world's experts on Rex Stout (and his official biographer), was a member. He came across my Stout collection, first remarking that there were a couple of books he did not have, and then pulling various volumes from the shelf and discussing them in what became an amazing half-hour lecture. Shortly before he died, John told me Rush Limbaugh had done a show talking about how good the Nero Wolfe stories were. This triggered a giant spike in interest in Wolfe, and as John was listed as an expert in the media directories, he had calls from networks and major newspapers and his phone had not stopped ringing.

Unfortunately, my friend Jim Duval inherited a genetic defect that caused the males in his family to die young. He left behind a wife, two young children, and a lot of sad Sherlockians. A number of his "finds" are now members of the BSI.

Every year at the Speckled Band's dinner, someone, usually Joel Schwartz, would say to me, "You should go to the Friends of Irene Adler dinner." To get there, I'd need an invitation from Dan Posnansky. I gave Dan my name and address several times with no result, and was beginning to think he just didn't like me. It turned out that forgetting to send out the invitations was normal for him, and eventually, he remembered. Dan had founded the Friends of Irene Adler more than 40 years ago so that Sherlockian women in the Cambridge/Boston area would have a place to go, the Speckled Band being male-only. For the first 30 of those years, the meetings were held at one of Harvard's private dining clubs.

Let's look at what it took to put on one of these old-style dinners. The Friends meeting is always the third Friday in December, so it becomes a Holmes Christmas dinner: pea soup with ham, roast goose with chestnut stuffing, brussels sprouts, and trifle. Every year, we would have to contact the club's new president, explain who we were, and negotiate the "rent." This was always a sort of payment in kind—the Friends would agree to replace the dishes and/or glasses that students had destroyed during the past year, to have the ancient stove repaired, or to fill some similar need. Someone would then go to the club to inventory the china and glassware to make certain we had enough, order linens, print the menus, rent the set-up, contract a chef and wait staff, and arrange for clean-up afterwards. In order to provide an open bar, we would check our own inventories to see what needed to be purchased in addition to the cases of wine. There was wood for the fireplace to be got, and finally there were the geese, which would arrive frozen and needed to be picked up several days early and brought to the club to thaw. The day after the dinner, we went back to the club to arrange pick-up for the tables and chairs, and then returned the linens to the laundry.

The Friends dinner was then, and remains today, a great convivial evening. There are toasts, the quiz, scholarly papers, and program additions such as auctions, concerts, or a movie. One becomes a member of the Friends by presenting a paper. Dan Posnansky then bestows an "appellation" (a quote from "A Scandal in Bohemia") on the new member. While I have been the titular head for the last 24 years, Dan still does much of the behind-the-scenes work. Through all these years, Joel Schwartz has been a most effective secretary and treasurer.

The toasts are unique. With the exception of the toast to the Queen which, until her health intervened, was always given by Anne Cotton, the toasters are always asked that night, forcing them to prepare their talks during the cocktail hour. It is amazing what many have created in so short a time! At one point, the toast to the Baker Street Irregulars was given by the youngest person present. In the early years, this person could truly be a youngster, as a number of members brought their children.

Another toast has been discontinued. It was the Toast to Moriarty, always given by Dirk Struik, a retired MIT professor. He came to the dinner on his own, via public transit, until he was in his mid-nineties, and then was driven until he was 102 or 103. Dirk's toast presented a positive image of Moriarty, "a fellow mathematician and Irish freedom-fighter." He would add to this praise items of current topical interest, and deliver his toast with no notes. Like the Professor, Dirk had an interesting history. During the McCarthy era, he was fired by MIT as a Communist—and thrown out of the Speckled Band. He sued and got his job back, then waited until every member of the Band involved in his ouster had died, and returned for one dinner.

I have developed a few traditions of my own, centered around the Baker Street Irregulars dinner in New York. I've met three BSI leaders ("Wiggins"): Julian Wolff, Tom Stix, and Mike Whelan. I've told them more than once, "I don't care where you seat me, or who you seat me with, because all Sherlockians are interesting people." This is no exaggeration: if you are at a table of eight Sherlockians and a random subject arises, at least six of them will be able to speak intelligently about it. The topic is rarely Holmes, but the conversation is always interesting.

For many years, I drove Scott Monty and Richard Olken from Boston to New York for the BSI weekend. Scott moved to Detroit, but the next year he called from the airport when Richard and I were on the Wilbur Cross Parkway. We chatted with him by speakerphone, and he did impersonations of several Sherlockians, keeping us in stitches until we were well along the Merritt Parkway. He has done that every year since, and Richard and I get nervous if the call comes late.

Until he stopped coming to New York, Dan Posnansky and I went to the opera on the Thursday before the Dinner, and often again on the ensuing Saturday. In the years when the dinner was at 24 Fifth Avenue, Charlie Adams and I would walk to the Village after the meal and visit a jazz club. After a set or two, we would walk up Sixth Avenue to the Algonquin, which would still be packed with Sherlockians. The time I spent talking with Charlie remains my favorite experience of the BSI weekends.

Thomas J. Francis (Scituate, Massachusetts) is a life-long reader, Sherlockian, and fan of Arthur Conan Doyle, who plays the saxophone daily and at 73 still plays ice hockey three times a week.

THE ADVENTURE OF THE AMATEUR MENDICANT SOCIETY

CHRISTOPHER MUSIC

"The year '87 furnished us with a long series of cases of greater or less interest, of which I retain the records. Among my headings under this one twelve months I find an account…of the Amateur Mendicant Society, who held a luxurious club in the lower vault of a furniture warehouse." ——The Five Orange Pips

* * * *

Enthusiasts enter the Sherlockian world through different doors. For many Sherlockians, a typical "How I Met Sherlock Holmes" tale begins with discovering the Holmes stories at age twelve or thirteen (often with "The Speckled Band" or *The Hound of the Baskervilles*). This first meeting with the Great Detective opens up for them an exciting new world—a Victorian world of hansom cabs and gas lamps—and gives them a new hero to worship. The young Sherlockian in this common scenario will then dive into all the remaining stories, becoming hooked for a lifetime.

Many others enter Holmes's world through the door of film and television (or even stage and radio in past generations). Interest in Sherlock Holmes tends to come in waves, and depending on one's age, this first introduction could have been with Basil Rathbone, Jeremy Brett, or Benedict Cumberbatch. Often the screen adaptations are satisfying enough, but sometimes fans are inspired to seek out the original stories, with some then becoming diehard Sherlockians.

These common experiences, however, were not my experience. As embarrassing as it might now be to admit—and while I was always a very active reader from a young age—I don't actually recall ever reading a Sherlock Holmes tale in my youth. I didn't stumble across an old copy of *The Adventures* on a dusty bookshelf; I never had a teacher or relative recommend a favorite story to me. And to make matters worse, I somehow also missed any classic screen adaptations of Sherlock Holmes (Jeremy Brett would have been the most likely).

My story is unique in that my very first entry into the Sherlockian world came through the door of the scion society, the local group of enthusiasts.

This happened in my mid-twenties, and the story—briefly—is this. A colleague of mine kept a handsome Sherlock Holmes statue in his office. My career then (as now) was in corporate finance—not a field where one usually finds opportunity for literary conversation. But after a time, I asked him about it. It turned out that he had been a fan of the Holmes and Watson stories for many years. More importantly, for my purposes, he said that he belonged to an actual club that met regularly over dinner and cocktails to discuss these stories seriously (something he referred to as "the Game"). Most intriguingly, this group had a mysterious sounding name: the Amateur Mendicant Society of Detroit. What kind of group was this? And what was an Amateur Mendicant, anyway? I simply had to find out—and I accepted his invitation to join him at an upcoming dinner.

What a scion to be introduced to! It turned out the AMS had a long and rich history dating back to the 1940s, and I learned that it was one of many local chapters of an even greater organization, the Baker Street Irregulars of New York City, established in 1934. These groups from around the globe all met to discuss—improbably to me—Sherlock Holmes and his world. They played the "Game" I had heard about, treating Holmes and Watson as if they were real people, with Arthur Conan Doyle acting as a literary agent. This all sounded too good to be true, and I knew I had to become a part of it.

The founder of the Amateur Mendicant Society of Detroit was Russell McLauchlin, columnist and theatre critic for the *Detroit News*. He once wrote to his friend Vincent Starrett in Chicago—for many the greatest Sherlockian ever—asking for his advice on starting a local club. Starrett wrote back: "Your credentials look excellent from where I sit, wherefore welcome to the BSI. I do things quicklike and by fiat...so by all means found a Detroit chapter if you can, being careful to let in only the right people—i.e. such as are capable of contributing a bit of spurious scholarship...whether they ever do so or not." So McLauchlin did. The twelve founding members of the Amateur Mendicant Society had their first meeting in April 1946 at a Detroit restaurant named Cliff Bells, which, like the AMS, still survives.

The AMS soon drew the attention of Edgar W. Smith, editor of the *Baker Street Journal* and Commissionaire of the Baker Street Irregulars. Smith was an executive with General Motors in New York City, and his work often brought him to company headquarters in Detroit. A letter he wrote to BSI founder Christopher Morley in 1947 gives some insight into the AMS in these early years: "I have to report my attendance last Friday evening at the dinner of the Amateur Mendicant Society in Detroit—easily, under Russell McLauchlin's guidance, the most erudite of the scions. There were seventeen present, and the opportunities for earnest and completely satisfying discussion were in sharp contrast to those presented at the same melees our BSI over-gatherings have become. Let this be noted for our future thought. Incidentally, there were two cocktails, two highballs, excellent food—and all for the sum of one guinea—at the old exchange."

I clearly had the good fortune to stumble into the right club. The Amateur Mendicant Society had a great heritage and honored traditions, and was the home of many great Sherlockians over the years, including legendary Irregulars from the forties and fifties like Russ McLauchlin, Robert Harris, and Bill Rabe.

Having discovered this exciting new world of Sherlock Holmes scholarship and sodality, I jumped in with the enthusiasm of the converted, trying to make up for lost time. I read everything I could get my hands on: the original 60 stories first, then that trove of scholarship known as "the Writings." Dozens (hundreds) of books, journals, articles all devoted to studying the glorious minutiae found in the Holmes stories. Which university did Holmes attend? How did he spend the three years of his hiatus? How many times had Dr. Watson been married? Or maybe Dr. Watson was a woman? As it is said, never has so much been written by so many for so few, and spending time studying something at a level of detail that never was intended turned out to be great fun.

Different Sherlockians have different fields of interest. The traditional scholarship as played in "the Game," chronology, pastiche, film, TV—the list is as varied as the many Sherlockians involved. But thanks to my own unique entrance into the Sherlockian world, through the scions, and my fortune at finding myself in a group with a long and rich past, my own particular interest became studying the history of the Sherlockian movement. That includes the Baker Street Irregulars, the scion societies, and the fascinating and interesting lives of the men and women involved in this wonderful pastime.

This interest in Sherlockian society history led me to become the archivist of the AMS, allowing me to study in depth the various records and documents from our group dating back to our very beginnings. Being in physical possession of these documents transported me to a long-lost time when people sent telegrams, postcards, and wrote letters to each other with a scholarship, humor, and erudition that might never be seen again (quite literally, in our age of email and other digital communication). This experience led me to write my first article for the *Baker Street Journal*, sharing my experience as a scion archivist and encouraging other groups to establish their own archives so that we could all preserve our rich histories. The experience also resulted in me publishing a book documenting the archival history of our great society (*From the Lower Vault: Treasures of the Amateur Mendicant Society of Detroit*).

My interest in the history of the Sherlockian movement put me in touch with other like-minded individuals, and gave me the encouragement to travel the country to attend dinners and gatherings of other "golden age" societies formed in the same era as the Amateur Mendicants, including the Speckled Band of Boston, the Hounds of the Baskerville (sic) in Chicago, and the Sons of the Copper Beeches in Philadelphia. Later I was fortunate enough to be invited to join the most famous Sherlockian society of them all, the Baker Street Irregulars.

Lately, I've been fortunate to be asked to play a small part in the BSI's own archival efforts, working with the Baker Street Irregulars Trust, and in recent years have even been asked to edit the Sherlockian Societies section of the *Baker Street Journal*. It seems that my work has come full circle.

But all of my effort in this area, both locally and with the BSI, is done in the hopes of helping in some small way preserve for future generations the memories of the societies and the great Sherlockian men and women who came before us.

Still, the best part of being a Sherlockian will always be the time spent with friends at my local club, the Amateur Mendicant Society of Detroit. The traditions first established in 1946 continue today—along with a fine mix of scholarship and sociability—but always with an emphasis on the latter. My belief is that the local groups are where the most fun is had, and where the strongest friendships are formed. As Sherlockians we get to make lifelong friendships with people we otherwise would never have met in the course of our normal lives, all through a shared love of our heroes Sherlock Holmes and Dr. Watson.

For me, this great adventure started from a brief conversation with a colleague concerning a statue in his office—a conversation that would ultimately change my life forever. I hope that a future scholar, many decades in the future, will look back and see what fun times we all had.

Christopher Music (Clarkston, Michigan) is the Commissionaire of the Amateur Mendicant Society of Detroit. He is a member of the Baker Street Irregulars, edits the society reports for the *Baker Street Journal*, and is a volunteer with the BSI Trust.

THE ADVENTURE OF
THE IRREGULAR HISTORIAN

HARRISON (TERRY) HUNT

In my 65 years, I have had two abiding interests: history and Sherlock Holmes. It is no surprise, then, that I get a special joy in approaching the Canon as an historian. What was surprising to me, though, is how Christopher Morley, founder of the Baker Street Irregulars, quite unexpectedly came to focus my interest in things Sherlockian.

First and foremost, I am a history geek, and have been since childhood. I was raised on stories of my family which made history come alive for me—Dad's forebears had settled in the American colonies in the 1600s, and Mom's family had been in the village where we lived since 1900. I loved family vacations to Williamsburg, visiting historic houses (mostly with Dad, as Mom thought they "smelled funny") and exploring the heritage of my community. I started a history club in my high school, and even received a grant in twelfth grade to publish a history of my home town. *Nerdus historicus* without a doubt.

So, when I read the Holmes stories for the first time—also in high school—I was hooked. They took place in my favorite era and captured the period perfectly: frock coats, top hats, gas lamps, steam-powered trains, horse-drawn vehicles and even a couple of early cars. And Holmes! Not only did this brilliant detective exhibit all the qualities of a first-rate historian, gathering evidence from disparate sources, evaluating it and reaching a demonstrable conclusion, he *was* a first-rate historian. I was (and remain) delighted that the Master had become so conversant with ancient handwriting that at one glance he could date the manuscripts of the Musgrave ritual and the story of the hound of the Baskervilles. He even relaxed by doing research into early English charters ("The Three Students") and the origins of ancient Cornish ("The Devil's Foot")…a true kindred spirit!

I, in turn, enjoy myself by analyzing the Holmes stories with the eye of an historian and researcher. It is great fun playing the Grand Game by constructing back-stories for the adventures, and puzzling out possible solutions for some of Watson's apparent contradictions, all the while trying to look at things from a period point of view. This involves consulting Victorian and Edwardian encyclopedias, books and articles, and scholarly studies of the era, in order to imagine what would have been familiar to Holmes and Watson, and eliminate the biases and preconceptions of our

21st-century minds. I've used this approach for numerous papers. One discovered that there were actually three crowns that might have been the "diadem [that] once encircled the brows of the Royal Stuarts" found in "The Musgrave Ritual." Another, following extensive research, proposed answers to what Elias Openshaw of "The Five Orange Pips" had done to earn the animus of the Ku Klux Klan, what was in his strongbox, and what Holmes's "American Encyclopedia" actually was.

Two studies reflected specialized knowledge I gained as an American Civil War reenactor portraying a Union Army surgeon. By looking at Watson's treatment of Victor Hatherley's thumb ("The Engineer's Thumb") through the lens of late 19th-century surgical practices rather than those of the late 20th century, it became clear that the good doctor did not deserve the accusations of malpractice that many Writers About the Writings had made. Similarly, an examination of period accounts and surgical manuals backed up Watson's description of his wounding at Maiwand. A significant part of this was the revelation that, using the period's teachings about the appearance of wounds, it is arguable that Watson could have identified the type of bullet that hit him by its entry laceration, even though modern medicine rejects this possibility.

All of which does not lead us to Christopher Morley. My connection with that seminal Sherlockian, and the major influence he had on me, came through my job. After getting my bachelor's degree (in history, naturally), I earned a master's in history museum studies and was hired as a curator with the Parks Department of Nassau County, Long Island. I married and had a family, and my Holmesian studies took a back seat; I actually sold most of my Sherlockian books when my children needed something that wasn't in the budget. At work I had several assignments over the years, finally serving as senior curator of history and supervisor of seven of the department's historic sites, one of which was Christopher Morley's little writer's retreat The Knothole, which he had constructed in 1935 next to his house in Roslyn Estates, Long Island, as a quiet place to work away from the distractions of his growing family. The building is a rustic one-room cabin boasting a fireplace, a convenient bunk bed, and a futuristic modular bathroom designed by Morley's friend Buckminster Fuller. A few years after Morley's death in 1957, The Knothole was moved a few miles to what is now Christopher Morley Park to preserve it as a literary shrine.

Supervising this site marked my introduction to this underappreciated author, and the reawakening of my interest in the Canon—an interest that came into full bloom when helping the Baker Street Irregulars plan a trip to The Knothole in commemoration of the group's 75th anniversary in 2009. Following that event, my last duty before retiring, I became active in several Sherlockian groups and, with my wife Linda, began researching Morley and the early years of the Baker Street Irregulars.

The Irregulars has matured a great deal as an organization since Christopher Morley convened the first meeting on January 6, 1934. The nascent group consisted of several of Morley's friends who he felt shared an interest in the Holmes stories. For the first few years of its existence, Morley continued to determine the guest list, inviting a mix of old friends and newcomers he thought would add to the Sherlockian gathering because of their interest in the Master or some specialized knowledge they possessed—like that of Harrison Martland, the Essex County, New Jersey, medical examiner and one of the top pathologists in the United States.

During the 1930s, the Irregulars (like the rest of the clubs Morley brought into being) was loosely structured at best; it would not be until Edgar W. Smith became involved in the 1940s that the Irregulars began to be organized into the society we know today. It was a gathering of Holmes aficionados who came together to eat, drink, enjoy some good conversation, and play the Grand Game, accepting Arthur Conan Doyle as Watson's literary agent and nothing more (to the consternation of ACD's sons). Under Morley's direction, the Irregulars established practices that not only have endured, but have come to characterize and unite American Sherlockian societies: ritual toasts, quizzes, celebrating Holmes's birthday on January 6, delivering papers (scholarly and otherwise), socializing over drinks and a meal during or after the meeting and, first and foremost, an abiding love of the tales of Baker Street, where it is always 1895.

Of course, over time there have been changes in the way things were done in Morley's day, too, many reflecting changes in society over the past 80-plus years. Women, who were excluded from the BSI for decades, were finally admitted in 1991, and one of the last of the traditional all-male scions, the Speckled Band of Boston, voted to follow suit in 2017. The serious imbibing that characterized many Sherlockian meetings in decades past has decreased in this age of social responsibility, to the point that the wives' group of the all-male Sons of the Copper Beeches in Philadelphia—affectionately known as the Bitches of the Beeches —no longer has to fulfill its original function of gathering together to drive their too-jolly husbands home. The cigar and cigarette smoking that was once common at meeting places has disappeared at all but the annual meetings of The 140 Varieties of Tobacco Ash society in Indianapolis. And the Irregulars now openly recognize and discuss Arthur Conan Doyle as the creator of Sherlock Holmes. But the biggest change of all is nevertheless rooted in the group that first gathered in 1934: Morley's single club has inspired the creation of hundreds of similar associations across the world, scholarly conferences, and extensive Writings About the Writings, all dedicated to keeping green the memory of Sherlock Holmes.

Harrison (Terry) Hunt (Catskill, New York) is a retired history museum curator and author. He is a member of the Baker Street Irregulars, the Adventuresses of Sherlock Holmes, and other societies. He and his wife, Linda, lead the Grillparzer Club of the Hoboken Free State, commemorating Christopher Morley, and are working on a volume of biographies of early Irregulars.

A CASE OF IRREGULARITY

ANDREW J. PECK

I find it hard to believe I have been a Baker Street Irregular for almost 45 years.

When did I begin reading the Canon? The answer of course is elementary—elementary school, that is. I started my Sherlockian collection with the Doubleday one-volume *Complete Sherlock Holmes*, Bill Baring-Gould's *Sherlock Holmes of Baker Street*, and Vincent Starrett's *Private Life of Sherlock Holmes*. From them, I learned that a group called the Baker Street Irregulars existed. After some hesitation, in June 1965 (at age twelve) I wrote to Julian Wolff (whose address was in Baring-Gould's book) and naively asked if I could join the BSI. He politely advised me that one had to be invited to join, but that I could subscribe to the *Baker Street Journal*. I asked my parents for an advance on my allowance, and subscribed. Subsequently, Dr. Wolff advised me that there were two "junior Sherlockian" organizations—the Baker Street Pageboys and The Three Students Plus—and in 1967 I wrote off for their mimeograph publications. I had a few letters to the editor and articles in *Baker Street Pages* (the editor of which is the editor of this volume, so things have come full circle in 50 years).

Then, out of the blue, I received an invitation to the January 1970 BSI dinner. I was a 17-year-old high school student, and this was more exciting to me than being asked by a girl to the prom (which my high school canceled that year, but that's another story). The dinner was at the Players Club on Gramercy Park South, and one's place at the two long tables was according to "seniority" order—I got the last seat, but was happy just to be there. Other Irregulars now joke that I have not changed from one BSI dinner picture to another, but if you look at the 1970 dinner picture on the BSI Trust website, that is the only BSI picture where I do not have a mustache. That adornment made its first appearance in the 1971 dinner picture (and has remained on my lip, albeit grayer, to this day). The 1971 dinner also was my first appearance in deerstalker, which I (and others) continued to wear for a while in those days before black tie was customary.

At the January 1973 BSI dinner (at the Regency Hotel), I was awarded the Morley-Montgomery Award for the best article in the 1972 *BSJ*, for "The Adventure of the Solitary Man-uscript." (Thanks are due to Peter Blau, who had informed me that Arthur Conan Doyle's original manuscript of "The Solitary Cyclist" was in the Rare Book Room at Cornell

University, where I was a student.) That was my fourth BSI dinner, so I admit that I was slow to leave the podium, just in case Julian was going to present me with an Investiture. He whispered "sit down" to me, and I figured I should, like the Dodgers' famous saying, wait until next year. So imagine my pleasure when, after several other Shillings were given out, Julian called me back up to be invested as "Inspector Baynes of the Surrey Constabulary."

I was extraordinarily lucky to be invited to BSI dinners at such a young age, because I met and became friends with Sherlockian luminaries who have long since passed beyond the Reichenbach. I did not meet Christopher Morley, Edgar Smith, or the first generation of Irregulars, but did meet the "second" generation, who were very kind to the youngster and budding collector that I was then—John Bennett Shaw, Bliss Austin, Nathan Bengis, Morris Rosenblum, Bill Jenkins, Rev. Leslie Marshall, Isaac Asimov, Norm Nolan, Chris Steinbrunner, and many others. There are not many BSI left who can say we received our Shillings from Julian Wolff.

I missed the 1975-77 dinners because I was in law school, but have not missed a Dinner since—even the year I was on trial (as a lawyer, not a defendant) in North Carolina (the only day of a nine-month trial that I missed). The January festivities in the 1970s and 80s were not the multi-day festivities that they are today. There was the Martha Hudson breakfast Friday morning at the Algonquin Hotel, where I didn't eat, but would show up to see people, usually with a briefcase full of recent acquisitions to get inscribed. Then off to the Gillette Luncheon, the Dinner, and a Saturday informal cocktail party.

The BSI was purely stag in those years. So the Adventuresses of Sherlock Holmes held their own dinner on the Friday night, and some of the BSI and ASH would get together after the two dinners ended. For a young BSI in that period, the ASH were more my contemporaries than the "older" BSI, so I tended to hang out with them, including dinner after the Saturday cocktail party. When they sang about "pity to poor BSI," they traditionally looked at me and I hissed in response. I also managed to date a few of the ASH over the years—my ASH investiture is "The Date Being—?", which I chose not only because of my chronology book by that title, but also because of its dual meaning.

Besides longevity, I guess I am known in Sherlockian circles for having been a completist collector. I blame that affliction on coming under the influence of John Bennett Shaw and Peter Blau at an impressionable age. My collection now includes original Paget and Steele drawings, first editions of the Canon and Doyle's non-Sherlockian books (some in dust jacket and some signed by Doyle), *Strand Magazine* appearances of the stories, as well as commentaries, parodies and pastiches, and much more. But I understand my West Coast counterpart, Jerry Margolin, is writing about collecting, so I will only add that my non-collector wife is less than thrilled that our New York apartment contains twelve bookcases (double shelved) filled with Sherlockiana, as she made clear when the BSI toasted her as The Woman a few years ago.

I was lucky enough to combine my Sherlockian interest with my work as a lawyer, representing Dame Jean Conan Doyle (and producer Sy Weintraub) in the lawsuit filed against them by Granada Television seeking to be able to show the Jeremy Brett television series in the United States. Fortunately, I was able to settle the case, allowing PBS to show the Brett series, so I did not get lynched by my fellow Sherlockians. I got to meet Dame Jean, who was a delight, and whose interest was protecting the integrity of her father's works, not making money. And it was amusing to defend the deposition of Dame Jean's then American agent, BSI Otto Penzler, and listen as he tried to answer Granada's lawyer's question as to how one becomes a BSI.

Once I became a Judge (in February 1995), New York law allowed me to perform weddings, and I performed the first surprise Sherlockian wedding at a scion meeting. (The surprise was not as to the bride or groom—no shotguns—but to most of the guests, who at first wondered if the ceremony was a skit or was for real.)

One last point deserves mention. Chris Redmond and I started as junior Sherlockians and were accepted by the old guard of the BSI. Alas, we are no longer young Sherlockians. For the BSI to survive into the future, it must always be accepting of new Sherlockians, even if they come to Holmes more from Cumberbatch than from the written Canon, and even if they celebrate or write about Holmes in different ways than more "mainstream" Sherlockians. Some curmudgeons have grumbled about the Baker Street Babes, as I suspect some did in the 1960s about ASH or long-haired male junior Sherlockians. The editor of the *BSJ* has published and supported today's version of the 1960s me—and we all should do the same.

I hope to attend many more BSI Dinners.

Andrew J. Peck (New York, New York) is "Inspector Baynes of the Surrey Constabulary" among the Baker Street Irregulars. He is the author of *The Date Being—?: A Compendium of Chronological Data*. In real life, he is a lawyer who has been a United States Magistrate Judge since 1995.

THE ADVENTURE OF
THE WINDY CITY GIANTS

AL SHAW

"It is 4:00 in the morning and here I am poring over my copy of William Baring-Gould's *Annotated Sherlock Holmes*. My Rathbonean bent pipe is blazing away and, as a neophyte Sherlockian, I am out of my skull with pleasure as I sit there wide-eyed drinking it all in." Thus begins a paper I wrote back in the very early 1970s. As I re-read those words, my mind drifts back to when it all began. That was a great time and there were great Sherlockians. I realize now that I was privileged to walk among giants.

There are seminal moments when one transitions from "a guy reading the Sherlock Holmes stories" to being a "Sherlockian"—a student of the Canon. The 1960s had just ended. My brother was in the Peace Corps in Africa. He took only one book with him: *The Complete Sherlock Holmes*. In those days, the Peace Corps (and sometimes the government) would open your mail. So, my brother wrote to me in the dancing men cypher so that our letters would not be understood by others. This rekindled my interest in Sherlock Holmes.

My interest was further sparked by another event. In 1971, Hugo's Companions, a scion society of the Baker Street Irregulars, was featured in an article in the Chicago *Tribune*. They posted a notice that they were hosting their annual birthday party for Sherlock Holmes. I decided to attend and my reservation was graciously accepted. The dinner was a very formal affair, with everyone in jackets and ties or dresses. This was my first experience with a large group of people with a common interest. It was also my first experience with a group of Sherlockians "playing the game." The members, recognizing me as new, greeted me warmly. By the end of the evening, the members made it clear that I would be welcome at their regular meetings. Their sincerity made me believe their offer to be genuine. I knew that this group was something special and it was something of which I wanted to be a part.

Two months later, I attended my first regular meeting of Hugo's Companions. How can I paint a picture of what it was like to walk into the private room at King Arthur's Pub on Wells and Adams in Chicago? A haze hung over the room from the cigarette, cigar, and pipe smoke. When you glanced around the room, everybody had a libation in their hand. Since everybody was smoking, I took out my pipe—several people took out their tobacco pouches and offered me a sample of their particular blend of "shag." It was a simultaneously relaxing and intimidating environment. In my twenties, I was one of the youngest people present. Despite my youth and inexperience, they greeted me warmly and immediately welcomed me into their banter and badinage. The quizzes were notoriously tough. In fact, those questions stand today as some of the most difficult quiz questions about the Canon. ("You can cock a rifle. You can cock a gun. In this story what did Holmes cock?" Answer: His eye.) To top it off, many questions had a humorous twist that only the *cognoscenti* could divine. I know this to be true because I have saved many of the quizzes. The jesting and joking continued throughout the meal. Although I cannot remember what the particular presentation was at that first dinner, future presentations were given by a Jack the Ripper expert (who later became a famous author on the Ripper) and a forensic pathologist from Florida who showed us wonderfully gory slides. There were also presentations by future Sherlockian celebrities like Jon Lellenberg, Robert L. Fish, and Otto Penzler.

It was at those meetings that I formed my "Theory of determining the age of a Sherlockian by their choice of one's Favorite Sherlock Portrayal." I mentioned to someone sitting next to me that I thought Basil Rathbone portrayed the quintessential Sherlock Holmes. The retort was "Eille Norwood was the best Holmes in film." Who the hell was Norwood? I was to find out that every generation chose their own Holmes as portrayed on film or television, and, if you knew who their favorite Holmes was, the odds were that you could guess their age better than a carnival con man could.

In those days, the average Sherlockian was incredibly erudite, sophisticated, and educated. The remarkable thing about the community is that I was accepted into the fold without having to first establish credentials. In fact, my Sherlockian credentials were ascertained by my very participation with those people. When that gavel fell in a meeting, one would little suspect the day-to-day identity of the person you sat next to. And so, though I little realized it at first, I was permitted to walk among giants. Rather than list all these great people that I encountered at my table during various dinners, permit me to introduce you to a few that I remember best from a particular evening.

It was my first meeting, and I was at the bar of King Arthur's Pub throwing some darts (I was going through my Irish-pub-and-darts phase) waiting for the meeting to start. A tallish chain-smoking gent asked to play a few games while we waited. It was the first game of what was to become a pre-meeting ritual. The humble guy in a green tweed jacket was John Nieminski, who, I later discovered, was manager of the Midwest Regional Office of the US Civil Service Commission. He authored *The Hounds of the Baskerville (sic): A History of Chicago's Senior Sherlockian Scion Society, 1943-1983* and twice co-chaired the annual Bouchercon (the national Anthony Boucher Memorial Mystery Convention). Mystery scholars prized his notable bibliographies of *Ellery Queen's Mystery Magazine* (1974) and *The Saint Mystery Magazine* (1980). He co-founded the quarterly *Baker Street Miscellanea* (and was primarily responsible for publishing my previously referenced paper in its pages). John also compiled histories of Sir Arthur Conan Doyle's visits to Chicago in 1894 and the 1920s and authored "Sherlock Holmes in The Tribune."

Of course, John and I sat together at a big table. I turned to the guy next to me. "Hi, I am a programmer trainee. What is it that you do?" He replied, "I play French horn in the Chicago Symphony." I had never even seen a French horn except in pawn shop windows. Across the way, a little rumpled Columbo-esque man was telling a series of jokes, most with a Yiddish accent—"Vell. Dat's hacting!" John elucidated: "That's Ely Liebow. He's the chairman of the English department at Northeastern Illinois University." I later found out that Ely took part in the historic 1965 Selma march! In 1982, he would present me with one of the first copies of his book *Dr. Joe Bell: Model for Sherlock Holmes*.

Next to Ely, Dave Stevens was saying, "I will put that joke in the magazine." Dave was an editor for *Playboy*! (A magazine to which, at the time, I faithfully subscribed for the fine articles.) Also sitting with us were Dave Levinson, an attorney specializing in worker's compensation law as well as being a science fiction writer published in *Galaxy* magazine under the name Louis Newman, and Dick Schwartz, who was both an MD and an attorney, not to mention a collector of 19th-century Greek philosophy volumes.

I was beginning to feel sweat form on my upper lip. "Am I worthy of this group?"

At a table across the way, I recognized Jay Marshall from his TV show *The Magic Ranch*. He was busy demonstrating the pencil-through-the-dollar-bill trick for the guys seated there. Incidentally, Jay appeared on *The Ed Sullivan Show* 14 times. Looking on were Paul Smedegaard, a life-master in competitive bridge, and Bob Mangler, friend of Vincent Starrett and corporation counsel for the Village of Wilmette, as well as Master of the Hounds of the Baskerville (sic).

My shirt at this point was soaked. "Why would these guys want me as a member of this group?"

A toast was given by John Bennett Shaw, who was a great raconteur. Though he was retired to Santa Fe, where he founded The Brothers Three of Moriarty, he was a frequent visitor to the Chicago group. My first personal letter from him arrived soon after and began, "Well what do you know, another Shaw..." Receiving that missive was a hell of a thrill for the new initiate, I must tell you.

Also in attendance that night and at future meetings were George Armstrong, host of *The Wandering Folksong* show on WFMT, and Tom Evans, composer of essayistic presentations on such pertinent topics as London fog, The Origins of the Detective, and Dr. Watson's ethnic heritage. I am privileged to attend meetings with Tom to this day. Other notables included Marshall Blankenship, MD; John Brousch, Jr., author of *Sherlock Holmes and the Voyaging Vampire*, who was our artist in residence; Fred Levin, director of government compliance and director for toxic substances, and holder of more than 20 patents; and Matt Fairlie, vice-president of the technical committee that inspects all of the Indianapolis 500 race cars. Matt was the founder of Hugo's Companions. Space does not permit me to list at least a dozen more.

That first meeting ended with Bill Goodrich reciting "221B." Bill was a bank vice-president and was at the time working on his book which would be published as *Good Old Index: The Sherlock Holmes Reference Guide*. When he found out I was writing a paper on Holmes and pipe smoking, Bill gave me mimeographed copies of his manuscript to aid in my research. (There was no internet, boys and girls.)

When we finally adjourned to the bar, I was sweating profusely. I thought, "They are going to know. I am an imposter. What am I doing here? I am faking it. I am a 20-something programmer trainee in the company of some of the most accomplished people I have ever met." Nieminski and Liebow came up to me. John said, "Let me buy you a drink. We expect you to sit with us at the next meeting." I was in!

So, the next time you're at a meeting where they stand up on the terrace for some deceased member, listen to their biographical obituary. Most of them were great men and women in their youth. I am thankful that I was given that opportunity to walk among giants.

Al Shaw (Chicago, Illinois) has been a member and officer in many Sherlockian societies, including Hugo's Companions and the Hounds of the Baskerville (sic). He creates still life cards and calendars from his collection of pipes and Sherlockiana. He notes that much of the biographical data included here is the result of legwork by Julie McKuras.

THE NARRATIVE OF
THE COPACETIC MATRIARCH

SUSAN RICE

I have been fortunate to live a robust Sherlockian life for a great many years. My passion was born 63 years ago, and I met my first Irregular and had my first experience of the great Holmesian sodality-and-soda some 54 years ago. In the decades since that introduction I dived in with enthusiasm, joining scions in several parts of the country, speaking at conferences, writing for publications, present at many occasions important in our collective history. My life has been filled past the brim with wonderful stories and sights, with wit and humor, and with tales of some of the remarkable Holmesians I have known and loved.

While I am a native Detroiter, fifth generation no less, I moved to Chicago in 1977 and enjoyed my time there until New York called with a better offer in 1980. During those years in Chicagoland I was as active a female Sherlockian as I could be, attending meetings of Hugo's Companions when I was permitted (and a couple of times when I wasn't) and propping an elbow on the Criterion Bar. I made strong friends among Chicago's fine flock of Sherlockian scholars like Bob Hahn, Ely Liebow, John Nieminski, and Richard Smith, but none of those stalwarts was there for this brief and haunting confrontation.

If I were to take a guess (a shocking habit) I would date a certain incident to 1978, but it really doesn't matter. I was working in an office building just south of the Art Institute, and in good weather I drifted into the habit of lunching on one of the benches near the museum. On this occasion, I was carrying a tote bag entirely decorated with a large silhouette of the Master, filled with reading materials, papers, and crossword puzzles. Moving toward an available seat I noticed a homeless woman, advanced in years, and surrounded by bags and a shopping cart that appeared to hold all her possessions. As I walked by her, she remarked loudly, "Sherlock Holmes—he turned 124 this year."

I stopped short, stunned by her knowledge of his birth year, a supposition which had graduated to a fact for a few hundred extra-scholarly insiders at most. Standing before her, utterly gobsmacked, I was attempting to ask her how she knew this tiny fact when I felt a presence behind me and turned to see two uniformed policemen with determined expressions, preparing to remove the homeless woman from public view. I turned to them in full bristle and said "Wait! You can't...", but stopped when I realized that the rest of the sentence would be "... arrest her, she knows Sherlock Holmes's real birth year!" These were not words that would change a policeman's mind or impress him with her capability to care for herself. After a few wordless gestures I slunk away, took my seat, and tried to enjoy my lunch while overwhelmed with feelings of helpless futility.

It's a small story with an unhappy ending, and no answer to the question of how she knew that extremely obscure fact, but it's something I will never forget.

Now another story. My first job after graduate school was to teach fifth grade at Cranbrook School north of Detroit, and I remained there for seven years. Since the elementary school where I taught shared the 300-acre campus with the boys' prep school and the girls' prep school, many of my former students returned after school to visit.

For some reason beyond my understanding, an interest in Sherlock Holmes chanced to develop among them, and I realized slowly that we had the makings of a scion society. In 1969 we began planning, spurred on by a member of my first class, Lucy Chase Williams. We named ourselves the Trifling Monographs, and each of us chose one of Holmes's studies as an investiture—I was told I had no choice, and as the only adult I must be the Master's *magnum opus*, *A Practical Handbook of Bee Culture with Some Observations on the Segregation of the Queen*. Each of the others chose their investitures, and so our meetings were populated by the tracing of footprints, the typewriter and its uses in crime, and other monograph names. Lucy wrote all of our ceremonies and customs, and we began to have full-fledged meetings in 1970.

By that time, an article about the club had appeared in our local newspaper, the *Birmingham Eccentric*, and it chanced to be read by another young Holmes enthusiast still in high school in a neighboring suburb. He wrote to ask if our club were limited to Cranbrook students, and was delighted when we welcomed him at our next meeting. He was hoping to be an actor. His name was Curtis Armstrong.

At the end of the school year in 1972, I decided to leave teaching to move to Greece. The Trifling Monographs went on for a year or two, but ended as more and more members graduated. I enjoyed an enchanted two and a half years in Greece, but after a country-wide mobilization there, and a small war with Turkey, I returned to my family in Detroit. A year or so later a friend invited me to see "A Midsummer's Night's Dream" at the Meadowbrook Theater in nearby Oakland County. We were in the midst of conversation as we took our seats, so I didn't open the program before the performance started.

You may recall that Puck makes his appearance at the beginning of Act II of this delightful fantasy, and the moment I heard his voice my attention was grabbed. I stared at the actor, a short, slender man who was a becoming shade of green, and then opened my program to discover it was Curtis, who had grown to adulthood while I was on another continent. I enjoyed the rest of the play, and at its conclusion wrote out a note to Curtis and found a theater employee who agreed to carry it to him. Moments later

Curtis appeared, still wearing about half of his make-up and a full grin, and we enjoyed our reunion.

I always hoped the messenger opened the folded note on the way, as it read, "If you are indeed The Polyphonic Motets of Lassus, then A Practical Handbook of Bee Culture with Some Observations upon the Segregation of the Queen awaits you above."

After teaching for seven years I proffered my resignation and set out to devour the world. I was hungry for experience that was not to be found in my neighborhood. I knew already that my first port of call would be Greece, as I had made that country's history, mythology, and ancient language the center of my years of study. I took a deep breath and departed my homeland with a roiling mix of excitement and fear.

I arrived in Athens equipped with the complete Sherlock Holmes, a deerstalker, and a plastic meerschaum. While I was packing I knew I wanted to have some representation of the Master in my new home, though I knew I would be unlikely to encounter another Holmesian in the Mediterranean. I lived on the corner of streets named for a philosopher (Philolau) and a courtesan (Phryne), and in my living room I set up the volume accompanied by the pipe and the hat to display my true faith. Everyone who visited always pointed at the assemblage and said phonetically, "Serloch Cholmes." Every single person who came by knew who those objects represented, though none had read the tales.

One day I was walking briskly through the streets of Athens when my eye fell on a popular magazine named *Phantasio* at a newspaper and magazine stand. On the cover was a box with a familiar silhouette—it was Holmes in Athens! I bought it, of course, and then sat at a cafe with a lemonade to puzzle out the Greek. It was indeed our ratiocinative friend in the midst of one of the *Adventures*, and I was about to learn how the Canon sounds in a language very different from his and mine. At that moment I was nearly overwhelmed with a feeling of homesickness; the glimpse of Holmes in the bright sunshine made me want to share my glee, and I knew no one in the country with whom to jump up and down and laugh and enjoy figuring out the Greek. Hungry for contact, I wrote a letter to the *Baker Street Journal* telling them of my delight at Holmes's appearance in Greece. I felt I had brought the incident to a proper conclusion, but I had actually started a whole new game.

The mail started the following week, and the first two notes arrived from John Bennett Shaw and Peter Blau. Both of them wanted copies of any story in *Phantasio* for their own collections. This was my first contact with either of them, yet both of these great collectors wrote talkative letters. John was chatty about his family and his Sherlockian contacts, and Peter suggested I seek Holmesian companionship at the USAID library. I was chuffed to be in contact with the two great collectors, and took care in responding when I'd readied their copies of the Hellenic Holmes, but that was only the beginning. More mail arrived from America, Canada, and England, perhaps two or three a week for months. Some wanted copies of *Phantasio*, others wanted a full collection of the stories bound together in book form.

I located the biggest bookstore in the city and was glad to find it was the one I was already using, just off Syntagma Square. Using my best and most formal Greek, I approached the counter and asked if they carried the Sherlock Holmes stories in Greek. Yes, they replied and brought me a thick book with a yellow dust jacket. "I'll take this one and another one, too." While an eyebrow was raised, he sold me both copies with pleasure. But letters kept rolling in, and so I kept returning to that bookstore. At first we continued to trade remarks that were careful and formal, but soon I would appear at his counter and he would say, "Hi there, my doll, how many do you need today?"

Susan Rice (New York, New York) is an Adventuress of Sherlock Holmes, one of the original 1991 class of women admitted to the Baker Street Irregulars, and author of *A Compound of Excelsior*, a Sherlockian volume about, of course, bee culture.

THE ADVENTURE OF THE COPIOUS CORRESPONDENCE

ALAN BRADLEY

"A Sherlockian must have someone with whom to share and savor his discoveries." So wrote Canadian Sherlockian Chris Redmond (in *Baker Street Pages*, June 1967) at a remarkably tender age, and I couldn't agree more with his sentiment. The only thing worse than being a lone Sherlockian is being a lone *Canadian* Sherlockian where the solitude is aggravated by the vast distances. Comparatively speaking, New York and London are but villages, where one has only to hail a taxi or revert to shank's pony for a civilized evening of refreshing conversation concerning the Canon.

And so, if memory serves, it was sometime in 1975 that I caused to be inserted in the *Baker Street Journal* a notice begging correspondence by mail with any interested party. Although the response was not overwhelming, it would soon prove to be more than sufficient.

The first respondent was Bruce R. Beaman, of Stevens Point, Wisconsin, who brought with him into the fold Andrew Malec, of Minneapolis. Andrew would go on to achieve fame for his work with the Sherlock Holmes Collections at the University of Minnesota Libraries, repository of—among many other things—the fabled collection of the late John Bennett Shaw, and now the largest Sherlockian library in the world.

For want of a better name, we three decided to call ourselves *The Unanswered Correspondents (sic)*. Bruce, as prime mover and editor of our little journal, *From the Mantelpiece*, was to be addressed as "The Transfixer", Andrew, "The Jack-Knife", and myself "The Mantelpiece."

An organizational chart was drawn up with each of the Holmes cases numbered, from "The Gloria Scott" (1) to "His Last Bow" (60), according to the sequence given in Baring-Gould's chronology as it appeared in *The Annotated Sherlock Holmes*. In strict rotation, each of us, beginning with Bruce, was to kick off discussion on his assigned case(s), with copies retained and sent in duplicate to the other two Unanswered Correspondents. The time period allotted was to be 30 days from the date of the first letter.

The Rules of Engagement covered two tightly spaced pages, covering everything from how much side discussion would be allowed to the dates of mailing, which were to be staggered to allow for the rather longer transit time from the Canadian prairies than the more speedy postal hop from Wisconsin to Minnesota. Each page of each letter was to be labelled

"TWC" (Three Way Correspondence) to keep it separate from any possible side chatter.

Bruce's first commentary on "The Gloria Scott" is dated September 17, 1975, and lists People and Places, as well as notes on Holmes himself: Humor; The Case; Habits; Character; Pursuits; Religion; Drinking; His "Art"; Knowledge; Publication of his cases; and finally, Seasons and Misc. (which included Allusions to God: "Oh, my God, it is as I feared!" (379); "which may kind God Almighty grant!" (381); "… by God! You'll learn to bless my name…" (382); "My God! Was there ever a slaughter house…" (383). This was followed by several tightly packed pages of Remarks, Notes, Observations, and Questions, all of them very perceptive and each, as is the tradition in Sherlockian scholarship, raising far more questions than they answered.

The TWC was active for five years, ceasing operation sometime around Christmas of 1979, by which time the membership had somehow ballooned to an astonishing 35, including such Sherlockian luminaries as Peter E. Blau, and eight honorary members, among whom were Ronald Burt De Waal, Michael Harrison, John Bennett Shaw, Donald A. Redmond, Dr. Julian Wolff, and (in memoriam) Luther Norris. Not too shabby for a little group founded to warm the cold Canadian winters!

Looking back on it all rather fondly after more than 40 years, I see that a remarkable amount was accomplished, mostly due to the tireless efforts of Bruce Beaman, who even persuaded the Governor of the State of Alabama, Fob James, to proclaim January 6, 1980, to be "Sherlock Holmes Day"; a proclamation which notes "The Unanswered Correspondents (sic)" to be "a corresponding scion society of the Baker Street Irregulars."

It was in the pages of *From the Mantelpiece* (No. 4) that my paper (with William A.S. Sarjeant) "The Woman" was first printed: an essay which nine years later would be published, in much expanded form, as the notorious *Ms. Holmes of Baker Street*.

Michael Harrison, too, contributed an article to that slender, mimeographed journal, not only acting as sounding-board to our heretical ideas, but even going so far as to make a personal appearance by long-distance telephone from England on the legendary *Wal & Den Show*, Saskatoon's long-running and popular morning radio entertainment. John Bennett Shaw also supported us by satellite during an appearance on the CTV television network. The world had suddenly shrunk, and Sherlockiana had caused it to do so. A single lonely reader on the winter prairies was now directly in touch with Santa Fe, with London, with Toronto and New York.

Although it was not strictly a Canadian Sherlockian society, *The Unanswered Correspondents (sic)* had at least one foot of its tripodium anchored firmly in Canada, a fact of which I am still inordinately proud. The TWC overlaps, chronologically, the foundation of The Casebook of Saskatoon when, according to a document in my archives, "A meeting was held on Wednesday, December 4, 1974, at the home of Gary Shoquist…to discuss the possibilities of organizing a local Sherlock Holmes Society. Present at the meeting were Allan Cushon, Dr. W.A.S. Sarjeant, Gary Shoquist, and Alan Bradley." It was noted that, at this formative meeting, "Dr. W.A.S.

Sarjeant was unanimously voted president, following assurances that such High Office carried with it only the responsibility of proposing toasts."

It was also noted that "At one point, Mr. Bradley bled copiously upon Mr. Shoquist's living-room carpet. Dr. Sarjeant immediately identified the event as a quiz, and submitted the correct answer—'The Second Stain'. No prize was given for this speedy deduction, as the bloodletting had been entirely spontaneous. Apologies are offered to Mr. Shoquist, who insisted that no damage had occurred. (Although it wasn't his finger.)"

Over the years, my Sherlockian archives, having been lugged from Saskatchewan to British Columbia to Malta and the Isle of Man, have been seldom—and never completely—unpacked. These few notes, extracted gingerly and a bit mustily, are meant merely to shed a little light, and to illustrate Chris Redmond's most percipient thesis: "A Sherlockian must have someone with whom to share and savor his discoveries."

Alan Bradley (Douglas, Isle of Man) is a retired radio and television engineer and a full-time writer, creator of the Flavia de Luce mystery series. He was co-author of the Sherlockian classic *Ms. Holmes of Baker Street*.

THE ADVENTURE OF
THE DANCING HOUND

JOANN ALBERSTAT

A *Hound of the Baskervilles* tap dance-ballet for children was my first foray into the world of Sherlock Holmes. It was 1986, and a fellow journalism student had asked me on a date. As a result, there we were in a Halifax arts centre auditorium on a Saturday afternoon, surrounded by dozens of noisy children and their parents.

But my date was cute, and the show—with its dancing, live music, and gothic atmosphere—was intriguing. Even stranger still, we weren't the only adults in the audience without little people in tow. For example, in the row behind us was a man in a wheelchair wearing a tweed cape and deerstalker. After the show, I met the late Paul Gouett and other members of the Spence Munros, Halifax's Sherlockian society, who were also in the audience. Little did I know this was the beginning of a lasting friendship with these fans, Sir Arthur Conan Doyle, and his work.

I was familiar with the stories, having read *The Memoirs of Sherlock Holmes* as a child. The grey-covered volume that belonged to my father as a boy is now tattered and worn but still sits on a shelf in my mother's house.

Another reason I was drawn to the society was the serendipity that my adopted home city is mentioned in the Canon. The Spence Munros gets its name from "The Copper Beeches". In that story, Violet Hunter is seeking a new position as governess because her previous employer, Colonel Spence Munro, has moved to Halifax, Nova Scotia, with his family. There are only a handful of Canadian references in Doyle's work and I still get goosebumps when I think that this colonial port city is one of them.

The Halifax club was established in 1982 by my husband, Mark—then a teenager—and Ron Lewis, a librarian at Saint Mary's University. The pair actually resurrected an existing society that was dormant. My involvement with the group began slowly during my university days, starting with Holmes's birthday dinners and special events. Needless to say, I became more active after I moved to Halifax permanently and then married the club's Colonel.

Our society gathers about half a dozen times a year, including story meetings in members' homes and outings to restaurants in Halifax and outside the city. We have long-time members in the Annapolis Valley, for instance, so a pub in that area called the Spitfire Arms beckons us regularly.

We've also had picnics at Truro's Victoria Falls, which we've dubbed "Reichenbach." Another favourite summer meeting spot is the fishing village of Prospect, where we have picked cranberries on the "moor" and enjoyed yet more picnics on the granite boulders that line the coast. We've also attended many local Sherlock-themed stage or musical productions over the years. Movie nights, held at our house, were introduced more recently and have also been well attended.

At our regular meetings, we tend to eat, drink, and socialize as much as we discuss the adventures of Holmes and Watson. However, I still learn about the Canon from members who are far more knowledgeable than me. The quizzes also help me remember more of the names and places with which Doyle loved to pepper his writing. Besides a dedicated quiz master—a few people have faithfully held this role over the years—a newer tradition is the story-themed craft that a member and her daughter bring to meetings. Whether the creation is a poison pill or a wooden bookmark featuring a canonical quote, there is always a sample for each of us to take home. I always look forward to seeing what they have come up with next.

The Spence Munros' membership has remained small but relatively stable over the years. There have been as few as eight active members. These days, the number is closer to 20. Some of our members have been involved for as long as the society has existed in its resurrected form. One of those long-time Sherlockians is also active in the Sherlock Holmes Society of London, and keeps us informed of the events held there.

Sadly, we've lost more than one dear member, and their loved ones, over the years. But we've also had others who have gone away to study or work abroad—though not in Mecca, Lhasa, or Montpellier—and later rejoin our ranks. We have also gotten younger recently, which is a good thing.

Motivations for getting involved with the group have also changed over the years. Members used to be drawn to the society because they were fans of the Jeremy Brett series. These days, they're watching *Sherlock, Elementary*, or the Robert Downey, Jr. movies—and perhaps all three. Recruiting efforts have also changed. The society used to recruit members through occasional newspaper articles and CBC Radio interviews. These days, we use social media and Kijiji to spread the word.

The club quietly celebrated its 30th anniversary in 2012 in our typically understated fashion. We realized after the fact that we had missed our silver anniversary. We marked our 30th year, however, by creating a commemorative pin.

As for the larger Sherlockian world, I've discovered it more recently through involvement with *Canadian Holmes*, the magazine of the Bootmakers of Toronto. Mark became the journal's Bootprint in 2009, with me as co-editor, since I'm the household grammarian. Since then, we've done more travelling with Holmes as our guide, although not as much as either of us would like. We attended the SINs conference in Toronto, as well as a

221B Con in Atlanta. Mark (BSI "Halifax") is also a regular attendee at the Baker Street Irregulars' weekend in New York.

Most enjoyable of all are the visits we—and the society—have received as our network expands beyond the local club. Sherlockians from throughout Canada, the United States, and as far away as Australia have travelled to Nova Scotia and looked us up. When Mark and I travel, we now make a point of seeking out Sherlockians, both in Canada and beyond. One of our most memorable trips was meeting up, while in Tokyo, with members of the Japan Sherlock Holmes Club. What a kind, enthusiastic group with whom to spend an enjoyable evening!

Then there is the world of Sherlockian scholarship—books, podcasts, journals and more. I've only just begun to discover the treasure trove of resources that are out there.

In fact, you could say keeping up with the ageless Holmes and his Victorian era is a bit like a dance—in particular, a mix of tap and ballet. The steps are set to eerie music and feature a tale about a larger-than-life canine. That performance three decades ago may have been meant for children. But it also managed to captivate a journalism student, connecting me to the Spence Munros and the broader world of Holmes in a way that continues to evolve and grow all these years later.

JoAnn Alberstat (Halifax, Nova Scotia) is currently re-inventing herself in the communications field after three decades as a journalist. She is co-editor of *Canadian Holmes*, and an aspiring member of the Red-Headed League.

THE ADVENTURE OF
THE OTHER EMPTY HOUSE

WILLIAM R. COCHRAN

When you come face-to-face with your own mortality, you begin to reflect upon many facets of a long life. How many hours were wasted in various activities, so absorbed in the task that their relevance seems to unexpectedly vanish like the yellow fog of a London street! But with regard to my Sherlockian life, I have no such regrets. Each special moment in the 40-plus-year study of the "Sacred Writings" has been well spent. The multitudes of Sherlockians I have met, the friendships I have made which often transcend borders and oceans, all have been special.

But the study of the original 60 canonical adventures has expanded my knowledge to a degree I would never believe possible when the journey began. You begin to notice the subtle points of interest in Watson's narratives which did not seem to be there upon the first reading. I learned this from Newt and Lilian Williams, who spent years reading together the many editions of *The Sign of the Four*, searching for irregularities in the texts.

If you had told me on January 22, 1977, that an upstart scion society would last for more than 40 years of monthly meetings, I would have suggested a visit to a psychiatrist. The "Occupants of the Empty House" were born in a small town in southern Illinois with a population of 5,908 at the last census. We had 22 participants at the first meeting, and since many had not read the entire Canon of Sherlock Holmes, it was decided that we should meet monthly and study each of Watson's narratives in the order of William S. Baring-Gould's *Annotated Sherlock Holmes*. The decision was made simple by the fact that this publication was responsible for introducing us to the concept of starting a society. My friend Michael Bragg and I were not sure if the Baker Street Irregulars even still existed in 1976, as we formed our plans. We had no idea how we were supposed to accomplish our task. All we did know for certain was that we had to meet once a year and present Canonical toasts.

Newt Williams did not arrive at our front door until the second meeting. We discovered he knew Ben Abramson of the Argus Book Store, the legendary publisher of the Old Series of the *Baker Street Journal*. He also mentioned he had corresponded with John Bennett Shaw and Peter Blau, though none of us knew who they were at that time. This was the curious incident that helped to change the face of our little scion. However, Newt admitted that it never dawned on him to start his own scion. Then he asked if we had registered the group with the BSI. This was one of the seminal moments of our scion, but Newt was always humble, and always asked me if he could take care of the necessary correspondence. Thus in those early years we assimilated each new member and it made our foundation stronger as the result.

This theme would repeat itself each year as new members entered the doors of Camden House. In 1978, Gordon Speck became a member. He was quiet at first, observing, evaluating, cerebrating, about becoming an Occupant. Shortly after he arrived on the scene, Newt started suggesting I should become the president, since my co-founder had departed. I was reluctant to take on the responsibility. However, ever since Newt was elected secretary when Paul Battaglia moved away, his desire was to let the Sherlockian world know about our scion. His next vision was to install me into the office of president, and he nominated Gordon as vice-president.

At our third annual meeting, after much deliberation, I yielded. But the presidential sobriquet, "Lord High Sherlockian," was too intimidating a title. New titles for the officers were plucked from the narrative of our titular story, "The Adventure of the Empty House." The president became "The Master of the House"; the vice-president was "The Waxen Image"; and Newt, the secretary, selected "The Old Book Collector." My first and last executive order as president was to ban the "minutes of hours wasted," and to dispense with *Robert's Rules of Order*. We were not politicians, nor were we executives. We were equals, all drawn to the meetings by a shared love of the tales featuring Sherlock Holmes. We would offer positive constructive criticism, if necessary, during the discussion of the presentation. Every member read from a copy of the paper as it was read by the presenter. Thus, each one had the opportunity to add their input into the final result. Again, the common bond was the love of Sherlock Holmes.

For me to call Newt Williams a profound influence on my development as a Sherlockian would be a gross understatement. I was somewhat like the fledgling detective in "The Gloria Scott" in those early years. But Newt had plans for me, and I soaked up his wisdom and knowledge like a sponge. As his health started to fade, Newt passed the torch to Gordon Speck, who was at my side every step of the way for 38 years. I emphasize these details to reinforce the idea that the OEH works because it is a shared experience. No dictator need apply. The vote that sent me into an office was the last time we ever officially voted on anything. Any new project that came along, I would simply ask if anyone was interested. The discussion would follow, and each member became a part of the project. It may not work for every society, but it has served us well all these years.

A case in point would be the creation of the legendary Door to Camden House. Newt had encouraged me to start by attending Sherlockian events and conferences, but Gordon's urging had greater success than Newt's. In August 1984 I ventured forth to my very first Sherlockian conference. The opportunity to meet John Bennett Shaw and Michael Harrison at the conference in Dubuque, Iowa, was too tempting to resist. I met my first Irregular there, a gentleman by the name of Tom Stix, the son of one of my favorite Sherlockian scholars. The younger Stix would soon ascend to the office of "Wiggins," head of the BSI. Of course there were many BSI in attendance, but he was the first I met, and my fears subsided with each new introduction.

I also met Michael Harrison, an Edwardian gentleman who preferred to carry on a conversation with a glass of single malt scotch in his hand. He sat next to me during the famous Shaw Quiz. I was not fond of quizzes because I feared a test of canonical knowledge might intimidate new members. It was the reason I refused to attend any Sherlockian function. Harrison did not care for quizzes either, so we were "forced" to chat. We became friends, and I told him the story of the first Sherlock Holmes book I had ever owned.

As a youngster, I had bought my own copy of the Sherlock Holmes stories. At the time, I believed there was only one, the twelve stories collected into *The Adventures of Sherlock Holmes*. I could only afford to buy an old and worn tome, a tattered old cheap edition found in an old book store, published by A.L. Burt in 1920. Michael Harrison listened with delight, but revealed nothing. Within a few months, I received a package from Hove, Sussex. Pasted inside the front cover of the book was this simple typed message:

> In giving this Sherlockian present, I am reminded that far too often, we, in giving a present, wonder if we have made the right choice. 'I wonder if he will really like it...'
>
> About this present, I have no such misgiving, and that I am able to give it (and thus, as I know, pleasing beyond doubt my friend, the recipient) has something of the miraculous about it.... Well, I judge it to be quite miraculous to feel that I had the companion volume—also battered, but in good condition. So with my best Sherlockian wishes, here it is: the 1922 A.L. Burt edition of *The Memoirs of Sherlock Holmes*.
>
> Michael Harrison
> Hove, East Sussex, 8th May 1989

It was a humbling experience to realize the great Sherlockian author embarked on his journey in the same manner as I. It changed my perspective on Holmes and Watson, and reminded me that I would have never befriended Michael Harrison if it were not for William S. Baring-Gould.

A few years later, Gordon and I were headed to a conference in Dayton, Ohio, at the invitation of Al Rodin, whom we had run into at the airport on our way home from the 1988 BSI weekend. We had attended them all from that time forward. Then one year Tom and Ruthann Stetak decided to have a poster competition. The directions gave a size stipulation, and the idea was to tell each scion's story with this poster for all to enjoy.

I told the members of the Occupants: "We only have a week to make this poster. Is anyone interested in helping with the design?" Three hours later, with every member involved, we had our plan. The group divided the project into work groups. Some were involved in deciding on the sections of what turned from a single poster to a poster-sized book, telling the varied interests of our scion: the presentations at the meetings; the monthly *Camden House Journal*; the Christmas Annuals; the Camden House sympathy card collection; "the idea behind the single rose at the head of the casket at a member's funeral"; the picnics. Some built the "door" proper, while others were honored with the assembly and mounting of the posters inside the shell. We were not concerned about winning, we only wanted to relate the OEH experience.

Gordon and I picked up the final project in West Frankfort on our way to Dayton. Gordon, who lived an hour from DuQuoin, had been at the meeting to be a part of the planning session, but he had no idea what it would look like until that morning. The "book cover" was a representation of the door to Camden House, number 111 Baker Street. This was the discovery of St. Louis Sherlockian Gray Chandler Briggs in the early part of the 20th century. When our door opened, the story of our scion was displayed page by page. When we arrived and placed our "poster" on the table, everyone started to remove their posters from display. We did not know it was a competition. We asked them to replace their posters, and to be proud of what they had done. We offered to withdraw from the competition if need be. To be honest, we should have been disqualified, but one of the competitors pointed out that the rules did not stipulate we could not make the poster into a book. It is important to share one's passion for Sherlock Holmes.

Indeed, the running joke was that wherever Gordon and I went, people would ask about the size of our scion. The answer would inspire a wry smile followed by the proclamation their high school was larger than the whole town of DuQuoin. But it is not the size of the town that matters, nor is it the number of the members, it is the size of their love of Sherlock Holmes.

We can only hope everyone understood our message. The most important element is to share the experience with each member. "To enjoy the prime detective is the prime directive!" If you enjoy the experience, then you have succeeded—you have won. It is not the goal of our scion to be the best at anything, except the enjoyment of Sherlock Holmes. Having monthly meetings and pretending to be a great literary society is a game we play, but it is not the only game in town. If you play it right, you cannot help winning.

William R. Cochran (Carbondale, Illinois) is a Baker Street Irregular, a former editor of the *Baker Street Journal*, author of *Thinking Outside the Tin Dispatch Box* and other works, and co-founder and Master of the Occupants of the Empty House.

THE ADVENTURE OF PONDICHERRY LODGE

JAYANTIKA GANGULY

The first time I met Sherlock Holmes, I was a bored bookworm in my twelfth year of existence, rapidly outgrowing the recommended list of books deemed appropriate for my age. The children's mysteries were too light and easily solved. The superheroes were in a slump. The classics were interesting, but they were usually just stand-alone tales and there were no fresh adventures for my favourite characters, leaving me sulky and irritable. That is when my father decided to introduce me to Sherlock Holmes, one of his own favourites.

The book I received was *The Return of Sherlock Holmes*—a battered copy that had once belonged to my grandfather. Of course, in less than a week I had been given my own brand new copy of the Canon and finished reading it. It was as if I had met the man of my dreams. How magnificent was this man, with his brilliant mind and heroic conduct! And yet there was a certain vulnerability, a fragility to him, that served to make him even more attractive. I was besotted; ensnared for life.

After that, I pretty much spent the rest of my school life (and later on, my law school life) looking for pastiches and adaptations of Holmes, and making up adventures in my head when I could not find one. Pastiches were rather hard to come by in India back then; I mostly relied on the magnanimity of indulgent foreign relatives for procurement. (Thankfully, it is much easier to get hold of books nowadays, and there are Indian editions of pastiches, too.) In fact, the first pastiche I ever read—*The Seven-Per-Cent Solution*, by Nicholas Meyer—was a gift from my American aunt. In the absence of Holmes, I read through whatever books I could lay my hands on, regardless of genre, in every language I could read, in the hope of meeting another person as incandescent as Mr Holmes. I am still searching, and although I have met (and religiously followed) several spectacular characters over the years, no one ever surpassed Sherlock, and probably no one ever will.

However, it was not until about four years ago that I discovered the existence of Sherlockian communities and contemplated the idea of joining in. I knew of online fan-fiction and associated groups, of course—I had been devouring these since high school (they still remain my guilty pleasure, and I have found many gems out there), but I had more or less existed in my own little isolated bubble of Sherlockiana. It was sheer coincidence, and boredom, that led me to the website of the Sherlock Holmes Society of London; further exploration opened my eyes to the existence of the Sherlock Holmes Society of India and the Baker Street Irregulars. I dug deeper, and to my amazement, found a completely new world—one that existed outside of my head, in the "real world"! I signed up for membership in the Indian society immediately, and soon after, the London society as well. Membership in the Baker Street Irregulars went onto my bucket list, too. (Is it any wonder I was over the moon last year when I received my BSI investiture?) Thanks to the internet, I was soon communicating with brilliant Sherlockians not only in my own country, but in various parts of the world. It was exhilarating! I had to rethink and reassess so many things, including my own erroneous idea that I was the biggest Sherlock-worshipper around. I was nothing compared to the people I got to know; after all, I am only "Holmesick", while so many Sherlockians/Holmesians I know are already in the "StockHolmes Syndrome" category! (What I am talking about is this "Holmes Mania Quotient" I devised a few years ago. Basically, there is a score-based test to see where one falls amidst these five: Holmesfree, Sherlocked, Holmesaddicted, Holmesick, and StockHolmes Syndrome, the last being the acutest form of the mania. Further details can be found in my book *The Holmes Sutra.*)

Thanks to the ease of communication in modern times, I got to learn so much about the Sherlockian world and fellow Sherlockian souls, especially in the USA and the UK. Our Sherlock Holmes Society of India is still nascent, and we take our cues from the international societies. We are probably akin to a slightly troublesome but adorable little niece vying for the attention of our big, powerful, and benevolent relatives by emulating them (or so I like to think). We are a scion society of the Baker Street Irregulars, after all. We do have some achievements under our belt—our e-magazine (*Proceedings of the Pondicherry Lodge*) is my pride and joy. It is bi-annual, full-colour, online and free for download and distribution (we Indians love free stuff; even our membership is free). Anyone interested can find all the issues online at www.sherlockholmessociety.in.

We try and meet up annually (fourth weekend of August, in a different Indian city every year). We have a Facebook page and a Twitter handle. Our gorgeous brand was designed by the renowned Czech artist Petr Kopl, whose series of Sherlock Holmes graphic novels remain the best I know of. To be honest, we get by thanks to the support we receive from our Sherlockian friends all over. I find myself amazed every time I sit down to edit the e-magazine—I often feel that I am not even remotely qualified to edit half the submissions we receive. The scholarship, the sheer talent!

To this day, I remain as obsessed with my hero as I was the day I first met him. Being a Sherlockian is a substantial fragment of my existence, and certainly the most interesting one. For me, Sherlock Holmes has played many roles through the years: he has been a friend, a confidante, a mentor, a guardian angel, a hero, a deity, an anti-depressant, a good-luck charm, and much, much more. I would not be exaggerating if I said he has saved my life on more than one occasion. He has opened my eyes to a new world and broadened my horizons. He is an unrivalled presence in my life, and as dear and important to me as my own family. I will also confess that I have even made several (unsuccessful) attempts to deify him (to which he takes great offence).

Of course, my tale is not unique. I have met many Sherlockians across the globe, and a significant number have similar stories. It never ceases to amaze me how easy it is to converse with Sherlockians in any corner of the world, even at the first meeting, and even for socially awkward persons like myself. We may differ in age, profession, education, language, culture, geography, nationality, ideology, race, religion, and pretty much every other aspect of a functioning adult's life in a civilised society, but being a Sherlockian is an element so wondrous and innately unifying, that despite all other factors being variable, we are able to find a common ground and get along splendidly. That sense of familiarity, of fraternity, is something I hold most precious. Sherlock Holmes has given me more than a hero to worship; he has given me the most enriching part of my life. For a man who eschews sentimentality, is it not ironic that he invokes quite a whirl-wind of emotions amongst his followers? I am certainly not complaining, though. Quite the contrary—as a beneficiary, I am rather pleased with it.

Jayantika Ganguly (Kolkata, India) is a corporate lawyer and general secretary and editor for the Sherlock Holmes Society of India. She is a Baker Street Irregular and a member of many other Sherlockian societies.

THE ADVENTURE OF
THE THREE GATHERINGS

MONICA SCHMIDT

There is an incredibly rich history of Sherlockian academic and pseudo-academic research (the so-called "Grand Game") that dates back to Monsignor Ronald Knox's 1912 essay "Studies in the Literature of Sherlock Holmes." Over the last hundred-odd years, thousands upon thousands of aspects of Sherlockiana have been explored, ranging from color themes in the Canon, to the state of Sherlock Holmes's mental health, to the "real" chronology of the Canon, and many, many more. The phrase "never has so much been written by so many for so few" really does apply to our noble hobby. Many of these papers are found in Sherlockian journals, anthologies, and booklets.

But growing up in rural Wisconsin, one does not come across such essays in the local public library. And even if one can find a collection of essays, nothing compares to being able to hear a presentation on these subjects in person and being able to ask the researcher or expert questions about their area of study. Therefore, the importance of attending Sherlockian conferences cannot be overestimated. Conferences are an opportunity to take part in the tradition of the Game while simultaneously meeting other Sherlockians from around the world.

My own experience in attending three of the Sherlockian conferences jointly sponsored by the Norwegian Explorers of Minnesota, the Friends of the Sherlock Holmes Collections at the University of Minnesota, and the University of Minnesota Libraries shows how, over the course of a six-year period, one's experience of the event can change drastically.

In late summer 2010 I was visiting a friend in Minneapolis and came across a notice in the newspaper about a Sherlock Holmes conference at the University of Minnesota, run by the Norwegian Explorers, a Sherlockian literary society founded in 1948. It was a three-day conference held over an extended weekend, and indeed it was already in progress as I learned about it. A bad experience with Sherlockians online years before had soured me on the prospect of engaging with the community, but I thought, a decade later, it might be worth giving the community a second chance. After deliberating most of Friday night as to whether I should visit the conference despite missing the first day, I decided to show up and see what I had been missing.

It was the best decision of my life. Early that Saturday morning, I walked into the Elmer L. Andersen Library not knowing what to expect. I received a few puzzled glances after I walked in ("who is this newbie?"), but those running the conference, and the attendees, were incredibly welcoming. Despite being a stranger and one of the younger people in the room (nine-year-old Soren Eversoll was the youngest), I was greeted like an old friend. One member of the Norwegian Explorers, Ray Riethmeier, took time to take me around the room and introduce me to as many people as possible. He also made sure I wasn't alone for lunch. It was a touch of kindness that I didn't expect or anticipate; the warmth of the crowd was almost overwhelming, but in the most wonderful of ways. Along the way, I even met Dr. Richard Caplan, the founder of the Younger Stamfords, the Sherlockian society in the place where I was living, Iowa City; it would later become my home scion.

I spent the remaining two days of the conference listening to all the presentations and soaking in everything I could. I was absorbed in the material, which led me to think about the minutiae of the Canon in ways I had never imagined. I was witness to quality academic-style presentations on Sherlock Holmes, providing a legitimate stamp on a personal hobby that I had kept to myself for nearly two decades. The more questions I asked about the conference, the more I realized how much of an honor it is to get a presentation slot at the largest of the Sherlockian conference events in the United States: only the heavy hitters in the community get a coveted invitation to speak. I even ventured to think that someday, maybe, I would get to speak at this conference. Of course, that line of thinking was secondary to my personal revelation: for the first time in my life, I felt I had found kindred spirits in Sherlockiana. I had found my tribe.

My 2013 Minnesota Conference experience was different and still better than the one I had in 2010. I wasn't walking into the conference blind as I had done three years earlier; I knew what to expect, and so I was far less anxious about attending. Besides, by that time I had three years of local scion experience in Iowa City and was (starting in May 2013) the Stamfords' president. As a novice who was thrust into the position of a society president, I decided I needed to learn more about this unique community and the people in it. So, I printed up some Sherlockian business cards at great expense at the last minute and decided to use them as an ice-breaker at the conference.

I took full advantage of the opportunity the conference offered to learn from the veterans about community history and how other scions run meetings. I had the privilege of meeting and chatting with so many wonderful and amazing Sherlockians from across the US and Canada. I finally got to hang out with Chris Redmond of Sherlockian.net, whose website I had followed since 1996. I spent some time getting to know scholars like Susan Rice and Evelyn Herzog. I met some of my kindred spirits in Eric Swope from Indianapolis and Lindsay Hall from Minneapolis. And I also participated in a long-standing Sherlockian tradition, as I delivered my first Sherlockian toast—to Dr. Watson—at the conference's banquet. Several of my new Sherlockian friends and I shared a final post-conference meal at

Matt's Bar (a Minneapolis burger joint which President Obama visited a year later). I left Minneapolis once again feeling that I had spent a weekend on cloud nine among my fellow Sherlockians—my friends.

Between 2013 and the next conference in 2016, I made good on my quest to get to know the community. I started exploring the rich history of Sherlockiana in Chicago, and had been made a member of the Hounds of the Baskerville (sic) and the Criterion Bar Association. I also made the journey northward to Minneapolis to attend other Norwegian Explorers events, and had attended several of the "BSI and friends" weekend conclaves in New York and spent time hanging out with the best and the brightest Sherlockians from around the world. By the time of the 2016 Minnesota conference, thanks to my travels and involvement on a local, regional, and national level, I knew most of the conference speakers and attendees and felt as if I were attending a family reunion.

In that three-year period, I had also made several weekend trips to Minneapolis for the purposes of using the archive at UMN to research the subject of Holmes and addiction. As a licensed mental health counselor specializing in the treatment of substance abuse, I wanted to provide a specialist's viewpoint on Sherlock Holmes's cocaine use in the Canon without treading upon already-covered ground. Because of my research efforts, this time I wasn't just an attendee at the 2016 Minnesota Conference; I had been asked to be one of the speakers. Presenting at any event is a great honor, but it was especially meaningful for me to speak at this conference. I had come a long way from the 2010 Saturday morning walk-in and the nervous young woman delivering a toast to Dr. Watson in 2013. Now I was one of the experts on stage putting forth my research and conclusions to an audience of my peers.

Over the years, I have received a great deal of guidance and support from multiple quarters, including Iowa City, Minneapolis, and Chicago Sherlockians. I received a lot of helpful nudges from these kind people to write, present, and attend events. They reached out and provided me with lots of opportunities to shine, and I'm not embarrassed to admit I took full advantage. A mere six years after my first official Sherlockian event, I was on the same stage as those I idolized in 2010. I am so incredibly thankful that I had found the family I never knew I had. And this is all because I took a chance and attended the triennial Minnesota conference.

Monica M. Schmidt (Solon, Iowa) is president of the Younger Stamfords in Iowa City and a member of the Adventuresses of Sherlock Holmes, the Hounds of the Baskerville (sic), and other societies. She works as a mental health counselor specializing in substance abuse.

THE CURIOUS INCIDENT OF THE UNAVAILABLE BAR

JULIE MCKURAS

When soliciting essays for this book, Chris Redmond described his vision of the finished work: "The book will embrace the world of traditional Sherlockian societies and friendship, as well as creators, scholars, the fandom, collectors, and other branches of this amazing adventure." I can't think of any theme for an article that would encompass all of these subjects more than that of Sherlockian conferences.

I've engaged in the "amazing adventure" of working on conferences for some time. It all began in 1998, shortly after I assumed the presidency of the Norwegian Explorers, the long-time Sherlockian society in Minneapolis-St. Paul. Plans were under way for our "Founders' Footprints" gathering in August of that year to celebrate the Explorers' 50th anniversary. Of course I agreed to help; how hard could it be? Besides the obvious facts that I really didn't know anyone outside of our Twin Cities group, didn't have a deep background in either Sherlockian authors or their writings, and had only attended one previous conference (when the University of Minnesota Libraries welcomed the arrival of John Bennett Shaw's collection), I couldn't find a reason not to participate. I didn't know what I didn't know, but I was enthusiastic about what we could do as a group. With that in mind, it was time to look back on my previous experience working on and organizing events.

When our children were involved in youth sports I co-chaired several large soccer tournaments. For a tournament one needs a budget, a responsible committee, teams to participate, hotels for traveling teams, volunteers, fields, schedules, referees, good communications, concessions, emergency numbers, and a program. We realized it would be a good idea to have a disaster scenario if teams or referees didn't show up, we were rained out, or we were confronted with screaming coaches or parents.

While it seems one can't compare a physical youth athletic event to a more cerebral literary affair, the similarities outweighed the differences. With a conference, we have to determine a budget, decide on a broad-ranging theme, contact and confirm speakers and make sure their subjects don't overlap, register attendees, prepare a program and communicate well with all involved. A disaster scenario would be needed for speakers who might not be able to make it or for miscommunications with the hotel. We wouldn't need referees and we probably wouldn't have to call the police (yes, that happened in the soccer experience) or ambulances (that happened too). I'm happy to report that so far that's been the case with our symposiums.

When looking for guidance on how to begin our Sherlockian conference planning in those early days, I turned to the writings of Dr. John H. Watson for sage advice. I found it in "The Disappearance of Lady Frances Carfax": we would need a "small, but very efficient, organization." A second pearl of wisdom was found in "The Speckled Band" when Mr. Holmes, in his questioning of Helen Stoner, said "Pray be precise as to details." With a good committee and a close eye for detail, our 1998 symposium was successful.

What I learned then has continued to be applicable in all of the triennial conferences I've worked on. All of them have been co-sponsored by the Norwegian Explorers, the Friends of The Sherlock Holmes Collections and the University of Minnesota Libraries. While things don't always run smoothly despite best-laid plans, the key to doing your best is to have good communication within the group. We meet frequently, document all decisions, and have an excellent secretary-treasurer who considers such issues as the minimal cost to break even. You have to decide how much you can afford to lose should costs exceed income; hopefully it doesn't come to that.

We go into it knowing that not only do we want to succeed, but our audience wants us to. People don't attend symposiums looking for flaws and hoping you'll fail. Armed with that knowledge, and a workable group of companionable souls, planning a conference is quite simply a process.

That process begins with choosing a theme, one broad enough to allow selected speakers to expand creatively. Out of a number of conversations comes a final agreement about the title. Over the years we've chosen "Founders' Footprints," "2001: A Sherlockian Odyssey," "A River Runs by It: Holmes and Doyle in Minnesota," "Victorian Secrets and Edwardian Enigmas," "The Spirits of Sherlock Holmes," "Sherlock Holmes Through Time and Place," and the most recent, "The Misadventures of Sherlock Holmes." Each of those allowed for a wide interpretation of subjects.

Once the general topic is decided, we consider who has a level of expertise on a topic that fits within the broad heading. Reviewing Sherlockian publications and attending other events enables the committee to gather names. We want speakers, including at least one member of the Norwegian Explorers, who can put together a well-researched, educational, and entertaining presentation, and will do it because they love the subject and possess the imagination to expand upon the premise. The ideal presenter is one who embraces the idea as a means to enhancing his or her own knowledge and is able to relay that to everyone in the audience. For instance, in "Sherlock Holmes Through Time and Place," we had speakers discussing collection mania over the years, as well as Victorian travel and transportation, setting Holmes in the appropriate time and place, to name just a couple of the talks.

Another aspect of selecting topics and speakers is that it must appeal to an audience. People who come to symposiums have all levels of knowledge, from novice to expert, as well as varying degrees of experience with planned Sherlockian events. They're spending their time and funds to participate. Over the years we've had any number of people tell us that not only is it their first time at one of our Minneapolis events, it's also their first time at a Sherlockian conference. The aim is that everyone walks away from our weekend having learned something and with new friends.

One has to have a suitable venue for the long weekend. We've been fortunate to utilize several good hotels close to the University of Minnesota and the Elmer L. Andersen Library. Arrangements are made for room blocks, catered meals with various dietary needs, audio-visual equipment, and a rather dizzying number of small personal requests. But no matter how well you think you've arranged things, something outside your control might happen. For instance, the hotel we'd used for years was undergoing renovation in 2013 and the management assured us that all would be ready for our conference. The Ronald Reagan phrase "trust, but verify" was applicable here. Three months before we were to begin, I called my hotel contact and learned that the hotel restaurant, ballroom, and catering operations wouldn't be "quite ready." They were willing to work with us, but when I asked the question "will the bar be ready?" and the response was "not quite," I knew it was time for the disaster planning. We found another wonderful hotel and I spent countless hours notifying people of the need to cancel and change reservations. As is often the case, it all turned out for the better.

Communication with vendors, venues, speakers, and attendees is vital. People want specifics, particularly if they're coming to an unfamiliar city. We make sure to let them know that we received their registrations, the best transportation options from airport to hotel, and where to park or dine. And make no mistake, people want adequate free time to socialize, and a timetable helps to plan their time. They're not only seeing old friends, but making new ones as well.

One might ask "what have you learned from all of this?" I feel that I've learned quite a bit.

- We've assembled a committee and asked who will manage specific tasks. A better approach that I hope to utilize is to identify the tasks that need to be done and then look for those people who best align with those tasks.
- You can never start too early. We sometimes start to brainstorm a week or two after the conclusion of the last conference.
- One has to consider exactly what kind of event is envisioned. We want ours affordable but we don't want it to appear cheap. We want the audience to know how much they're valued and want their experience to be a positive one.
- You can't communicate enough. During my first conference one of the presenters told me he needed video equipment to play a recording. I arranged it but less than two hours before he presented, he said "You got a Beta player, right? Not a VHS?"

When I asked him why he hadn't asked for Beta he told me he thought I would have assumed that. Fortune smiled on me that day. I ran across the street to a video equipment store and the clerk was able to convert his material from Beta to VHS in short order.

- In the list of priorities that any committee sets, first and foremost should be the conference attendees and the speakers, and the experience that they take away. With the opportunities that social media provides, their experience both during and after the event ends turns into our conference reputation.
- Be prepared for the unexpected. A speaker might not be able to make it due to a last minute emergency, or a visual presentation might not work. During the 2016 conference, I didn't expect to be in a knee-high walking boot due to tendonitis. Was it a problem? Yes. Did people offer to help me in any way I needed, including helping me get up the few stairs, without benefit of handrails, to the elevated presentation platform? Yes, they did.
- Don't be afraid to try new things. In 2016 we decided to have, with one notable exception, speakers who had never presented at any of our conferences. Was there anything wrong or inadequate about previous speakers? Absolutely not, but sometimes new people deserve a chance.
- Be open to serendipitous occurrences. When Michael Dirda gave an entertaining presentation about Langdale Pike, every one of the other speakers managed to work Mr. Pike into their own talks. One day before another conference began, the Minneapolis newspaper ran an article about the upcoming event. They had interviewed me and I highlighted the holdings of the library, including its four copies of the 1887 *Beeton's Christmas Annual*, which the article misstated I owned. Gary Thaden began his welcoming remarks with a notice from the University of Minnesota police and the Apple Valley Swat Team (I live in Apple Valley) that the home a "person of interest" was being raided as he spoke, in order to retrieve the stolen items. Our latest conference opened with Bill Mason talking about pastiche and parody, and then going into a brilliant recitation of the various names given by authors to their Holmes character. We couldn't have planned any of these, but they became highlights everyone remembered and had fun with.

In closing, I'd like to emphasize that despite the hard work and long hours that have gone into planning our conferences, I've never regretted the outcomes, which I feel have been successful in so many ways. The co-chairs I've worked with, Dick Sveum and Gary Thaden, will be my friends for life. Over the years I've met people who now make the symposiums feel like family reunions—the reunions you wish you had. It's been such a learning experience.

My advice is not to be afraid to try new things, and that includes working on conferences. There is much to be gained from it. Hopefully, when your symposium concludes after months of planning, you, your committee, and your attendees will be able to utilize a portion of Holmes's quote in "The Five Orange Pips" when he said, "So perfect was the organization of the society, and so systematic its methods" that it was a conference to be remembered.

Julie McKuras (Apple Valley, Minnesota) is a former intensive care nurse and a devoted grandmother. She is a Baker Street Irregular, edited the BSI Trust newsletter, is one of the Adventuresses of Sherlock Holmes, was a long-time president of the Norwegian Explorers of Minnesota, and is active with the Friends of the Sherlock Holmes Collections.

THE ADVENTURE OF
THE APRIL LANDMARK

CRYSTAL NOLL

Before Sherlock Holmes, my love was Arthurian legend; in fact, I was quite ignorant about the Great Detective and his Boswell until well into my twenties. I wasn't one of those lucky people who was forced to read the stories in high school. I can recall seeing representations of Holmes in the media all throughout my life, specifically one of my favourite *Doogie Howser, MD* episodes. But it wasn't until BBC's *Sherlock* that I truly started to pay attention.

My dear friend Heather Holloway is completely to blame. We were visiting our alma mater, Georgia Southern University, when she mentioned that we needed to be back to the hotel by a certain time and did I know if they had PBS? Needless to say, they did, and we detached ourselves from our friends in enough time to watch the new episode.

We weren't even out of John Watson's bedsit before I was hooked. One of her favourite stories to tell about that day is when they introduced Mycroft. "They want us to think that's Moriarty but I think it's Mycroft. How much you want to bet?" she said.

"Shut up, I'm watching this," I replied.

My own favourite memory from that day would come later. We had taken ourselves down to Waffle House for a late dinner, like you do in Statesboro, Georgia. In the middle of gushing about how good the episode was, I realised that they had already aired in the UK and we had the internet (don't worry, BBC, you've collected a *lot* of my money since then).

I often joke that I was late to the party but I came in with fervour, because after that I enjoyed what I lovingly call my "Victorian Christmas." It was during this time that I discovered the Canon and began soaking in as much Sherlock Holmes as I could get my hands on.

Fast forward to May 2012, the month that series 2 of *Sherlock* aired in the United States. What you may not realise was that during Memorial Day weekend that year, there was a *Doctor Who*/*Stargate* convention in Atlanta called TimeGate (now known as Wholanta). And that at this con, two groups of friends would all go to a panel about Sherlock Holmes hosted by past BBC employee Louis Robinson.

I came out of his panel 55 minutes later thinking that if I knew half of what he had probably forgotten about Sherlock Holmes I would be set and happy for life. What I didn't realise was that five other people in that room were thinking along the same lines. Somehow we congregated on a couch outside the room, discussing all the different topics that could have been panels of their own, when one of our group finally said, "Someone should put on a Sherlock Holmes convention."

"*We* should put on a Sherlock Holmes convention," someone else responded. And that is how 221B Con was formed.

We'll be the first to tell you that, as we found out later, we did everything wrong, but we did strike when the iron was hot. We've since learned that you should have thousands of dollars saved, be an LLC or a non-profit, and take at least two years to plan your event. Yeah, oops.

Less than a month after the idea for 221B we had a hotel contract, about $100 of our own money, and donated web hosting. Nine months after that, we had a convention, 221B Con of 2013.

The original hotel contract, to be honest, seems almost laughable now. We speculated that maybe 75 to 150 people would want to come and spend two days talking about Sherlock Holmes with us. We even wondered what we would do with the three meeting rooms we'd arranged. We certainly did not imagine that in less than a year we would be making 680 close friends and renting out entire hotels. When we tell people that 221B is like a family reunion for us and our members, we truly believe it.

Going on six years later, we're still amazed that this small conversation between six people at a *Doctor Who* convention has become such a large part, not just of our lives, but also of so many others'. We still tear up at the thank-you emails and hugs. We still marvel at the panels and cosplays. We still look for new things we can offer or talk about. And most of all, we're still learning. Our little two-day event has grown to span three days, with more than 115 hours of programming, and brings together 600 to 800 people every April. We cover everything from the Arthur Conan Doyle Canon to the modern and futuristic representations of Sherlock Holmes.

On behalf of myself, Heather Holloway, Liz Elberger, Taylor Blumenberg, and Cathy Bruhnke, you're all invited to come to Atlanta and celebrate ACD's creations every April. And before I close, let me pass on the greatest piece of advice for convention planning we were ever given: "Don't buy what you can rent. Don't rent what you can borrow. Don't borrow what you can steal. And don't steal what you can find in a dumpster." Trust me, it will come in handy one day.

Crystal Noll (Warner Robins, Georgia) is an Olivier-Award-winning theatre producer, a Colorado Avalanche fan, one of the directors of the annual 221B Con (221bcon.com), and a member of the Confederates of Wisteria Lodge, the Beekeepers of Sussex, and the Sherlock Holmes Society of London.

THE ADVENTURE OF THE WEIRD COUSINS

HEATHER HOLLOWAY

There's a difference between being a Sherlockian and being *in* Sherlockiana. All it takes to be a Sherlockian is an appreciation for Sherlock Holmes in any of his incarnations. But being in Sherlockiana is like marrying into an extended family with a ton of at-first-inexplicable traditions and a network of weird cousins. You might not always know what's going on or even why, but it's family, and sometimes you're just expected to show up with potato salad.

I've been a Sherlockian since I was 14 and Mrs. Phyllis Bright assigned "The Speckled Band" during our first semester of ninth grade. All that really did was make my parents have to listen to in-depth and super-extra-excited fangirl paeans to the Great Detective and how "seriously, amazingly awesome all these stories are. Seriously. You should read them." But please, weep not for my parents; they were old hat at tuning out blow-by-blow synopses of every episode of *Star Trek: The Next Generation*. I'm sure they barely remember it.

The adventure of Sherlockiana, however, waited far over the horizon during the crazy days just after series one of BBC's *Sherlock*, when all the world was aflutter with Holmesian love. In 2012, Liz Elberger, Crystal Noll, and I attended Timegate, a Doctor Who convention in Atlanta that was destined to change our lives. There we met Taylor Blumenberg and Cathy Bruhnke, two Sherlockians from the Charleston area, who, like ourselves, couldn't fathom why no one had ever put on a Sherlock Holmes convention. In short, we did that, eventually capping registration at 700 and realizing that one does not simply underestimate the timeless appeal of Arthur Conan Doyle's most famous creation.

As we promoted the con, I met more and more Sherlockians and learned of a world I had never imagined. I was aware of the online communities for fanfiction and meetups, but I had no idea about the scion societies and organized gatherings being held all over the world.

There was a bit of a generation gap at first. After learning of the existence of scions, I immediately looked for a nearby group. I found the Confederates of Wisteria Lodge, based in Atlanta. This is now my home scion, and I love every single member of this group and cherish our time together, but initially the name gave me pause. As a young, liberal, social-justice-minded woman on the cusp of Gen X/Millennial status, I find the evocation of Confederate terminology troubling. I discussed the name with other friends and ultimately decided to give the group a pass.

This seemed like a good idea when I later met two members and was told that I wouldn't fit in, that it was for older people, and that I probably wouldn't like it. If I had never met Marilynne McKay, the group's Gasogene and all-around amazing human, I probably would have never given them a chance. However, she encouraged Crystal and me to join, insisting that we would love it. Thank goodness she is so convincing!

I attended my first scion meeting warily, waiting to be judged. By this point, I had heard horror stories of the "Old Guard" testing your knowledge, laughing when you couldn't quote the Canon, and cavorting with Goody Proctor in the woods. Turns out, they pretty much just drink and talk about what's going on in their lives. I can do that!

I think this is the most confusing aspect of the community for the poor unfortunate souls not of our tribe: they wonder how we can spend so much time talking about nothing but one old detective. They have no idea of the millions of delightful conversations we have about an army doctor, a long-suffering landlady, the entire Victorian constabulary, and no less than four Violets. But even these fascinating subjects don't always come up. We spend just as much time talking about the last play we saw and our children (well, your children; my cats) as the exploits of Sherlock Holmes and company. Then, should conversation wane, we can always turn to the Canon, the latest movie, or even an obscure fact of Victoriana to get it started again.

We have a common ground, a place to start where others long for an icebreaker. Jacquelynn Morris told me she sees her excellent annual symposium, A Scintillation of Scions, as a Sherlockian family reunion. Sherlock Holmes isn't just a detective in some old stories; he is a shared strand of DNA that links us all.

Over the last six years, I've been privileged to meet some of the most diverse and interesting people on the planet. I've been at O'Lunney's at 2:21 a.m. I've sung cartoon theme songs with pajama-clad women at 221B Con. I've chanted Vincent Starrett poems at the top of my lungs at the end of formal dinners. I've toasted subjects as odd and varied as a Jezail bullet and Dr. John Watson's moustache. And I have made dozens of new friends whom I can always count on for a quick online chat or, if we are near the same zip code, dinner and some conversation.

Sherlockiana has been, to me, the greatest pool of potential friends I've found since college days. That's the secret, folks! The older you get, the harder it is to make friends. Everyone is married or already has enough friends, or, even worse, they don't get any of your references. Other than work and church (if you go), there is no playground for adults, no dormitory common room where you are bound to meet like-minded people with at least a few things in common. But with Sherlockians, no matter how different our backgrounds, how disparate our ages, how antithetical our politics, we have one grand starting point: how did you discover Sherlock Holmes? It's a question everyone is asked, a question everyone asks, and no one ever gets tired of it. Yes! I would love to tell you my story! I would love to hear yours!

Heather Holloway (Griffin, Georgia) is a co-founder of 221B Con and a member of the Atlanta-based scion The Confederates of Wisteria Lodge. In her spare time she enjoys traveling, volunteering, and watching some of the worst movies ever made.

THE ADVENTURE OF
THE BOY IN BUTTONS

BETH L. GALLEGO

I am a Watsonian. Maybe you're one, too.

Possibly, you're wondering what a Watsonian is, and why someone would claim that title in a book about being a Sherlockian. The short answer is that being a Watsonian means that I am a member of the John H Watson Society, which officially "seeks a level of equality in scholarship and enthusiasm for the life and work of John H Watson, MD." It is "an open and inclusive Society, seeking the collegiality and conviviality of Members worldwide and at all stages of involvement in Watsonian, Sherlockian and Holmesian interests. Mostly, we are about having fun."

The longer answer—what it really means to be a Watsonian—requires a look back at how I got here. I came to Baker Street the long way around. I was a voracious reader as a child, but Victorian London just didn't appeal. I was in my late thirties before I realized how fascinating the world of 1895, and all the worlds that have spun off from that original, could be.

It was a knitting podcast that did it. I was in college while the internet was blossoming, and by the time I finished a graduate degree in library and information science, websites had gone from novelty to necessity. I moved from central Illinois to southern California to start a job as a children's librarian in a small branch of a very large library system. Outside of work, I knew almost no one. It wasn't quite "a comfortless, meaningless existence," but the longing for "a friendly face in the great wilderness" was something I could understand.

Among its programs, the library hosted a series of knitting classes, drawing on the sudden rise of "the new yoga" to bring in patrons. Outside the library, too, knitting groups were an easy way to socialize in my new city. Knitting blogs and podcasts popped up all over the internet, followed by a social networking site called Ravelry, offering even more opportunities to connect with others.

As the hot knitting trend cooled, a certain detective was gaining popularity among a new generation. The films directed by Guy Ritchie were successful at the box office, and two television shows aimed at modernizing the stories appeared on the small screen. The hosts of one of my favorite podcasts, *Knit 1 Geek 2*, raved about the BBC's *Sherlock*. In mid-2013, the first two series were available to stream on Netflix. One summer evening, I decided to watch "A Study in Pink" on my laptop.

I fell in love.

Like anyone in the early stages of new love, all I wanted was to know more about the object of my affection. I picked up a two-volume paperback of the complete stories at my favorite used bookshop and started reading. Not content reading alone, I looked for others to talk to about my new obsession.

Unsure where to start, I turned to my favorite social network: Ravelry. In the years since its debut, the site had developed a robust discussion forum with groups focused on any topic you can imagine. On a site with more than six million registered users, the groups provided a space to find those who shared an interest besides creating things with yarn, whether that interest was running, travel, or...Sherlock Holmes.

The biggest Sherlockian group on Ravelry, by far, was simply called "221b." I jumped in, and it quickly became my primary online social outlet. Within the group, there were discussion threads for analysis of past episodes, speculation about future episodes, commentary on interviews with the cast and crew, and anything else members wanted to talk about. There was a thread for gardening, a thread for cooking, and a thread (of course) for knitting and crochet. There was a thread for people who wanted to read and discuss the Canon stories that were likely to be referenced in the then-upcoming third season.

Through the discussion boards, I got to know three other regular posters in particular. We were spread across the country, but the internet allowed us to have an ongoing conversation for months before any of us met in person. In 2015, we were roommates at 221B Con in Atlanta—the first time all four us were in the same physical room together.

Sherlock Holmes and the internet gave me some of the best friends of my life. It is rather fitting, I think, given the friendship that lies at the heart of the Canon.

Which brings me—at long last—to Watson. Sherlock Holmes is, to put it mildly, an interesting character. For over a century, readers have followed his adventures and then produced reams of analysis and opinion about everything from whether he attended Cambridge or Oxford to whether he might, in fact, have been a woman. But no one has ever been, or ever will be, as fascinated by Sherlock Holmes as was his friend and biographer, Dr John H Watson.

It is no wonder that readers who fell in love with the Sherlock Holmes stories came to call themselves Sherlockians (or Holmesians). He is the towering figure around whom all else revolves. It is easy to forget that the man who is almost always by his side is an exceptional and extraordinary man himself.

Not unlike Mr Holmes, some Sherlockian institutions can be a bit intimidating at first. They have long histories and their own rituals. As a newcomer, unsure what to say or do, I felt most welcome when I happened upon the web page of the refreshingly relaxed John H Watson Society.

The Society itself is a living monument to friendship within the Sherlockian (Watsonian!) world. Founded by Don Libey in 2013 as a birthday gift for a friend and fellow Sherlockian, it grew quickly, welcoming all who wanted to join. Its home and meeting place was a website where members and visitors from around the world took part in weekly discussions and tricky canonical quizzes. In August 2013, teams and individuals competed for the first time in a devilishly difficult 100-question test of canonical knowledge known as the Treasure Hunt.

Every member of the Society is assigned a "bull pup moniker." Don took "Buttons" for his moniker; I was given "Selena" as mine.

"Buttons" was a force of nature. A well-known author and speaker in his field of direct marketing, he somehow found time to pursue his varied interests, from studying Japanese poetry to making wine. He "edited" *The Autobiography of Sherlock Holmes* (2012) and *My Brother, Sherlock*, by Mycroft Holmes (2013). He referred to himself as a "seven-decade Sherlockian" and was a member of the Napa Valley Napoleons of S.H. before moving to Florida in 2014.

The Watson Society was Don's labor of love. And he did much of the actual labor himself: creating the site, posting something to the blog nearly every day, devising weekly quizzes and the annual Treasure Hunt, and thinking of discussion topics every week. He took on the persona of "the Boy in Buttons" (from "A Case of Identity") when discussing Society housekeeping.

His enthusiasm was contagious, and he had a way for spotting talent and drawing it out of those he met. One of his greatest gifts was his ability to immediately bring newcomers into the fold.

From my first posted comment on the site, before I even became a member, "Buttons" made me feel that I was welcome and that I could be as much a part of the discussion as those who had spent decades thinking and writing and reading about the Canon. After learning that I had some small experience in website maintenance, he invited me to take on the role of associate webmistress. I eagerly began organizing, categorizing, and tagging the hundreds of posts on the site, along with other behind-the-scenes technical matters. In addition to keeping the Society's home tidy, I wanted to make it even more interactive. I linked a Facebook page and a Twitter account, and I started investigating options to enhance the social component of the site.

Less than six months later, our "Buttons" passed away. It was sudden, and there was no process in place for transferring leadership. It took a team to continue carrying out the duties he had shouldered himself, but the Society had been important to him, and it was important to us. We were determined to preserve his legacy. "We can but try" became, indeed, the motto of our firm. I kept a handle on the technical aspects while another member took on the role of "Boy in Buttons" and became the face of the Society for a year before recommending me to take her place.

It has been a challenge like no other I've known. Working with people via telephone and email across thousands of miles to maintain a group with no physical home presents difficulties unique to this very 21st-century experience. The *Watsonian* editorial team includes members from at least three states and two countries, all of whom work together to produce a journal twice a year, distributed in print and electronic format to more than 170 members worldwide.

Again and again, when thinking about my Watsonian experience, and what it means to be a Watsonian, I come back to these words: "We are an open and inclusive Society, seeking the collegiality and conviviality of Members worldwide and at all stages of involvement in Watsonian, Sherlockian and Holmesian interests. Mostly, we are about having fun."

When I first found the Watson Society, it was like coming home. It remains a community of individuals from all walks of life and from around the world. That community includes men, women, and those who identify with neither gender. It includes college students and retirees, traditional scholars and new media artists. Like our original "Buttons," I want everyone to feel welcome to participate in and enjoy everything on offer.

People talk a lot about Sherlock Holmes, the smartest man in any room. But I hope to live up to the example set by the best friend one could ever hope to have, Dr John H Watson.

Beth L. Gallego (Los Angeles, California) is current "Boy in Buttons" (leader) of the John H Watson Society (johnhwatsonsociety.com) and a member of the Curious Collectors of Baker Street and the Sub-librarians Scion. She talks about yarn, tea, and Sherlock Holmes at thistangledskein.com.

THE RETOOLING OF
SHERLOCK HOLMES

THE ADVENTURE OF THE SINGULAR FRIEND

NICHOLAS MEYER

Memory is a funny thing. It plays tricks on you. What I remember may not be what happened. I can only hope to come close. Alas, no one living except myself can verify what follows, so perhaps it's as well to take this with a few grains of salt.

I do not remember how old I was when my father—I am sure it was my father—gave me the complete, one volume edition of the Holmes stories, with an introduction by Christopher Morley. Was I ten? Eleven? What prompted him to give it? I cannot say. Was I interested in detectives? Not that I recall. I don't believe it was a formal present, i.e., not for my birthday, or anything like that. Just something he intuited I would enjoy.

But whatever the occasion and however old I was, I do recall plunging into *A Study in Scarlet* and a certain bafflement that overtook me when I turned the page and found myself in an entirely different narrative, this one set in the wilds of Utah.

I didn't know much about printing books—and still don't—but I imagined a printer's error of some sort, in which another story had been inadvertently grafted to the Holmes tale I'd been happily imbibing. Not quite sure what to do (a frequent occurrence with me), I kept on reading, and lo and behold, the two stories conjoined.

After that, there was no let-up. I can't say I remember my feelings reading the 59 cases that followed, but do remember my first time encounter with each, which has never been surpassed, even as my sophistication as a reader matured. I was at the perfect age (whatever age that was!) to get hit right between the eyes by Holmes and Watson. I took everything at face value. It did not occur to me that perhaps Watson was a bit of a dunce (Watson, *c'est moi*) nor was I troubled—if I noticed—by any of Doyle's narrative inconsistencies. The name of the landlady, the location of Watson's wound, etc., all these, I maintain, gave my younger self no pause. I was, and remain, infatuated.

As to what it was, particularly, about Holmes and his world that excited my sympathetic imagination, it is hard for me to say. Notwithstanding my admiration for Holmes's specialty, I am not myself by nature a very analytical person, but I hazard a guess that the stories existed far enough in a romantic past, complete with damsels in distress and horse-drawn conveyances, that the detective himself assumed the trappings of knight-errantry, but close enough to the allegedly "modern" world I inhabited so that many of its appurtenances—telegrams, revolvers, motor launches, etc.—were reassuringly familiar. Holmes's world was at once distant and immediate, while the detective's eccentricities and foibles were as memorable as Watson's were endearing.

Already a scribbler, in no time I was penning imitations of Holmes. I believe I'd read some of my father's efforts and his use of the phrase "my singular friend" set me off and running. I cannot mimic anyone, but I can mimic a mimic. And I did.

Around this time (the mid-fifties), "My Fair Lady" was all the rage. The heady combination of Shaw plus Lerner and Lowe was heard everywhere in New York. Long before I got near the show, I knew all the songs by heart. And when I did manage to see it, something tickled the back of my mind. Professor Henry Higgins of 27a Wimpole Street and his roommate, Colonel Pickering (just back from India!), in the household presided over by Mrs. Pierce, did strike me as eerily reminiscent of Sherlock and his ménage at 221B Baker Street, with Mrs. Hudson in charge and roommate Watson just back from Afghanistan. I wondered (there was no internet to make my wondering simple), then became convinced, that Shaw had brazenly ripped off Doyle.

And if Shaw's rip-off had made a great musical, wouldn't the original make an even better one?

I set to work concocting a musical based on Holmes, which I called "Baker Street." Ignorant of such niceties as copyright, I did not trouble myself about them, but blabbed my whole idea to anyone who would listen. Brought by my parents to a cocktail party where I was introduced to a Broadway producer, I gave him the whole kit and kaboodle. If I been anywhere as observant as my hero, I might have noticed the grave attention with which he heard me out. Grownups don't often give strange children as much air time as this gent was giving me.

At breakfast week or so later (my memory, remember), I was poring through the theatre section of the *Times*—always my first stop; I never bothered with the front or sports pages—and was flabbergasted to read that this same producer was negotiating with the Doyle estate to produce a Sherlock Holmes musical, tentatively titled—get this!—"Baker Street!"

When my father showed up, I expostulated. He was only marginally sympathetic. "What'd you expect?" I think he said, "You told everyone your idea. Besides, you're only a kid."

If memory serves—(see above)—"Baker Street" opened in the fall of 1964 to indifferent notices, and I received a telegram from my father (I was then a freshman attending the University of Iowa): "Congratulations. Knew they couldn't do it without you."

Cold comfort. This experience put me off Holmes for at least the next several years. I wanted nothing more to do with the Great Detective. It wasn't until a year or so after college, when a chance encounter renewed our relations.

I was back in New York, living in a three flight walk-up on Second Avenue, next to Elaine's, then the trendiest place in the city, which, it goes without saying, had no use for me. Accordingly I made my watering hole of choice a bar called Eric's, more or less across the street from the yellow awning that was Elaine's. It was there one night that I found myself engaged in conversation with an attractive young woman and somehow the subject of Holmes came up.

Where was Watson wounded? She asked me. I didn't know. What was the curious incident of the dog in the nighttime? Damned if I could remember. What was the name of Mycroft's club? I never saw this person again, but the encounter sent me reeling back to the Holmes stories, and I was once again hooked.

Another strand of my involvement must be cited here. In high school when kids learned my father's profession, I was asked, "Your old man's a shrink? Is he a Freudian?" I did not know the answer to this query and put it to my father, who responded by saying, "It's a silly question." "Why?" I wondered. "Why is it a silly question?"

"Because it is no more possible to discuss the history of psychoanalysis without starting with Freud than it is to discuss the history of America without acknowledging Columbus—or the Vikings, if you wanna get cute—but to suppose that nothing has happened since Columbus is to be pretty rigid, pretty doctrinaire. When a patient comes to see me," my father went on, "I listen to what he says. I listen to how he says it. I am especially interested in what he does not say. I am interested in how he's dressed, curious as to his body language. Is he on time? Et cetera. I am in short, searching for clues, from him, as to why he (or she) is unhappy, and against this I apply a background of some clinical experience and expertise."

Suddenly I knew whom my father had always reminded me of. But it wasn't until my conversation at Eric's bar years later that I began to connect the dots. Re-reading the Holmes stories, I fell to wondering just what Doyle had known about the life and writing of Sigmund Freud.

Both Freud and Doyle were doctors; they both lived—and died—in London. Within nine years of one another. Both men were involved with cocaine. Doyle had studied ophthalmology (in Vienna, no less!) and it was as an anesthetic used in eye surgery that Freud wrote his first paper on cocaine.

These titillating coincidences—if they were indeed coincidences—stayed with me as I drove west to seek my fortune in Los Angeles, where they kept the movie business. There by chance I stumbled onto the next component of my infatuation with all things Sherlockian, the writings about the Writings. It began with a book by Trevor Hall, and from there I began haunting second-hand bookstores (does anyone remember "first hand" bookstores?) collecting all the jolly and ingenious "criticism" which "played the game." In this sub-genre of Sherlockiana, as we all know, Holmes is considered to be a real person, Watson (not Doyle) his chronicler, and the latter sometimes described or dismissed as the "literary agent." The tomfoolery begins by attempting to reconcile Doyle's sloppy details (where *was* Watson wounded? How many times had he been married?), in the process learning Victorian arcana (is it Cambridge or Oxford that has quadrangles?).

No one I knew at the time excepting myself was interested in this nonsense, but when the Writers Guild (of which I was and remain a proud, card-carrying member) went on strike in 1972, my friend Michael Scheff and Sally Connor, the woman with whom I was then living, both urged me to use my sudden free time to write "that book you're always talking about." Having literally nothing better to do (screenplays were off limits and picketing for three hours outside the Goldwyn studios every day was not very interesting), I sat down and wrote the novel that became *The Seven-Per-Cent Solution*.

I wrote the book for my own pleasure and as a corrective to other Holmes imitations (chiefly films) that I couldn't abide. Basil Rathbone might have made a great Holmes, but asinine Nigel Bruce was never Watson, his able chronicler. (And why, pray, does a genius hang out with an idiot?) Nor did I care for yanking Holmes out of period and a number of other (to me) unpardonable liberties taken by what I took to be insensitive hands.

I was prompted by the egomaniacal conviction that I and I alone was capable of channeling Arthur Conan Doyle, and even though no one else might ever read what I attempt, I'd have the satisfaction of knowing that I'd got it right.

To my surprise, my book and two succeeding pastiches were published to agreeable success and acclaim. As the years passed, expert imitations by "divers hands" followed, disproving the theory of my unique qualifications and abilities.

This, to the best of my recollection, constitutes a brief history of my discovery of Sherlock Holmes and what came of it. Some details may have escaped me, but the whole, I venture to say, more or less sums it up.

I remain a committed Sherlockian. I find that many of my initial enthusiasms—Holmes, Bizet's "Carmen," Gilbert & Sullivan, the Marx Brothers, Robert Louis Stevenson, H. Rider Haggard, Anthony Hope— have never left me. Other passions have piled atop these—*Middlemarch*, Philip Roth, Woody Allen, ad infinitum—but there's not much that I've jettisoned. Even when I think I'm sick of Holmes, re-reading one of the stories (like everyone, I have my favorites), brings back happiness in a brain-wave of pleasure.

Nicholas Meyer (Los Angeles, California) is a novelist, screen writer and director of such films as *Time After Time* (1979), *Star Trek II: The Wrath of Khan* (1982), *The Day After* (television, 1983), and *Star Trek VI: The Undiscovered Country* (1992). A television series, *Freud: The Secret Casebook*, is in the works. His Hollywood memoir *The View from the Bridge* was published in 2009.

THE ADVENTURE OF THE BAZ AND THE NAZIS

NICK CARDILLO AND CATHARINE CARMODY

Pennsylvania, 2016: "Catharine, I have a proposition for you."

Winters are cold in Pennsylvania—perhaps not as biting and bleak as they're portrayed in *The Valley of Fear*, but cold nonetheless. It was on just such a cold January afternoon that Nick approached Catharine with a scheme. Nick had loved Sherlock Holmes since the age of six when he had been introduced to the detective in *The Great Illustrated Classics* edition of *The Adventures of Sherlock Holmes*. That blossomed into a full-blown passion which had—for better or for worse—taken over a large portion of his life. (He'd be inclined to say that it was for the better.)

Nick knew that Catharine was not as well versed in all things Sherlockian, though she was hardly a stranger to the Sherlockian world as a fan of the Robert Downey, Jr. movies, *Sherlock*, *Elementary*, and *The Great Mouse Detective*. In short, she was the perfect partner to take the plunge and dive into that corner of the internet reserved for all things Sherlockian.

Nick's scheme was simple: start a blog which reviewed a host of Sherlock Holmes films, books, TV shows, and anything else which fell in that general region. In doing so, Nick and Cat would explore just what it meant to be a Sherlock Holmes fanatic and discover just how the world had been shaped by the great detective.

Cat said yes.

The blog, *Back on Baker Street*, officially launched that month. After creating the Google account, selecting the theme, designing the site, and collaborating on the introductory post, one big question was left: where to begin?

Perhaps the best place to begin was with the low-quality silent features which starred Eille Norwood. Or the John Barrymore version of the William Gillette play from 1922? Of course, one had to start with the Arthur Wontner films of the early '30s. After all, those words from Vincent Starrett saying that "Surely no better Sherlock Holmes than Arthur Wontner is likely to be seen and heard in pictures in our time" now resounded in Nick's head like a symphony.

And then, the obvious answer presented itself: Start with the 1939 version of *The Hound of the Baskervilles*, starring Basil Rathbone. Really, in retrospect, it was all quite elementary.

The Sherlockian community has been writing about the great detective for decades. The stories have been analyzed and picked apart time and time again, their characters examined with the same minute detail which Holmes might have given to a doctor's misplaced walking stick. Was there anything new left to be said about the filmed exploits of the world's greatest detective?

In short: yes. You see, what we think works so well about *Back on Baker Street* is the fact that our knowledge of Sherlock Holmes is so different. We can bring two diametrically opposite points of view to the same material, often prompting in-depth discussion. Often it is the outsider who can bring the objective viewpoint to the table and put things into perspective. And there were certainly times in the run of the original Basil Rathbone and Nigel Bruce portrayals that an objective viewpoint was certainly required (*cough* Pursuit to Algiers *cough*).

The process of watching all of the original Rathbone Holmes films took seven months. As two young, college-bound Sherlockians, we did have other things to tend to in that time, but it all began on yet another cold day in January. Before it came time to pop Nick's DVD copy of *The Hound of the Baskervilles* into the player, he insisted on a short history lesson.

* * * *

Hollywood, 1938: We weren't there, but we hope it was one of those swanky Hollywood parties, the kind you hear about in stories or see in movies. In our minds' eye, it's perpetually black-and-white; the men are dressed to the nines and sporting fashionable pencil-thin mustaches; the women are clad in elegant gowns. There's lots of smoking, drinking, schmoozing, and—what with this being a Hollywood party after all—lots of movie industry talk.

Not unlike the question of who fired the "shot heard 'round the world" commencing the Revolutionary War, there's no way of knowing for sure who broached the subject of turning the beloved Arthur Conan Doyle Sherlock Holmes stories into movies. According to Hollywood lore, Daryl F. Zanuck, Gregory Ratoff, and Gene Markey hit upon the idea of launching the series at Zanuck's company, 20th Century Fox. After all, Fox made their bread and butter with mystery movies: the Charlie Chan series had been a staple for the studio since 1931, and by 1938, the studio had also produced four films in a Mr. Moto series. If the world's greatest detective were to take up home in Hollywood, Fox was the place for him to do it.

But who would possibly fill the giant shoes (and infinitely larger deerstalker) of the detective? After all, Holmes was no stranger to the silver screen. He made his formal film debut in 1901 and since then had been personified on screen by actors including William Gillette, John Barrymore, Clive Brook, and Arthur Wontner.

And then someone mentioned Basil Rathbone. And if Hollywood lore is to be believed, almost as soon as Rathbone's name was mentioned, so was Nigel Bruce's. And so, a chapter of both cinema and Sherlockian history began.

* * * *

Over the course of the seven months that we spent in the company of Basil Rathbone and Nigel Bruce, we tried as hard as we could to document the reactions and discussion points which arose during the movies themselves. Our thoughts overall? Well, first things first: chances are, Sherlockians are well acquainted with the Rathbone/Bruce films. If you're reading this book and are not, we highly recommend setting this passage aside for a little while and watching them all now. It will be well worth your time. We'll be here when you get back.

* * * *

Did you see through that disguise in *The Adventures of Sherlock Holmes*? How about the killer's true identity in *The Scarlet Claw*? That one was pretty surprising, wasn't it? Oh, how about that moment when Watson asks the Washington D.C. police "what's cooking?" Hilarious, right?

Watching the Rathbone/Bruce films, one wonders why these films have stood the test of time. They're not, strictly speaking, adaptations of the Canon, and that could put some fussier Sherlockians off at once. Both Fox and its successor with the Rathbone franchise, Universal Studios, portrayed Watson as a bumbling idiot, to the detriment of the character until, perhaps, Doomsday. And they're not necessarily big-budget films. *The Hound* and *The Adventures* feel like there's some scale to them, but the Universal films are the very definition of 1940s B-movies, with a revolving cast of actors turning up time and time again.

So, why do we love these movies so much? To be simple and devastatingly vague, they just feel so right. But, what does that mean? What is *right*?

At the heart of the Canon is the friendship between Holmes and Watson. The true, driving force of the canonical narrative is what drives these two men—brothers not in blood, but by bond—to stick together and solve mysteries. The best writers of pastiches make sure to include glimpses of the true men beneath the veneer of personality traits which Holmes and Watson exhibit, and the best films do the same. The Rathbone/Bruce films succeed brilliantly in this department.

Sure, Watson is reduced to comic relief, but he and Holmes seem like genuine friends. Nigel Bruce's Watson, though hardly the sharpest knife in the drawer, really does seem to humanize Holmes. A lovely moment in *The Adventures* finds the detective admonishing the good doctor, calling him an "incorrigible bungler," only to pat him reassuringly on the shoulder seconds later to make amends. These little moments are scattered throughout the series and are all so telling.

Both Rathbone and Bruce carry themselves with a stalwart Britishness which adds to their characters and the movies. Particularly in the first three films made at Universal—*Sherlock Holmes and the Voice of Terror*, *Sherlock Holmes and the Secret Weapon*, and *Sherlock Holmes in Washington*, making up what we dubbed the "Nazi Trilogy"—the wartime sentiment of "Keep Calm and Carry On" seems to be personified by Holmes and Watson, and that attitude carries through right to the closing frames of the final film, *Dressed to Kill*. Rathbone never ceases to look stoic, even when he's sporting a faintly ridiculous haircut in the early Universal films, and somewhere in the back of your mind you know that no matter how dire a situation may be, and no matter how many times Holmes faces death, he will emerge victorious.

But The Baz and Bruce didn't do it alone. They were accompanied by a veritable repertory company of character actors who popped in to add tremendously to the films. There was Dennis Hoey's lovably dim-witted Inspector Lestrade forever trying to win approval from Holmes and receiving only glares from Watson. Then, there is Mary Gordon's Mrs. Hudson, who acted as Holmes and Watson's surrogate mother, keeping peace and order at 221B throughout all 14 films.

Character actors like Lionel Atwill, Paul Cavanaugh, Hillary Brooke, and Henry Daniell appeared on several occasions in the series: Atwill and Daniell both conducted a battle of wits with Holmes as Moriarty, and Hillary Brooke rose through the ranks from supporting player in *Voice of Terror* to be the goody-two-shoes heroine in *Sherlock Holmes Faces Death* and then *femme fatale* in *The Woman in Green*.

Even behind the scenes, little changed. Except for *Voice of Terror*, Roy William Neill helmed all of the films at Universal and, though the studio only afforded the series B-movie status (usually ending up on a double-bill with an Abbott and Costello comedy), Neill and his company managed to make each of the films feel sleek and polished. And, when the script called for it, Neill managed to infuse his films with enough atmosphere for two movies. See *The Scarlet Claw* for specific reference: the fog is so thick in that film you could reach into your TV and cut it with a knife. Actually, bad idea there.

The films made at 20th Century Fox and Universal Studios were incredibly successful, appealing not only to fans of the great detective but to casual film-goers as well. Their popularity has not waned since their glorious black-and-white images first flashed up on a movie screen seventy-some years ago, and they do not seem to be going anywhere any time soon.

While the debate will forever rage on as to who is the best Sherlock Holmes on screen, for many, Basil Rathbone will forever be the face and voice of the great detective. And, while a number will hold Jeremy Brett, Peter Cushing, and Benedict Cumberbatch in our hearts (don't we all?), just as many will look back to Basil Rathbone and Nigel Bruce as the finest pair of actors to have played the detective and his Boswell.

* * * *

Our blog officially closed a chapter of Sherlockian cinema history in early September of 2016. Many today argue that it is the greatest chapter in the great detective's legacy on film, but we are not quite ready to make that judgment yet.

The task of slowly making our way through the next 70 years of screen history is certain to thrill us. But, above all, our *experiments*, plunging headlong into the world of the great detective, will excite and entertain. And one has to assume that we are not the only ones who have marveled at Holmes's screen adventures. The detective's ability to stand tall as one of the finest heroes of literature, film, and TV is an indicator of his enduring popularity. Something will always be happening *Back on Baker Street*.

Nick Cardillo is a student of history and secondary education, with a minor in theatre, at Susquehanna University, co-writer of the blog *Back on Baker Street*, and author of Sherlockian pastiches appearing in *The MX Book of New Sherlock Holmes Stories*. He muses on film of all kinds at Sacred-Celluloid. blogspot.com.

  Catharine Carmody is pursuing a major in English, with a focus on creative writing and secondary English teaching certifications, at Lycoming College, and is the co-writer of *Back on Baker Street*.

THE ADVENTURE OF
THE RATIONAL ACTOR

JOHN C. SHERWOOD

Journalism has been my career, but my semi-professional hobby is acting. I'd like to tell you how a set of intriguing circumstances placed me in the character of Sherlock Holmes.

A lot.

Encouraged by two noted Sherlockian scholars, I can assert that I've played the part more than any other living person. I've spent more professional time in the role than Jeremy Brett and Basil Rathbone combined. Benedict Cumberbatch has nothing on me, although Jonny Lee Miller is barking at my heels. Of course, William Gillette holds the record for the most time spent in the role, and I imagine his record may never be broken.

My own small claim to Sherlockian distinction was attained simply, just like Gillette's great achievement—one performance at a time. In fact, it began with my own utter shock that any audience—indeed anyone—could imagine me as Sherlock Holmes.

In the early 1980s, I performed in a series of Christmas parlor programs at the Victorian Villa Inn, near Union City, Michigan. The owner, Ron Gibson, had hired me to do my magic act, and my friend Brooks Grantier to provide the music. At first, our wives were part of the program, but over the years the gig became a two-person variety act.

Whenever Brooks and I sensed a certain staleness, we sought fresh material to entertain repeat guests. In 1985, I proposed a brief Sherlock Holmes skit. When it became something of a hit, our boss had one of those Big Ideas. Ron asked us to develop a mystery-weekend format for the inn, during which guests could solve cases with Holmes and Dr. Watson. We'd perform it repeatedly over the course of the year, extending our professional presence at the Villa well beyond Christmas. Wow! Great!

However, in the face of the deathless Rathbone and Brett, I was terrified. Who was I to try to re-invent the role? Who was I to try to write cases for the Master to help modern Baker Street Irregulars to solve?

As a journalist, however, I'd long reported on police and crime news. I wasn't a mystery buff, but like so many well-versed young Americans I'd read the Holmes stories several times. What was needed was a focused re-reading, and I spent the next few months studying little but the stories and others' writings about them.

Gibson, Grantier, and I decided not to dramatize existing stories by Sir Arthur Conan Doyle or others. After all, some guests might have read these and know their solutions. The Villa's cases had to be new works, yet true to the format Doyle had established, of real-world dilemmas fairly solved in a real-world manner.

Also helpful was the fact that a large number of the Holmes stories had been placed in a manor-house setting, and those particular stories inspired us to find new twists from which we could develop new mysteries. There was much to iron out.

My personal challenge was to present Holmes properly and believably. Everyone, it seems, has a notion—caricatured or otherwise—about Holmes and his abilities. But certain things are set in stone by those who've absorbed the details of each tale, as well as the informed conjectures by such writers as W.S. Baring-Gould and Vincent Starrett.

We adopted such "facts" as Holmes's birth on January 6, 1854, in the North Riding of Yorkshire, the existence of his more intelligent brother Mycroft, and his retirement in 1903 to keep bees in Sussex. We kept Holmes and Watson alive in the modern era by inventing an elixir Holmes distilled from the royal jelly his bees produce, but they would wear clothing reflecting their Victorian roots.

The first mystery event was launched in mid-1987. The script had withstood questioning, revision, and study. Actors had been hired and rehearsed. But I still had precious little faith in myself as Holmes. In fact, I made myself downright ill. During that first dinner, I spent an hour lying on a restroom floor, trying to regain my equilibrium after too much tobacco (I'm no smoker!). So, here's a big tip to others who tackle the part: Use that cherrywood as a prop, not a pipe.

It also took me several attempts to grow comfortable and allow the role to "possess" me. Eventually, I came to understand what Doyle, Rathbone, Brett, and others have meant when they've said the character has a disconcerting life of its own.

In time, I gained a new admiration for Doyle's ability to create plots as frequently as once a month. I found it tough to produce a new script once a year. Over time, however, we developed 13 distinct mystery events performed repeatedly at the Villa over 22 years—approximately 110 performances in all—for groups ranging in size from 6 to 100.

During each weekend performance, Brooks and I maintained the personas of Watson and Holmes for some 18 to 20 hours, typically without relief—or breaking character. It was the most intense acting experience of my life, and the most satisfying.

Since then, I've been asked: Is there a "trick" to playing Holmes? Well, there's more to playing him than sticking a pipe in your mouth and a deerstalker on your head. The challenge is to be recognized as Holmes without such stereotypical pieces of equipment.

Certainly, reading all of Doyle's stories repeatedly provides an advantage. Memorizing some of the famous quotations is a plus (you definitely should be able to rattle off "When you've eliminated the impossible, whatever remains, however impossible, must be the truth"). It also helps if you're a man, if you happen to be slender and about six feet tall, and if you can manage a reasonably cultured British accent!

But none of these factors is essential to conveying the character completely. As those acquainted with the work of the Beacon Society well know, a short, female teacher certainly can portray Holmes in order to teach her students something about logic. The character is universal, and therein lies the key to portraying him.

If there's an essential "trick," it's to shove one's own personality aside and gently allow Holmes to speak and behave for himself, in whatever fashion one's informed imagination will permit. One must allow one's inner version of Holmes to emerge and have his say.

Deep down, there's a bit of the masterful in each one of us—a rational, methodical self who's somehow wiser and more cautiously insightful than we otherwise might tend to be. The more you allow that side of your nature to emerge, the more "Sherlock" you will become.

I discovered this phenomenon only after portraying Holmes for a few years. Often, and eerily, I found myself saying surprising—and unscripted—pronouncements that seemed uttered by an entity quite different from my own self.

As the knack developed, I shared another experience with Rathbone, Brett, and Cumberbatch: A small fan club emerged around my version of Holmes. I was the recipient of gifts and honors, including oil paintings and sketches of myself as Holmes, invitations to give away brides at weddings—in character, of course—and a reputation that preceded me when I moved my home from Michigan to the East Coast; there, my version of Holmes found new life as a frequent dinner guest and speaker at school functions from Baltimore to Nashville to Savannah.

When Holmes and Watson strolled into a school library, or the streets at a book fair, they often were approached by children ranging in age from 8 to 13 who not only had read many of the stories—notably "The Speckled Band"—but who seemed to know many Sherlockian details far more accurately than the adults.

A wonderful magic occurs at such events, especially when young people gather 'round to ask questions or to bask in Holmes's Victorian glow. There are extremely few characters in 19th century British fiction—perhaps Mr. Hyde or the Time Traveler are among them—who hold such interest for young students today. It's an honor to become Sherlock for these growing minds, and to give them a chance to meet one of their heroes in the flesh, even if we all understand that it's just pretend.

But, for honors and distinction, nothing can surpass a curious incident that occurred at the Villa during one of those first mystery weekends. A guest was a distinguished retired judge in his mid-70s who'd spent several hours taking part in the mystery. On the second day, he and my version of Holmes were seated alone in the parlor while the rest of the guests were "out sleuthing."

"Mr. Holmes," the judge said. "I have something to say to you."

"I am all attention," I replied as Holmes.

"When I was a boy," he said, "I discovered Dr. Watson's accounts of your career, and I read every one. Your adventures were an inspiration.

They were so exciting, and the way in which you solved each case so plausible and understandable, that I made up my mind then and there, as a boy, that I would study criminal law.

"I firmly believe that reading those stories helped me to choose my career. And, long ago, I vowed that, if I ever had the opportunity to meet you, I would tell you how grateful I am to you for having put me on the right track. So, Mr. Holmes, thank you—thank you very much."

I was thunderstruck, almost immobilized. On the outside, as Holmes, I was gracious, and thanked him for his kind words. Inside, I realized something astonishing had happened. My own self, as an actor, had disappeared. I was serving as a conduit between the character of Holmes and this man's boyhood, his memory of his aspirations and self-understanding. I heard myself channel Holmes, saying that, given this man's nature, he'd have found his proper course, whether or not "I"—that is, Holmes—ever had existed.

These thoughts and these words didn't occur to John Sherwood. Holmes was speaking now, offering wisdom and insight from the deep well of the logical human psyche.

The judge, deeply moved, suddenly seemed a boy again, years evaporating from his face. He stood up, shook the hand of Sherlock Holmes and thanked him profusely. He left the parlor—and I took Sherlock Holmes out for a little stroll around the Villa, to help ourselves come to terms with what had just happened.

Such extraordinary experiences don't happen to actors confined to a stage. Theatrical performers can barely see their audiences beyond the footlights. They can't hope to experience such personal, profound magic, the kind that happens between individuals, face to face.

To create such an experience with another person who is utterly in earnest is nothing but stunning and unforgettable—and I experienced it while being Sherlock Holmes.

It wasn't make-believe. It happened. And for that, I thank the great Sir Arthur and all those who join me from time to time in the world he conjured.

John C. Sherwood (Marshall, Michigan) is a retired journalist and an incorrigible magician and actor. He details his world of Sherlock Holmes at SherlockVisits.com. An earlier version of this essay was written in 2008 for the Beacon Society and appears on its website.

THE ADVENTURE OF FINDING BOSWELL

DAVID HARNOIS

It always a pleasure when skills you've obtained over the years can be used for something you enjoy doing. I started doing theatre at age eleven as an actor, and worked my way backstage into scenic construction, as well as lighting and sound design. Twenty years later, I'm still doing all those things. I was also a karaoke DJ for four years, which gave me experience with live sound mixing and audio recording equipment. And in 2014 I was able to combine acting, sound design, and sound mixing into *I Am Lost Without My Boswell*—an entirely volunteer-driven effort to create free audio dramatizations of the entire Sherlock Holmes Canon.

Like most people, when I was growing up I knew the name Sherlock Holmes and had a vague idea who he was. I saw the Wishbone adaptations of "A Scandal in Bohemia" and *The Hound of the Baskervilles*, and surely would have seen *The Great Mouse Detective*. I knew the deerstalker, and the pipe, and the Inverness cape. But I didn't really know Holmes. My journey to Sherlock Holmes began in 2009, with the release of the first Robert Downey, Jr., movie. The movie's accuracy aside, I decided I needed to read some of the stories. I picked up the first volume of the IDW collection, which was attempting to publish the stories in chronological order, and started plugging away. (IDW is normally a comic book publisher, having done a serialization of *The Seven-Per-Cent Solution* in 2016, but they publish books as well.)

I confess that I fell off the Canon-reading wagon, but that had everything to do with my schedule doing theatre, and not with the stories' contents. A friend turned me on to the BBC *Sherlock* series not long after, and my fascination was fixed. I started researching Holmes here and there, trying to make sure that I was getting my facts straight when discussing him. I learned more about the Baker Street Irregulars and the so-called Great Game, and started listening to podcasts like *I Hear of Sherlock Everywhere* and *The Baker Street Babes*. An idea took root. While I might not have the stereotypical Holmes body type, I wanted to play Holmes if I ever got the chance.

That chance came in 2013. At the time, I was working for the Waterloo Community Playhouse/Black Hawk Children's Theatre in Waterloo, Iowa, as the technical director and lighting designer. We were going to do

Katie Forgette's "Sherlock Holmes and the Case of the Jersey Lily," and I wanted the part of Holmes on top of my normal workload. I spent the next few months preparing: going back to material I had read before, starting to re-read the Canon again, very happily discovering the Granada series, and taking in bits and pieces of other interpretations as well. I absorbed whatever I could before going into the audition.

The work paid off, and I portrayed Holmes onstage in November 2013. Jeremy Brett was my biggest influence on how to approach Holmes on stage both physically and vocally. (I had my deviations from Brett, though; I always prefer a soft "a" in Lestrade as opposed to the harder "a" that Brett employed.) The show received positive feedback from the public, and we had an immense amount of fun doing it.

Towards the end of 2013 and into January 2014, a combination of reminiscing and changes in my personal life led me to think about starting a new project. A part of me just couldn't let Holmes go; I wasn't done with him. I needed to focus my creative and personal energy into a project outside of work, and then an idea cropped up. I asked my Facebook friends: what if I were to do audio dramatizations of the entire Canon? The response was a resounding affirmative. Shortly after that, I started adapting "A Scandal in Bohemia" into a script.

Turning a story into a script is usually at least a three-pass process. It takes me at least that many times to make sure I have all the lines broken up correctly and attributed to the right person, and that I have the sound effects denoted. A beauty of the modern age is that the text for the Canon is available very readily online. I copy and paste the script into a new document, and start going through and breaking it up into something easily readable for my actors. I leave every bit of the text in, just denoting what not to say by making it bold. I also indicate what will become sound effects with italics, underlining, or separate notes. So, for example, a passage from "The Five Orange Pips" comes to look something like this:

> WATSON: *(SFX: DOORBELL)* "Why," **said I, glancing up at my companion,** "that was surely the bell. Who could come to-night? Some friend of yours, perhaps?"
> HOLMES: "Except yourself I have none," **he answered.** "I do not encourage visitors."
> WATSON: "A client, then?"
> HOLMES: "If so, it is a serious case. Nothing less would bring a man out on such a day and at such an hour. But I take it that it is more likely to be some crony of the landlady's."
> WATSON: Sherlock Holmes was wrong in his conjecture, however, for there came a <u>step in the passage</u> and a tapping at the door. He stretched out his long arm to turn the lamp away from himself and towards the vacant chair upon which a newcomer must sit.

Landing on the title for my project was surprisingly easy. For whatever reason, the line, "I am lost without my Boswell," from "Scandal" just started running through my head and I knew that was what I had to use.

Looking back, the reason for this was two-fold: we were going to start with that story, and that specific line challenges the adapter to find the right interpretation. Depending on how you view Holmes and Watson's relationship, it can be as sarcastic or as sincere as you want it to be, and I don't think either reading is necessarily wrong. In doing these new dramatizations, we would have to create our own interpretations of the stories, and give context for certain moments and dialogue within the stories.

The hunt was now on for members of the team. My friend and stage manager for "Sherlock Holmes and the Case of the Jersey Lily," Caitlin Hurban, came on board as our producer. Margot Taylor, another friend, was our original graphic designer and still serves as our website manager, and one of my best friends, Jens Petersen, was cast as our Watson. Our sound designer for "A Scandal in Bohemia," Riley Germann, had to leave the *Boswell* team after that story. Recently, we welcomed Nicole Linderholm as our new graphic designer.

Once we had a Watson in place, we started holding auditions for other cast members. One of my goals was that distance should not be an exclusionary factor if people wanted to perform. For our first outing everybody was local, save for Irene Adler, who was played by my friend Amanda Lynn Juhl in Toronto. At the time of writing this essay, we are producing "The Man with the Twisted Lip," and I'm happy to say that everyone, save for Watson and myself, is from out of state or indeed outside the country.

The first read-through for "Scandal" was an incredibly exciting and somewhat nerve-racking experience, but I was surrounded by friends who were all excited by the project, and believed in what I was trying to accomplish. We ended up guerrilla recording in the theatre after hours, which got me in trouble, but at this point I'd say it was well worth it.

When I started *Boswell*, I didn't know how to promote the project, or connect with people who could help. I thought we might do an interview on a podcast, but that was really about it. In March 2014, our friend John Molseed wrote an article about *Boswell* for the *Waterloo/Cedar Falls Courier*. This was picked up by the Associated Press, got published in Des Moines, and made its way out to Washington as well. That article opened the gates to the Sherlockian community. A letter arrived from Richard Caplan, who founded the Younger Stamfords in Iowa City. We had a lovely phone conversation, and he pointed me towards the woman who would become my Sherlockian big sister, Monica Schmidt, who is now leader of the Younger Stamfords. I spoke at a meeting of the YS, and connected with more people who love Sherlock Holmes.

From that fateful meeting, I have spoken with people from all over the country. I've had a written interview with *I Hear of Sherlock Everywhere*, attended and presented at a meeting of the Crew of the Barque Lone Star in Dallas, and at a meeting of the Iowa Valley of Fear in Marshalltown, Iowa. I was thrilled when asked to present at A Scintillation of Scions in 2016. I have to sincerely thank Scintillation and its founder, Jacquelynn Morris, because they are now also our sponsors, and the whole *Boswell* team is incredibly grateful.

Every time I go someplace new, I meet wonderful, warm, welcoming people who are excited about what I'm doing. My usual joke is that I'm a glutton for punishment, but at least I didn't hate myself enough to start the project with one of the novels. But at this point, Boswell has really become about connecting with Sherlockians. We are helping bring the Canon to people who've never experienced the stories before, and giving those who have been around the block with Holmes and Watson a new treat to enjoy. (Our work is online at iamlostwithoutmyboswell.com.) There are so many people I never would have met if not for *Boswell*, and I'm so happy I have. We all may not play the Game quite the same way, but we certainly all do it for love.

David Harnois (Washburn, Iowa) is a member of the Younger Stamfords, the Iowa Valley of Fear, and the Crew of the Barque Lone Star. He works as a customer service representative for Copyworks and Limited Edition Comics & Collectibles, and freelances in technical theatre when the time allows.

THE ADVENTURE OF
THE CASTLE DUMMY

HAROLD E. NIVER

In 1968 there was a flu epidemic—the Hong Kong flu—and I caught it along with pneumonia at the same time. I was in bed for almost a month. After a while you do tire of watching *Gunsmoke, The Flying Nun*, and *My Three Sons*. For some reason I had never read a Holmes story, at least not that I could remember. I did have a volume of detective stories that contained *The Hound of the Baskervilles,* so I read it and wanted more. Well, that didn't happen for a while as I went back to work. Working in Hartford, Connecticut, I visited the biggest, and oldest, bookstore in the city. I selected a book that contained several of the Holmes stories.

While in the check-out line I asked the clerk about more books on Holmes and he said to turn around and ask the man in back of me. I turned and there stood a fellow about my age wearing a deerstalker! We chatted and he told me about the *Annotated Sherlock Holmes* book by Baring-Gould. He also told me about the Baker Street Irregulars and Julian Wolff, then the BSI's Commissionaire. Needless to say I hurriedly purchased a deerstalker cap, lit up one of my curved briar pipes, and started reading and corresponding.

I subscribed to the *Baker Street Journal* and learned of scion societies in neighboring states. There were the Hudson Valley Sciontists in New York and the Cornish Horrors in Rhode Island. I wrote and called Sherlockians such as Al Rosenblatt and Al Silverstein. Both gentlemen were extremely gracious and invited me to attend their various meetings.

The people I met were very friendly and helped educate me in both the scholarly and pseudo-scholarly world of Sherlock Holmes. An enthusiasm for Holmes can extend into every part of life: for example, I belong to a cowboy target-shooting organization in which each member uses an alias, and mine is Hawkshaw in honor of a comic strip detective who was popular in the early 20th century.

In the meantime I had met, and married, a young woman named Theodora Czerepuszko—Teddie—who shared my interest in Holmes. We purchased a house in Rocky Hill, Connecticut, and started collecting Sherlockian items.

The British production of William Gillette's play "Sherlock Holmes" came to the Bushnell Theater in Hartford. Some people connected with the theater had heard about our interest in Mr. Holmes and asked us to assist in the publicity for the play. We showed up on opening night dressed in Sherlockian attire and talked to people in the lobby. We were asked if there was a Connecticut-based Sherlockian society. We said "No, but give me your name in case one were to start up."

A local TV reporter interviewed us and learned that we had a Sherlock Holmes collection. They asked if they could visit our home and do to the interview there, as promotional publicity for the play. Naturally we said yes and made a quick phone call to Teddie's mother, who lived with us, and asked her to quickly clean up the house. The interview was a success.

At that point we gave serious thought to starting a scion. While attending a BSI weekend one January and talking with other Sherlockians, one of them came up with an idea. Since we lived in Rocky Hill and a tor, as mentioned in *The Hound of the Baskervilles*, is basically a rocky area, why not name the group The Men on the Tor? And so, starting in 1977, The Men on the Tor scion society was founded.

Julian Wolff honored me with the Investiture "The Man on the Tor." Teddie, thanks to Tom Stix, was later given the Investiture of "Carina." Like Carina, she is a singer of note.

I also became a collector of Sherlockiana. In fact, our house has a Sherlockian theme. It is an English Tudor, and on the big wooden front door there is a brass plaque that says "Baskerville Hall." The doors to the various rooms have plaques as well. The door to Teddie's mother's room says "Mrs. Hudson" and the door to the main bathroom says "John H. Watson"—after all, in American the bathroom is sometimes referred to as the john. The wallpaper in the library is a scarlet color: the study in scarlet, of course.

John Bennett Shaw, the ultimate Sherlockian collector, became a good friend and mentor. He gave me the names of reliable dealers in Sherlockiana and always told me of an item that I should purchase.

Teddie and I happen to live in the perfect state for a Sherlockian: Connecticut, the birthplace and residence of William Gillette. Yes, William Gillette, who brought Holmes to life on the stage and helped create the iconic image of Holmes, the curved pipe and deerstalker cap. For a time, the Men on the Tor were able to hold some of our meetings at Gillette Castle in East Haddam, Connecticut—though the landmark building's proper name is The Seventh Sister, originally the name used by mariners on the Connecticut River for the hill on which the castle stands. Built between 1914 and 1919, the castle has 24 rooms and 47 solid oak doors, fixtures by Tiffany and Quetzal, and a system of mirrors so that William Gillette could glance out from his bedroom to see who was arriving downstairs and who was already at the bar.

A memorable evening for the Men on the Tor was the one devoted to "The Sussex Vampire," when there was an actual, live bat flying around inside the historic building. Another meeting, on a foggy fall evening, was devoted to Jack the Ripper, and it was eerie to see people in Victorian clothes strolling on the castle's terrace. One of the funnier incidents took place when the great Sherlockian author Michael Harrison visited

Connecticut (he stayed at our home) and attended a Tor meeting at the castle. Thanks to the state legislature, the castle was officially dry—no liquor permitted—but Harrison was undaunted, as he always carried a flask on his person.

For eleven years now, Teddie and I have volunteered our services at the castle to portray the Gillettes. I am Mr. Gillette, with deerstalker, cape, curved pipe and lens, and Teddie is his wife, Helen, in appropriate Victorian attire. We educate and entertain visitors from all over the United States and the world. When they arrive they might know something about Sherlock Holmes and Mr. Gillette, but we tell them how Conan Doyle and Gillette became connected and develop the character. A memorable event was the 2015 wedding of two Sherlockians, Ashley Polasek and Paul Hyde, and we made sure the Gillettes were on hand to welcome them.

When company is expected at the castle, Teddie is usually stationed in the bedroom, and I take my position on the upper floor, in front of the library bookshelves. There is a window nearby that looks down upon the Connecticut River. One day there was a lull in visitors and I was standing near that window, quietly holding my pipe to my mouth, when a new group entered the library behind me. I turned around, unaware of them, and one of the tourists let out a scream. She had thought I was a mannequin! I quickly realized that there was fun to be had. Nowadays I often sit in an old canvas-and-wood director's chair with one knee folded, my pipe in my mouth and the lens up to my eye. I don't move or even blink—which is hard sometimes—and when visitors enter they aren't sure whether I am a dummy or the real thing. When I feel the crowd is just right I suddenly move and say "Hello!" and there is usually a shriek. When we leave the castle, shortly before closing time, we go to the Lily Pond near the park entrance and wave to the visitors leaving, and they invariably wave back.

We also cherish a number of little connections between ourselves and the Gillette household: for example, Gillette's butler and friend, Yukitaki Ozaki, had a brother who was mayor of Tokyo, Japan, and whose wife was, like mine, named Theodora. Charles Perkins, a neighbor of the Gillette family in Hartford, founded a law firm, still in existence, who have been our lawyers since long before we had any involvement with Gillette. We also note that October 16, my birthday, was the date in 1906 when Gillette's play "Clarice" opened—and the date in 1970 when the Gillette exhibition opened at the nearby Nook Farm visitors' center.

When William Gillette's long-lost 1916 film was rediscovered recently, the castle hosted several weekend showings of the film, and Sherlockians came from all over, even as far away as Canada, to see it in that evocative location. The Friends of Gillette Castle were kind enough to pay the expenses of the Gillettes—that is to say, me and Teddie—to attend the world premiere of the restored film at the Castro Theatre during the San Francisco Silent Film Festival in May 2015.

Mr. Holmes has been good to us. Through him we've met many interesting and wonderful people and been places and done things that wouldn't have been possible without that person who never lived and can never die:

Sherlock Holmes. I wonder, if I hadn't caught the Hong Kong flu, would any of this have happened anyway?

Harold E. (Tyke) Niver (Rocky Hill, Connecticut) spent 50 years in the retail piano business. He and his wife Teddie founded the Men on the Tor society in 1977 and are both members of the Baker Street Irregulars and other Sherlockian groups. They published *A Sherlockian Songbook* in 1983.

A CASE OF ART IN THE BLOOD

JERRY MARGOLIN

I was born a collector. I inherited the collecting gene from my mother, who was an antiques dealer and had her own collection. She was also an accomplished artist, hence my interest, throughout my entire life, in art. Interestingly, my brother, who is four years older, collects nothing and has never been interested in anything to do with this passion. However, I do acknowledge and thank him for my total interest in all things Sherlock Holmes. At ten, he introduced me to the world of Mr. Holmes by presenting me with *The Complete Sherlock Holmes* to read. After that I was hooked, though it would be many years before I started on my own personal journey of collecting everything to do with Holmes.

My second lucky break on this journey to collecting madness, beyond the comics, baseball cards, and vinyl LP's I already collected, was meeting the late Norman Nolan. From New Jersey, he was one of the great Sherlockian and mystery and detective fiction collectors. He not only took the time to teach me about the art of book collecting, but also very kindly took me to my first Baker Street Irregulars' dinner.

My collecting of Sherlockian books actually started on my honeymoon, 45 years ago, where we spent 15 days in London, England. I purchased a few early paperback books not really knowing if they were important or not, but those were the first of what came to be many. From there I began in earnest, with Norm guiding me, towards building a fine book collection. In New York, where I was working at that time, there were always bookstores to explore. During this period I began building what was to become a massive Holmes library. Even more portentously, I began to purchase Sherlockian original art. My very patient wife, known to many as "St. Judy," never really said much as bookcases seemed to be added in our home with disturbing regularity.

When we moved to our present home in Portland, Oregon, where we have now lived for 27 years, every room in the house, with a few exceptions, filled up with books, statuary, and art dedicated to Mr. Holmes. The movers were not terribly pleased when I showed them the 200-plus cartons of books that needed to be moved along with the household material. The statuary and art filled my parents' basement until it also could be moved to the new residence. About nine years ago, I realized it was time to sell the book collection and end a 45-year obsession, or at least a part of it. As I like to say, "collectors never die, they just move on to other things."

So, though the books were mostly gone, I did keep a bookcase full of Sherlockiana, and the art collection began to grow with quite a bit of speed. I was never afraid to call or write to any artist whose art I wished to acquire. As a result, I became friends with Will Elder, of *MAD Magazine*—he and Harvey Kurtzman were responsible for *MAD*'s "Shermlock Shomes" and "Shermlock Shomes & The Hound of the Basketballs." It was the same with Gahan Wilson, the great cartoonist and illustrator responsible for many Sherlockian-themed cartoons for *Playboy* and other books and magazines. I possess several pieces of great art from both of these masters and many, many others.

My crown jewels would be my original Sidney Paget drawing for "The Resident Patient," which shows Holmes sniffing a cigar and holding a cigar case. I also have an original Frederic Dorr Steele drawing for "The Musgrave Ritual," which was done for the Limited Edition Club set. It shows Holmes pulling papers from a dispatch box. The Paget is something that, as a young collector, I could not have dreamed of owning, and after owning it now for more than 25 years, I am still amazed that it hangs on my wall.

The collection has grown to close to 3,000 pieces and there seems to be no end in sight. As I sit here writing this essay, I am waiting for the postman to ring my doorbell and deliver a 1950's cartoon piece from Argentina. Collecting is a wonderful obsession. There is always something new or old to look forward to adding to the collection, and the excitement never ends.

Jerry Margolin (Portland, Oregon) has been a member of the Baker Street Irregulars since 1977. Retired after a 20-year career in the software industry, he is an art collector and an enthusiast of modern cinema, music, and the New York Yankees.

THE ADVENTURE OF
THE CANDLELIT DINNER

HARRISON KITTERIDGE

I honestly can't remember my introduction to Sherlock Holmes. If I had to guess, I'd say it was one of the old black and white films of *The Hound of the Baskervilles*, and the only reason I have any recollection of it is because I was so young that the cheesy rendition of the hound was enough to scare the living daylights out of me. I was into mysteries, though—Nancy Drew and The Hardy Boys, Encyclopedia Brown, Trixie Belden—and have never wavered in my love of the genre, but for some reason Sherlock Holmes never really made much of an impression. I suppose I saw myself and my friends in the likes of Encyclopedia Brown, and wanted to be a clever child detective, too. I learned the craft and formed a young detectives club (yes, I was that kid). At the age of eight I knew all the characteristics of fingerprint patterns and what a photofit was. But I didn't relate to an old Victorian man smoking a pipe and wearing a funny hat. I liked the stories well enough to read them and enjoyed the films and television series when I came across them, but it was all too far removed. I read more Agatha Christie than Arthur Conan Doyle, but Miss Marple and Hercule Poirot didn't get much love either. I wanted to read about other children. I wanted to see myself in the protagonists. In that way, I suppose it's fitting that my love for Sherlock Holmes came in adulthood.

Trawling for free classics in the Kindle store is how I wound up devouring the entire Sherlock Holmes Canon. In the years that followed, I found myself re-reading the stories periodically, and, as much as I enjoyed the cases, there was something about Sherlock Holmes, the man, that I was drawn to. It went beyond being amazed by the acuity of his mind, though. I *liked* him. I thought he was funny and strange and fascinating and troubled. He was a hero, but he was far from perfect, and somewhere in that imbalance, I believe, lies the key to Sherlock Holmes's immortality. There is something mythopoeic there—the blessing of a great intellect coming with the burden of an unquiet mind; valour and bravery joined with intense melancholia; the pride of a warrior assailed by the cravings of an addict. I liked Dr. Watson, too: how put-upon he sometimes was, how well and how little he understood Holmes, the unassuming quality of his immense loyalty. Holmes and Watson were both damaged but not broken. I liked them together—sort of a Victorian-era Bert and Ernie. While the cases were the points of interest, the underlying relationship as seen through Dr. Watson's eyes is the real foundation of the stories for me.

I was of course aware that queer readings of Arthur Conan Doyle's stories sprang up almost immediately, and could see clearly the subtext of the "confirmed bachelor" who had an "aversion to women" in Holmes. Even so, I never really paid it much mind. In hindsight, I can see that my indifference to the matter stemmed from my only ever hearing the theory discussed from an academic perspective: I'd never read an actual story about Holmes and Watson as a romantic couple. That changed when I discovered the explosion of fanfiction that arose around BBC *Sherlock*.

I was late to the party, discovering the show after the first two seasons had already aired. I binge-watched the episodes over the course of a weekend and was an immediate convert. I enjoyed the contemporary setting and familiarity—Holmes and Watson were now Sherlock and John, and they had mobile phones and laptops and ordered Chinese takeaway. It was all more relatable, more intimate somehow, than the original tales. I thought it was brilliant. The show nodded directly at the queer interpretation of Sherlock Holmes in the first episode when John seems to make a pass at Sherlock, and Sherlock rebuffs him. In that moment, the fanfiction power pairing Johnlock was born.

I knew nothing of fanfiction and learned the word—and learned of the existence of Johnlock—through sometimes unfairly unflattering articles about the intense fandom the show had spawned. Out of curiosity, I googled "Sherlock fanfiction" and discovered Archive of Our Own, a website run by the non-profit Organization for Transformative Works to provide a depository for fan works. No one would deny that there is a lot of terrible fanfiction out there, but I got lucky and almost immediately stumbled across high-quality stories that delved thoughtfully into Sherlock and John's relationship. Not all of them saw Sherlock and John as a romantic couple, but the overwhelming majority did. Most of the stories were set in the universe of BBC *Sherlock*, but some created alternate universes or timelines for the show's characters, and there was a fascinating mélange of stories ranging from hunts for serial killers, to adventures in outer space, to John and Sherlock playing at Wimbledon. The creativity was staggering to behold. The fanfiction took the "Bert and Ernie" analogy to its logical conclusion: Sherlock and John were a lifelong romantic couple. Once I got on board, there was no getting off that train.

I haven't actively participated in any fandom since my early teens, and I consume most of the content I enjoy, including early *Sherlock*, in relative isolation. I'm the classic lurker, and I had limited interaction with the wider fandom. I'd never have used the word "Sherlockian" to describe myself, and wouldn't have described myself as a fan of "Sherlock" in the traditional sense, but I knew I shipped Johnlock and shipped it hard. While I wasn't part of the new audience the new series introduced to Arthur Conan Doyle's stories, the show and the fanfiction forever changed the way I see the characters. I'd always thought Holmes and Watson were like an old, bickering married couple, but I'd only ever scratched the surface of what that meant emotionally, and the fanfiction gave me a lens to explore their relationship more thoughtfully. I had a new perspective on the original texts and appreciated much more profoundly the depth of the characterisation ACD had managed to achieve.

I don't believe for one moment that a queer reading of Sherlock Holmes is compulsory, but Holmes and Watson, in whatever incarnation they arise, are always "ride or die"—willing to make the ultimate sacrifice for each other. Combine that with the themes of romantic love, and you have the ingredients for a powerful story. Recognising this is what led me to take a run at writing my own re-telling of Sherlock Holmes's story. Had I never been exposed to the free-wheeling creativity of the fanfiction community, I can say with certainty that I never would have found the inspiration.

Sherlock has been that rare TV show that truly captures the zeitgeist, and it has forever changed the way people see Sherlock Holmes. I don't think it will be possible to have future conversations about the cultural impact of Sherlock Holmes without discussing the show. Nevertheless— given the "date scene" in the first episode and John repeatedly declaring, "I'm not gay!"—a queer reading of the show was, and will remain, inevitable. Steven Moffat and Mark Gatiss, the show's creators, played both the date scene and John's adamant defence of his heterosexuality perfectly straight, so to speak, and most of the audience went along with them and either didn't see the subtext or ignored it.

Had Moffat and Gatiss chosen to switch the gender of either Sherlock or John and an attractive woman had been sitting across from an attractive man over a candlelit Italian dinner, they would have set in motion the "years of angst-filled, unresolved sexual tension because these two idiots don't realise they're in love" trope that would have eventually culminated in a loving, carnal embrace. The show being billed as a modern, intelligent reboot of the Sherlock Holmes stories meant that some modern, intelligent fans who don't assign heterosexuality as a default thought the romance was part of the story being told.

While I saw the romantic subtext (and, let's be honest, actual text), I never thought that was the show that was being produced. For all its grand 21st century stylings, *Sherlock* is thoroughly mainstream, and, therefore, a bit retrograde culturally—it doesn't have a shred of transgressiveness anywhere in its DNA. There was no way the show was overtly queering up one of Britain's most well-loved, enduring cultural icons. What seemed obvious to me wasn't to others, though, and the fandom became embroiled in a civil war of sorts, at the centre of which emerged something called "The Johnlock Conspiracy" (TJLC).

TJLC is explicitly described by its founders and adherents as a "belief system", and the core belief is that Johnlock becoming canon was always the endgame for *Sherlock*. TJLCers weren't arguing for a queer reading of *Sherlock*, they were insisting that the show had actually been conceived and was being executed as queer. Steven Moffat and Mark Gatiss repeatedly shot down (sometimes rather crossly) the idea of a John and Sherlock romance, stating as unequivocally as possible that it wasn't in the cards. Nevertheless, the "movement" was not to be deterred, and no argument was to be brooked. Those who expressed doubt that Johnlock would become canon (even long-time, hardcore Johnlock shippers) were attacked. The battles toxified the *Sherlock* fandom so much that many fans simply left.

In the run-up to Season 4, a few TJLCers baldly asserted that Johnlock was already canon by dint of them having been clever enough to have declared it so. Following the end of Season 4 (in which there was no Johnlock in sight), increasingly bizarre conspiracy theories were put forth.

The addition of new, Johnlock-free canonical material in Season 4 meant TJLC had to revise its catechism in the face of the series' total repudiation of its beliefs. They began by arguing that that the footage of the finale had been faked up (something to do with the Russian leak of the episode). In the weeks and months following the airing of the finale, the tinhattery culminated with the assertion that the producers of *Sherlock* had created an Alternate Reality Game (which they had bafflingly failed to promote) and had sprinkled clues throughout the Season 4 episodes, in their interviews and social media posts, and all over the internet. Once the game was complete, a "Lost Special" would air. Stalwart TJLCers were the only ones clever enough to have unearthed the plot and follow the trail of the imaginary breadcrumbs. As with prophecies about the end of the world, the rapture kept getting postponed.

The passage of a few months without the airing of the "Lost Special" has thinned TJLC's ranks, but the continuing toxification of the *Sherlock* fandom has created a breach that may never be healed and has driven even more fans into the wilderness. (In addition, Season 4 was polarising, and for myriad reasons having nothing to do with Johnlock, other fans (myself included) who were disappointed by the direction of the show have also peeled off.)

TJLC is a "When Fandom Goes Wrong" moment, and, while I found it horrifying, it was also fascinating. Particularly because these weren't the stereotypical sobbing, acned teenage fanboys and fangirls. They were in the same phylum as the condescending male chauvinists who threw embarrassing, sexism-crazed tantrums over the all-female reboot of *Ghostbusters*, claiming it was "destroying their childhoods". Adults, some of them middle-aged, are poisoning fandoms because they revel in rejecting context and take a fundamentalist approach to the interpretation of fictional work. I loved the first two seasons of *Sherlock*, thought season three wasn't very good, and hated season four rather a lot, but it never even occurred to me to care whether or not Johnlock became canon. I don't want to participate in any kind of community where allowing my opinion of a fictional TV show to change with the emergence of new episodes makes me some sort of apostate.

Appreciation is the basis of fandom. But it often becomes married to intense passion that borders on devotion, and this is the place where I always become uncomfortable and start looking for the exits. Nevertheless, I firmly believe that creativity is the foundation of culture and is the most important human quality behind empathy. Artists should be appreciated, perhaps even revered, but none of their work is sacred, and our interpretations of it certainly aren't. When I say I'm a Sherlockian, what I'm really saying is that I greatly appreciate Arthur Conan Doyle's stories and many of the novels, films, and TV series that have been inspired by it. When I say I'm a Johnlock shipper, what I'm really saying is that this interpretation of the Sherlock Holmes oeuvre moves me emotionally. To me, there is no conflict there. My relationship to Sherlock Holmes is fluid and has been changing since I was a child. It will keep changing as I continue to learn and grow—and as more works, fan-created and otherwise, emerge.

Harrison Kitteridge (Mandeville, Jamaica) is a "recovering attorney" and the author of the novels *Before Holmes Met Watson* and *Sherlock Holmes and the Adventure of the Paper Journal*.

THE REMARKABLE INCIDENT OF THE SHIP

PRU HOLCOMBE

If someone had told me ten years ago, at the age of twenty, that in just a few short years I'd find myself hunched over my computer, caffeinated and delirious, telling stories about how two characters from someone else's book or movie or TV show are totally in love, I would have laughed in confusion while sidling slowly away.

Five years ago I would have laughed nervously and sidled away, wondering how they had found my online alias. Today, I'd probably hear them only saying something that vaguely sounded like the word "fic" and I'd be stampeding toward them with a business card detailing my Twitter, Tumblr, and AO3 account info, and phone number. (I swear I really haven't done this. Ever. At all.)

It's amazing how we grow as people, isn't it?

As it goes, Sherlock Holmes fic is especially fun—there are a virtual ton of different adaptations to draw from. From ACD-Canon to any number of movies, books, television shows, heck, even plays, we fic readers and writers live at a time where we can count ourselves truly blessed. We can play around with elements from so many of those mediums, and explore the things that catch our notice. Fanfiction, and its somewhat more scholarly literary cousin the pastiche, can range from gritty and gripping subjects with mind-bogglingly intricate mysteries to stories that are as silly as an episode of *Scooby Doo*. There are more than 120 years' worth of transformative works to read and enjoy!

Some people might frown and ask, "But what's the point? Why don't you just pick up a different book, if you want to read about something like X? Why can't you just write original fiction that delves into the stuff you want to talk about?"

Sure, we could do that. But obviously anyone who might say that hasn't experienced the bewildering, life-affirming joy of *Sherlock Holmes* with dinosaurs, a movie put out by Asylum Films.

Or just imagine: Holmes and Watson run a coffee shop. Maybe the "Baker Street Cafe" serves as a front while they're investigating a case, or maybe it's a legitimate business venture, and maybe we have to solve the Adventure of the Disappearing Cafe Chairs. (Spoiler: it was definitely Wiggins, the newest employee, who was moving them into the back alley, right beside the skips, while he cleaned the floors. They kept getting picked up by the bin men who mistook them for abandoned furniture. Wiggins figured it out early on, but was really embarrassed to admit it was something he'd done.)

Between Watson and Holmes, which one of them would have to deal with fussy customers, and who would just hide behind the espresso machine, scowling at the beans? It's easy to imagine Watson getting ridiculously twee in his descriptions of just about any attractive person to come through the doors, and really amusing to think of the way Holmes might study a person for half a second before deducing their coffee order with 98 per cent accuracy. Oh, and what if the rival coffee shop across the street is run by a certain retired professor who's turned his public interests into more entrepreneurial avenues. How would that work?

The joy in reading and writing fic, especially in the broad Sherlockian universe, is the essence of what it means to still let yourself play, really. I love the odd little club we accidentally form—we can create things or find and enjoy things with a common shorthand. We can incorporate in-jokes and everyone gets to play along. As a writer and an avid consumer, it genuinely delights me to see the profound diversity of stories and ideas to be found when we let our minds wander.

This "play" is essential: for so many writers—many of whom may only ever be hobbyists, others who eventually move on to more professional avenues, like myself—fanfiction can serve as a beautiful seedling nursery. Given the tight-knit community and the popularity of the various Sherlock Holmes-based franchises, most authors are exposed to a wealth of support and suggestions for how to hone their craft, as well as fanatic encouragement when they write something particularly enjoyable. Heck, some of my favorite comments are thoughtful and in-depth, but the ones I print and hang in my office are the ones where the commenter just incoherently smashes buttons on the keyboard like they'd tripped and spilled a bowl of alphabet soup in their haste to sing my praises. Personally, if I've made someone forget how to use the English language, I'm doing what I set out to accomplish.

Truth is, though, you can't throw a rock very far in the fanfic camp without hitting creations where writers involve their ships, whether or not it's the focus of the work.

For anyone who may not be aware, "shipping" is what happens when you thoroughly enjoy or believe in the (usually romantic) relationship between two characters. This can be a Canon relationship (think, John Watson and Mary Morstan), or ones some fans want to explore (I personally know a one-woman army dedicated to Sherlock/Wiggins from BBC's *Sherlock*). This is the meat and potatoes for slash writers like me. Oh, slash? That's the nickname for the genre, usually revolving around a romantic/sexual pairing, typically of two male characters—in this case, Sherlock Holmes/ John Watson. See it? That slash between their names? We're a clever lot.

If you ask a hundred Sherlock Holmes/John Watson shippers, you'll get *two* hundred different reasons for doing what we do. I can't pretend to speak for even a fraction of us, but I can definitely (and verbosely) offer up my own experiences. Well before I considered myself a Sherlockian, I discovered fic and slash almost at the same time. The early Aughts and Geocities webrings made it an ideal time for a pre-pubescent caterpillar to start the metamorphosis to fandom butterfly. I dabbled in a roleplay thread for a sci-fi series I loved in middle school (*The Dragonriders of Pern* series by Anne McCaffrey), and stumbled onto fully-written stories some of my roleplay partners had written, with new and existing characters. It blew my world wide open.

It became second nature to play around with characters, to notice plot holes (or "unanswered questions," if we're feeling generous), to pick up on themes and subtext and symbols. Granted, it took a rather long time to make anything I'd be proud to show someone, but for me, fanfiction has always been A Thing.

Part and parcel with that, then, came the shipping. Sure, some mainstream couples are really well done, and I will forever love them. But for me, a queer kid from the south, there were so many other "friendships" that read just the same, but without anyone calling it a relationship.

And that's what brings us back around to being inducted into Sherlockiana. I came into it, yes, from the BBC show with Benedict Cumberbatch, purely from curiosity (although personally, I was excited about it because I'm a long-time Martin Freeman fan). Within the first 30 minutes, I was already seeing enough to pull out my phone and tab open AO3 (otherwise known as archiveofourown.org, possibly the most popular archive of transformative works currently). I couldn't help seeing the ship beginning to sail, so to speak. I inhaled the first two seasons and then dove headfirst into the fandom.

After that, I got curious about ACD Canon: the original Sherlock Holmes stories by Arthur Conan Doyle. Whatever modern franchise any of us comes from, that always winds up being a touchstone, I think. And to be fair, I did go into it without the ship-goggles (the idea that if we pointedly go looking for something, nine times out of ten we'll find it). I expected to find the cut-and-dried partnership I vaguely remembered being exposed to when my second grade class read "The Red-Headed League." (It could have been that the teacher helped us along with it or simplified it in some way, but I definitely remember Paget illustrations and a character copying the dictionary!) But yet again, certain things kept catching my eye.

There were the simple, obvious things like the fact that Mary, now married to Watson, was perfectly fine with him taking off in the middle of the night to dash around London, or the fact that she let her husband build his BFF his own guest room. There was the way Watson would describe Holmes, and his language would get just as flowery about him or other guys as it would about his own lady-wife when he first met her.

Later on, I tumbled into the literary rabbit-hole of essays on queer-coding specifically within ACD Canon. Queer-coding is a way of describing a person or relationship as anything other than heterosexual in a way that would be recognizable to a queer audience, but pass under the radar of a heterosexual audience (a device typically employed because doing otherwise was quite unsafe). Certain aspects of coding have hit the mainstream understanding over the years, including stereotypes about what certain people look like or how they act, but largely, from generation to generation, these subtle cues can be lost as culture and society evolve. For a really easy example on coding, just consider about every other character from anything written by Oscar Wilde—one of Doyle's contemporaries, mind you. Jack and Algy, anyone?

Through exploring Canon, I met a cache of what we call aca-fans, or fans who come from a more academic angle. These are the nerds who write the best essays on analysis of Canon I've found. That was how I found the history of "shipping" and "queer-coding" as it pertains to Sherlock Holmes: it turns out generations of people—including some of Doyle's original fans—have been analyzing the relationship between the two men. It was definitely empowering to know that there have been generations of people far smarter than me who have picked up on the things I've noticed, who can better analyze and explain their hypotheses.

So for me, this is why I write slash, especially as a Sherlockian. I still mumble my affiliation with Watson/Holmes (or, in the younger BBC *Sherlock*-specific crowd, Johnlock) when it gets brought up in polite company, but that comes from a lifetime of having people around me rolling their eyes with varying levels of fondness and annoyance, and denying what seems plain as day to me. I write slash because I see something beautiful and underrepresented there. I write it for myself. I write it to add to the dragon's hoard so that future generations will have more. I write it for other queer kids like me, for that first time they side-eye something and go, "Wait a second…"

Whether it means, as it might to some, that John Watson and Sherlock Holmes are somehow fluffier, lovey-dovey versions of themselves or having wild sex all over 221B—that's down to personal preference or how an author might choose to explore a given story dynamic. I love all of that and more. I love the sorts of creativity I stumble across in myself and in others, all because we enjoy two fictional sarcastic British men.

After all, if it weren't for one mustachioed guy sitting down more than 120-some years ago and writing what may or may not have been "real person fanfic" of a buddy or two of his own, none of us would have the Canon material that has lent itself to so much of English-speaking culture ever since.

Pru Holcombe (Easley, South Carolina) is a long-time member of the Sherlock Holmes fandom, and has written more than 40 works focusing on Sherlock Holmes and John Watson. She has since branched off into parts unknown with a patreon dedicated to an original fiction series, the Under-London series, inspired by one such early fanfiction.

THE ADVENTURE OF
THE SCARLET THREAD

WENDY C. FRIES

Humans can be fond of itty bitty boxes.

You like *that* team? You read *those* books? You think *this* show is good? Sherlock Holmes is gay, a warlock, a 21st-century man...are you *crazy*?

Maybe that's why, when I joined the Sherlock Holmes fandom, I expected some itty bitty boxes. A bit of Us and Them. Old-guard Holmesians strictly hewing to Canon over here, lovers of Basil and Brett over there, Cumberbatchians in a different room entirely, and none meeting in the middle.

Yeah. Right. To paraphrase a modern Holmes: I was wrong, wrong, *wrong*. Instead I found that fans of this century-old character are usually on the same page, and it rarely matters if you first fell in love with Holmes as a Victorian gent or a posh modern man; most don't care *how* you came to Sherlock, they're just glad you're here.

After all, stories about the great detective didn't stop when Arthur Conan Doyle laid down his pen. Fans started creating new tales for the legendary sleuth in ACD's lifetime. If they hadn't, we might well have lost Holmes to attrition or new trends long before now.

Instead, the famous and not-so carried on writing Sherlock Holmes stories. *Peter Pan* creator J.M. Barrie wrote sardonic parodies for his friend Arthur, actor William Gillette gave the detective true love in his 1916 film *Sherlock Holmes*, and half a century later Nicholas Meyer beset the man with secrets best soothed by a seven per cent solution. William S. Baring-Gould gave the fictional detective a biography, a birth date, and another brother, and meantime there were films, television shows, and more films.

And the creation continues 130 years later, in ever-expanding iterations. There's a resurgent *Strand* magazine; the tidal rise of fan fiction; and publishers producing hundreds of Sherlock Holmes pastiches, parodies, and academic works.

Titan Press gives us crossovers galore, as the famous men of 221B Baker Street head to Castle Dracula, find themselves on the trail of Dr. Jekyll and Mr. Hyde, or take on the wrath of the white worm. Improbable Press adds romance to Canon and contemporary mysteries, with novels and anthologies that presume a world where Sherlock Holmes and John

Watson's relationship goes beyond friendship. MX Publishing gives us its popular series of "big books" of new Canon short stories, and just about everything in between, from graphic novels to Swearlot Holmes, from modern tales to children's books.

Along with being the acquisitions editor for Improbable Press, I've been privileged to write essays about Holmes and his fandoms, as well as a couple of books. One of those, *The Day They Met*, is 50 stories of other ways Holmes and Watson could have met, best friends *foreva*. A sequel, *The Night They Met*, contains 19 longer tales of how these legendary men could have met—and begun to fall in love.

As innovative as today's magazines and book publishers can be, probably nothing beats the world-building, the genre-, gender-, and story-expanding vibrancy of fan fiction. Like the science fiction and romance genres, fan fiction copes with the lack of respect it receives by...ignoring the lack of respect it receives. As a result, in fan fiction you'll find thousands of iterations of Holmes and Watson, of Adler and Trevor and Lestrade. There are fan fiction novellas, novels, and short stories; there are writers aged 13, 30, 60, and more. In fan fiction there are new writers learning where their gifts lie, and just as many professional writers, some who write TV scripts and books in their day jobs. All of these creators breathe new life into this legendary character for the sheer love of him.

Has everyone liked every one of these iterations, whether book or comic or fic? Doubtful. Yet just as some prefer Brett to Basil, or Robert Stephens's melancholy Holmes to Robert Downey Jr's more vigorous man, few deny the benefit of *more*. More adventures, more friendship, more mysteries. Even if every story isn't to every taste, the world's most famous—and only—consulting detective *lives*.

When I came to the fandom, I thought being a Sherlockian would mean defending turf or justifying preferences. Instead I've been to Sherlock Holmes society luncheons where an 80-year-old Swiss man admired Sherlockian T-shirts bearing likenesses of Benedict Cumberbatch. I've found a group of college kids listening to a 70-year-old Japanese woman recounting her trip to the Reichenbach Falls. I've learned that a love of Sherlock Holmes unifies far more than it divides, and as new fans discover this long-lived character there's no end in sight.

We love Sherlock Holmes.

This is the indivisible fact and by far the more engaging, the one that starts conversations, encourages commentary, and leads to new Canon. Building on what *was* to create a what *is* is the province of everything living. Nothing remains static, and so creation and recreation is what we fans *do*. Sure birth (and rebirth) is a sprawling, messy business, but while I may not want a trunk, I'm pretty sure the elephant loves hers.

So it doesn't matter if I see the natural progression from a Bohemian Holmes to a foul-mouthed private dick. Someone else did and went ahead and joyfully wrote that book. Another connected the fairytale of a fluorescing hound with the modern chemistry that would have lit up that hound, and they went ahead and wrote *that*. Still others see John and Sherlock's attachment to one another as a deep and romantic interest and so they tell those tales. More than a century on, the scarlet thread running through each of these is this: Sherlockians read between Sir Arthur's lines and do their part to keep the ageless detective alive.

That's what unites us, that's what makes us Sherlockians. Every press, every fan, every fandom, we're on the same page and on that page is this: *Once upon a time there was Sherlock Holmes and John Watson.* The rest of that story is up to us, all of us.

Wendy C. Fries (Dublin, Ireland) is the author of *Sherlock Holmes and John Watson: The Day They Met* for MX Publishing and, as Atlin Merrick, *The Night They Met* for Improbable Press (improbablepress.co.uk), for which she is acquisitions editor.

THE ADVENTURE OF THE QUEER DETECTIVE

ELINOR GRAY

Sherlock Holmes is queer, and so am I. I'm not going to try to prove the first half of that statement to you, but I am going to use the second half to illustrate something else. Stick with me.

Allow me first to list my Sherlockian credentials, in an attempt to convince you to take me, a queer cis female fan/scholar under 30, seriously. My first Sherlockian society was Watson's Tin Box of Ellicott City, Maryland, which I joined in 2013. Then I joined the John H. Watson Society as a charter member in 2014. I moved to London in the autumn of 2014 and joined the Sherlock Holmes Society of London, and during the 16 months that I lived in the UK I co-founded the Retired Beekeepers of Sussex, based in Brighton. I moved back to the United States in 2016 and joined my newest local scions: the Noble and Most Singular Order of the Blue Carbuncle of Portland, and the Sound of the Baskervilles of Seattle. While in London, I attended Queen Mary University of London for my Master of Arts degree in human geography, and wrote my thesis on 19th-century women's transportation as portrayed in popular literature—specifically, ladies' bicycling in Sherlock Holmes.

So far, so good: perhaps this laundry list of memberships will have convinced you to keep reading.

The next part of my identity forms and is formed by my participation in the Sherlock Holmes community. I was out of college and in the wild world for a few years before I found words that described my own queerness. I had been surrounded by LGBT+ friends for years, and in queer-run fandom spaces for even longer, but for whatever reason they hadn't stuck. In London, immersed in Holmes and his aficionados, I finally figured it out. Thanks to the way I began to perceive Dr. Watson's love for his friend, and for his wife, I pinned it down.

Reading the books as a kid, I was in it for the adventures and the mystery. As an adult, I find more and deeper meaning in the stories. The Holmes/Watson friendship became the most important thing, and, primed by fandom and my own queer soul, romance followed. It's not that I think Doyle intended Holmes and Watson to be a romantic couple, necessarily. I make no claims to know what good old Arthur meant when he wrote anything down. He hardly took notes and made a lot of things up, and you know it. Intent is not the point. Interpretation is where the magic happens. I can read whatever I want into a text because once it's published it is the property of the readers (please note, the Death of the Author as a literary concept does not require the literal death of any author, although it is convenient that Doyle is long gone). Readers make meaning, separate from authorial intention. Readers bring their context into the bedroom with the book, and asking them to separate themselves from fiction for the sake of purity is ridiculous.

I'm not asking you to believe me. I'm just asking you to see it as a possibility. Holmes and Watson have been robots, mice, gender-swapped, and on the moon, but being romantic partners is too much of a suspension of disbelief? Everyone, *everyone*, knows at least one person who identifies as queer. No one is on intimate terms with a robot.

I was listening to a Baker Street Babes podcast episode that was a recording of a panel of Sherlockians discussing some element of the Canon; the particulars are unimportant. A woman in the audience asked the question I dread in public Sherlock Holmes forums: had the panelists heard of this notion that Holmes and Watson were in love with one another? One panelist jumped in, clearly experienced with fielding this sort of question, and explained that whether or not they were in love is not provable in the Canon, because there is no evidence one way or another. One cannot prove a negative, and so the reader is free to interpret as they like. I felt like I'd dodged a bullet listening to this recording, but the gun hadn't really been fired yet.

"Oh, no," another panelist chimed in. "Reading Holmes and Watson as a couple is a mistake."

It pierced me to the core. "A mistake." According to this panelist, who unfortunately holds a view I've heard time and time again, my reading was an error. I was reading the books wrong. My interpretation was invalid. Simultaneously, though not intentionally implied by the panelist, my identity was invalid.

A Sherlockian friend and I sat down at a certain convention in Atlanta in 2017, and this story came up. How, my friend asked, could not reading two fictional characters as lovers invalidate my own personal identity?

The key, I explained, was not in disbelieving, but in denying. Not perceiving Holmes and Watson as life partners wasn't the problem; it's the scoffing dismissal of that romantic reading as possible, as if anyone who sees things that way must be mad, that I object to. Reading Holmes and Watson as romantically involved is not "a mistake," because being queer is not a mistake. Queerness is not an insult to the characters, because being queer isn't a bad thing to be. It's just a thing. The notion that Holmes and Watson couldn't possibly be in love or because one reader didn't see them that way, and that thinking such a thing was ridiculous or absurd, is where the insult lies.

Here's the thing: I want to participate in traditional Sherlockian fan interactions. I love the idea of dinner clubs and quizzes and toasting the Queen and sharing papers on cryptology and train timetables. The time-honored objective of the Grand Game is to look for clues, fill in the gaps, make meaning where there is nonsense, and extrapolate. But I'm bringing my queerness with me wherever I go, and it extends to my readings of literature. This is how I "play the Game." Our own conclusions and perceptions of Holmes and Watson (or, as they say in the internet fandom, "headcanons") are built on the foundations of our own lives.

As a reader, seeing oneself reflected in fictional characters is not a foreign concept. As a queer woman, seeing queerness in my favorite heroes is not unreasonable. Holmes and Watson mean to me what they mean to you: they are friends, they are gaslit crime-solvers, they are gentlemen of quality who protect the meek and punish the wicked, all for the sake of a good puzzle. They are on-and-off bachelor flatmates who spend 20 years together and can't seem to thrive when they're apart. Why *can't* they be in love? Why deny them that?

I could point out dozens of passages in the Canon where Watson fixates upon Holmes's eyes and hands. I could show you the references to crucial moments in queer history. I could count for you the number of times Holmes calls Watson "my dear," or show you the way Holmes distances himself from female beauty and masculinity while Watson dotes upon handsome men. But I won't, because I don't have to. Other scholars have done it already. The curious appearances of double-bedded rooms have been recorded, analyzed, and archived. This version of the "Game" is being played all the time.

I don't need you to believe. I just need you to let *me* believe, and not have it chalked up to "a mistake." I'm not saying I'm right, only that I'm not necessarily wrong. And in return I'll leave your Irene Adler fantasies alone.

Elinor Gray (Portland, Oregon) co-founded the Retired Beekeepers of Sussex in Brighton, edits the bi-annual journal *The Practical Handbook of Bee Culture*, and is the author of *Compound a Felony: A Queer Affair of Sherlock Holmes*.

A STUDY IN SEMBLANCE

LYNDSAY FAYE

I make my living, at least in part, writing Sherlock Holmes fanfiction that also happens to qualify as pastiche. But allow me to begin this discussion from the heart rather than from any perceived intellectual distinction between the F-word and the P-word I've just cited: I adore Sherlock Holmes stories.

All of them. Well, most. Allow me to explain.

Firstly, Arthur Conan Doyle's adventures held my hand through the process of growing from a socially anxious, gleefully nerdy child into a socially anxious, gleefully nerdy adult who employs pawky humor and frilly dresses to ease my path; they also introduced me to twin lifelong obsessions, loyalty and courage, which are major themes in all my published works (and my unpublished ones, at that). Next, fanfiction taught me that you don't need formal training to put what you're feeling into words, gifted me with tales that are passionate about Doyle's characters while also being deeply personal, and caused me to meet some of my favorite people in this wide, wonderful world. And finally, pastiche quite literally changed my life by way of changing my career.

So forgive me, I beg, if I wax poetic on this topic. There's a lot to unpack. And I wouldn't have missed a second of it for all the French gold in the vault of the Coburg branch of the City and Suburban Bank.

I've read *a great many* Sherlock Holmes stories, penned by a great many people. Well written, poorly written, hilariously written, morbidly written. Sharp and lugubrious. Witty and plodding. Banal and poetic. Clever and nonsensical. (One of the nonsensical ones is by a fellow whose initials were ACD, and its title rhymes with "The Adventure of the Feeping Fan.") Like Holmes's cases, not all are triumphs. But even when they are not successes to my mind—and I forever insist that *de gustibus non est disputandum*—most of them are written out of admiration for the marvelous originals. At times, the closest imitations are also the least inspired; at times, the oddest incarnations are also the most loyal. They strive to restore, or renew, or even remake the immortal characters Sir Arthur created for us, from a young Daniel Stashower pitting our heroes against grenade-wielding lizards to Paul Attanasio and David Shore transplanting them to Princeton Plainsboro Teaching Hospital.

To every one of these storytellers regardless of experience or efficacy, which are in the eye of the beholder anyhow: I see your love, and it looks like mine. And I hereby shake your hand and call you sibling.

I say "most" post-Doyle Sherlock Holmes stories were written out of sincere affection for two reasons. First, occasionally people attempt to cash in on Holmes as a low-hanging and lucrative fruit, and when that happens, the savvy among us smell blood in the water. And second, occasionally a popular published work might posit Holmes was in fact Jack the Ripper, for example, and the author's devotion to shock value against all demands of character integrity makes some of us cringe. But for the most part, we write about Sherlock Holmes and John Watson because we're compelled to do so. We engage with their dual biographies because we witness bravery that we aspire to emulate, or isolation that we're afraid we share. Or we are hooked by the beautiful relationship we wish all human beings could experience—that elusive alchemy of kindred spirits that can make the reflection in a polished coffee pot seem fascinating or the crude summons, "If inconvenient, come all the same," sound enticing.

I wrote *Dust and Shadow: an Account of the Ripper Killings by Dr. John H. Watson* because I couldn't stop myself any longer. The thing was begging for its freedom for better or worse, clawing and scratching its way out of me. Mostly this was because I'm trained as an actor, not as a creative writer, which means that I bristle in annoyance if I hear Watson say "Great Scott!" when he ought to say "Good heavens!" We learn to mimic speech patterns, syntax, and regionalisms as performers, and to strive for naturalism above all else, so it likewise rankles to me when Holmes talks in relentless abstruse paragraphs, stringing clauses together *ad nauseam* and never calling over his shoulder, "I'll be back some time, Watson," before vanishing into the night. After finding yet another published pastiche to skim through during my lunch break at a long bygone Borders, and noting minutiae I would have executed differently, I finally took the bait and accepted Watson's challenge from "The Abbey Grange." What good would nitpicking do if I never sat down and attempted to channel Doyle's remarkable prose myself?

I figured in my happy delirium after finishing *Dust and Shadow* (no one is more surprised than the author when they complete their first novel, trust me) that if no Sherlockian small press wanted it, then I could always publish it as an e-book, and still be able to talk about it at geeky dinner parties. To my everlasting astonishment, it sold to Simon & Schuster and was released in hardcover in 2009. And to my continued chagrin, it sold approximately as well as manure sandwiches, and was remaindered, which means the first edition copies were sent to that Great Wood Chipper in the Sky. But this isn't about the trials of the mystery novelist—I was thrilled that after penning *Dust and Shadow*, I was very quickly asked to contribute short stories to anthologies. And remarkably soon after that, I landed the accidental gig of a lifetime: regularly writing new Sherlock Holmes adventures for the revamped American version of the *Strand Magazine*.

Over the course of several years, I was honored to write ten short stories for the *Strand*. The onus of being that particular publication's go-to

Sherlockian author wasn't lost on me, and I sacrificed sleep fretting over Henry Mayhew's *London Labour and the London Poor*, trying to come up with feasible Victorian deductions—or at least ones as plausible as claiming that wearing an unbrushed hat means a man's wife has ceased to love him. Occasionally my dear husband (whose hats I never ever brush) would watch me stewing and remind me that Doyle thought snakes drank milk, so could I please calm down and stop rhythmically banging my brow against my laptop, since it was alarming the cats? I'd often listen to this wisdom, and I remember specifically the times I caved and invented from thin air a species of red leech, a deadly Amazonian poison akin to ricin, and a secret passage in the Thames Tunnel. But for the most part, I tried to invest my pastiches with the ring of historical truth, the way I treated the all too real Ripper murders in *Dust and Shadow*. The mendicant who has repeatedly exposed himself to frostbite in "The Beggar's Feast," for instance, was based on Mayhew's study of the desperately indigent, and "Colonel's Warburton's Madness" drew heavily on my research for an unpublished novel set in 19th-century San Francisco.

I say all this to admit that I took writing for the *Strand Magazine* eminently seriously. But I was never *frightened* of doing it, and that lack of fear wasn't about hubris, or at least I hope it wasn't—I truly believe it was about love. If you love something fully, love it with wild abandon, that can be enough to stoke the fires of self-confidence. Potentially, you can become much less afraid of other people judging you unworthy of your own obsession if only you're obsessed *sufficiently*. I attribute learning this kindly principle wholly to my experience with fanfiction. Every fandom has its trolls, its flame wars, its infighting, its cruelty, and its drama. But I was reading Sherlock Holmes fic before the Warner Brothers films came out—and after, and during the frenzied fannish renaissance that was BBC's *Sherlock*—and for the most part, the community is simply and sincerely delighted to add new creators to its fold. One seldom encounters bullies and even fewer self-proclaimed gatekeepers. Constructive criticism abounds; beta readers readily volunteer their services. It's all in the name of camaraderie and plumbing the depths of the characters, which at the end of the day is what all of my pastiches are about.

Pastiche writing often focuses on the creation of intricate plots and authentic voice; fanfiction often explores the inner workings of flawed people and gaps in the original narrative. I like to hope that my short stories strive for both. All pastiche is fanfiction, though not all fanfiction is pastiche, and since I've never considered either term a pejorative, I've at times been mystified when readers have leapt to my defense over what they perceived as insulting terminology. I remember when I first discovered that someone wrote modern-day fanfiction about my antebellum New York original character Valentine Wilde of *The Gods of Gotham*—I was so flattered, I practically threw myself a parade. Several of my Sherlockian shorts, which are now collected in the volume *The Whole Art of Detection*, were certainly conceived as plots. What would happen if a man was kidnapped multiple times but released unharmed? What would happen if Watson presented Holmes with a Dupin-esque armchair mystery to solve?

After having written 18 pastiches total, my hat is forever off to Sir Arthur for doing yeoman's work: he was utterly crackers to have come up with 60, and if I could go back in time, I'd bring him a medal and a slice of the banana cream cheesecake from Billy's on 23rd Street in Manhattan.

Plots are a tough nut to crack. But other thought exercises that led to my new tales, and some of the most dear to me, were based entirely on relationships. What sort of case would it take for Lestrade to tell Holmes how he truly felt about the Hiatus? What could Holmes have possibly wanted with the Duke of Holdernesse's money? Following the deaths of his dearest friend and his beloved wife, could grief nearly drive Dr. Watson away from London entirely? In this way, my short stories seem to me to be an intersection between what pastiche attempts and what fic attempts, with neither one influencing my narrative goals any more than the other. I want to write a clever conundrum; I also want to pick apart these people's insides and see what makes them bleed.

My husband's oldest niece is a very meticulous, dare I say exacting, individual. When she was a kid, she started learning to cook with her dad when her mom was busy, and one day as they were making pasta, my brother-in-law suggested adding an herb that wasn't in the recipe to their sauce.

"Why?" asked my niece.

"Because I think it might taste better," replied my brother-in-law.

"Dad, I don't want it to taste *better*," she told him soberly. "I want it to taste *right*."

In brief, I try, like so many fanfiction authors, to do my Best. And I also try, like so many pastiche authors, to get it Right. The two have never been mutually exclusive. So I attempt, as so many others have done so well, to blend a bit of the new in with the old, and hope only at the end of the day I've done justice to Doyle, to my readers, and to myself.

Throughout all of these happy exercises in creative expression, there is love. Love of the originals, love of my fellow Sherlockians, love of language, love of the permission to carry on a noble tradition. Love of London. Love of the fact that Watson would chase down devil hounds for Holmes, and that Holmes would face a watery death alone for Watson. Sherlock Holmes stories—real and derivative—have provided me with more meaning than I can possibly express, and it's my greatest joy and privilege to be allowed to share my tributes with a larger audience than I ever expected. Multiple people have approached me and said that they were given or picked up a copy of one of my chronicles, and that it inspired them to read the Canon for the first time. Well, thank God for that, I say. And like Mary in *The Sign of Four*, I can only hope that after having been introduced to the wonderful world that is Sherlockiana, they say thank God too.

Lyndsay Faye (Queens, New York) is the best-selling author of six novels and one short story collection. *The Gods of Gotham* and *Jane Steele* were both nominated for the Edgar Award. She is a Baker Street Irregular and an Adventuress of Sherlock Holmes—and one of the Baker Street Babes.

HIS LATEST BOWS

THE ADVENTURE OF THE GREATER LIGHT

TIMOTHY J. JOHNSON

It is best to tell the truth. My primary motive in applying for a special collections curatorship at the University of Minnesota had little to do with Mr. Holmes. I was more interested in a collection of Swedish-American imprints. Nineteen years after the fact, I feel safe in telling you this. In reality, it was mostly about family and a love for this little part of the world. My ancestral roots—planted shortly after the American Civil War—sink deep into Dakota prairies and Minnesota forests. Some of my people, in their own extraordinary ways, were early Norwegian explorers. After two decades living and working in the City of the Big Shoulders (and home to Abe Slaney), with recently retired parents settled on northern prairies, near lakes, it was time to seek a position closer to home. I began to look.

The Minnesota vacancy presented itself in early 1997. By midsummer, university officials confirmed receipt of my application materials. For months I waited and heard nothing. Two days before Christmas, a telephone call informed me that I was no longer under consideration. We celebrated the holidays, awaited the New Year. Ten days into 1998—a day before departing on a two-week trip to Israel—the university called and wondered: could I come for an interview after all? I agreed on a date two days after my return from Tel Aviv (and a day after Denver defeated Green Bay—two other places important in my personal history—in Super Bowl XXXII).

My all-day interview began at eight in the morning, concluded some twelve hours later, and included moments of Sherlockian slumber. During my mid-afternoon public presentation on a topic (now forgotten) related to some aspect of special collections or rare books in an academic library, the late and beloved Allen Mackler fell asleep. Seated as he was—first row, front and center—Allen's snooze, combined with my Israeli time shift, proved disconcerting. He awoke, I believe, during the question and answer session; I don't remember if he asked me anything. So began my relationship and friendship with Allen, and with this tribe named after a consulting detective.

My relationship with Mr. Holmes predates my companionship with Allen, but that is a topic for another time. Suffice it to note here that I read the Canon as a kid, was captivated as an adult by Jeremy Brett's portrayal of the Master, did not consider myself conversant about Holmes's world, remained ignorant of the existence of any Sherlockian societies save for the Baker Street Irregulars, and later lamented living within a stone's throw of a Chicago treasure—Ely M. Liebow—without realizing it, or him.

A short time after my interview, University Librarian Tom Shaughnessy called to offer me the position. I was not the university's first choice, but I was their last one, and the right one. Shortly after my acceptance, I received a call from another Sherlockian, Dr. Richard Sveum. I vaguely remembered Dick in attendance at my public presentation and made a blunder on the phone by referring to him as the "elderly" gentleman seated in the back. (His beard can fool you!) I'll never know what possessed me to regard—much less comment on—Dick as elderly; it was so out of character and a thing I never did in conversation. Perhaps I was overly excited about the new position. Dick has long since forgiven me this *faux pas*, a thing we can chuckle about. His reason for calling, besides congratulating me on the position, was to make me aware of an important group of supporters—The Friends of the Sherlock Holmes Collections—and of an upcoming conference: "Founders' Footprints," the 50th anniversary celebration of the local Sherlockian society, the Norwegian Explorers of Minnesota.

My Minnesota career began July 1, 1998. In anticipation of the conference, I re-read the Canon; familiarized myself with Norwegian Explorers' lore; dined with E.W. McDiarmid (whom I had met in graduate school) and Bryce Crawford (whom I had not); prepared an exhibit with third-generation aficionado James (Jamie) Hubbs while chatting with his father, George, the first president of the Friends; met past and present Friends and Explorer leaders such as Dr. C. Paul Martin, Bruce Southworth, Pj Doyle, and Julie McKuras; conversed with predecessors (now elevated by their Irregular investitures), Andrew Malec and Austin McLean; and generally (yet cautiously, with Scandinavian reserve) dove into this northern pond of Holmesian enthusiasts. It was an exhilarating and, for an introvert like me, exhausting time. So went my debut in the Sherlockian world.

This prelude to my eventual partly Sherlockian career resonates with existential themes. They are the melodies defining what I do, who I wish to be, how I relate to others, and what I wish to become. Bound into this music are elements of self-discovery, pilgrimage, friendship, remembrance, honor, faith, hope, and love.

Dr. Watson, I am bold to say, was wrong. At the very end of "The Solitary Cyclist" Watson noted that

> In the whirl of our incessant activity it has often been difficult for me, as the reader has probably observed, to round off my narratives, and to give those final details which the curious might expect. Each case has been the prelude to another, and the crisis once over, the actors have passed for ever out of our busy lives.

As a curator, I might make a similar observation (and confession), with one major difference: In the whirl of incessant activity it has often been difficult for me to round off my duties and to give those final details which the donor or researcher might expect. Each case (in my instance, an interaction with a collection, creator, donor, or scholar) has been the prelude to another, but the actors will never pass for ever out of my busy life. I am terrible at remembering names. It takes three or four exchanges for a name or face to sink into my consciousness. But I make the effort to remember. Thankfully, others are there to assist me, to help us collectively to remember. Memory is the important thing.

We are called to remember, and in that act of remembrance to share the joy and honor and pleasure attached to those memories. I live and move and have my being in a land of ghosts. They are good ghosts, congenial ghosts, but ghosts all the same. For example:

I never had the pleasure of knowing John Bennett Shaw, whose Sherlockiana now makes up an important part of the Minnesota collection. Yet I am touched by his work and spirit every day. I stand amazed in his presence, awed by his energy, confounded by his networks and depth of knowledge. I am a steward of his good works. But I will never reach his heights.

Vincent Starrett haunts my halls. His papers swirl around me, his writings infect my soul. I whispered quiet words of appreciation over his grave in Graceland, yet never knew the man. I am a custodian of much that was, and is, this good person.

I read her scripts, listen to her dramatic presentations, marvel over her creativity. And yet, I will never have the honor of being in the presence of Edith Meiser. For me, she will always be The Woman, albeit in an ethereal relationship. I remain a guardian of her sonic waves and sponsored texts, ever eager to share them with a new listener or reader.

And who could ever forget the good doctor and his wife Mary. Amidst the rolling hills of southeastern Minnesota they amassed a trove of Sherlockian treasure—and then gave it away. Mary Kahler and Philip Hench departed decades before I arrived, and yet I am surrounded by the radiance of their pursuits. I remain astonished at their careful notes, overwhelmed by assembled imagery, humbled by cherished volumes, benumbed by generosity. I am a keeper of their legacy, a master of their fate. It is a solemn calling.

Other collectors and admirers, great and small, followed these leads. All are worthy, all commendable, all special. The halls I stroll, the aisles I roam are charged and sacred spaces. I walk on just and holy ground. Many friends, past and present, join me in the pilgrimage. These creators, friends, and supporters of the collections at Minnesota provide a clue to future endeavors, voiced in a passage from "The Naval Treaty":

> "There is nothing in which deduction is so necessary as in religion," said [Holmes], leaning with his back against the shutters. "It can be built up as an exact science by the reasoner. Our highest assurance of the goodness of Providence seems to me to rest in the flowers. All other things, our powers, our desires, our food, are really necessary for our existence in the first instance. But this rose is an extra. Its smell and its colour are an embellishment of life, not a condition of it. It is only goodness which gives extras, and so I say again that we have much to hope from the flowers."

"It is only goodness which gives extras...." This Holmesian hope, a faith which "is the substance of things hoped for, the evidence of things not seen," points me to vibrant and sensory embellishments of life; new technologies and modes of communication; diversities in fandoms young and old; Canonical, Apocryphal, and perhaps even non-Canonical adventures that in combination catalyze growth in the Minnesota collections in new and exciting directions. I want to find that extra thing. I wish for roses. "Our highest assurance of the goodness of Providence seems to me to rest in the flowers."

Finally, there is a sense of the divine, and of justice, embedded in a rose. Holmes and flowers and friends (and, we might add, music) belong together. It is what binds us. Watson unwittingly expressed this binding in a different context: "Always there was this feeling of an unseen force, a fine net drawn round us with infinite skill and delicacy, holding us so lightly that it was only at some supreme moment that one realized that one was indeed entangled in its meshes." In those ultimate, sometimes intimate moments we celebrate our entanglement. It is Holmes observing our hands while perceiving "a spirituality about the face." It is all about mind and body and spirit and heart.

I am drawn to Holmes through the faces and hearts of friends and fellow travelers, pilgrims on the way—those present and remembered. I am particularly drawn to those who came before; I am biased toward the past. One of my favorite seasons in the Christian liturgical year, as noted in the Book of Common Prayer, is the "Commemoration of the Faithful Departed." Holmes was not one to pray, although as "Sir Henry lay insensible" in *The Hound of the Baskervilles*, "Holmes breathed a prayer of gratitude." I have a sense that Holmes divined meaning in a prayer he might have heard as a student, or later over the radio. The words come from the Bidding Prayers in the Service of Nine Lessons and Carols held annually in the Chapel of King's College, Cambridge: "Lastly, let us remember before God all those who rejoice with us, but upon another shore, and in a greater light, that multitude which no man can number...."

Let us remember...and celebrate.

Timothy J. Johnson is Curator of Special Collections & Rare Books and the E.W. McDiarmid Curator of the Sherlock Holmes Collections for the University of Minnesota Libraries. He has an undergraduate degree in history and graduate degrees in library science and theological studies.

THE SIGN OF THE NERD

MATTIAS BOSTRÖM

"Granddad, ask me something," the nine-year-old boy said. They were out on one of their long walks, along the river and in the university area of the town. The boy always to the left, where Granddad had a better sense of hearing.

Granddad thought for a while and then started asking questions about history, science, culture, whatever he might think would be a challenge for the boy to answer.

This was their pastime, their game to play.

* * * *

I have a very understanding wife.

One Saturday, in February 2012, we were driving through a snow-storm on our way down to Bjertorp Castle in western Sweden, for a romantic weekend away. It had been booked for months, long before the TV schedules had been published.

The art-nouveau manor house, built in the early 1900s, was the perfect setting for afternoon tea in a comfortable armchair followed by a three-course dinner in the dining hall a few hours later. We had requested the earliest possible sitting—we had an appointment to keep and we wanted to avoid rushing the meal.

After dinner we retired to the room, and turned on the telly. I pulled out my laptop and went online. It was time for me to provide commentary, via Twitter, during the second series of the BBC's *Sherlock*.

* * * *

Twenty-five years earlier, in 1987, I saw the first episode of another Sherlock Holmes series, with Jeremy Brett as the master detective.

It was ten to eleven at night, and I was sitting in the old green sofa at my grandparents' place in Uppsala. Over on Channel Two, the day's broadcasting had just come to an end. I walked over to the set and pressed the top button, tuning in to Channel One, the only other channel that existed in Sweden.

I had been 16 for a week, and my teenage heart was filled with enthusiasm for the English detective and the world he inhabited. Earlier that day, Granddad and I had taken the train down to Stockholm. The House of

Culture were inaugurating a centenary exhibition about Sherlock Holmes, which also gave me the chance to meet other Holmes devotees for the first time, including Ted Bergman, Sweden's leading expert on the subject. Ted and I had been writing to each other for a few months.

I had found Ted's address on the last page of a Swedish edition of Sherlock Holmes stories. It also included contact details for three Sherlockian periodicals. I wrote to all of them: the *Baker Street Journal*, the *Sherlock Holmes Journal*, and the Danish magazine *Sherlockiana*. And then I wrote to every single active Sherlockian society I could find the address to. Soon my correspondence became so big that I, in the best Pavlovian way, brightened up as soon as I saw a mailman, *any* mailman, anywhere.

A new world appeared before my eyes. A world of playful, quasi-academic research about a man who never lived, yet who for me was more alive than anything else. This was not an escape *from* reality, but an escape *to* it.

I realized that what I previously had believed was literature was in fact a wealth of possible knowledge. Persons, items, addresses, plots, dates— there were zillions of details that could be treated as facts. For someone who normally ate knowledge for breakfast, lunch, and dinner, that was the revelation that really got me hooked. It would actually be feasible to learn everything about Sherlock Holmes, and for once this digesting of knowledge would have a purpose—to play the game.

My growing fanaticism about all things Sherlock Holmes was viewed with some scepticism by those around me. It was a rather peculiar interest, at a time when peculiar interests stuck out. The word "nerd" had only recently reached Swedish shores, and it had a ring to it that was anything but flattering. Finding like-minded people was difficult. I simply had to impose my newly discovered fascination and knowledge on friends and family alike. It worked best on the school bus—twenty-eight minutes' worth of journey before the person next to me could escape.

Finally I managed to convert at least one person: my grandfather. He studied the literature and understood the conditions.

He and my grandmother went to London that summer, in 1987. They took a river cruise down the Thames, and Granddad reported in a letter: "I hope I will be forgiven for the surprise I gave my fellow passengers by shouting out just after our departure from Tower Bridge. On the starboard side I noticed a large black sign, with the words 'Jacobson's Wharf' on one of the docks. This was of course where Sherlock Holmes had found the missing boat in *The Sign of Four*!"

My mission, to make the whole world love Sherlock Holmes, was off to a good start. One person down.

* * * *

That night in 2012, I tweeted frenetically from our hotel bed. The episode was packed with allusions to Arthur Conan Doyle's original stories, and I wanted to convey as many of them as possible to newly-won and long-time followers alike. How anyone was able to read my tweets while simultaneously watching the programme was a mystery to me, but I could tell that they were appreciated. For my part, it was quite simply my Sherlockian duty to share this knowledge with the twittersphere. Questions were flooding in, and I was answering all of them, hours after the episode had finished. I ended up being temporarily blocked by Twitter for having sent too many messages—I had never even heard of such a limit.

With each episode I tweeted, I gained hundreds of new followers. My inner nerd was given full expression, and I didn't need a school bus to keep my audience captive.

Sometimes, a thing as simple as my wife's understanding about what this meant to me is all it takes to make a romantic weekend.

* * * *

In the midst of my hotel-room tweeting came a request from one of my Twitter followers.

"When's the book out?" read the message.

"The book?" I was puzzled. Then it dawned on me. If there was ever a time to write that big Sherlock Holmes book I had contemplated so many times over the years, it was now.

I started the next day.

* * * *

From Holmes to Sherlock has transformed my life. A book can do that, especially if you are the author. However, something else important happened that night in February 2012. It was the moment when I made the transition from Sherlockian to researcher.

The way I wanted to write my book, as narrative nonfiction, made it necessary for me to find small details that could add spots of colour and life to the story. I have quite a big collection of books concerning Sherlock Holmes and Conan Doyle, but few of them provided what I was searching for. I needed to know personal things about *Strand Magazine* editor H. Greenhough Smith, radio writer Edith Meiser, illustrator Frederic Dorr Steele, and lesser-known persons in the history of the Sherlock Holmes success, like Arthur Whitaker, Tony Harwood, and Henry E. Lester, all of them only briefly described in the books in my collection. I wanted to come closer to these persons than just mentioning their names and what they had done. I needed correspondence, autobiographies, biographies, interviews, old press cuttings.

Me turning into a researcher was therefore just for practical reasons. Me not wanting to be anything but a researcher was something entirely different.

I remember late one night when I was trawling the online historical newspaper archives for information—*any* information—about the *Lippincott's* editor Joseph M. Stoddart, for whom Conan Doyle wrote *The Sign of Four*. I desperately needed it for my book, to make Stoddart come alive. Usually I could find biographical data in obituaries, and all kinds of tidbits in other, quite unrelated articles. This night I found a short interview with Stoddart in an issue of the *New-York Tribune* from 1905, containing a previously unknown anecdote from his famous meeting with Conan Doyle at the Langham Hotel. That dinner has been so thoroughly researched by others that I couldn't believe my eyes. I shouted "Yes!" and literally jumped for joy. "I have never seen you this happy," said my wife. And I was! I can still remember exactly how I felt that night, trembling, bubbling, in love with an anecdote.

It is an addiction. You understand that when you start to randomly research things, with no other purpose than to see if you find something interesting. It happens all the time—I have quick and easy access to the newspaper archives on my iPhone, and it's a fun pastime to just search for "Sherlock Holmes" or "Conan Doyle" in any random month and year of the late 19th or early 20th century, a perfect occupation when I'm on the commuter train or elsewhere with a few minutes to spare.

A few years ago, on a Friday afternoon, I was sitting next to my two-year-old daughter on the floor of her room. She was busy with her toys, and at the moment I wasn't part of the game, merely observing and being at hand. I had a quick glance at the phone and happened to notice the sensational news of an old man in Scotland finding in his attic an unknown Holmes story by Conan Doyle. While Molli continued playing with her toys, I spent a few minutes on the phone to see if I could verify what the Scottish man claimed. I really wanted to do that. However, I failed. Instead I found enough evidence to write a blog post for *I Hear of Sherlock Everywhere* later the same day, disproving the claim. Some 100,000 persons visited that blog post, and it reached top-ten at the web content rating website Reddit. Sherlockian research is hot, hot, hot. Being a nerd, too, nowadays. Tell that to my 16-year-old self.

The online historical newspaper archives are powerful sources—there are hundreds of millions of pages in them, fully searchable. Articles must of course be treated with some scepticism, there are many errors in them, but they are good starting points for further research. I normally also re-search a subject by checking Google Books to see if there are any books, old or new, that either could be read online or should be ordered from second-hand booksellers. And I visit the online resources HathiTrust and archive.org for more old books and magazines.

When I researched Ouida Rathbone's early career as a screenwriter— for a *Baker Street Journal* article and for some last-minute editing of *From Holmes to Sherlock*—I combined facts from all those sources. Some normal googling is always added, just to see if any further information can be found. My extensive research into the Mdivani family (Nina Mdivani was married to Conan Doyle's son Denis) has shown that at least half of the web texts that I find contain too many errors to be useful, so the tricky thing is to spot those errors. Normal googling, using clever search strings, will however often provide a few really useful documents, since so much old material has been digitized and is searchable through Google.

Using all these sources so frequently has also made it possible for me to help others. When I notice a friend on Facebook or Twitter needing research help, I just make a quick check in the different online archives to see if there are any documents or facts that could be of interest. It takes only a few minutes, and I'm often able to help people, which is a most rewarding feeling—and actually a nice way of having a social life. I have the research tools and I should use them. I know that subscribing to all of these newspaper archives is quite expensive, so it's not something that is recommended to someone who is just searching for single facts for a single project. Or, it should be added, who doesn't have research as an addiction.

For me, knowing a lot is knowing where and how to search. At the same time as I stepped out in that unknown, unbounded terrain of new Holmes and Conan Doyle facts to discover, I stepped away from the more general desire for knowledge that had been with me since those long walks next to Granddad in Uppsala. I'm not interested in being a Sherlock Holmes expert or a Conan Doyle one. I have no longer any need to store and show off knowledge. I just want to find it and then give it to others. The true excitement is in the work, in the research. If you ask me anything specific, I'm most likely not able to give an instantaneous answer, but give me a few minutes at my computer or around my books and in my archive, and I will in most cases return with what you need. Give me a few hours and you will get an article about it. Add some more time and I will write a book on the subject. There are no limits what you can do when you start researching.

If there is ever a strategy in what I'm doing, it's to find as much new, or at least quite hidden, knowledge as possible. There is no actual plan for what I'm about to research next time; it depends on what project I happen to be involved with. However, debunking myths and correcting false claims are hobbies of mine. And there is one ongoing research project that has become the base in my Sherlockian and Doylean life—the *Sherlock Holmes and Conan Doyle in the Newspapers* project. Whatever other things I have done or will do in the future, that project will forever be my most important contribution to the study of Conan Doyle and his master detective.

Back in 2014, when the original edition of *From Holmes to Sherlock* had just been published in Swedish, I had numerous piles of research material all around in my study. In those piles there were hundreds of newspaper articles that I had found and printed out from the newspaper archives. It felt like a giant waste to keep them only to myself: this was a treasure that had to be shared. Almost none of these articles was previously known in the Sherlockian/Doylean world—a few years previously, in a not-so-much-digitalized world, it would have been tiresome work to find these mentions of Conan Doyle and Sherlock Holmes just by randomly browsing through old newspapers. What I realized was that someone had to start transcribing these newspaper texts, search for even more articles, collect them in book form, and make them easily accessible to other researchers. That was not really a task I had been dreaming about as a young boy, to spend endless hours for the rest of my life transcribing barely readable newspaper texts. I asked my friend Matt Laffey if he would be equally interested in doing this—on a not-what-I-had-dreamt-of-but-I-must-do-it-anyway level. For some reason I believed he would say yes, and he did.

For each volume we produce (we have now reached 1894) we slowly change the way we all look upon the importance of Conan Doyle and the development of Sherlock Holmes, just by showing how their contemporaries looked at them. The truth is not in the facts, but in the context. We need a massiveness of texts and mentions to understand the true roles of Holmes and Conan Doyle in their own time. I am not necessarily the one to draw all the conclusions from this huge material. I am the researcher. And that is my life.

* * * *

I have a very understanding wife. She gave me a fridge magnet a few years back, with the text "You are so weird—but I love you." She knows and accepts my need to spend time on Sherlockian and Doylean things. But there must be a balance in everything, even if you have an obsession for research. There is a life going on. I just can't help that Sherlock Holmes is such a big part of it.

"I have never seen you this happy," said my wife that night in 2012 when I found the Stoddart anecdote. There was a touch of sadness in her voice.

Mattias Boström (Bålsta, Sweden) is a publisher, a husband and father, and a gregarious Sherlockian. His landmark book *From Holmes to Sherlock* has been published in several languages, including English, in mid-2017.

THE ADVENTURE OF
THE IRONIC MONSIGNOR

SUSAN E. BAILEY

"Deutero-Watson." That was the word that changed my life and sealed my fate forever as a Sherlockian.

The first scion meeting I ever attended was in January 2013. It was the annual potluck of Watson's Tin Box, called The Mycroft. One of the members had brought a number of books that were duplicates in their collection and offered them up to the group for the taking. I had arrived at the event alone and fortunately found myself in the one empty seat at a table with several long-time members. I discovered that my table-mates were friendly and encouraging, and they urged me to go select a book. I felt as though this might be some sort of test that would determine my fate.

I was right. Included in the books on offer were a number of pastiches, even some by well-known authors. But what attracted me was a small book that had an academic appearance. It was T.S. Blakeney's *Sherlock Holmes: Fact or Fiction*. I felt that I wanted to take my burgeoning exploration of the Canon in a scholarly direction, and this book looked like just the kind of text I needed. When I showed my selection to my table-mates, they praised it—but I didn't yet know why.

I started reading the book later that day, but I'm not sure I got much past the preface on that first reading. It's because I encountered this sentence:

> We should welcome a critic who would grapple with this task [of literary criticism of the Holmes stories] as Mr. J.M. Robertson tackles Shakespearean problems, sifting the wheat from the chaff, the accretions of the pseudo-Watson (to say nothing of deutero- or trito-Watsons).

This sentence stopped me in my tracks. There is only one kind of person who would use the word "deutero-Watson," and that is someone who is familiar with Biblical criticism. Could I really be seeing what I thought I saw? If so, my mind thrilled, these are my people! I approached an online friend who I knew was knowledgeable about matters both religious and Sherlockian and she told me that I was correct in what I saw. She told me about Monsignor Ronald Knox and encouraged me to read his writing.

When I read Knox's famous essay, "Studies in the Literature of Sherlock Holmes," it became clear to me that the Sherlockian community is where I need to be. You see, my academic background is in religious studies. My undergraduate major is in religious studies and I have two master's degrees in the field as well. The tone of his writing was clearly humorous and satirical, but Knox was obviously steeped in the same way of thinking that I was trained in, and it felt so entirely familiar and comfortable to me to read his writing. I felt that I was participating in an "in-joke" that I hadn't known I was part of.

As an undergraduate, I took a seminar entitled "The Quest for the Historical Jesus." We read about the German tradition of the historical-critical method that dated back to the 19th century, and about the contemporary scholarly views of Jesus that have continued to come out of that line of inquiry. For example, the type of questions that scholars of the historical Jesus might ask would include: Did Jesus speak any Greek? What was the socio-economic status of Jewish carpenters in the 1st century? Is there any evidence that Jesus was or wasn't married? How familiar was Jesus with the Hebrew Bible?

This method of inquiry is fundamentally the same as the way that Sherlockians who play the Great Game or investigate Holmes's historical context think. It is precisely the way that I think and was trained to think, and as a result, traditional Sherlockian scholarship is a lot of fun for me. At the end of my academic career, my area of specialty became the religions of India. However, the way that I asked questions or used historical evidence did not vary depending on the content of my study. Rather, it was the tools that mattered. Similarly, Sherlockian scholars ask questions about what we can know about Holmes and Watson from the text and what their Victorian historical context tells us about their behavior or language or the objects they used. We are constantly looking to the text for clues about Holmes's and Watson's personalities and characters. The investigation of trifles (have we not been exhorted by the Master to pursue trifles?) might open up for us a whole world that has since gone out of existence.

It is ironic to me that we as a Sherlockian community have so warmly embraced a type of historical and literary inquiry that Knox found worthy of spoofing. Perhaps it could be that we can indulge in our inquiry of the Canon because it has no actual soteriological significance. Whether or not Knox's 1911 paper "Studies in the Literature of Sherlock Holmes" had a heart-felt appreciation of Holmes, it is certainly an intellectual exercise in the cause of fun, and that is something I appreciate. Knox apparently had no intention of starting a movement of literary or historical investigation into the life, world, and mind of Sherlock Holmes, but that seems to have been the result. It could be that we owe this tone of solemnity not to Knox as much as to his followers, such as T.S. Blakeney and H.W. Bell, both of whom published serious works of Sherlockian scholarship in 1932.

Just because Sherlockian scholarship might be serious, it doesn't follow that it is not also serious fun. Now that I have shown how and why I approach the material the way that I do, I'd like to provide a few examples of how my way of thinking manifests itself in what I do. For a number of years I either participated in or led weekly tweetalongs (sponsored by

Sherlock DC) of the Granada Holmes series featuring Jeremy Brett. Being one never to let details slide by unnoticed, I would often insert historical information or photographs into my tweets. For instance, while watching "The Man with the Twisted Lip," I tweeted a link to the Wikipedia page for the word "lascar," which appeared in the both the original story and the television episode.

As the current Gasogene of Watson's Tin Box, I research the historical details of the story that we read each month and offer them during the story discussion if they become relevant. A few months ago we discussed "The Mazarin Stone." Did you know that there is a historical Cardinal Mazarin who actually bequeathed his collection of 18 diamonds to the French crown, and that they are on display today in the Louvre? Or that Cardinal Mazarin's niece Hortense was a mistress of King Charles II? I particularly love this last detail because my favorite story is "The Musgrave Ritual" and it connects the two stories.

My academic training taught me to always search for new questions to be asked, and there are still so many that remain to be asked about the Sherlockian Canon. Whenever I get an idea for a topic to research in depth, one of the first things I do is look to see if this is a topic that has already been addressed. I am not interested as much in covering ground that has already been trod as I am excited by new territory that has yet to be mapped. Every time I read the stories, new details or passing references catch my eye as potential topics of research. Inspired by "The Naval Treaty," I researched who may have performed a search of one of the suspects in the disappearance of the treaty, Mrs. Tangey. The results of my research were published in the spring 2017 issue of the *Baker Street Journal*. In the summer of 2017, I went to London and Edinburgh to look at archival documents pertaining to Dr. Watson's and Sir Arthur Conan Doyle's medical education. What I found will, I hope, shed further light on the Canon.

Like many other women of my generation, I first encountered Sherlock Holmes on screen in the form of Benedict Cumberbatch in BBC *Sherlock*. What might make me a little unusual is that I took that interest in an entirely different direction. I suppose this makes me somewhat of a traditionalist, so much so that my interest harkens back to the very beginning of Sherlockian scholarship. Movies, shows, and actors all come and go, but the core of who we are as a community remains, and that is the original text and the characters of Sherlock Holmes and Dr. John Watson. I am grateful that through this, I was able to be drawn into a community and a hobby that has a place for someone like me.

Susan E. Bailey (Sterling, Virginia) holds master's degrees in religious studies from Harvard Divinity School and Duke University. She is a member of Watson's Tin Box of Ellicott City, Maryland, and of the Scintillation of Scions organizing committee.

THE ADVENTURE OF
THE MAGIC DOOR

DOUG WRIGGLESWORTH

He was a tall, lean man of middle years, with the garb and demeanor of a rumpled academic. He had a kind face and a rare wit, and he became my personal introduction to bibliographic Sherlockiana. The late Cameron Hollyer was the man, and by pure serendipity, he was my seatmate at my first ever meeting of the Bootmakers of Toronto. So began over a quarter-century of immersion into that wonderful world-wide collection of "kin-sprits", as Christopher Morley liked to call us. Adventures across Canada and in the United Kingdom and United States were important contributors to my list of friends and acquaintances.

It did not take long for Cameron to introduce me to the wonders of the Arthur Conan Doyle Collection at the Toronto Reference Library, and to enlist me in some early escapades. Typical of these were attempts to have an appropriate plaque placed on the birthplace of Vincent Starrett, or at the site of his grandfather's Toronto bookshop where a young Vincent loved to read. Trying to explain to a recently arrived Asian family why we wanted to mount a plaque on their home was an awkward task.

During these early years, in 1994, my friend Doug Elliott and I, with the assistance of The Battered Silicon Dispatch-Box, organized a Boot-maker visit to the Shaw Festival. The William Gillette play "Sherlock Holmes" was being produced, with Jim Mezon as Holmes and Robert Benson as Watson, directed by Christopher Newton. Doug Elliott and I prepared some lovely reproductions of historical material for participants. We were all treated royally by Festival staff, visited with the cast on stage after the performance, and were treated to a private performance of "The Painful Predicament of Sherlock Holmes" by the Shaw Festival Academy players. A special edition of the script was published, with additional material by Bootmakers and Shaw Festival staff, and made a lovely memento. I was privileged to share the closing night performance with Christopher Newton—a rare pleasure indeed.

The usual Toronto suspects revisited the Shaw Festival in 1998 to enjoy their production of the Conan Doyle play "Waterloo", starring the venerable Tony Van Bridge as Corporal Brewster. Mr. Van Bridge proved a most amiable lunch guest. When concern was expressed about his being mobbed for autographs, the octogenarian actor responded, "That's what we actors live for!"

An investiture as a Master Bootmaker in 1994 was an honour that really made me feel a member of the Tribe!

Having always been a serious book-lover, I was enticed by the tales of the early Sherlockian bookmen, such as Starrett and Baring-Gould, to join the ranks of Sherlockian bibliophiles and to begin to gather a collection of vintage Sherlockiana and some of the incunabula that flowed from the pen of Sir Arthur Conan Doyle himself. This has resulted in an overflowing home library—a challenge many readers may appreciate.

In 1997, on my first tour of duty as "Meyers", president of the Bootmakers of Toronto, and with a decision made in all youthful innocence, a group of Bootmakers joined me in mounting an international conference, "Lasting Impressions". With the help of a strong and supportive committee, and that of the Toronto Public Library, all went well. Ostensibly mounted to celebrate the 25th anniversary of the Bootmakers, it became an international success despite a June heat wave that made our venue, the venerable Arts and Letters Club, an inferno. Happily, a supply of fans arrived—"Holmes" branded, believe it or not—to ease the problem somewhat.

A highlight was a special display in the Toronto Reference Library Gallery of original Sherlockian artwork, some on special loan from a local collector and some from the library's Arthur Conan Doyle Collection. The ACD Collection is the repository of a wondrous treasure trove of material by and about Arthur Conan Doyle. Of course, it features his most famous creation, with Sherlockian artifacts literally from the sublime such as rare first editions (including a *Beeton's* in remarkable condition) to the numerous examples of the thousands of literary and video products of the tortured imaginations of Sherlockians. The collection is found in splendid rooms, part of the new Marilyn and Charles Baillie Special Collections space.

"Lasting Impressions" was, for me, a real introduction to the international world of Sherlock Holmes. It also raised in me, and for some others, an urge to help keep the importance of the ACD Collection in the minds of local decision makers, as well as renewing its profile among Sherlockians and Doyleans around the world. The result of the conference was the Friends of the Arthur Conan Doyle Collection, which began with a 1997 meeting of a few interested people in Cliff Goldfarb's Bay Street board room. Over the next two decades, the Friends have gathered members from around the world and sponsored a regular newsletter, *The Magic Door*.

The annual Baker Street Irregulars weekend in New York also called to me. Under the influence of friends such as the late Maureen Green, Edwin Van der Flaes, Doug Elliott, and Cliff Goldfarb, I was privileged to attend a number of the fabled BSI dinners. An investiture as "The Retired Colourman" in 2004 was indeed an honour, one that is a highlight of my Sherlockian career.

Of course, London is not far from a Sherlockian's imagination, and the Sherlock Holmes Society of London is a wonderful group with whom to share Sherlock's city. Several trips to London have allowed me to share many escapades with them. Among happy memories are annual dinners in the House of Commons Dining Room at Westminster; tea on the Terrace of the House of Lords overlooking the Thames; the unveiling of the Sherlock Holmes statue on Baker Street; travelling the route Holmes, Watson, and Mary Morstan took from the Lyceum Theatre to Pondicherry Lodge (this was guided by the legendary Bernard Davies as we travelled in a restored 1930's London Transport Omnibus); finding an actual Colourman Store, and sharing the news of my BSI Investiture with a puzzled owner. A personal highlight that will be hard to surpass was a personal visit with Richard Lancelyn Green at his book-lined flat, then sharing with him a lovely dinner at Simpson's in the Strand.

An early project of the ACD Friends was to mount another conference in 2002, "Footprints of the Hound", to celebrate the centenary of *The Hound of the Baskervilles*. Again, with the help of a great organizing committee, the Bootmakers, and the staff of the Toronto Public Library, we were able to gather a strong list of speakers, such as Mrs. Georgina Doyle and Catherine Doyle Beggs, Richard Lancelyn Green and Sir Christopher Frayling. Once again, the world came to Toronto and a grand time was had.

In honour of the late Cameron Hollyer, first curator and founder of the ACD Collection, the Friends have hosted an annual Cameron Hollyer Lecture featuring speakers from a wide variety of sources.

I was honoured to chair the Friends, and shepherd the publication of its newsletter *The Magic Door*, for almost two decades, with the capable assistance of a board, but especially Cliff Goldfarb. Supportive library staff were vital to its success, particularly Peggy Perdue, the curator of the collection, and David Kotin, who was head of Special Collections during our early years.

After surfing through the treasures in the ACD Collection, I soon began to realize how much more there was to the life of Arthur Conan Doyle than Sherlock Holmes. What a thrill it was to visit the churchyard of All Saints in Minstead and see those appropriate and memorable words inscribed on his tombstone: "Steel true, blade straight." Any review of one of the score or more biographies of the man soon provides evidence of all these qualities throughout a truly adventurous lifetime.

It has been a great privilege, with my wife Nancy, to meet, and become friends with, a wonderful woman who has a direct link to that life. Georgina Doyle is the widow of Conan Doyle's nephew John Doyle, son of his brother Innis. (Very recently, in early 2017, after many years as a widow, Georgina has married a long-time friend, Sir Barry Wilson, KCB, and is now known as Georgina, Lady Wilson.)

Our first memory was joining Georgina and a gang of the usual Toronto suspects for dinner at a Toronto eatery on an evening in October 2003. It was during this dinner that news arrived that our first grandchild had been born. Since then, Georgina has always been interested in how Sarita was getting along (very well, thank you).

Since that memorable evening, Nancy and I have enjoyed Georgina's hospitality several times at her home in Dorset. Thanks to her we now have our own "London Club"—the Victory Services Club, which provides economical and central accommodation on our London visits. Happily, we have also been able to host Georgina several times in the Toronto area, with her step-daughter Catherine as a frequent companion. On a 2014 visit, Georgina and Catherine met our Toronto family and she was able to meet a blooming young Sarita in person.

We were happy to join Georgina and her family and friends at a special 2006 birthday party for her in London. Georgina and I inspired lots of chuckles with our joint reading of ACD's short story "The Grey Dress." It also has been a pleasure to be Georgina's escort at a few Sherlock Holmes Society of London dinners at Westminster, and to know that she continues to enjoy some of the wonderful outings that society arranges.

A most rewarding experience was to assist her in the publishing of *Out of the Shadows: The Untold Story of Arthur Conan Doyle's First Family.* Conan Doyle's life can be seen as consisting of two distinct eras: before his marriage to Jean Leckie and after she became Lady Doyle. Many existing biographies tend to have limited information on the earlier period, as this part of his life was essentially neglected and buried as much as possible by his second wife, and because of the efforts of her two sons, Adrian and Denis.

Georgina was determined to fulfil a wish of her late husband, that a proper account of the first Conan Doyle family, with his wife Louise (Touie), and children Kingsley and Mary, be made available. Her work to restore proper respect for Conan Doyle's first family was a labour of love for her. She spent many years in detailed research, and the result was a huge collection of information on that family, its genealogy, and the relationships among the various family members. The next step was to get this information published, and happily we Doyleans in Toronto were able to find a professional editor to work with Georgina to polish the text, and a publisher willing to produce the book. Not only were the results of her research put into words, her huge collection of photographs was an important addition to the process.

What a gratifying experience! Georgina and the editor worked together through the magic of the internet to create a fine volume. The publisher (Calabash Press) produced a lovely book that has since become an essential resource. *Out of the Shadows* is constantly being quoted in the literature as an important reference by scholars—demonstrating its true value. Introducing the book to interested audiences brought further adventures. We gave a pre-publication preview in Toronto at an ACD Friends event in the autumn of 2003. Another happy adventure was a publicity trip to join the Norwegian Explorers of Minnesota at their 2004 conference as we introduced Georgina's book to an appreciative audience.

My most recent visit to London with this Gracious Lady was 2014 to join in celebrating the 125th anniversary of "the Lippincott Luncheon" at the Langham Hotel with Georgina and her family. Again, a delightful time giving such fond memories of the people, the places, and friends.

When I sat down beside Cameron Hollyer on that evening in the fall of 1990, I could not have imagined the adventures that lay before me.

"Experiences on three continents and several countries" only hints at the pleasures and people that have graced my life.

Doug Wrigglesworth (Holland Landing, Ontario) is a retired educator with a keen interest in the history and literature of late Victorian and Edwardian London. He is a Baker Street Irregular, a Master Bootmaker, and founding chair of the Friends of the ACD Collection at the Toronto Reference Library.

THE ADVENTURE OF
THE IRRELEVANT AVOCADO

VINCENT W. WRIGHT

Most people are terrified to speak in front of others. They freeze up with fear. They get clammy and shaky. Their voice cracks. They say "but, umm" a lot. And the only thing they want is to finish. It's when they're told later that they did a good job that they feel relief. But the more they do it, the easier it gets. The nerves subside, the sweaty palms go away, and comfort sets in. I've been on stage in some way my whole life—plays, band, chorus. I'm used to it. But my first time in front of a Sherlockian group terrified me. My hands shook relentlessly, and I was so glad when I was done. But, as I said, it got easier, and eventually I decided to give a presentation at a major Sherlockian conference.

Imparting knowledge to a crowd is a nerve-racking thing. You're either going to have something everyone remembers, or you're not. And in order to have a memorable presentation you have to show them something they've never seen before. Now remember, a Sherlockian meeting or convention isn't a boardroom setting. There may be charts and graphs, but no jobs are at stake. The worst that can happen is to not be invited back, or to have no one remember your talk.

In that original situation, I went with a question that had been bugging me: how had Holmes found the flat on Baker Street? Was it through a friend? By word of mouth? Or something else? Then it hit me: where does one go to find info about places to rent? The newspaper, of course. I began looking for ads for places to let on Baker Street at the time. I found several, but none satisfied the known facts of 221B. Then I saw one for 23 Baker Street from January 1881 that worked. So, I built a paper around it. Happily, the more I researched, the more cool stuff I found, and after several months I had a decent paper. However, I was about to introduce a radical idea to a group of experts, and I'm sure my fear was palpable.

I introduced myself to PowerPoint. I wanted my pictures and illustrations enlarged on a big screen. (I made some rookie mistakes with the program, but soon got better.) When the time came to start I squared up my sheets, said hello to the audience, pulled out my glasses, dropped them, retrieved them, and began. The projector came to life and there was no turning back. Unexpectedly, oohs and ahhs were what I encountered. People shook my hand afterwards, even pulled me to the side to share their thoughts. They couldn't stop talking about it. I was congratulated over and over. The pressure was off. Later, interest in the piece followed me. Within a year I had given it in four different states.

Then, while looking over the paper for places to add new data, I discovered that I had made a huge mistake. 23 Baker Street could not have been the true location of 221B. I was devastated. (I had sent this paper to a major Sherlockian newsletter, and had won second place with it in a big essay contest.) Did I cancel my talk? No. I went ahead with the paper as planned, and explained that my proposal was impossible. The paper was dead. Why did I do it? A friend of mine told me that that is the essence of research. You work on your theory until you either prove or disprove it. If you prove it, you've changed the field it relates to. If you disprove it, you now know where not to look for the answer. Said Thomas Edison: "I have not failed. I just found 10,000 ways that don't work."

By the time I retired that paper, I had given several others as well. I didn't realize it then, but my first presentation used a pattern that I would almost always employ: state your idea up front, digress from it with a bunch of neat tidbits in the middle, and have a huge payoff at the end. It works very well for me, people have come to expect it, and I think it makes for a great talk. Granted, the stuff in the middle has to be just as good. It has to be interesting, understandable, and relevant to the main idea. But it's fine to have fun with it, too. I once gave a paper about the terrible things that could happen to your body if you were unlucky enough to die in Victorian England. It was a grim paper, but I still threw in the occasional chuckle because it's necessary. If your talk is about a non-humorous subject, slip in some levity to distract everyone for a moment. Otherwise, you might have a bunch of bored, disgusted, or sleepy folks in front of you. After all, there are three things to accomplish to have a good Sherlockian presentation: *Educate, Entertain, Enjoy.*

The title of your creation can be to the point, or can leave everyone wondering what's in store. I never give away anything with my titles. By the end, though, its meaning falls into place. (Still, I fret over them, and often it's the last thing I put down.) I once talked about the initials on the cover of the 1902 *The Hound of the Baskervilles* that seemed to have been ignored by scholars for a century. I called it "Initially Seen, But Not Observed." It's still my favorite title.

So now you have everything you need to do a great paper, but what about yourself? Don't worry about what to wear, or whether you forgot to floss. You need to worry about tone, inflection, volume, and speed. You must talk clearly. It doesn't matter if you have a good speaking voice—you only need to be heard and understood. Try not to repeat words unless there aren't different words to use. (I give talks about Sherlockian chronology. Try finding synonyms for that!) Be mindful of "umms" and things of that nature. Don't go too fast. Look up at your presentation (if it's a visual one) from time to time. Don't be monotone. (A droning voice is a terrible thing. It's even worse if your talk is scheduled right after lunch. Heads will be a-bobbing.)

Italicize words you want to emphasize. Make a notation on your pages for when you need to advance the slide, or just make a separate page for every point. Highlight the words that match what's on the screen. Make the word(s) bold or underlined. Put a star beside them. Use a different font. Make them a different color. Anything to prompt you to go on to the next thing, or to know when you're discussing something that is also on the screen. I change what I do for this with every paper so I don't get too accustomed to one thing.

Make good eye contact. Keeping your head down and reading doesn't make the crowd feel involved. At the spots where it's fun or funny, make sure you react appropriately. (Don't expect them to get the joke if you don't act like there was supposed to be one.) Smile. Use your hands. Step away from the podium from time to time. Walk over and point at things on the screen. Interact with them and your creation.

Finally, know the difference between something that's only to be read, and something that's to be read aloud. Open any book of essays and read part of one of them out loud. Record yourself and play it back. If it sounds boring to you, it will be boring for others. (I have seen too many speakers who didn't know the difference.) Have someone read you an article from a newspaper. Listen to the pace of the writing. See how monotonous it is? That's because it wasn't meant to be read aloud. Now get a book by Dr. Seuss. *That* is meant to be read aloud. It stimulates the mind, senses, and emotions. That is what your piece has to do. People should come away from your talk having had their feelings trifled with. They are there to hear papers from people with differing points of view or new takes on old ideas. You have to give them something to remember. They must recall the emotions they felt, or the laugh they had, or the wonder of a new way of looking at a topic. Make sure you deliver.

It is possible to present a great paper without using visuals. I know a Sherlockian who gives fantastic papers, and has sworn off PowerPoint. He does read the paper just like he has written it, but he knows the difference between a piece for a publication versus one to be read to others. He uses inflection and emphasis. He smiles when he's supposed to. He looks up at his listeners often. People want to hear what he has to say because he and his works are engaging. Personally, though, I like having things for folks to look at. I know some say you shouldn't use words on your visuals as people can't read and listen at the same time. That's likely true, but the trick is not to read exactly what's on the screen. Mix it up a bit with like terms or slang. Shorten it. Lengthen it. Do whatever, but never repeat what's on the screen exactly. Also, have something to add to help keep it interesting. Example: if on the screen the line 'Holmes liked avocados' is displayed, look up at it (remember the prompt on your sheet?) and say something like, "Also, Holmes had an affection for disgusting avocados." (I'd say that because I think they *are* disgusting.) Then add a bit like, "Avocados weren't terribly plentiful in Victorian London, but you *could* find them in places like Westminster and Fulham." See what I mean? Have fun with it and keep it fascinating at the same time. (Be careful here, though. If you put up too much your audience will be concentrating on the screen and not you. Do it in small sections. An entire slide of words or sentences up will drag the audience away from you.)

I'm not saying my way of doing this is the only or correct one, I just know it works for me. I'm nothing special to look at, don't have the greatest voice, and I'm not famous. So, I use what I have: good research abilities, the capability to think outside of the box, and the skills to put together clever presentations with solid facts and interesting visuals. Go and do likewise. And remember to have fun. After all, that's what this is all about.

Vincent W. Wright (Indianapolis, Indiana) is creator of the Facebook site Historical Sherlock and a 20-year member of the Illustrious Clients of Indianapolis. He has been hooked since discovering *The Annotated Sherlock Holmes* while in high school and seeing Jeremy Brett in the Granada series.

A STUDY IN SILK AND SATIN

TIFFANY KNIGHT

Armor.

Not made of metal or mail, leather or canvas, or a Kevlar breastplate. Armor constructed of satin and lace, trims and ruffles, pearls and stones. Armor that deflects the eye, attracts the attention, and builds a character without ever needing a word.

The simplest way to declare one's intentions is donning your battle armor. The same way Irene Adler in the BBC *Sherlock* series chooses nudity, Neville St. Clair in "The Man with the Twisted Lip" makes up his face, or Holmes in "The Empty House" becomes an elderly bookseller, the choice of clothing allows the wearer to hide in plain sight.

Costuming was always the simplest way for me to proclaim my devotion or knowledge of a fandom. The detailing and designs are ways to exemplify knowledge and allow it to speak freely for me. You don't need to find a way to start a conversation with regular pleasantries when you have an outfit to do it for you.

When I created a steampunk Sherlock Holmes outfit, every inch of it was a hidden Easter egg from the Canon. There are the obvious clues, of course: the deerstalker, an Inverness, the distinct plaid pattern, the pipe—those are the signs that would allow any individual to realize that this is somehow involved in the world of Sherlock Holmes.

What makes it a talking point are the other details. In the middle, you have a test tube of green liquid strapped onto an arm, a magnifying glass, a journal with a picture of a woman, a book on beekeeping, a revolver—these are the things for a passing fan of the Canon or television shows. Then come the smaller details: a chatelaine with references to the Canon, like a rose or hound, a lock-picking kit, a bullet from an air rifle, a map of the London Underground, tickets to Dartmouth, a telegram tucked in the pocket, makeup along the veins, a wax and makeup kit, a lock of red hair, litmus paper, a jar of honey…all details that you might look at or display that only a seasoned Sherlockian would expect or ask about. These are also the things that draw them to you, the things you can discuss when they do come forward. It adds up to the ability to walk into a room, draw a crowd to you, and then have a talking point without the pleasantries.

The most simplistic example of course is the deerstalker. There's always the question: "Does it count as a costume?" But consider the fact that a costume, according to Merriam-Webster, is "the prevailing fashion…an outfit worn to create the appearance characteristic of a particular period, person, place, or thing...a person's ensemble." The second definition quite definitively places the deerstalker as a costume. While it is not out of the realm of possibility that an individual *might* wear a deerstalker as a fashion statement, if you go into a meeting with other individuals interested in Sherlock Holmes, it is difficult to argue that you are not dressing in the style of the character.

It's the easiest way to identify other people who also have a dedicated interest. I can wear an Inverness and bustle gown and not necessarily get recognized as a Sherlock Holmes enthusiast, but if I wear a deerstalker in the supermarket, at least one person will likely ask "Sherlock fan?"

Wearing it to a meeting? Simple way to discuss the accuracy, origin, and your own history with your hat.

It's easy then to take it a step further, especially with the history of costuming in the Canon. The mysteries of Holmes's cases were always interesting, but the moments that kept me were the disguises: his ability to don a second skin, immerse into a character so deeply that even his best friend cannot recognize him, and the final unveiling leaves you gasping.

These are the moments that let me connect with him, the fun that can be had in putting on a mask and still watching the world from just behind the inner skin. For a moment, you can be anyone—people tend to remember the dress and not the face, or remember what you wore and not what you said. You remember parts, you'll still remember an excellent conversation, but there's a range of space and allowance given to you by the spectacle you've arranged. After all, you've proven your worth by your outer wear. You've made a statement.

Depending on what you want to discuss, you can play to different strengths. If I want to discuss BBC *Sherlock* I can go Adler-inspired with seamed stockings and vintage hairstyles, or a Sherlock-inspired purple shirt, black coat, and blue scarf. Jeremy Brett might be reflected in an Afghan or especially long scarf, and the recent films by Guy Ritchie have their own steampunk flairs to mimic. Each of these incarnations gives you a different audience and different talking point—what better way to meet people? Take a whole BSI weekend and choose a day—put on a deerstalker Wednesday, wear a Victorian ball gown Thursday, change to a cocktail dress printed with the Canon on Friday, and finish it off in an electric blue day dress on Saturday. That way, you've covered various incarnations of the Canon and fan base, and likely found ways to connect with all the different Sherlockians when otherwise you might have kept to the same circles.

It's hard to say what my official entrance into the Sherlockian community might have been without an armor fashioned from bustles and ruffs. I had read the Canon as a child, and continued to come back to it for years. I had loved the *Sherlock* series since it first aired in the UK in 2010 and I had to have it sent by friends—not knowing at the time if we'd ever see it in the United States. I went to the release of the *Sherlock Holmes*, Guy Ritchie-version in costume. I've gone as both Sherlock Holmes and Irene Adler for Hallowe'en for years without ever being recognized, and I've worn deerstalkers with the "isn't that a mystery thing?" I loved every random Holmesian reference in other series I'd read or watched such as *Star Trek*, *Detective Conan*, or *Doctor Who*. I would reread cases every few years, and had found a pointed interest in the community since I'd heard it existed—but I knew it as intimidating.

So instead of speaking words, instead of trying to explain a love for a character and for a series that has had such an impact on my life and times, instead of searching for an intangible emotion that the English language cannot quite exemplify?

I built the story instead.

And painted it onto my armor.

Tiffany Knight (New York, New York) is an actress who dabbles in costumes when she's not performing as an actor or musician. She found the Canon as a child and has continued to thrive with the support of local and far flung scions. She is a member of the Adventuresses of Sherlock Holmes and the Baker Street Babes.

THE ADVENTURE OF THE INEVITABLE ACRONYM

SCOTT MONTY

The internet is a strange place, full of contradictions. At once it can be a tool that reconnects you with people with whom you've lost touch for decades, and yet it can serve as a means for complete strangers to rain their vitriol down on you. You can enter a bustling online marketplace that rivals Covent Garden, or spend countless hours in isolation, almost as if you're in your own little nook in your own private Diogenes Club. But for those with a shared interest in Mr. Sherlock Holmes, the web serves multiple functions: a research tool, a news medium, a campfire, and the world's largest Sherlockian society.

Though a Sherlockian since the age of 14, I made my own first foray into the internet some seven years later, before there were modern web browsers. The world I discovered included the Usenet discussion forum alt.fan.holmes, followed by the email discussion group the Hounds of the internet. And soon after came the website Sherlockian.net, which acted as a central clearinghouse for everything one might wish to know about Sherlock Holmes that existed on the web.

Beginning in 2001, I served as business manager of the *Baker Street Journal*. Since the BSI was selling CD-ROMs of the first 50-plus years of the *Journal*—technology that required computers—I reasoned that such a product was practically begging to be sold online. (For reference, Amazon was just five years old at this point.) So, I developed a website and online ordering system for the *BSJ*, its CD-ROM and BSI Press publications, at bakerstreetjournal.com. But there still seemed to be a gap.

While the *BSJ* continued to arrive at its staid and steady quarterly pace, the rise of the internet made the wait between issues interminable. In the era when emails were instantaneous, it seemed both quaint and vexing to wait as long as two issues before a letter to the editor was published. Not to mention that the *BSJ* needed an additional boost of publicity.

Enter the *Baker Street Blog*, born in August 2005. Early updates were technical in nature, introducing to Victorian- and Edwardian-minded Sherlockians the concept of a regularly-updating website with a comments section. But its purpose was clear: to provide regular news and information of any sort about Sherlock Holmes in popular culture, and to act as a publicity arm for the *BSJ*. The early audience was small, but dedicated.

Fast forward to June 2007 when we added a companion site and yet another "new media" format: a podcast called *I Hear of Sherlock Everywhere* that would serve as Sherlockian talk radio. Co-host Burt Wolder and I mixed interviews with discussion shows where we talked about news and issues in the Canon. Each site fed the other, and the listenership and readership grew together.

The only challenge was keeping up the pace of two sites, with all of the writing, recording, and editing they required. The show burned bright through March 2008, and then, just as Holmes did, we went on a hiatus—popularly called "podfading." Professional life got in the way, as I was recruited to an executive position at the headquarters of Ford Motor Company. The Archive section of the site tells the story in plain numbers: there was a precipitous drop in frequency of posts from 139 posts in 2006 to 160 in 2007, and then to just 37 posts for all of 2008.

Life tends to do that to hobbies from time to time. The only difference is that when one is producing a regular cadence of content for an online audience, the audience is bound to provide feedback. From the concerned ("Are you okay?") to the curious ("What have you been up to?") to the disappointed ("I miss your regular updates"), I received notes that filled me with encouragement and guilt simultaneously.

It wasn't until the end of 2009 that things began to get back on track. The show re-started at Episode 19, and the frequency of articles began to chug forward like a large locomotive. We notched 59 posts in 2009, then 72 in 2010. By the time the 2011 BSI Weekend rolled around, I knew things had to change. This simply wasn't possible to sustain as a sole proprietorship (at least as far as the blog went; the podcast was and continues to be a two-person effort). I confided to Peter Blau that the site would begin to take on a Baker Street Irregular approach: a cadre of dedicated people who would like to contribute to the hobby. I had no idea how to make it happen, but saying it out loud to another Sherlockian imbued the pledge with a sheen of credibility.

To my surprise, some of our long-time readers were more than happy to lend their writing skills to the blog, and they quickly developed their own beats: for example, Gordon Dymowski did book reviews, particularly focusing on comic books and graphic novels; Chris Redmond lent his astute observations to matters historical, Canonical, and everything in between; Matt Laffey syndicated his *Always 1895* updates from Tumblr; and many more joined the fray over the years.

In 2013, it was clear to me that maintaining two separate sites—one for the blog, one for the podcast—not only was cumbersome, but diluted the brand. As I was no longer acting as business manager for the *Journal*, the *Baker Street Journal*/*Baker Street Blog* connection was less significant; and as we became this catch-all of Sherlock Holmes in popular culture, it only made sense to embrace the *I Hear of Sherlock Everywhere* brand. And so, on August 28, 2013, the *Baker Street Blog* made its last update before everything was ported over to *IHOSE*.

We had never intended to embrace the moniker "IHOSE" as part of the brand identity. While it's the logical and simple acronym for the site, in speech it sounds like some Apple device one might use in the garden. But fans embraced it, and so did we when we mention the site on the air. It's just easier to say.

Beyond our struggles with branding, there are a handful of instances that bear repeating. The first is our brush with internet notoriety. In 2007, Sherlock Holmes hadn't graced the movie theaters for some time; this was two full years before Robert Downey, Jr., took his first turn as Holmes. As always, Hollywood swirled with the occasional rumors of writers and directors who might be interested in taking on a project of some sort, but it was much too soon to attach the name of an actor to the role. We decided to create an article with just enough of a whiff of the truth that it might be plausible that Nicholas Rowe might be reprising the role he played in *Young Sherlock Holmes* some 22 years before. For those astute enough to catch it, we posted the article on April 1 (ihose.co/SherlockRowe). Well, we were a little more convincing than we had anticipated, as some Hollywood websites picked up on the news and ran with it, as if it were a fact. (Imagine our surprise when Rowe actually did don the deerstalker once more, as a cameo appearance in the 2015 film *Mr. Holmes*.)

Another article worth noting is one that was commissioned in response to a sensational piece of journalism that claimed a lost Sherlock Holmes manuscript had been found in Scotland. Reading like a bad pastiche, the news item went that a 1,300-word story had been found in someone's attic and was a missing Sherlock Holmes story. Since he is co-editing the Wessex Press series *Sherlock Holmes and Conan Doyle in the Newspapers*, we turned to Mattias Boström as a correspondent, to give him the opportunity to research and rebut what we thought was a ludicrous claim. As Mattias's research showed, our assumption was correct, and on the same day, we had a lengthy refutation, backed up with plenty of facts (ihose.co/ACD_not). And just as before, when a controversy arose, the press was quick to pick up on it. Within the next 24 hours, Mattias was interviewed by a number of international news organizations, and outlets across the internet were referring to his article as definitive (ihose.co/LostStory).

As we've grown the *IHOSE* brand, we finally settled into a regular cadence of shows, airing on the 15th and 30th of every month. We've spoken to authors like Rebecca Romney, Kareem Abdul-Jabbar, and Lyndsay Faye; playwrights and directors like Ken Ludwig and Nicholas Meyer; collectors like Jerry Margolin and Glen Miranker; publishers such as Steve Doyle and Otto Penzler; actors such as Fritz Weaver and Lara Pulver; and countless other Sherlockians of unique qualifications and interest.

And thanks to helpful feedback from our listeners, we discovered that many found some of our episodes a little too exclusive—"inside baseball"—for those outside of the BSI or Sherlockian circles. Not to mention that some episodes clocked in at nearly two hours. Some fans were just interested in learning about the stories, and some thought a shorter format would be easier to consume. As a result, we began a companion show called *Trifles* early in 2017. This weekly audio broadcast is just 15 minutes long; in it we discuss some of the minutiae in the Canon, from Holmes's dressing gown colors to his smoking habits.

These last dozen years online have been a long, strange journey. From the emergence of podcasts and social media, we've seen the landscape change, and we've been there to change along with it. We're in no danger of running out of content any time soon, and we know we'll continue to connect with people young and old, some of whom have just discovered Sherlock Holmes and others who are life-long Sherlockians. We hope to convey the same kind of excitement and wonder that we had when we discovered the wonder of the world of Sherlock Holmes ourselves.

Both the internet and Sherlock Holmes have demonstrated a remarkable ability to reinvent and repeat themselves for new generations. And *I Hear of Sherlock Everywhere* will be there to chronicle it.

Scott Monty (Canton, Michigan) is a blogger, speaker, and consultant in business, technology, communications, and marketing. He spent six years as head of social media for Ford Motor Company, and is CEO of Brain+Trust Partners.

THE ADVENTURE OF
THE PLUCKY HEART

SONIA FETHERSTON

There's a wonderful old story about writer and critic Alexander Wooll-cott, who crashed the first dinner of the Baker Street Irregulars in 1934. This he did in high style, clip-clopping up to Christ Cella's restaurant in one of the last horse-drawn hansom cabs in New York City. Wearing a deerstalker and carrying a magnifying glass, Woollcott ignored the blister-ing stink-eye bestowed on him by BSI founder Christopher Morley. Seat-ing himself at the sacred table, the man of letters began to make mental notes about his companions—among them boxer Gene Tunney, bookman Vincent Starrett, illustrator Frederick Dorr Steele, and actor William Gil-lette. He immortalized their evening in his "Shouts and Murmurs" column for the *New Yorker*, a piece which has become one of the great classics of Sherlockian rhapsody.

Woollcott had pluck.

It has long been an axiom of mine that the best Sherlockians share that trait. Like Woollcott, they pursue the Great Detective with a formidable trifecta of fearlessness, determination, and cheek—those marvelous quali-ties generously apportioned to all plucky people. I, too, am a Practitioner of Pluck, albeit at a level much more modest than Woollcott was able to achieve. Still, pluckiness has enabled me to savor a few Sherlockian ex-ploits of my own.

I can't remember how I first learned about the dollhouse that silent film star Colleen Moore created in the mid-1920s. Moore was, in her heyday, one of Hollywood's top stars. She enlisted film set designers to help build a stunning 14-foot high dollhouse where she could stow her collection of pricey antique miniatures. Moore thought it would be fun to include a Lil-liputian library, so she commissioned the binding of several dozen blank volumes, each as big as a postage stamp. These tiny books were distributed to her favorite living authors, including Sir Arthur Conan Doyle, with an invitation to write something inside and return them for her dollhouse li-brary. I'd seen references to these books in old film fan magazines from the 1920s, but after Moore's star finally flickered out around 1929 there were virtually no more mentions of them. I made discreet inquiries of longtime Sherlockians, and even of surviving members of the Doyle family. Most everybody was unaware of the tiny book in which Conan Doyle put pen to paper those many decades ago. Quite naturally I wondered what he'd written, and where the book is today.

Pluck got hold of me. I went on the bookish equivalent of a manhunt, scouring the internet, plunging into dusty archives, even interrogating modern members of the Academy of Motion Picture Arts and Sciences. The dollhouse, it turns out, now resides at Chicago's Museum of Science and Industry, where it is housed inside a huge Plexiglas box in a reverentially dimmed gallery. I asked for permission to come and examine Conan Doyle's little book. The head curator told me that I could buy a ticket and walk around the Plexiglas box just like everybody else. What she didn't seem to appreciate is that People of Pluck are *not like everybody else*. I wanted to see the book up close, to learn what Conan Doyle wrote in it, and to take that information to the Sherlockian world. So began my yearlong campaign to persuade her to open the tiny library for my inspection.

Month after month I worked my way up and down the museum's organizational chart. From volunteers, to line staff and managers, to members of the board of directors, nobody was immune from my pestering entreaties. I phoned, wrote, and emailed everybody I could think of to ask whether I could come and meet the tiny treasure in person. Then, at my darkest hour, a plucky idea began to glimmer. Eventually it would light the way toward a solution. As a veteran of more than 20 years writing folderol for the *Baker Street Journal*, I asked the museum's lowly media relations intern if she might help credential me—a *Journal*-ist—to gain access to Conan Doyle's tiny book. For good measure I chipped in a letter of endorsement from the *BSJ*'s editor. There, the intern's silver answer rang: could I present myself at the museum in three weeks' time? I instantly booked my flight. That's how readers of the *BSJ* learned about my pluck-induced appointment with the Moore/Doyle book…and what I found inked inside it. Being plucky saw me through.

Now, Chicago boasts a population roughly triple the size of some sovereign nations (Lithuania, for one). It's a far cry from a dusty frontier town of just nineteen hundred souls located on the underbelly of historic Route 66. Welcome to Moriarty, New Mexico. I went on location to listen for echoes of a group of old-time Sherlockians who, under the leadership of the renowned John Bennett Shaw, staged annual "unbirthday" parties there for Holmes's nemesis, the similarly named Professor Moriarty, back in the 1970s. For my auspicious day I donned a pair of green Sherlock Holmes socks that would serve as my plucky calling card. Moriarty, which looks a bit like the set for the TV show *Bonanza*, is small enough to just amble around in. I visited the community's police department, fire station, library, town museum, and other sites. I even ventured, lickety-split, down a dirt track called "Irene Avenue," dodging rattlesnakes that had set up housekeeping in the verges. Everywhere I went, I raised my pant legs, displayed the socks, and said only that I was a Sherlockian. While nobody was able to recall the times, more than four decades previous, when Shaw and his cronies came to town, nearly every person with whom I spoke made the connection between Sherlock Holmes and the name of their little burg.

The police chief bowled me over by reciting canonical quotes, and one of his officers named a half-dozen of his favorite Sherlock Holmes sto-ries—even pointing out those that featured Professor Moriarty. The librar-ian helped me locate Sherlock Holmes books on her shelves; incredibly, more than half of them were checked out! At the animal control office, the dogcatcher laughed and assured me there are no glowing hounds lurking on the mesa. I took pictures of a young man suited up in Moriarty Fire De-partment gear, and then he—something of a Pluckmeister himself—took a photo of my socks. A nice lady at the local museum, a cubbyhole smaller than my bedroom closet, managed to find two old news clippings from the 1970s about Shaw and his parties. If they didn't personally remember the old-time Sherlockians, these people made me feel ever so welcome. A few months later my reminiscences ended up as the lead story in the *Baker Street Journal*.

For my next adventure I said "Happy Trails" to Moriarty and "Aloha" to Honolulu. Actually, the journey started at home in Oregon while I was running an online archive search of references to "Sherlock Holmes" in historic out-of-print Pacific Rim publications. Suddenly, the name of an 1890s consulting detective in Honolulu—a man whose friends admiringly called him "Sherlock"—popped up. I skimmed through a few 120-year old articles about him, enough to see that he was a really appealing charac-ter, somebody I'd like to research and write about next. But first I needed to finish the task at hand; I decided I would come back to this Hawaiian Holmes the next day. Unfortunately, I neglected to jot down his particulars, relying on my faulty memory to reunite me with the old fellow. Of course I forgot *all* of the details, including the man's name! I spent *six plucky years* searching via hundreds of word combinations, trying to recreate the one that took me to him in the first place. During that time I went to Honolulu twice, cultivating contacts at the Hawaiian Historical Society, the Univer-sity of Hawaii library and archive, and other helpful resources. Nothing. All the while I kept plugging away, doggedly looking online:

> "Sherlock + Hawaii"
> "Hawaii + Consulting Detective"
> "Honolulu + Holmes"

I used every search parameter I could possibly think of. As Holmes himself once pluckily observed, "there is nothing more stimulating than a case where everything goes against you." So I kept at it and, finally, pluck paid off. I blundered into the right combination of words, and the tropical detective who was Sherlock Holmes's contemporary suddenly popped up on my computer screen. Much to my chagrin I saw that his surname, which had eluded me for years, was *Doyle*! With his name in hand I could finally research his life story and compose an article about his very colorful career as the Islands' top sleuth. The *Sydney Passengers Log* kindly published my finished work. Once more, pluck served me well.

There's a lot to love about being a Sherlock Holmes nut: fellowship... continuing education...creativity...putting a natural penchant for infer-ence and deduction to practical use. There's also pluck. Pluckiness for a

Sherlockian means the difference between passively reading or watching a TV show or movie, versus becoming a very active participant in a world where "it is always eighteen ninety-five." A plucky heart means an infinite capacity for taking pains—yes. But as Woollcott showed us, pluck is also the method by which one can attain the most extraordinary, the most thoroughly *Sherlockian*, undertakings.

Sonia Fetherston (Salem, Oregon) was for 15 years an advertising and public relations executive, and is now a busy freelance writer, as well as a veteran Sherlockian scholar and a Baker Street Irregular. She received the Morley-Montgomery Award for 2011, and the BSI published her book *Prince of the Realm: The Most Irregular James Bliss Austin* in 2014.

THE ADVENTURE OF THE
INEXPERIENCED ACADEMIC

ANGELA FOWLER

In the second chapter of *A Study in Scarlet*, Dr. Watson, puzzling over his mysterious roommate, makes a list titled "Sherlock Holmes: His Limits." The list begins with Holmes's ignorance and slowly works toward his mastery. I've always thought it was an odd way of ordering the list: wouldn't it be better to start with his profound knowledge of chemistry rather than his complete ignorance of the solar system? Perhaps Watson had glimpsed into the abyss of Holmes's capabilities (he still didn't know how Holmes knew he'd been to Afghanistan), and he needed to start with his limits: what he didn't know.

When I first became a Sherlockian, it felt a bit like staring into that abyss. The thing about Sherlock Holmes is that he's generated a lot of material. Film, novels, fanfiction, research, merchandise…there was so much to absorb. My first experiences with Sherlock Holmes had been radio plays from my parents' record collection and a few kid-friendly films (*The Great Mouse Detective* and *Young Sherlock Holmes*), but in my late 20s, when I began both serious fandom and research, I realized I'd only scratched the surface. There was so much that I hadn't watched and read, and I had the sneaking suspicion that there was still more I wasn't even aware of. All I could focus on was the limits of my own knowledge and experience.

What made everything harder was the fact that at the same time I was becoming a Sherlockian in the fandom sense, I was becoming a Sherlockian academic. I was getting my doctoral degree at Auburn University, and, after washing out of 18th-century literature, I'd jumped ahead about a century, becoming perfectly happy amid the New Women, aesthetes, and penny dreadfuls of the 19th century. I'd taken a class in Victorian literature with a focus on cosmopolitanism, so I was ready to take on the entire British Empire—or, at least, contextualize Victorian writings using the concepts of empire, travel, and British national identity. My plans were not so well articulated as I just so glibly put it, but I was getting there. So when my advisor asked me what kind of literature I wanted to focus on, I chose Arthur Conan Doyle and dove head-first into research.

And faced the abyss yet again.

After the first crawl through the database search and the first pile of books from the library shelves, I found myself drowning in information about Sherlock Holmes and his companion Dr. Watson. There were an-notated versions of the Canon, speculations about his fictional life, maps following his footsteps, discussions of every influence and adaptation. Hundreds of Sherlockians had taken up Watson's role as Boswell and had filled page after page with minutiae. While there was much less written about Conan Doyle's non-Holmes works, there were still enough biogra-phies of the author to make a beginning researcher despair.

I didn't fully realize at first that there were several aspects of Sherlock-iana wholly unique in British literary academia. While authors like Charles Dickens and Jane Austen had their own early fandoms that continue today, none had the type of active fan engagement that Conan Doyle enjoyed (or, occasionally, didn't enjoy). I wasn't aware that the work of early members of the Baker Street Irregulars, Adventuresses, and other groups were done half in earnest and half in jest. I knew about the Great Game (the type of writing that pretends Holmes and Watson really lived, and that Conan Doyle was Watson's literary agent), but I didn't know how pervasive it was in Sherlockiana, and how the serious research and the Great Game essays were often listed in databases side by side.

I think my misunderstanding came to a head when I read Rex Stout's "Watson was a Woman," published in the *Saturday Review of Literature* in March 1941. In this article, originally a speech given before the Baker Street Irregulars, Stout makes a case for Dr. Watson not only being a wom-an, but being Holmes's wife. His argument hinges on things like Watson noticing whether Holmes breakfasted or the one time Watson faints. I was livid. How dare he? How could anyone treat literary analysis so poorly? How could anyone call this serious research?

But no one had. I'd made several rookie mistakes. I'd dumped the ar-ticle into my to-read pile without checking the publication information. I'd also missed the, in hindsight, obvious clues that the article was meant to be facetious. I'd also missed further context, that this was a speech given at a BSI meeting, meant to entertain and perhaps ruffle feathers. In retrospect, I could have used this source to explore heteronormativity and how Holmes and Watson have been viewed as a couple, but I wasn't there yet.

At the moment, rather, I was learning how to navigate a long and var-ied conversation, with its own language, codes, in-jokes, and quirks. After much practice, I could not only navigate the conversation, but I could inter-pret it—and I could join it. I learned what would work for serious literary (publishable) research, as well as to recognize shoddy research. (Pro tip: never trust a source that says that Victorian men wore mourning armbands after "The Final Problem" was published, or that Conan Doyle got his knighthood because of Holmes.) I also developed my own Sherlockian pet peeves, becoming defensive of people saying that Conan Doyle hated Sherlock Holmes (he didn't) or that his interest in Spiritualism was a sign he was losing his mind (don't even bring up the Cottingley fairies).

Looking back, I realize I was (and in many ways I still am) a new, unpracticed voice trying to write a dissertation under the weight of what I knew and the fear of what I didn't know. Through my own stumbling efforts, the patient advice of my academic advisors, and the help of many kind people in the Sherlockian fandom, I found my voice and grew as both an active fan and academic. I became not only a Sherlockian researcher, but a Sherlockian teacher as well. I taught Sherlock Holmes whenever I could manage it. In my writing classes, I had the students become detectives as they investigated their topics, and I would pepper in Sherlockian quotes while sporting a deerstalker. In my literature classes, we read "A Scandal in Bohemia" and "The Speckled Band" and watched *Sherlock*, comparing Benedict Cumberbatch to Basil Rathbone and the original text. We made our own adaptations, and I now have a painting hanging on my wall of Basil of Baker Street, a gift from a student.

And even as I found a voice, I became more vocal. Early in my experiences as a Sherlockian, I was hesitant to participate in the fandom. I was writing a dissertation on Arthur Conan Doyle, I was teaching Sherlock Holmes, and I liked the stories, but did that make me a fan? Did that make me part of the Sherlockian community? There seemed, at first, to be a barrier that hadn't been there in the early Sherlockiana that I'd researched. Fan works didn't seem to be paired with serious scholarship any more.

That was what I thought, right up until the point when I walked into registration for the fan convention 221B Con. This convention, held annually in the spring in Atlanta, was my first real experience with what it means to belong to a Sherlockian community. There were people dressed in deerstalkers, people dressed in dark Belstaff coats and blue scarves, and people dressed as deer with flowers on their antlers (it's called "faunlock," and it's just as Sherlockian as deerstalkers). The panels were laid out to show the diversity of Sherlockiana: a panel about shipping (or supporting the relationship of) Sherlock Holmes and Moriarty (or Sheriarty) was held in a room beside a panel about villains in the Canon, which was also beside a panel about Victorian costuming. I felt like I'd finally come home. The next year, I signed up for three panels and got to be part of all three. I talked about what I knew—Conan Doyle's non-Holmes works, his relationship with spiritualism, teaching using Sherlock Holmes—and people were interested. So many people showed up for the panel about spiritualism the first year I did it, we had to move to a bigger room. At the same time, I learned so much and made so many friends. I not only understood the conversation going back to the 1890s, I felt part of the same community.

That's something I try to remember: I was once a newcomer, and now I'm in the ever-changing, ever-growing community. With new Holmes adaptations and new avenues of engagement, both in person and online, we're seeing a renaissance of Sherlockian fandom. It's tempting for older fans to get defensive, to try to test and exclude. How can someone be a Sherlockian if they haven't read the original stories? The thing is, they can.

Most Sherlockians, like myself, get introduced to the detective via an adaptation, and that adaptation changes with each generation. It used to be William Gillette, then it became Basil Rathbone, then Jeremy Brett, Robert Downey, Jr., Benedict Cumberbatch, Jonny Lee Miller…. I originally fell in love with a cartoon mouse named Basil facing off against a giant rat voiced by Vincent Price, and a gangly teenager at a boarding school fighting a cult using weaponized hallucinogens. A community (because that's what we are) can only grow and thrive through new members. Each new Sherlockian brings with them their own voice, their own interpretation, and their own engagement, and it's essential that more experienced Sherlockians include rather than exclude. At one point, we were all new fans.

Angela Fowler (Montgomery, Alabama) is an adjunct instructor at Auburn University whose PhD dissertation was on "Arthur Conan Doyle and British Cosmopolitan Identity: Knights, Detectives, and Mediums." She is the host of the podcast *Through the Pages of Sherlock Holmes*.

THE ADVENTURE OF THE SEEDS OF INTEREST

ROB NUNN

"I liked how Holmes was able to figure out so much about Henry Baker."—Jackson

"It was cool how the story started out about a hat and ended up being about a gem."—Duane

"I would be in a forgiving mood and let Ryder go too."—Jez

"I don't like how the villain didn't go to jail!"—Alyssa

In just two weeks, I think I might have made some future Sherlockians. At least that's what I tell myself after I finish teaching my Sherlock Holmes unit to my fifth grade class every November.

But it wasn't always that way. The first year I taught "The Blue Carbuncle" and "The Red-Headed League" to my students, the stories were received with lukewarm acceptance. But once my teaching started to mirror my own ever-growing interest in the Canon, some of those ten- and eleven-year-olds really took to Doyle's work.

As a Sherlockian, my personal journey started off with a Christmas gift 13 years ago. Because of cultural touchstones such as *The Great Mouse Detective* and *Sesame Street*'s Sherlock Hemlock, I was always aware of Sherlock Holmes, but once I cracked open that gigantic red-covered volume, I was done for. The stories! The adventures! The deductions! Eventually, I read all 60 stories, and that was that. I had thoroughly enjoyed the Canon and picked up a few pastiches here and there, but felt that I hadn't really gotten the full experience.

And then I discovered Sherlockiana, scion societies, and writing about the writings. Through these three avenues, I was able to really dig my teeth into the stories and discuss them with other people. This, my friends, is getting the full Sherlockian experience.

"The ending when the guys came up out of the hole in the ground was very unexpected."—Winston

"I felt like Doctor Watson. I didn't know what was coming next."—Lucas

"Hiring a guy just because he had red hair was very unique."—Julia

"I like how they caught the robbers at the end of the tunnel."—Tyler

When my second year of teaching Sherlock Holmes rolled around, I knew I wanted the kids to be more engaged, just the way I had become as a Sherlockian. I applied for and was awarded a Jan Stauber Grant from the wonderful Beacon Society. With that, I was able to buy class sets of *Classic Starts: The Adventures of Sherlock Holmes, Sherlock Holmes and the Copper Beeches* graphic novels, and scripts for the plays "The Red-Headed League" and "Sherlock Holmes and the Blue Carbuncle." Because of the Beacon Society's generosity, I was able to take a one week reading unit, and expand it into a two week cross-curricular event.

I started out the unit by taking time to introduce Holmes and his many incarnations throughout the years. With a PowerPoint presentation, the students were shown everything from books to comics and movies to puppets. Since it was an introduction that was meant to engage fifth graders, I spent more time on Batman and the Muppets than I did on Sidney Paget and Basil Rathbone. If I was going to get them hooked, I had to play to my audience.

The first Sherlockian book I had ever read was *Sherlock Holmes of Baker Street* by William S. Baring-Gould. Realizing that the stories could be put into different chronologies and that Watson wasn't always a trusted narrator was a revelation to me as a reader. After that, I reread the Canon through a new lens. Baring-Gould's annotated Canon and Vincent Starrett's *The Private Life of Sherlock Holmes* reinforced this new way of thinking. Every story now led to more questions. When did this take place? Could Moriarty or Mycroft be involved behind the scenes? Which wife is Watson referencing? What had originally been an entertaining stand-alone story now became a multi-faceted tale for me to analyze and pick apart.

That's what I wanted my kids to do with these stories, too. Instead of reading and then answering a few comprehension questions, I really wanted them to engage with each story in one way or another. I decided to focus on specific elements for each story.

At the end of "The Blue Carbuncle," the class discussed character motivations—which turned into a debate about whether Holmes should have allowed James Ryder to go free. Once the kids had to back up their opinions to their friends, they were much more invested in why Holmes and Ryder behaved as they did. Keeping that focus, we discussed how characters are written for the short story format, and mysteries specifically, when we read "The Red-Headed League." The students had seen Holmes's deductive powers at work before, but with this story, we really broke down his initial assessment of Jabez Wilson and why each of Holmes's interesting behaviors throughout the story eventually led to the capture of John

Clay. The "Copper Beeches" lesson focused on tension and rising action in a story, as well as how a story is presented differently in a graphic novel as opposed to a traditional text. The gothic atmosphere of this story is perfect to display an impending sense of doom that pays off in a climactic scene.

When we read "The Speckled Band," our lesson focused on the author's purpose and how Doyle's choices as an author moved the story along, as well as his use of red herrings with the mention of gypsies and a baboon. The students were particularly taken with the villain Grimesby Roylott, which led into a discussion of what makes a good villain. I saved "A Scandal in Bohemia" for last, just so I could kick off the lesson with the question: Can Sherlock Holmes be beaten? From there, we discussed how foil characters can be used to create conflict with a protagonist, and many of the students were blown away when Irene Adler bests Holmes at the end.

"It was weird that she had to cut her hair and wear a certain dress." —Jez

"It had a surprising plot."—Brody

"I didn't like it when the dog got shot." —Jarvis

"It was creepy and interesting." —Madison

I was taking in all of these great ideas through scholarly writings, and wanted to try some of my own. Knowing I definitely didn't have the knowledge base yet to tackle something as daunting as my own scholarly writing, I still wanted to contribute to Sherlockiana somehow. I had been a fan of IHearofSherlock.com for a long time, and decided to give it a try myself. I reached out to its creator, Scott Monty, through Twitter, and he was more than welcoming in allowing me to contribute to his blog site. I started out writing about my personal experiences in the Sherlockian world and doing book reviews. I eventually branched out into other avenues, such as interviews and researching a little-known Sherlock Holmes series that never made it to TV. After a time, I began to formulate an idea for a possible Sherlockian book of my own, and began to work my way through the research and writing process in depth.

In much the same way, as the class read through our stories over the two-week period, the students began working through the writing process and slowly built their own Sherlock Holmes stories. Starting with identifying elements for a mystery, the students mapped out their own mysteries and first drafts were written. After the story was down on paper, we took time to learn what it means to "see but not observe" by examining jackets and making deductions about their owners just as Holmes does with Henry Baker's hat. This lesson helped the kids to understand the importance of using details in their writing. The students then did rewrites of their stories, adding more details, and had them peer-edited by a friend in the class. A third draft was written, which was turned in to me for a final edit, and final drafts were at last produced. At the end of the writing process, everyone's

Sherlock Holmes stories were collected in a bound book that was placed in our classroom library. The students not only had a better understanding of the writing process, they had their own published book sitting right there in our classroom.

"I loved the bad guy and the snake."—Kolton

"This story gave me chills and felt very mysterious."—Julia

"I think it's sad that a stepdad would kill his daughters just because of money."—Alyssa

"The villain had a brilliant brain."—Ivy

"I felt scared reading this story. That was really cool."—Ella

After I was knee-deep in scholarship and writing, I wanted to discuss all my new ideas with other Sherlockians. I ventured out to my first scion meeting by joining the Harpooners of the Sea Unicorn in St. Charles, Missouri, for a discussion on "The Stockbroker's Clerk" and was welcomed by a small group that ranged in age from well into retirement down to high school. Going into that meeting, I didn't know what to expect, but by the end of the night, I couldn't wait to meet with more Sherlockians.

Luckily for me, the St. Louis area has a strong Sherlockian population, and as well as being a member of the Harpooners, I quickly joined the Noble Bachelors of St. Louis and the Parallel Case of St. Louis. These interactions with other Sherlockians are a true high point in our hobby, and I wanted my students to enjoy interacting with one another over Sherlockian discussions, just as I do.

To foster such discussions, I had the class break up into small groups and focus on elements of mystery stories in general. Each group had an abbreviated Holmes tale they would read in groups of four or five and focus on how a detective solves a case. After the groups had time to discuss, they then compared answers with members of other groups and readjusted their opinions on what it takes to think like a detective.

For the culminating activity of the unit, the students presented two Reader's Theater plays based on "The Red-Headed League" and "The Blue Carbuncle" using the scripts purchased with the Jan Stauber Grant. Each student picked out and practiced their parts for a week leading up to the performance, and took time to decide how their characters should move and what props and costumes would be appropriate. Their co-stars were quick to offer opinions, and the groups would complain each day when time was up and their practices had to end.

When the day of the performance arrived, six other fifth-grade classes joined ours in the school media center to watch the kids' hard work pay off. A rubber chicken inserted for Henry Baker's goose got the expected laugh, and the audience was rapt as a ten-year-old Holmes burst out from the chairs he was hiding behind to arrest John Clay. Not only had my students gained a deeper knowledge of Sherlock Holmes, they had, I hope, planted the seeds of interest in other fifth graders that day.

"I liked that Irene outsmarts Holmes and she dresses up like a dude."
—Samantha

"It was cool that Sherlock used different disguises."—Abbie

"I liked that a girl outsmarted Sherlock Holmes, but I don't know why she had to marry that other guy."—Sienna

"Irene's note was great!"—Jozie

As an educator, I feel that it is important for my students to know that I am passionate about subjects that I teach. It is so rewarding to see copies of *The Hound of the Baskervilles* being passed around from student to student weeks after our Sherlockian unit has ended, and the surprise on kids' faces when they read "The Greek Interpreter" on their own and learn that Sherlock Holmes has a brother. At the very least, I hope my students walk away each year with an appreciation for the world's greatest detective. But who knows? Maybe there are a few budding Sherlockians getting their start right now.

Rob Nunn (Edwardsville, Illinois) is the author of *The Criminal Mastermind of Baker Street* and blogs at interestingthoughelementary.blogspot.com. A graduate of Southern Illinois University at Edwardsville, he has been teaching for twelve years. In his spare time, he enjoys spending time with his wife and daughter, reading, and watching baseball.

THE ADVENTURE OF
THE BONES OF JUSTICE

CARLINA DE LA COVA

Being a Sherlockian, for me, is more than a hobby. It is a philosophy that encompasses all aspects of my life, including my personal belief system, moral code, and work ethic. Sherlock Holmes has been an integral part of my life since my childhood.

I had been exposed to both Peter Cushing's and Jeremy Brett's interpretations of Holmes whilst in grade school. *Young Sherlock Holmes* had also been released in my youth. However, my formal introduction to Sherlock Holmes came in my sixth grade English class as we were assigned "The Speckled Band" and watched the Granada adaptation starring Jeremy Brett. I had been a voracious reader as a child, and when I met Holmes, I was captivated by his intellect and his ability to see beyond the commonplace. However, as is the wont of young children with drifting minds, I started to read the Canon but did not complete it.

It would not be until the crucial and difficult years of my adolescence and teens that Holmes and I became reacquainted. At one point during the early 1990s I happened to be in my neighborhood antiquarian bookstore with a friend, looking for early comics. As we were perusing the comic books in their long white boxes, placed right below the fictional literature section, I happened to look up at the shelves for a moment. A copy of the *Reader's Digest* version of *The Adventures of Sherlock Holmes* stood out, its golden font captivating me. There was no hesitation on my part as I snapped the volume off the shelf. Each week I returned to purchase the subsequent books until I exhausted the shop's supply and completed the Canon.

The adolescent mind is far more complex, and in some respects needier, than the childhood mind. It is often a fragile, insecure, and rebellious structure seeking to shape itself and assert its identity in what it views as a turbulent world. Part of that definition of identity comes from one's confidence, their perception of themselves in society, any chosen role models, and their peer network. When I reconnected with Sherlock Holmes, I immersed myself in Watson's (as well as Holmes's) narratives. Whilst my peers were admiring teen idols, emulating Kurt Cobain, and dreaming about Brad Pitt, Holmes became my role model and my teacher on how to interpret the world, define justice, understand human behavior, comprehend when someone sought to do harm (and why), and be a proper, noble citizen. As I studied the detective, I learned how to interpret people, read into their behaviors, and observe their habits. My sense of just and unjust became thoroughly defined.

With maturity and age come new insights. Thus, as I grew from a teenager to an adult, my comprehension of the Canon, Holmes's personality and code of ethics, as well as the underlying messages Doyle imbedded in each story, expanded and became redefined. They would become the groundwork for many college papers and form the philosophy of not only my career in bioarchaeogy and forensic anthropology, but my life. I embraced Holmes's words and actions, and opted to dedicate my work and my life to bringing justice to the voiceless in both the historical and forensic contexts.

As a university professor and someone active in the fields of forensic anthropology and bioarchaeology, I use methods implemented by Holmes daily. My forensic work requires me to create a biological profile of a skeletonized individual, often discovered in dubious circumstances. This means I must perform an intricate examination of the anatomical features of each bone in the skeleton to assess age, biological sex, ancestry, height, unique identifying features, and possible cause of death (if observable). Furthermore, if I am called to the scene of discovery, which is not always the crime scene, I must not only examine the decedent's remains, but their positioning, any associated artifacts, disturbances associated with the scene, impressions, and any additional evidence that will tell me when, how, and where death occurred. Thus, like Sherlock Holmes, I must pay attention to the smallest details as they can have larger repercussions in the outcome of a case or identification. A series of minute observations, based on skeletal robusticity, size, shape, and length, allows me to create a biological profile. The slightest abnormality in bone provides me with possible hints about life history, disease process, trauma, or cause of death, further shedding light on the individuals I identify and study.

Forensic cases can be emotionally challenging, but as Sherlock Holmes says in *The Sign of the Four*, "It is of the first importance not to allow your judgment to be biased by personal qualities.... Emotional qualities are antagonistic to clear reasoning." Like the Great Detective, I turn off emotions whilst working a case or performing my academic research. Emotions are apt to cloud judgement, create error, and introduce bias. However, once my work is complete, I confront the reality of what I have discovered. Sometimes this is not pleasant, as I have seen humanity at its worst and been left wondering what it all means. Then I remember why I chose this occupation. Holmes's words from "The Three Gables" ring in my ears: "I am not the law, but I represent justice so far as my feeble powers go." I firmly believe that every individual I identify, or study, deserves some form of justice. In the forensic context, that justice comes from identifying the decedent and any factors tied to their cause of death, because regardless of who the individual was, and what they did in their lifetime, they had someone who loved them. My work has always been about bringing justice to these individuals and providing the decedent a voice.

Most of my academic research, however, is centered on the study of skeletal health of marginalized individuals in 19th and early 20th century America. The persons I study were curated in anatomical collections and dissected without consent. Although elements of their bodies have been examined extensively to create standardized methods of human identification and forensic profiling, few researchers have acknowledged who these persons were, let alone their origins. The majority were poor immigrants, African-Americans, and the insane, who died in public and charity hospitals and were voiceless with regard to their postmortem fate. Due to their poverty and the postmortem unclaimed nature of their remains, laws dictated that their bodies be dissected as a means of paying their debt to taxpayers who sustained them and provided their healthcare. My work has revealed how societal discrimination of these persons impacted their health and resulted in their deaths. Tangled in this has been the abandonment of institutional women and the negative health impacts of the Great Migration.

Whilst I have a strong emotional tie to my research, given my African-American background, Sherlock Holmes's methods and beliefs have also played an important role in this work. Like Holmes, I scrutinize all lines of data, including biological, skeletal, historical, and social, to reconstruct the lives of the persons I study as well as the diseases they suffered from. Furthermore, like the great detective, I am a firm believer in social justice. Holmes never discriminated against his clients based on sex or social position. He served each with the same fervor and sought to provide them some form of justice. My attitude is the same with the individuals I study. Whilst they were impoverished and non-consensually dissected, my goal is to provide them with some form of social justice now that corrects the contemporaneous social wrongs done to them. This means telling their stories and educating my colleagues on the ethics associated with studying these individuals.

Being a Sherlockian also means sharing this way of life, code of ethics (which may vary from Sherlockian to Sherlockian), and shared beliefs with a wonderful and supportive community of individuals. We may define what it means to be a Sherlockian differently, but we are united in regard to the emphasis and role Sherlock Holmes has in our lives. I also teach a university-level forensics course on Sherlock Holmes that allows me to share his impact on criminology and forensics with new generations of college students.

Lastly, to me, being a Sherlockian means walking in the footsteps of the great detective. I believe Sherlock Holmes was a true anthropologist and seeker of justice, both within and outside the criminal and legal system. He was cognizant of the impact of important criminal anthropologists like Alphonse Bertillon and Cesare Lombroso. Holmes was also familiar with Charles Darwin and scientific discussions of criminality. Furthermore, he had published on the morphology of the human ear, could calculate height from stride, was familiar with the identification of charred bone, and knew about physical traits associated with geographical differences.

However, underlying these forensic and biological aspects of anthropology (of which there are numerous examples in the Canon), Holmes was also keenly interested in human behavior and sought to comprehend why people behaved as they did. Perhaps this is why he kept bees in his retirement. Maybe he felt he could get at the root of human behavior by comprehending the complex social actions of bees. Modern social biologists still engage in studies such as these and apply their results to human interactions. Regardless, like Sherlock Holmes and as an anthropologist, I seek to understand human behavior. Why do we continue to marginalize those different from us? What are the broader health-related and social impacts of this process of othering? These are questions I have spent my career answering. My hope is that, like the great detective, my findings provide some form of justice, give a voice to those historically silenced, and initiate social change.

Carlina de la Cova (Columbia, South Carolina) is an assistant professor of anthropology at the University of South Carolina, with a research interest in forensic anthropology, Victorian medicine, and Watson's suggestion that the human femur has an "upper condyle." She also serves as a deputy county coroner.

THE ADVENTURE OF THE DISTANT FRIEND

ZSÓFIA MARINCSÁK

I love to read. As I remember, I was twelve when I first read the novels of Arthur Conan Doyle, beginning with *The Hound of the Baskervilles*. I was overwhelmed by the mystery and by the genius of Sherlock Holmes, and I was astonished by the unique methods he used to solve crimes. And, of course, the sleuth's special personality was also very attractive.

After that I got acquainted with the other adventures, and enjoyed them thoroughly. The first television adaptation I saw was the Granada Sherlock Holmes series starring Jeremy Brett. For me he is the perfect Holmes, the most definitive in the role. Over the years I have seen several other adaptations as well, but the Granada series remains the most loved one for me. I like to watch the episodes again and again, and I always find something new in them. I have also reread the novels many times, and they offer something new each and every occasion.

In Hungary, where I live, the name of the sleuth is widely known. Television channels showed most of the Holmes series, and you can still catch episodes of the Granada series now and then. The original stories and some of the latest pastiches are available in bookstores and you can purchase television or movie adaptations to watch at home, too.

In my own family, the assessment of Sherlock Holmes is variable. My father was a huge fan of the detective; he both liked the books and the different television adaptations, and enthusiastically followed the Granada series. My mother also read the novels, but she didn't like Jeremy Brett's Holmes. In my broader environment people are familiar with Sherlock's name, and younger people mention Benedict Cumberbatch as their definitive Holmes actor.

But there's so much more for which I can be grateful to the best-known detective in the world, not just the many enjoyable hours I have spent reading and watching. In particular I got to know a lovable girl, Adrienn Fray, because of Sherlock Holmes. She knows lots of things about the hero of Conan Doyle, and she encouraged me to found the Hungarian Sherlock Holmes Club together and to create an English website about the great sleuth.

We created sherlockian-sherlock.com to make Conan Doyle's immortal hero known as widely as possible. We wanted to show that Sherlock

Holmes is far more than a literary character. Of course he plays an extremely important role in literature, because lots and lots of people read his adventures around the world. But there are countless other themes that can be linked to him. We dedicate articles on the site to his famous creator, too. In relation to Holmes, it is essential to speak about the era in which he lived—that's why we deal with several aspects of the Victorian era in our writings. We show those famous personalities who were the models for Doyle in creating Holmes. He's not just a consulting detective, but a scientist as well, and he applied forensic science to solve his cases. For that reason we offer information on the first forensic scientist, Dr. Edmond Locard.

One cannot leave out the numerous pastiches, television and movie adaptations, and the effect the detective had on different branches of art. Because Jeremy Brett is one of our favourite Holmes actors, and because he is among the most well-known impersonators of the detective, it is a matter of course that we have several articles about him. We have an extensive piece on the many actors who have played Sherlock Holmes, and in a long article we list the most commonly believed errors around the character. Beyond all this, our site offers numerous interesting readings.

Through our common interest, Adrienn and I can talk wonderfully, but sadly just via online chat, because we live far from each other and we have met in person only twice. The shared work brought us really close, and I am proud to say that I have found a true and loyal friend in her. I can share my joy and sadness, we can talk about everything, and we always make decisions regarding our website together. And though we both have difficulties in our lives, it is a satisfaction to know that we can count on each other.

Zsófia Marincsák (Záhony, Hungary) lives quietly with her mother in a small town on the border with Ukraine. Her hobbies are reading and cross-stitching.

THE BOOK-CASE OF
SHERLOCK HOLMES

THE ADVENTURE OF
THE COLLECTION MANIA

DON HOBBS

There are two sorts of people in the world, those with the collecting gene and those without it. I definitely fall into the former category. When Sherlock Holmes tells Dr. Watson that Baron Adelbert Gruner "has the collection mania in its most acute form—and especially on this subject," it could have just as easily been my wife explaining me to any of her friends. I too have the collection mania in its most acute form, especially on the subject of foreign language translations of the Canon.

As long as I can remember, I have collected something. As a small boy it was rocks, small reptiles, baseball cards, and comic books. As a teenager, I progressed to record albums, surfer shirts, and girls' phone numbers. As a working adult, I began collecting books, and this eventually evolved into collecting Sherlock Holmes books. At first, I used the vacuum cleaner approach: I sucked up any and every book on Sherlock Holmes I came across. That is why I have a gazillion books today, worth about a nickel apiece. I soon revised my collecting criteria and started collecting with a more focused approach. I began buying books I could not read: foreign translations of the Canon.

This specialty might seem a bit quirky to many, but I did have sound reasoning behind my decision. The transition to foreign translation collector happened quite randomly, during a chance visit to a book fair in Austin, Texas, in 1991. It was there that I bought a circa 1920 edition of *Pies Baskerville'ów*. This Polish translation of *The Hound of the Baskervilles* was the first foreign language edition in my collection. At that same book fair I also bought a Spanish collection of short stories, *Las aventuras de Sherlock Holmes*.

The following week I was scheduled to visit John Bennett Shaw in Santa Fe, New Mexico. The invitation came via a phone call from John, who had heard I was a collector of Sherlock Holmes. I suppose that in the broadest sense of the term, it was true, but my meager collection was around 500 editions. I had read John was reportedly adding approximately 500 items a month to his amazing collection. Obviously I decided to accept his invitation.

After my arrival and all proper introductions were made, John took me to The Library (to me, it will always be The Library). Upon entering the room, an 18-by-18-foot square with shelving from the floor to the ceiling and books double-stacked, I found myself more in awe than ever before in my life. From time to time he would stop and pull out a specific volume and give me the short history behind that particular tome. I was amazed that not only did he know the story inside the book but also the story about the book and how it ended up in The Library.

Eventually we stopped in front of the shelves that featured translations. Back in 1991, there were 60 languages into which someone had translated at least one canonical story. Proud of my recent discoveries, I told him about the two books I had recently found in Austin. John was not familiar with either edition and began rifling through the shelves looking to see if they were there.

He owned neither! My first thought was how it could be possible that I owned books that he did not. He smiled at me and gave me one of his favorite axioms: "If you have one of something, gloat about it; if you have more than one, you should share." I was in a gloating mood because here was this neophyte Sherlockian collector standing in the Mecca of the Sherlockian World with possibly the world's greatest Sherlockian collector, knowing I owned something the great man did not own. (Eventually, years later, I found a second copy of the Spanish edition; but, sadly, it was too late to share it with John, who died in 1994, after sending the contents of The Library to the University of Minnesota.) But it was this experience that set the course I am on to this very day. This was when I became a serious collector of foreign translations.

Over the next 25 years I managed to expand the number of known languages to 108. To keep track of my ever-growing collection, I created "The Galactic Sherlock Holmes," an electronic bibliography. The GSH is not just my collection—with the blessing of Ronald B. De Waal, I extracted all of the foreign-language entries from his three mammoth bibliographies, *The World Bibliography of Sherlock Holmes*, *The International Bibliography of Sherlock Holmes*, and *The Universal Sherlock Holmes*. I combined these entries with those in my collection, placing them in alphabetical order by language. Then, they are arranged alphabetically and chronologically for each language. Finally, whenever possible, I add a book cover scan next to the bibliographic information. Therefore, Sherlockians who find a book they are unable to read will have a visual reference to guide them.

By its very nature, a bibliography becomes obsolete as soon as it is published. Because the GSH is electronic, when I find a new translation not listed in the GSH, regardless of when it was published, it can be added to its correct place in the listings. This eliminates the frustration of having "A," "B," and "C" entries as in the De Waal editions. Every few months I save the entire bibliography as a PDF, copy it to a medium such as a CD or flash drive, and distribute it on demand. I simply assign each saved version a number that is the year and month. So July 2016 would be GSH 16.7.

Of the many odd and interesting foreign translations I have added to my collection, several stand out particularly. I find the Inuit translation the most intriguing. *Baskervillekut kingmerssuat* was published in 1961 in Godthåb, Greenland, by Det Grønlandske Forlag. However, my first

Inuit edition was a reproduction published in 1999, limited to three copies. German Sherlockian Richard Kederele was visiting the National Museum of Denmark in Copenhagen in the mid-1990's. On display was the Inuit *Hound*. (Greenland is a territory of Denmark.) Mr. Kederele convinced the museum to allow him to photocopy the entire book. A couple of years later, he read about my collection mania and decided to publish a few copies of the book. Using a computer program that aligned the photocopied text, he produced three copies. The final page is dedicated to me as his inspiration. A few year ago, I tracked down an original 1961 edition.

One of my favorite stories is how I found a Macedonian translation. Using De Waal's bibliographies, I used to search the internet to try and find items I was missing from my collection. *Avanturite na Šerlok Holms* is listed in De Waal as the only Macedonian translation. Searching the internet for that title came up empty. Deciding to tackle the problem differently, I searched for Tome Momirovski, who was listed as the translator. I got a single hit for that name listed in the Macedonian Translators Union. This page also listed Mr. Momirovski's postal address, but no email listing. I wrote a letter asking if this Tome Momirovski was the same person who translated Sherlock Holmes in 1961. A month later, I received an email from his granddaughter. She said it was indeed her grandfather who did the translation as a graduate student. She said he was surprised and very happy someone remembered him for doing the translation. He apologized that he did not have any copies, nor did the university where he taught, but she said to rest assured that a Macedonian never forgets and they would find me a copy of the book.

A full year passed without further word from Bela, the granddaughter, or Tome. Then word came explaining that Bela had moved to London and her grandmother had passed away and her grandfather had been in mourning. But, she repeated, a Macedonian never forgets, and they would find a copy for me. She asked for my mailing address, which I provided.

Another year passed before I got an email from Bela that said they had found a copy and, again, please send her my mailing address. It seems that a Macedonian sometimes does forget, because nine months later, the book had not arrived. I sent Bela a message just to make sure the book had not been sent and thus lost. Six months later, she responded but not before asking me once again for my postal address, which I provided for the third time.

A few weeks later a signed copy of *Avanturite na Šerlok Holms* arrived in my mail box. I did not have the heart to tell Bela or Tome that in the four years it took to get the book, another Macedonia translation had been published: *A Skandal vo Bohemija* appeared in 2007.

The worldwide popularity of Sherlock Holmes can never be exaggerated. The lax enforcement of copyright laws since the earliest days has frequently allowed for the publishing of pirated editions of the tales. By 1891, there were Norwegian and Swedish editions, some authorized and some not. By 1893, Russian and Danish edition were available. The next year French and German translations were published.

To a collector, the process is never complete. There is always another edition to be found, catalogued, and added to the collection. There are plenty of languages without a canonical translation, and if one exists, there is a good chance I will eventually find it. It is just one of the many reasons I love being a Sherlockian—and especially one who collects books I cannot read.

Don Hobbs (Flower Mound, Texas) is a member of the Baker Street Irregulars, the Maniac Collectors, and other groups, and owns more than 6,000 books he cannot read. He works as an applications specialist for a radiology software company.

THE ADVENTURE OF THE GERMAN READERS

MARIA FLEISCHHACK

A couple of years ago I sat in my local Starbucks and giggled repeatedly and audibly while reading a slim volume. A girl approached me after a while, asking what I was reading that was so funny. I told her it was *A Study in Scarlet*, a Sherlock Holmes story. She did not seem to be familiar with it at all, though the name Sherlock Holmes seemed to ring a bell. She went to tell her parents, and I secretly hoped that she would start reading the stories—while simultaneously knowing that she would not find them quite as amusing as I did that day. I had just watched "A Study in Pink" and giggled at the brilliant way the adaptation had made use of quotations and references to the original stories.

That was also the year in which I realised that Sherlock Holmes was to become a household name for a new generation of Germans: high school and university students. The BBC's *Sherlock*, which had been available online and via imported DVD a long time before the German-dubbed version was shown on television and subsequently came out on DVD here, was a slow-burn success in Germany. However, because of the digital literacy of the students and free access to the internet, the growing fandom eventually took hold over here, too, and Sherlock Holmes, with the face of Benedict Cumberbatch, was once again a household name in Germany.

The Sherlock Holmes Canon was translated into German in its entirety in the 1960s (with early translations of selected stories appearing as early as 1903 and 1906) and is available in three different translations. Alas, all are riddled with mistakes, most of them resulting from a lack of understanding of British cultural conventions. In addition, Doyle's gorgeous prose and humour are often lost in translation. So while the books are widely read in Germany, though mainly by my grandparents' and parents' generation, they seem a bit stilted and dry to the younger generation.

Most famous, and very much unrelated to the Canon, is probably the German adaptation of the Austrian pastiche *Der Mann, der Sherlock Holmes War* (*The Man Who Was Sherlock Holmes*, 1937), in which two English detectives pretend to be Holmes and Watson in order to get more cases. Soon criminals, victims, and the police mistake them for the famous duo and they become involved in proper crimes, which they manage to partly solve. In the end, their identity theft is revealed and they find themselves in a courtroom. Arthur Conan Doyle personally saves them by revealing that Holmes and Watson are literary characters and not real people, and they walk free.

While this film is certainly the most famous German production, various plays, radio plays, and pastiches have been written and performed for the German market. Furthermore, most British adaptations have been dubbed and broadcast on German television. I remember watching a few episodes of the Granada series in German, and I have particularly fond memories of *Without a Clue*, which is still one of my favourite parodies. Interestingly, the first and third series of Granada Holmes were broadcast with German dubbing simultaneously in West Germany and the GDR in the late 1980s—in hindsight it's lovely to think about it as yet another uniting feature of Sherlock Holmes—bringing people together, even if they don't quite know it.

After I began teaching English literature at Leipzig University in 2010, I also taught some of the Sherlock Holmes stories and pastiches. At around this time, the BBC *Sherlock* had taken the UK by storm, but it was still relatively unknown in Germany beyond those who engaged in online fandom already, partly because the dubbing took a while, and partly because once it was broadcast, it was shown quite late in the evenings. So when I taught both *A Study in Scarlet* and "A Study in Pink" to a group of second semester undergrad students in 2011, showing them a few clips of the deductions and drawing attention to the direct quotations which were picked up by the series, some of my students immediately went out to buy the DVD.

Even though this was still the time before Netflix and Amazon video, internet fandom did a great service in spreading the word about the BBC series. By the arrival of series two, most of my students were not only familiar with the program, but proper fans. Their digital literacy allowed them to watch their favourite series in English and write about it online as well, which in turn had positive consequences for their language skills, as well as offering motivation to talk about these topics in university classes.

Teaching Sherlock Holmes stories to those students is now a joy, as they are familiar with the BBC adaptation (and most with Guy Ritchie's films as well) and are open not only to reading the original material, but also pastiches like Lyndsay Faye's *Dust and Shadow*, Mitch Cullin's *A Slight Trick of the Mind*, and Neil Gaiman's mashup "A Study in Emerald." Even though only a few years have passed since the first airing of *Sherlock*, it is quite obvious that young people have greater access to original content, and the market tries to accommodate these practices—merchandise for the BBC series has become largely available online, and the Canon stories have been republished in several new collections and forms. The new S. Fischer translation of the entire Canon by Henning Ahrens will be a very welcome new addition to the existing material.

When I was asked to write a German introduction to Sherlock Holmes which became *Die Welt des Sherlock Holmes* (*The World of Sherlock Holmes*), I realised that while there is a plethora of material available in the English-speaking world, very little secondary material has been published in Germany by Germans, apart from an out-of-print *Das umfassende Sherlock-Holmes-Handbuch* which had appeared in several editions, and several Wikipedia articles. As far as I am aware, there is a short excerpt of one Sherlock Holmes story in the English textbooks used by tenth-graders in the state of Saxony, but it is taken out of context and the stories themselves are not part of the syllabus.

Most Germans who have worked on Holmes took to the internet to write about the Canon, older adaptations, the Ritchie films, and the new series. While Michael Ross's bookshop Baskerville Bücher in Cologne specialises in Holmes and pastiche publication, there is still relatively little literary output. In fact, more academic books and essays on the Holmes stories, Arthur Conan Doyle, and detective fiction have been published than books that "play the game." A few pastiches have also been translated—among them Nick Rennison's *Sherlock Holmes: The Unauthorized Biography*, which has been repeatedly mistaken for an academic publication by students, Mattias Boström's brilliant *From Holmes to Sherlock* appeared in German in 2016, and some German authors have published their own Sherlock Holmes pastiches.

Yet, besides the generation of my students who came to the stories via the BBC adaptation, an even younger generation is growing up to know Sherlock Holmes rather as Cumberbatch than Brett or Rathbone. They are the children of the BBC series' fans. In late November 2016, I was invited to give a lecture on Sherlock Holmes for the Leipzig Children's University—a lecture series for nine- to twelve-year-olds. Our auditorium, which has 800 seats, was almost entirely full (though it was easier to spot the parents than the kids, some of whom could barely see over the tables in front of them) and one child proudly wore the deerstalker, announcing before the lecture that he had dressed up as Sherlock Holmes for this year's Fasching (carnival).

Most of these children, I realised, had seen the BBC series with their parents. Some of them were a bit confused that I used the Sidney Paget illustrations and screenshots of Brett to introduce Holmes's character and methods and not Benedict Cumberbatch's portrayal of Sherlock. Next to the BBC series, most kids seem to have watched the Sherlock Holmes films directed by Guy Ritchie as they could easily answer my question concerning Holmes's hiding place in the final scene of *A Game of Shadows* when he wears the chair's pattern as a disguise in Watson's study. A hilarious moment ensued when I showed them a collage of several different personifications of Holmes: The Great Mouse Detective, Tom and Jerry, Jeremy Brett (in several disguises), Vasily Livanov and Vitaly Solomin, Sherlock Hound, and a Japanese anime in which Holmes is a young girl.

They were quite fascinated to see just how many different versions there are of Holmes, especially that he could also be a girl (while none of them were in any way surprised that he could be a mouse or a dog). It was, in fact, delightful to see how many girls were visibly excited by that prospect, and several of them came to me afterwards to ask questions about detective work. It was heart-warming to see just how many kids were absolutely convinced that they would be a detective one day, several of them wanting to take up martial arts or at least look at things through a magnifying glass.

While I know that a lot of those children had been in previous contact with the stories, I do hope that my lecture inspired them to pick up the books and read the stories with a fresh, open mind, just as I hope that my regular students will continue to go back to the source material and read more than just the stories that my classes require. But, considering their digital literacy and their interest in the newest adaptations, and the fact that a new translation is now becoming available, I am sure that this generation will be quite aware of the many faces of Sherlock Holmes.

What remains to be said then, is that the character of Sherlock Holmes is quite popular in Germany, but perhaps the stories are not read as widely as they are in the English-speaking world. There are images of the deerstalker, pipe, and magnifying glass whenever a mystery is involved, math books and crossword puzzle books come with little images of Holmes, pipe and tobacco shops have the silhouette of Holmes on their placards. Sherlock Holmes is therefore immediately recognisable and definitely part of our cultural memory, but, as perhaps in many other places as well, far fewer people have read the stories than those who can identify the detective merely from his iconic features.

And yet, there is now a new generation who perhaps not only recognises the traditional image immediately, but also identifies the facial features, curls, and turned up collar as Sherlock Holmes—namely Cumberbatch's Sherlock, or, perhaps, what we could call, without any judgement, the millennial Sherlock.

Maria Fleischhack (Leipzig, Germany) is a research associate and lecturer in the Department of British Studies at Leipzig University. Her main research interests include the works of Shakespeare and late Victorian fiction as well as adaptation and film studies, and she regularly teaches classes on the Sherlock Holmes Canon and adaptations.

THE ADVENTURE OF
THE GRADUAL DEVOTEE

ALISTAIR DUNCAN

I won't lie: my introduction to Sherlock Holmes came via a certain Mr Basil Rathbone. Events conspired to ensure that I was in front of the television one day in 1982 when my mother changed channels to watch *The Scarlet Claw*. I became fascinated and ensured that I was in the same place every week afterwards to see the other films in the series. Naturally we eventually reached the end, and I was hungry for more.

My mother, in response to rather too many questions, mentioned that there were Sherlock Holmes books of which she had two. I asked to borrow one, and she ended up letting me read *The Adventures*. I got about two pages into "A Scandal in Bohemia" and closed the book in confusion. This was not the Holmes I had been watching on screen. In a strange way I felt betrayed. I felt entitled to more adventures of the amazing detective who battled Nazis and glowing men. I wanted more comedy moments with the silly Dr Watson. I wanted them now, and these stories were not giving me what I wanted.

Rathbone had lit a fire of interest in me for Holmes (or a version of Holmes), but without fuel it was a fire that was destined to die. I had to wait two years for that fuel—and it probably came just in time.

My mother had long had an interest in crime fiction and always made a point of watching new screen adaptations. Holmes was by no means her favourite (she is a devotee of Agatha Christie) but she was the first to notice, during early 1984, that a new ITV adaptation of Sherlock Holmes was due to be broadcast, starring Jeremy Brett. To the best of my recollection I gave the news a cautious welcome. I struggled to believe any adaptation could reach the bar set by Rathbone and Bruce. I very much feared an adaptation that would be as bad as I then felt the books to be. What's more, I had never heard of Jeremy Brett. On reflection this was no bad thing, as it ensured I had no expectations of his performance other than his need to live up to the standards of Rathbone.

The series began its UK broadcast on April 24, 1984 (thanks IMDB.com), and it very helpfully commenced with "A Scandal in Bohemia". I recall being initially disappointed, as this was the story that had spoiled Holmes for me, but it was also a blessing as it was the only written canonical tale I had even a passing familiarity with. Much to my surprise, I found myself getting completely absorbed in the programme. Partly this was due to the adherence to the story (what I knew of it) and the wonderful period setting, but it was mostly down to the sheer power of Brett's performance.

I came away from that first episode thoroughly impressed and with a renewed desire to read the books. I almost immediately reread "A Scandal in Bohemia" and was surprised to find that Brett had replaced Rathbone as the Holmes of my imagination. This, more than anything else, demonstrated to me the effect that Brett's performance as Holmes had on me.

However, it was not all down to Brett. As fond as I was of Nigel Bruce's silly Watson, I was blown away by the wonderful performance of David Burke as the dependable and not remotely silly Watson. For me Burke remains *the* Dr Watson—far eclipsing any performance before or since for his sheer fidelity to the character, compared to other actors.

It is completely true to say that the Sherlockian and Doylean I am today is down to the impact of Jeremy Brett on my view of Holmes. Basil Rathbone showed me a window on Holmes's world, but Jeremy Brett unlocked the door and let me in.

I watched all the episodes that Granada produced and bought (or sought as gifts) VHS videos of the series as they came out. Above and beyond this, I acquired copies of all the original stories and read them all from end to end. Without really realising it I had become a collector of Sherlockiana and was acquiring a solid knowledge of the Great Detective.

Despite all this, I was not a member of any societies. Holmes was my guilty pleasure and not one that was popular with my peers. To them the Granada series was just a period drama in much the same bracket as Dickens, Austen, and Brontë, and was something for girls. Once I became aware of their displeasure, I took my interest underground in the sense that I kept it to myself. In addition, being told that I was into something uncool prevented me from seeking out like-minded people. In fact I convinced myself, without any evidence, that my interest must be rare to the point of non-existent in people my own age.

The years that followed saw me work my way through school, college, and university. Holmes remained a part of my life but not one that consumed a lot of my time. It was not until I entered the world of work that Holmes gained more of my attention. Even then, I did not seek out societies. I was too conditioned to believe, even then, that my interest was out of step with my peers.

A pivotal point came in 2002 when my mother and I had a phone call in which we discussed her imminent retirement. During the course of the conversation she listed a number of things she was keen to do once she gave up her job. This got me thinking and I realised, much to my distress, that I had no real ambitions. After a few weeks' thought I decided that I wanted to write a book. I had no idea what such a book would be about, and that was as far as the idea got.

The years that immediately followed saw both professional and private ups and downs. Jobs came and went. Relationships came and went. In early 2004 I became engaged, and my wife and I were married at the end of 2005. Life settled down in 2006 and I began to return more enthusiastically to the Sherlockian world. This manifested itself in collecting. I had led a relatively transitory existence since graduation and tended to almost live out of a suitcase, but now I was, in the words of Dr Watson, a man who was "master of his own establishment" (okay, not quite master, I'm more 21st century in my attitudes than that). I was settled enough, and had the money, to collect again.

In March 2007, during a visit to my parents, I had an epiphany. I could write a book about Sherlock Holmes. On the train journey back to London I began to sketch out a structure for the book. The following month I overcame my fears and joined the Sherlock Holmes Society of London. I was not an active participant at that stage—I was simply content to read the twice-yearly journal.

In February of 2008 my first book, *Eliminate the Impossible*, came out. It had its supporters and detractors and I won't claim it was an original concept (very few Sherlockian books can claim to be totally original) but it was favourably commented on by Roger Johnson in the SHSL newsletter. This kick-started a conversation between us which led to Roger providing me with an invaluable reading list and much useful advice (a service he continues to provide). Four more books followed, as did a number of articles that were given an audience courtesy of several global journals.

Overall, my initial writings were well received, and this positive reception encouraged me to show my face at society events. Since 2009 I have attended numerous such events, given talks on Holmes and his creator, and been honoured with awards and nominations for my scribblings. I have also made many good contacts in the Sherlockian world, some of whom have gone on to become friends.

Not all the books I've written have focused on Holmes. In 2009 I joined the small subset of Holmes fans who have gone on to show serious interest in his creator. For me this interest in Arthur Conan Doyle arose while writing my first two books. Each of them contained a certain amount of biographical information on Doyle, and I became more and more interested in him during my researches.

A few months after the publication, in 2009, of my second book, *Close to Holmes*, I was itching to write something more and it occurred to me to have a go at a biography of Doyle. I had no desire to chronicle his entire life and it took a little time for an idea to occur to me. At the time I was living in South Norwood, where Doyle himself had lived, and the period he had lived in the area was one of the least documented as far as I could tell from the biographies I had read up to that point.

I sensed an opportunity to plug this gap and I felt that I was well placed (in geographical terms, at least) to make the attempt. The result of my efforts was *The Norwood Author*, which was published in 2010 and received the 2011 Tony and Freda Howlett Award from the Sherlock Holmes Society of London.

As the writing of *The Norwood Author* was coming to its end I became aware of the plight of Undershaw, Doyle's former home in Surrey, and became involved with the Undershaw Preservation Trust, headed by John Gibson. Lynn Gale, who was, effectively, Gibson's deputy, suggested to me that I ought to write a biography on the Surrey years of Doyle's life. I was reluctant but eventually gave in. Approximately 18 months later saw the publication of *An Entirely New Country*.

I was more than content to stop there, which I think frustrated some people who wanted to see me finish the job and, as it were, see Doyle all the way to his grave. I was hesitant for two reasons. The first of these was the sheer scale of the work to be done. *The Norwood Author* had been the account of three and a half years. *An Entirely New Country* had covered ten years. Following the same pattern meant that the next book would have to cover 23 years. It was something I found daunting to say the least.

That said, what scared me most was Spiritualism. The subject dominated Doyle's life during those last 23 years—especially post-1916. It was an area of his life that had tripped up more than one of his biographers. I always felt that it had done so because these writers had a position on the subject, be it pro or con, and they had allowed this perspective to dictate the tone of their writing. I felt that, regardless of personal viewpoint, it had to be handled in a neutral fashion. Regrettably, I felt unequal to the task.

For the best part of three years I continued to avoid the idea. However, throughout those years I was itching for a subject to write about and was failing to come up with anything that had any mileage in it. In the end I rolled up my sleeves and got on with facing my fears. I declared my disbelief in Spiritualism at the beginning and then went on to treat it as dispassionately as possible. The result, in August 2015, was *No Better Place*. I was praised for my even-handed coverage of Spiritualism and was short-listed for the 2016 Tony and Freda Howlett Award.

As you can see, many links make up this long chain of events; but, for me, the most significant is Jeremy Brett. For me, he simply *is* Sherlock Holmes. We Sherlockians get pretty close to elevating our favourite Holmes actors to the status of gods. In my case, Jeremy Brett is the Zeus of that particular Olympus. Without him and his influence, my interest in Holmes (and later Doyle) would have been a mere flicker and my life a lot less rich.

Alistair Duncan (Surrey, England) is the author of five books on Sherlock Holmes and Arthur Conan Doyle. A former Council member of the Sherlock Holmes Society of London, he is also a member of the Sydney Passengers and the Conan Doyle (Crowborough) Establishment.

THE REMARKABLE AFFAIR
OF THE AGONY COLUMN

DIANE GILBERT MADSEN

"I blame it on Sherlock Holmes," my mother said when she wanted me to do the dishes and found me hiding somewhere with my nose in a Sherlock Holmes story. Yes, I liked him more than I liked washing dishes. I still do. In fact, I liked him more than almost anything, and I consider myself lucky to have found him when I was very young. I'd walk to our local library each week and bring home a stack of books. One week I read "The Musgrave Ritual" and was immediately hooked on the world's first consulting detective. After that, I eagerly read every story, and thankfully there were many. Sherlock Holmes fueled my lifelong interest in the Victorian age, in the Restoration, in puzzles, codes, and in manners, murder, mystery, and mayhem.

Learning that Sherlock Holmes was based on Dr. Joe Bell, a real person, caused my interest in him to persist and spread. Posters of Sherlock Holmes and his London filled my walls. My brother Albert, now a noted wildlife artist, sketched out a scene based on a drawing in *Collier's Magazine* depicting Holmes and Watson in 221B Baker Street. At school, everyone knew I was an avid Sherlockian. I lobbied hard to get brand new microscopes at school, and I always carried a magnifying glass in my purse. Looking back, I must have expected a crime to be committed so I could investigate and solve it. While others my age were dating and listening to rock and roll, I was doing scientific experiments. To this day, don't ask my family about planaria and the State Science Fair. I even began assembling my own agony column, with bizarre and unusual news clippings based on my fascination with the agony column in the *Times* that Sherlock Holmes faithfully read. Friends and relatives still send me articles of curious incidents to include in my collection.

You might imagine that it's harder for a girl than a boy to like Sherlock Holmes. Not true. In my dreams I didn't want to fall in love with Sherlock Holmes, nor did I want to be a female Sherlock Holmes. No. I wanted to *be* Sherlock Holmes. In some ways perhaps it's easier for a girl to fully appreciate, embrace, and respond to the quirkiness of Sherlock's personality. He's so smart, compelling, and unique that he takes your breath away, and you want to be just like him.

After I had a full-time job, the first books I purchased were the two volumes of Baring-Gould's *Annotated Sherlock Holmes*, well worn and still on my shelves today. My first checking account was with Barclay's Bank, which offered special Sherlock Holmes checks. My first ambition was to become one of the Irregulars, but alas it was sadly still an all-male group. One truly memorable event in my life was meeting Ely M. Liebow, a great Sherlockian, and discussing with him Sherlock Holmes, Arthur Conan Doyle, and Dr. Joe Bell. Another was meeting Tom Joyce, a talented Sherlockian and rare book seller in Chicago, and being fascinated by his involvement in the world of Sherlock Holmes and all things arcane.

In all the Holmes stories I was amazed and excited by the breadth and depth of knowledge Sherlock Holmes displayed. This trait made him not just a detective, but a unique and great one. Poisons, tobaccos, early English charters, the ancient Cornish language, fingerprints, bloodstains, horseshoes, even Faber pencils, all evince the cachet of a savant. It's why we expect him to unerringly uncover the truth. It's why today we recognize Holmes as the first forensic scientist. That first story I read, "The Musgrave Ritual," piqued my lifelong interest in ciphers, in the Stuarts and the 17th century with its royal intrigues, the Scottish influence, and a monarch restored to the throne. Stories in which Holmes uses disguise, such as "A Scandal in Bohemia," are among the best, as are stories with animals—both domestic and exotic—especially when they end up doing murder. Other stories I particularly enjoy involve the burgeoning new discoveries of the Victorian age, such as bicycles, trains, typewriters, and photographs. Learning about the history of these inventions was one of my favorite pastimes, and my friends laughingly called me "the encyclopedia."

When I married, my husband Tom and I joined Chicago's Criterion Bar Association, and we still treasure the Cri Bar coffee mugs we were awarded on Outrageous Theories night when we produced a genealogy "proving" that Mycroft and Sherlock were the last of the deposed Stuart line. (Remember that Mycroft "will receive neither honour nor title, but remains the most indispensible man in the country.... His position is unique. He has made it for himself. There has never been anything like it before, nor will be again.... Again and again his word has decided national policy." It was a fact!)

Conan Doyle himself was an intriguing person. I loved his writing style and his clever plots and the clues he used. When he killed off Holmes at Reichenbach Falls, I was amazed that he did not foresee the flak he was destined to receive from all quarters. Sherlock Holmes would have predicted it, but Doyle completely underestimated the outpouring of great affection for his singular detective and the long-lasting impression he would make on the world.

With a master's degree in 17th-century English literature as well as an ongoing fascination with Sherlock Holmes and crime, it was inevitable that I would grow up to write mystery stories. My husband Tom swears that I walk, talk, eat, and sleep mysteries. My mother tells him that I've been that way all my life, and when my first mystery story was published, she wasn't surprised and once again commented, "I blame it all on Sherlock Holmes."

I started writing the DD McGil Literati Mystery Series, which uses events in well-known authors' lives and projects the results to current times and crimes, all to be resolved by heroine DD McGil. I often use articles from my accumulated agony column in my mystery novels, and I included Tom Joyce as a character in the series—the character my agent likes the best. After publishing several books, I was looking for another plot. My husband Tom, knowing my lifelong interest in Sherlock Holmes, suggested Arthur Conan Doyle. I initially rejected the idea as being presumptuous, but then, encouraged by my brother Albert, began considering it. I tackled the mystery of why Conan Doyle had nothing to say about the identity of his contemporary, Jack the Ripper, even though the case caused a sensation in London and throughout the world, and even though Doyle had a penchant in later years for solving real cases. The result was my third book, *The Conan Doyle Notes: The Secret of Jack the Ripper*. When I started the book, I placed a photo of Conan Doyle on my desk next to my computer and, using the Sherlockian method, I assembled a series of clues—clues I believe that Conan Doyle and Joe Bell, and by extension Sherlock Holmes, would have used to help solve the case. Information that my old friend Ely Liebow reveals in his book on Joe Bell was instrumental in developing part of the plot for *The Conan Doyle Notes*.

As might be expected, this wasn't the end of the story. While researching that book, I was struck by the variety of Holmes plots and the many different outcomes of the crimes. Some wrongdoers were severely punished, while others, even murderers, were excused by Holmes or escaped, and never faced the law or punishment. I was also struck by the various crimes Holmes and Watson committed in their quest for justice. So I decided to write a book on my findings and musings. *Cracking the Code of the Canon: How Sherlock Holmes Made His Decisions* is the result, and it covers Sherlock Holmes's attitude toward justice and how he handles the crimes, villains, victims, and police. Several friends as well as experts in British law lent their expertise. Coincidentally, the jacket cover is that very same sketch my brother Albert made back in high school of Holmes and Watson in 221B where "it's always 1895."

While I was working on *Cracking the Code*, I realized that many of my current likes, dislikes, passions, and prejudices can be traced to those I formed early on reading the Canon as a young girl. I still enjoy re-reading the Holmes adventures, and was recently captured by the idea that Sherlock Holmes had gotten himself engaged to Agatha the housemaid in "Charles Augustus Milverton," so I have written a Holmes pastiche entitled *Sherlock Holmes and the Queen of Hearts*. I do hope that future generations will get the same enjoyment and become enthusiasts of Holmes, Watson, and Conan Doyle as I have been.

The only thing missing in my history with Sherlock Holmes is that I was born in Chicago and not in London. Had I been a Londoner, I would have had the chance to walk in the footsteps of my fictional hero and visit many of the places I've read about and researched. I'd have hoisted a pint at the Sherlock Holmes Pub and spent a night at the Sherlock Holmes Hotel and visited 221B Baker Street and Simpson's on the Strand. Had I moved to London, undoubtedly my mother would have said, "I blame it all on Sherlock Holmes."

Diane Gilbert Madsen (Cape Haze, Florida) attended the University of Chicago and Roosevelt University, and spent many years in government jobs ranging from deputy village clerk in a town of 60,000 to director of economic development for the state of Illinois. She is now a consultant and a Sherlockian author.

THE ADVENTURE OF
THE GASLIT EDITOR

CHARLES PREPOLEC

I blame Ron De Waal and William S. Baring-Gould, on top of Arthur Conan Doyle, Doc Savage, comic books, a lifelong love affair with film, an innate weakness towards the wallet-emptying disease known as "collecting", and the timely heartbreak of a teenage romance ending, for making me the Sherlockian I am today.

For me, being a Sherlockian is all about the words, pictures, and people. It's about community. It's about sharing my love for a subject and adding, or giving something back, to the pool from which I've drawn, and continue to derive, so much pleasure. It's surprising to look back over the last 30-plus years to see just how much my life has been influenced by the world of Sherlock Holmes since fate handed me a particular comic book in the mid '80s. But I'm getting ahead of myself.

Once upon a time, in the 1970s, I was a nerdy only-child who found companionship in the pages of comic books at an early age. Through the medium I was introduced to the collecting bug—a compulsion to gather all the material in a given field or on a particular subject. In the pages of comic books, I met a character named Doc Savage, a 1930's pulp hero, whose original adventures were then being reprinted by Bantam books, so I progressed from collecting comics to paperback books. That brought me to Phil Farmer's *Doc Savage: His Apocalyptic Life*, a meta-fiction biography of the character that worked in Farmer's whole Wold-Newton universe linking a large variety of literary characters into one family tree. On one of the branches lurked some fellow named Sherlock Holmes. I felt compelled to investigate further, and so, at about ten or eleven years old, I read *The Hound of the Baskervilles*. Hated it. I wanted to read about Sherlock Holmes, but he wasn't even in half the book, so I wasn't impressed and didn't read any other Holmes stories.

A little less than a decade later I was in a comic shop and spotted a Dan Day cover on a new series called *Cases of Sherlock Holmes*. I picked it up for the art, which was spectacular, but was equally intrigued by the format. This series used Arthur Conan Doyle's original text running around the art, rather than being an abridged adaptation with dialogue balloons. It was my first exposure to ACD's short Sherlock Holmes stories. I promptly bought a copy of *The Adventures of Sherlock Holmes*. At about that time I had my first big teenage relationship come to a bitter end and was pretty depressed about it, so when I read the opening of "A Scandal in Bohemia" and was hit with the business about Irene Adler "of dubious and questionable memory" being *the* woman, and how the softer emotions were "a distracting factor which might throw a doubt upon all his mental results", I was hooked. Happily, the Jeremy Brett Granada Sherlock Holmes series was just hitting television screens, so yes, my love for Holmes came about largely through coincidental timing and the complete disintegration of my teenage love life.

In Holmes, I found a superhero with seemingly attainable powers, a beacon of rationality to inspire me to find order in my own disordered world, and some damned fine writing as a bonus. The collector's bug bit deep, and it wasn't long before I stumbled across two titles that truly changed everything about how I viewed Sherlock Holmes. These were *The Annotated Sherlock Holmes*, by William S. Baring-Gould and *The World Bibliography of Sherlock Holmes*, by Ronald De Waal. With the former, I discovered that other folks took this character seriously too and there were "Writings About the Writings". With the latter I discovered just how much writing there actually was and learned the meaning of a delectable new word to me—pastiche—but more importantly, I learned that there were such things as Sherlock Holmes societies! It's a revelatory and eye-opening experience to suddenly discover that you are not alone. It feeds a desire to connect and compare, to move from the solitary "I like" to "he or she likes" to "they like" and finally the much desired and inclusive "we like". De Waal provided addresses for these societies, so I took pen to paper and naively sent out letters across the globe. Responses arrived from all quarters, often with little souvenirs enclosed, and I ended up on newsletter lists, subscribed to journals, ordered booksellers' catalogues, and became part of the receiving end of the Sherlockian grapevine. I learned about the Baker Street Irregulars, of what it is to be a scion society, of the Canadian umbrella group the Bootmakers of Toronto, and thanks to a timely newspaper article in the summer of 1987, of a society that had recently started up in my home city of Calgary. So, that September, at the age of 21, a year or two after picking up that singular comic, I joined my first Sherlock Holmes scion society and took tentative steps on the path towards being a Sherlockian. What I didn't see coming was how the path I'd chosen would so strongly affect the rest of my life.

There I was, a university student majoring in history and education, with a mind completely tuned to the world of Sherlock Holmes. I had a hero and literature that spoke to me, and I was utterly pleased to be learning about this amazing new/old world. I wanted desperately to be part of it all somehow. Of course, things got fairly thin on the ground fairly quickly in a city the size of Calgary, so I was relying more and more heavily on mail order for treasure from mystery and detective fiction specialty shops. A thought struck and a light clicked on. Calgary did not have a mystery or detective fiction specialty shop, but maybe it should? So, in June of 1989 I opened Mad For a Mystery Books. This was the first major life change initiated by my exposure to Sherlock Holmes. I now had a vested interest in Sherlock Holmes. Unfortunately, I was a better collector than seller, so I ended up closing the doors after only five years, but not before accumulating and reading hundreds of Sherlockian pastiches, to say nothing of befriending a publisher's rep named Jeff Campbell.

It was a happy time for me. I was active with our local scion, I was gaining knowledge about the Sherlockian world, I was becoming known in Calgary as "the Sherlock Holmes guy". I was invited to speak at a local school, I had an actor turn up looking for insight on playing Holmes in a then forthcoming play, I was in touch with Sherlockian book dealers and specialty publishers in the USA, Canada, and the UK, and I even ended up selling books to the legendary John Bennett Shaw. This was me being a Sherlockian. This was, I naively thought at the time, me giving back to the Sherlockian community in some way, even if there was an element of financial gain attached.

When I closed the doors for the last time in the mid '90s I was at a loss as to how I could continue making myself useful to the world of Sherlock Holmes. And that really was a palpable concern, as I had decided on contributing to the wealth of material. One day seeing my name immortalized in print amongst the greats in some future volume of De Waal's ever-expanding bibliography was somehow important to me, even if I had no idea how I might achieve that goal.

Since I could draw a bit, and I was feeling inspired by the wonderful annual cards issued by Jerry Margolin, I decided that I would sketch various Sherlockian actors and issue my own card every Christmas. Maybe after twelve years I'd produce a calendar featuring the first dozen drawings. The film books of David Stuart Davies, Robert Pohle, Chris Steinbrunner, Peter Haining, and others became my guides, and I devoured everything I could about the media presence of Holmes. I also discovered *Scarlet Street* magazine, with its regular coverage of Holmes film material. Then, one day, there was the internet, and the world was at my fingertips.

While there were certainly many individuals who were keen on the internet (Chris Redmond and Willis Frick come to mind), Sherlockian societies, on the whole, were a tad slow embracing the online world. I saw an opportunity to make a difference and launched Bakerstreetdozen.com, a site for our local scion, but more importantly a focus for my own Sherlockian output. I began writing reviews of pastiches, articles profiling various actors, and guides to DVD releases, and when the Matt Frewer television films started production, I got in touch with the production company looking for info to share with the wider Sherlockian world. That, in turn, lead to the publication of my telephone interviews with Frewer, Welsh, and the director, alongside a review, appearing in *Scarlet Street* magazine, my first professionally published work. Shortly thereafter, because of my film interests, I ended up editing news for actor Christopher Lee's official website. I was still drawing, and had produced a couple of Christmas cards, but my focus had swung from pictures back to words.

In those younger days I was a rather too serious and traditionally minded Sherlockian and so was unimpressed with a great number of pastiches I'd been reading. Fortuitously, I got together for drinks with my old publisher's rep and friend, Jeff Campbell, and by the end of that meeting, after multiple "Can we do this? Sure, we can" moments, we'd decided to produce a print journal of Sherlockian short fiction written by Sherlockians, for Sherlockians. We sent out the call for stories, Phil Cornell came aboard to provide art, and thus was born *Curious Incidents: Being a Collection of the Further Adventures of Sherlock Holmes*. Two former Canadian booksellers, an Australian artist, and an online community of writers had produced a Sherlock Holmes book, however amateurish. We got it into a few specialty shops in Toronto, New York, and Seattle, and sold the rest through eBay and direct mail order through bakerstreetdozen.com. Selling out in a matter of months, we began work on Volume 2 for release in 2003.

Thanks to *Curious Incidents* contributor, friend, and Edmonton Sherlockian, the late Peter H. Wood, I found myself invited to the 2003 annual dinner of the Baker Street Irregulars. My first ever Sherlockian event, and it just happened to be on my Sherlockian bucket list! For the first time, but not the last, I was truly amongst my tribe, and I was more star-struck and nervous than I'd ever been around film or television actors. Here was Susan Rice, there was Brad Keefauver, or the Rodens, and hey, isn't that Jerry Margolin? These were some of the people I'd practically worshipped for their contributions to the ongoing legacy of Sherlock Holmes. I felt like a total fraud for my own efforts in such company, but that was down to my own insecurities as everyone was utterly marvelous throughout my first BSI weekend and every other I've attended since then. To my everlasting amusement, when I discussed *Curious Incidents*, and my plans for a second volume, with a couple of Sherlockian publishers that weekend, both told me never to print more than 100 copies as I'll be sitting on them for years. We promptly published 150 copies of Volume 2 and 50 additional copies of Volume 1, and once again sold out in less than six months.

Instead of a third volume, Jeff and I turned our minds towards producing a Holmes/horror mash-up anthology. Rather than publish it ourselves, we arranged a meeting with Brian Hades, head of Edge Science Fiction and Fantasy Publishing, plunked the two volumes of *Curious Incidents* on the table, and said we'd like to do something similar with a fantasy/horror theme, but we'd like you to publish it. As Harry Potter had been a success in print and on screen for a number of years, and two different Sherlock Holmes films had just been announced as going into production, he readily, and sensibly, agreed. We had a publisher, a waiting market, and most importantly, a budget that meant I could ask professional writers, whose work I had read and admired, for stories. We got Barbara Hambly to open and Kim Newman to close the book, with a mix of other authors and a couple of Sherlockians along to round it out, plus wonderful illustrations again by Phil Cornell. *Gaslight Grimoire: Fantastic Tales of Sherlock Holmes* launched at the 2008 World Fantasy Convention (which fortuitously featured Barbara Hambly as guest of honor) and sold out its initial print run of 2,000 copies within seven weeks. Even before the launch our publisher had requested a follow-up volume (which became *Gaslight Grotesque: Nightmare Tales of Sherlock Holmes* and in turn begat *Gaslight Arcanum: Uncanny Tales of Sherlock Holmes*), so I was able to actually ask a good many writers for stories in person. The one thing that was driven home to me as a commissioning editor is that almost every writer I approached had at least a respect for, or was inspired on some level by, Sherlock Holmes stories and was pleased as punch to have an opportunity to write one. The realization that not only was I giving something back to the community, but empowering certain writers to do so too, still stands as the ultimate expression of what it means to me to be a Sherlockian.

Ten years on from *Gaslight Grimoire* and I'm pleased to be working on a fourth "Gaslight" volume. As always, even after 30 years, it's about sharing the love and giving something back to the community that has given me so much joy and many friendships and shaped the world within which I live and work. Being able to give back words and pictures? That to me is being a Sherlockian.

Charles Prepolec (Calgary, Alberta) is co-editor, with J. R. Campbell, of five Sherlock Holmes anthologies, as well as works about Professor Challenger and other science fiction. He is a member of the Bootmakers of Toronto and other societies.

THE ADVENTURE OF
THE CULTURAL LEGACY

TOM UE

I research, teach courses, and supervise dissertations in the Department of English at the University of Toronto Scarborough, where I am currently the Banting Postdoctoral Fellow and a Lecturer. I also hold an appointment at University College London as an Honorary Research Fellow in the Bentham Project in the Faculty of Laws. My interests, both in teaching and in scholarship, have concentrated on the close correspondence between canonical and less canonical Victorian writers, the commonalities and differences in their thinking, and the persistence of their concerns in our own times. I regularly incorporate Sherlock Holmes, his contemporaries, his disciples, and his incarnations into my teaching, with the aims of introducing Arthur Conan Doyle's and his contemporaries' oeuvre to new generations of students and encouraging existing fans to revisit the Canon afresh.

In my 2011 Cameron Hollyer Memorial Lecture, I explored some of the connections among Conan Doyle, Shakespeare, and George Meredith, and traced some of the (dis)continuities in their reading practices. Teaching and lecturing on Holmes have broadened my own thinking, furnished me with fresh insights, and tasked me with new research questions. I have consequently contributed entries to a number of works of scholarly reference, most recently the *Companion to Victorian Popular Fiction* (McFarland), edited by my friend and colleague Kevin Morrison, and reviews and features to periodicals such as the *Times Literary Supplement*.

As for many others, my earliest run-in with Holmes was with *The Hound of the Baskervilles*, a novel that I found—and continue to find—endlessly fascinating. Although, in early readings, I was drawn to its red herrings, Conan Doyle's evocative descriptions of the moor, and the story's pacing, further encounters with the text and conversations with students, colleagues, and fellow Holmesians have spurred me to attend to its treatment of ethics and its use of the epistolary form, something that seems inextricably intertwined.

Nicholas Ferguson's *Young Sherlock: The Mystery of the Manor House* (1982) and Barry Levinson's *Young Sherlock Holmes* (1985) led me to think more about the fictional biographies that have been created for Holmes by his fans, while exposure to a great many different Holmeses on screen prompted me constantly to shift my allegiances. The six-book series

Boy Sherlock Holmes (2007-12), by the Canadian novelist Shane Peacock, followed by a succession of excellent pastiches, inspired me to develop a major research project to frame and explore some of these texts in a more collaborative context.

Supported by the Joint Faculty Institute of Graduate Studies, the Public Engagement Unit, and the Volunteering Services Unit at UCL, *Sherlock Holmes: Past and Present* began as a series of four international conferences that encourages Holmes enthusiasts into sharing their insights. The events brought together more than 200 academics and members of the public and attest to the global interest in Conan Doyle's writing as well as the numerous critical and theoretical frameworks in which he is under consideration. The four meetings not only have explored previously under-examined aspects of the Canon, including its incorporation of earlier texts and its response to the dramatic social and cultural changes in the Victorian period, but have revealed the cross-pollination between Holmes and his contemporaneous sleuths, between Conan Doyle and his contemporaries, between Holmes and his disciples, and between Holmes and his adaptations across numerous periods and cultures.

I have discussed some of my own findings in *Newsday* and *The Times*, and my Facebook and Twitter channels continue to be important forums whereby research and information relating to Holmes, the Victorians, and cultural studies are widely disseminated, reaching a weekly audience of over 12,000 readers. This forum encourages creative writers to share their work-in-progress and fosters collaborations amongst Holmesians.

In response to the enthusiasm of contributors and readers, I am in the process of editing two works: a collection of essays titled *Mapping Conan Doyle's Modernities: 1887-1929* (Manchester University Press) and a special issue of the *Journal of Popular Film and Television* on "Imagining Sherlock Holmes". The former argues for Conan Doyle's literary and cultural importance. It attends to his stories about Holmes and Professor Challenger with particular focus on his changing attitude to issues such as narration, form, and literariness; print and material contexts; and faith and identities. Underscoring fundamental features of modernism and modernity, while showing how they combine the Romantic imagination with Enlightenment reason, this anthology provides helpful context for students, scholars, and enthusiasts. My own essay is partially motivated by my own experience of Holmes. I return to *The Hound* to explore the ethical implications of Holmes's delay in apprehending Stapleton, reveal some of the commonalities in *The Hound* and Twain's "A Double-Barrelled Detective Story" (1902), and explore the extent to which Conan Doyle's and Twain's concerns about ethics were in the air.

If *Mapping Conan Doyle's Modernities* has focused on Holmes in the Victorian and Edwardian periods, then the five essays in *Imagining Sherlock Holmes* are somewhat more forward-looking. This issue of the *Journal of Popular Film and Television* responds to the global interest levelled at Holmes and reassesses his cultural legacy on screen. This journal issue addresses Holmes's metaverse, positioning some of his extensions in relation to different sociocultural climates, and brings together essays on the modes for approaching Holmes's popularity, on issues of "authenticity" and "faith," and on the relations between reality, fiction, and metafiction. The issue analyzes a wide range of adaptations including James Hill's *A Study in Terror* (1965), Paul Morrissey's *The Hound of the Baskervilles* (1978), Bob Clark's *Murder by Decree* (1979), Mark Gatiss and Steven Moffat's *Sherlock* (2010-), and Bill Condon's *Mr. Holmes* (2015), based on Mitch Cullin's 2005 novel *A Slight Trick of the Mind*.

My own essay juxtaposes *Sherlock* and *London Spy* (2015) to reveal how the two series characteristically tax their central focalizers' (and the viewers') trust and, in so doing, argue for the importance of taking a leap of faith—in essence, a (re)turn to trust. This rhetorical move, I suggest, separates *Sherlock* from the Holmes stories, where Watson could rely more comfortably on demonstrations of Holmes's abilities.

What I cherish most about more than a decade's work on Holmes is the friendships and collaborations with his fans, the most generous and supportive of communities. I have benefited significantly from discussing Conan Doyle's creation with Holmesians of many stripes, from the comic book artist Daniel Corey to the Canadian theatre director Andrew Shaver, and from journalist and scholar Michael Dirda to the playwright Simon Stephens. I constantly rely on Steven Rothman for stimulating conversations about Victorian writers and matters relating to book history, Peggy Perdue for research help, and Ian Duncan and Michael Saler for supportive reading.

I look forward to exploring the new and emerging creative work of so many Holmesians: Corey's *Moriarty: Endgame VR* (2017) is an immersive Virtual Reality version of his comic book, and Peter Davidson has directed a short-film adaptation of the Professor Challenger story "The Disintegration Machine" (1929). In his introduction to the conference that inaugurated *Sherlock Holmes: Past and Present*, John Mullan argues that we are as separated from Holmes as we are in awe of him, that we are, in fact, closer to Watson. Our community of Watsons, I think, has both embraced the enjoyment of the Canon and greatly expanded the knowledge economy on the character, his creator, and Victorian literature. I, for one, will relish my return to that "long, low curve of the melancholy moor."

Tom Ue is a postdoctoral fellow at the University of Toronto (Scarborough). His 2011 Cameron Hollyer Memorial Lecture at the Toronto Public Library was titled "Sherlock Holmes and Shakespeare".

THE ADVENTURE OF
THE LIVING CHRONOLOGY

DAVID MARCUM

Like so many Sherlockians, I started young. I acquired my first Holmes volume, an abridged copy of *The Adventures*, when I was ten in the mid-1970s. But I wasn't prompted to read it until I came across *A Study in Terror* (1965) on television a short time later. I jumped in and read my only Holmes book, and there was no going back. I found a paperback of *The Return*, and read about Holmes's return from the Great Hiatus before I even knew why he was gone. I borrowed ahead on my allowance and got the complete Doubleday edition.

Soon after, before I'd read much more of the Canon, I was given William S. Baring-Gould's definitive biography, *Sherlock Holmes of Baker Street* (1962). I bought Nicholas Meyer's *The West End Horror* (1976) and loved it. I began looking for Holmes stories, both Canon and pastiche, wherever I could find them. I quickly determined that some pastiches followed the traditional model, and sadly, some didn't.

Right from the start, I've played the Game with deadly seriousness, and it was quickly established in my mind that both the pitifully few original 60 stories presented by Watson's first literary agent, Arthur Conan Doyle, and so many of those others by later literary agents, had equal importance. The Canon is the wire core of the rope, and all the pastiches are the strands wound around it. I, like most of the rest of the world, had no doubts that Holmes was the world's greatest detective. But showing *why* he was in just canonical stories was not enough.

As I grew, I knew enough to buy Holmes books when I ran across them, because I might not ever find them again. My collection grew and grew, now encompassing novels, short stories, radio and television episodes, movies and scripts, comics and unpublished manuscripts, and fan fiction. In my thirties, I went back to school for a second degree in civil engineering, and this gave me access to the internet, the university inter-library loan program, and unlimited printing in the computer lab, which allowed me to seek out and print every traditional pastiche on the web that I could find—and I was good at finding them, along with tracking down many other pastiches which had previously escaped my attention.

Before long, with the books I'd bought over the past several de-cades, along with the online stories I'd found, I had more than a thousand adventures. All were traditional Holmes stories—no alternative universe tales for me, thank you!—waiting for me to dive into. And I did. In the mid 1990's, I started reading all my old favorites, and all the new things I'd acquired over the previous few years. Along the way, I was making notes in a small binder I'd assembled, with maps of England and London, noting the dates that each story took place, in and around the Baring-Gould chronology. (I don't agree with everything that Baring-Gould proposed, but he's a great jumping-off place, and he explains things better than some other chronologists who seem to work solely on intuition.)

After I finished this great read-through of all my Holmes stories, I realized that I had a rough chronology—not just of the Canon, but of *all* of Holmes's career. There are many canonical chronologies (I believe that I have all of them) and too many people get off in the weeds of just trying to systematize and analyze those few 60 stories. I had constructed a chronology that showed the *entire* lives of Holmes and Watson, from birth to death.

When I finished, I was still in a Holmes mood, so I started again, this time at the chronological beginning, refining my notes, and working in new stories that I'd added to my collection in the meantime. At the eventual end of this next pass through all these stories, my chronology was more polished and much bigger. And I was still in a Holmes state of mind—I always am, really—so I kept reading and adding more and more traditional stories to the big picture.

I've found, when looking at the overall gestalt of these various stories, that they all fit together like threads in a Great Holmes Tapestry. Often, one story will have just a breakfast conversation on a given day, and then nothing else will happen. Actually, a lot happened in other parts of that day, related to other cases. But Watson, in his wisdom, only pulls out those threads that are relevant to the tale that he's telling from the big tangled skein.

When reading stories to see how they fit, I break them down by novel, short story, chapter, or even paragraph into the correct year, month, day, and even hour. The hard work is done now, and I've found that when reading new adventures, they quickly sort themselves into the right place.

In the twenty-plus years that I've been constructing this chronology, I've created a living document, well over 600 pages of small, dense text that will never actually be finished, because new tales about our heroes are constantly being pulled out of that amazing tin dispatch-box. Many people have asked if I'll publish it, but I'd hate to draw a line under it that way, since it would immediately be out of date. Also, a lot of "editors" of Watson's notes might not like it when they see how I disagree with them in certain places. You see, I include notes about things that are incorrect, such as when they have a case in the wrong year, or have Watson publishing in the *Strand* in the 1880s, before that magazine was even in business, or when they have Watson living in Paddington when he was actually in Kensington. And there are worse mistakes. Some of these editors make egregious errors that simply don't fit with the big picture, either from ignorance or to suit their own agendas. If it's too big of a mistake it cannot be excused or rationalized, and it doesn't go into the chronology.

Rationalizing is a big part of it. There were a lot of giant rats encountered by Holmes and Watson, as well as red leeches and boulevard assassins named Huret. One must figure out the correct explanation—for example, in 1894, there was apparently a whole nest of Hurets whom Holmes defeated. In 1895, there were quite a few tobacco millionaires in London, and Watson lumped all of their different narratives under the name John Vincent Harden.

Watson did a lot of obfuscating, likely for a number of reasons—national security, protection of the innocent, or simply carelessness. One cannot take his notes at face value. In some cases, his handwriting caused problems, such as the conflicting dates in *The Sign of the Four* and "The Red Headed League," or when he places "Wisteria Lodge" in 1892, while Holmes is missing during the Great Hiatus. Some intelligent reasoning has to occur to correctly place both the canonical tales and the later stories, and this essay, with its limited word count, is sadly not the place to explain all that. But trust me, it all fits together—amazingly so.

After reading and chronologicizing all of these thousands of adventures for so long, I was finally able to "edit" some of Watson's tales myself, to positive responses. This led to the idea of soliciting tales for a new collection of Holmes stories that I would edit, with the royalties going to the Stepping Stones School at Undershaw, one of Doyle's former homes. This now ongoing series of books, *The MX Book of New Sherlock Holmes Stories*, has raised funds in over five figures to help support the school and its activities. In addition, it has brought me into contact with dozens of other "editors" of Watson's notes from around the world. This has been amazing for me, as I previously enjoyed my studies of the Master in solitude for decades.

Since I was 19, I've worn a deerstalker as my only hat, from fall to winter, wherever I go—to work, to the store, to the movies or on walks, to church, on camping trips and hikes—and in all that time, no one in the eastern Tennessee area in which I've always lived has ever come up and said, "Sherlock Holmes? I like him too!" (One person did smugly, if ignorantly, call me "Inspector Clouseau.") By meeting the participating authors in the MX anthologies, both in person and through the internet, I've connected with some really amazing folks, proving to me that Holmes people are the best people!

Still, to me, it all comes back to the stories, both original and new. Some people are Sherlockians because they love to study all aspects of the Canon, and *just* the Canon. Others are in it as a social activity, with Holmes being the common starting point. But I'm here for what Holmes actually *did*, and after assembling and maintaining the chronology now for so many years, I've realized that he did a lot more than what literary agent Doyle shared with us. Pastiches sometimes aren't for everyone, and keeping a chronology of this magnitude certainly isn't. After all, some people are overwhelmed trying to keep track of just 60 stories, let alone thousands.

But for me, it adds even more life to that amazing detective and doctor, and I wouldn't have missed it!

David Marcum (Maryville, Tennessee) has collected thousands of traditional Holmes pastiches, including novels, short stories, radio and television episodes, movies, and other items. He has written many such stories himself, and edits the continuing *MX Book of New Sherlock Holmes Stories*. He is a civil engineer.

THE ADVENTURE OF
THE STEPPING STONES

STEVE EMECZ

In the last decade, the Sherlock Holmes publishing world has expanded exponentially. Pastiches have always been popular, but fueled by the new film and television franchises there are tens of millions of new Sherlock Holmes fans. My firm, MX Publishing, is one of the publishers that have ridden that wave. It's been a fascinating journey that has introduced me to some brilliant Sherlockians. But it's not been without its challenges.

My wife, Sharon, and I originally set up MX in 2006 to publish mainly NLP (Neurolinguistic Programming) books for children with learning disabilities. Things took a somewhat different direction two years later when I was approached to produce a fascinating book which reviewed the entire Holmes Canon. *Eliminate the Impossible* grabbed my attention, quite beyond the clever title. Alistair Duncan had produced a riveting review of the Arthur Conan Doyle stories and the actors who had portrayed the main characters, and had been brutally frank. Previous Canon analyses had generally been quite forgiving to the weaker stories, but Alistair pulled no punches. With his outspoken book, our Sherlock Holmes publishing range had begun. In the next two years, we produced multiple historical and biographical works including two ACD biographies by Alistair, one of which (*The Norwood Author*) won the Howlett Literary Award (Sherlock Holmes Book of the Year) in 2011. Alistair completed the trilogy of biographies with *No Better Place* last year, covering ACD's controversial later life.

The release of the first Warner Brothers *Sherlock Holmes* movie in 2009, followed shortly by the BBC *Sherlock* series, led to a significant increase in approaches for Sherlock Holmes fiction. Fast forward to 2016 and MX has more than 100 authors with 250 books, and enjoys fans in more than 50 countries. One significant factor in our growth has been the massive changes in the publishing world. It seems that every couple of years, seismic shifts hit the industry: the move from bookstores to online (led by Amazon), from bulk printing to POD (Print on Demand), from traditional marketing to social media, from print to e-books, and lately to audiobooks. By being a small, independent press we have been able to pivot to a certain extent in response to the changing environment.

Sharon and I, with one part-time administrative assistant, run MX in our spare time—spare being defined as in the morning before work, in the evening when we get home and at the weekend—as a vehicle to support two key causes. The first is Happy Life Children's Home, a children's rescue centre in Nairobi, Kenya. The program rescues abandoned babies from the streets of Nairobi, and in the last 15 years has saved the lives of more than 400 babies. The ultimate goal is to have the kids adopted, but some naturally end up staying with Happy Life long-term. We have spent the last four Christmases in Nairobi volunteering at the centre, and the three weeks we spend with the kids are the best of our year. The program has expanded to a second centre in the village of Juja Farm where Happy Life have built a church and school and now house 60 of the older children. There are a host of projects we're working on with them, including the building of a medical centre. In 2015 my wife and I wrote and published *The Happy Life Story*, which tells the amazing story of the program that has grown from saving four children initially to a large organisation in just 15 years.

The second project we are able to support is Stepping Stones School at Undershaw. This has brought me into a wonderful circle of Sherlockians passionate about the future of Sir Arthur's former home at Hindhead, Surrey. Since 2009 we've been fundraising, originally for the protection of Undershaw itself (partnering with the Undershaw Preservation Trust), and since 2014 working with the DFN Foundation on restoration projects as the house has been turned into the new home for Stepping Stones School for several dozen children with learning disabilities. I'm proud to now be a patron of the school, and we continue to work to raise funds and awareness for Undershaw's new role.

So, what have been the most exciting projects we've been involved with? It's difficult to know where to start, but perhaps it's best to talk about the largest. *The MX Book of New Sherlock Holmes Stories* is the brainchild of writer and editor extraordinaire David Marcum. What started as an idea for a "small anthology" for Undershaw that expanded beyond our own author base has become a phenomenon. With five volumes, nearly 2,000 pages, and 100 authors already, as of early 2017, and two more volumes already in the making, it's the largest collection of new Sherlockian stories ever compiled. David is a tough taskmaster, too—all the stories have to be traditional pastiches set in the canonical timelines. Volume V, *Christmas Adventures*, published late in 2016, is a hefty 560-plus pages with 30 new stories. It's been an amazing collection to be involved with, and with all authors donating their royalties to Stepping Stones it provides a great support too.

Through our association with Undershaw we have run dozens of fundraising events, including a Guinness World Record attempt at bringing together the biggest crowd of people dressed as Sherlock Holmes. We had half a dozen TV crews in attendance for that one. There have also been live theatre performances and the Great Sherlock Holmes Debates which brought together experts from all over the world to debate the merits of the new films and television programs. It's been great to meet lots of eminent Sherlockians—too many to mention in case I leave anyone out, but I would like to thank Alistair Duncan, David Marcum, Phil Growick, Roger

Johnson, Luke Kuhns, Bonnie MacBird, Dan Andriacco, and Jay Ganguly for their help and friendship over the last decade.

One series that has been a delight to work on has been the graphic novels of Petr Kopl. I have the wonderful Jay Ganguly to thank for that. Jay implored me to translate Petr's amazing art from his native Czech into English. We started with *A Scandal in Bohemia*, which had won the Czech Republic Comic Book of the Year Award, and we used Kickstarter to raise awareness and funds for the tough job of translating from Czech to English. It proved a big hit and we have published three more of his works (*Hound of the Baskervilles*, *The Final Problem*, and *The Lost World*).

A very different product, and one that has certainly grown our fan base amongst younger Sherlockians, has been the performance biographies of Benedict Cumberbatch. *Benedict Cumberbatch London and Hollywood* last November was the third book in four years reviewing his work—of which BBC *Sherlock* is a central part. The first book (*Benedict Cumberbatch: In Transition*) was also translated into Japanese, Chinese, and Polish, which helped us reach out into new territories.

As of early 2017, we publish four or five new books each month. We hope that will continue, and we're excited to see whether the rapid growth in audiobooks we've seen will expand beyond the United States, where it is strongest. We'd like to do more foreign licensing. We have an amazing partnership with Mondadori (Italy's largest publisher) who have taken a couple of dozen of our novels, and one with Jaico in India. With the fourth series of BBC's *Sherlock* just aired, and CBS's *Elementary* going strong, the future looks good for Sherlock Holmes fans. The challenge will be the publishing industry itself, which continues to be a tough and rapidly changing area in which to operate.

Steve Emecz (London, England) describes himself as a social enterprise entrepreneur. Alongside his day job in e-commerce he runs MX Publishing, which since 2009 has become one of the world's largest independent publishers of Sherlockian books.

THE ADVENTURE OF THE ANONYMOUS SKETCHBOOK

REBECCA ROMNEY

Rare book dealers make a living by knowing what others do not. Yes, the same could be said of the surgeon, the lawyer, the teacher. But in the case of the rare book dealer, it's the seemingly extraneous details, the ones others overlook, that form the very foundation of our trade.

A.S.W. Rosenbach, the most famous antiquarian book dealer of the 20th century, loved to recount dramatic examples of this principle. For example, in 1923, he made special note of an unremarkable publication, a "dull theological work" that was described only in broad strokes by the auction house. Because of his extensive reading and memory for details, Rosenbach was able to identify this imprint as the Eliot Indian Bible—the first Bible printed in the American colonies. He purchased it for $250; just a year later a fully described copy sold for $34,000. The rare book dealer's method is a form of living by one's wits. It's just a bit less street urchins (like the Baker Street Irregulars) and more bibliographies, collation formulae, and watermark catalogs.

The other side of the equation is the rare book collector, whose habits betray certain Sherlockian traits. Indeed, I do not think it is a coincidence that many Sherlockians collect in one form or another. Collecting is an excuse to study minutiae and develop expertise in niche topics. You know, those topics that make your friends raise a single eyebrow while you suddenly remember to pause for air mid-rapture. The difference between collectors and hoarders (weary loved ones, take note) is that collectors seek to create systems. Their ultimate goal is to organize their data into a narrative. One cannot make bricks without clay; collectors hunt for that clay.

Remarkably, the Sherlockian community as a whole promotes collecting through a robust cycle of production, distribution, and preservation of material related to Holmes. These objects range from the highest levels of the rare book world—a *Hound of the Baskervilles* in the dust jacket, or an original Sidney Paget illustration—down to ephemera saved from scion society events, and everything in between. We'll save napkins if they retain scribbles from a Person of Interest. Note too that, for us, such a Person doesn't have to be a famous author; he or she could simply be a beloved member of a Sherlockian society.

In this hunting and gathering we see evidence of one of my favorite traits of Sherlock Holmes: the long shadows he casts. From pastiches to playing cards, the man and his mysteries inspire others to creativity in a variety matched by few other literary characters. We Sherlockians become inspired; we produce; we collect; we organize it into something new; again we become inspired. We are a self-feeding cycle. Each trip around we find another way to engage with the texts, with each other, even with our cherished memories of previous cycles.

Collectors, in imposing their idiosyncratic order, know that sometimes it is simply new framing that can illuminate discoveries. This is one of the reasons "The Sussex Vampire" is one of my favorite Holmes stories. While everyone else is distracted by the exotic story of vampirism, Holmes knows to look for another way to frame the data. Our detective is able to find the solution because he looks at the facts with an entirely different perspective from that of others. "Did it not occur to you that a bleeding wound may be sucked for some other purpose than to draw the blood from it?" Once we have reframed the context, our assumptions betray themselves for what they are. That clears the path for a new explanation, one that accurately represents the facts. In his memoir, Dr. Rosenbach explains one reason the other bidders overlooked the Eliot Indian Bible: they made the assumption that the publication place, listed only as "Cambridge," meant England, not Massachusetts.

I linger on the philosophy of the collector because we rare book dealers are collectors ourselves. Some of us deny it. Yet we follow the same steps: we gather, we organize, we find the narrative. The difference is that we accomplish these tasks in order to sell the books to someone else. But even in selling our books, we use methods that echo the strategies of Holmes. We bring to bear our specialized knowledge and observation of seemingly unimportant details not just to find the books, but to write our catalog descriptions. These humble paragraphs constitute our big reveal, just like Holmes's announcement of the solution to the mystery.

That moment carries a bit of magic simply because Holmes skips all the steps in between. Edgar Allan Poe consciously crafted this idea into story structure, a puzzle in which the author deliberately leaves out the logical steps leading to a conclusion. He called the result "tales of ratiocination" (wonder why that didn't stick). Yet the whole process seems mundane when the steps in between are revealed, as Holmes himself was well aware. "Watson, confess yourself utterly taken aback," Holmes says in "The Dancing Men," "because in five minutes you will say that it is all so absurdly simple."

Those steps in between do make it look simple, but they are the heart of the method. The rest is simply showmanship (admittedly not unknown to Holmes or to rare book dealers). Those are the steps one must walk in the dark, without the path already laid out. When I use this method in research, I call it "Sherlocking," with apologies to Mr. Poe.

I Sherlocked a book the other day, a stunning early 20th-century sketchbook reproducing an artist's observations of art and architecture from across England and Europe. Neither previous owners nor scholars could identify the artist of many of the lovely watercolors, which were mysteriously initialed "S.K.M." Who was this S.K.M.? Even a printed postcard, laid into the sketchbook, included an attribution "by S.K.M." only.

After some creative Googling, I came across a digitized copy of Richard Glazier's *Historic Ornament* (1899), the most famous art textbook used in the early 20th century. I was surprised to discover my first clue: in many of the illustrations, the manner of captioning, down to the style of lettering, mimicked what I saw in this sketchbook. Moreover, many of the illustrations were also labeled "S.K.M." Did Glazier borrow sketches made by a friend for this book, then include that attribution where required?

Clearly there was a connection of some kind between Glazier and the sketchbook in front of me. But what? I researched Glazier a bit further and learned he was a member of the South Kensington Circle, an artists' group I had never heard of. I did know a few of the other names associated with it, however: Owen Jones and Henry Cole, two instrumental figures in the founding of the Victoria & Albert Museum. This anonymous sketchbook was suddenly becoming quite intriguing.

Now I had material to Google even more creatively. I focused on this Circle and the works depicted in the sketchbook. Bingo: one of the stained-glass pieces appeared in a 19th-century notice that announced its acquisition by the South Kensington Museum. I hadn't heard of this museum before, so naturally I had to follow that trail. Then I came upon something unexpected: an historic name change. Around the turn of the twentieth century, the South Kensington Museum was renamed the Victoria & Albert Museum.

Theory: "S.K.M." wasn't a person. It was a place, now known as the V&A. Or so I suspected. Before sharing my hunch with my bookselling partner, I had to cut through the red herrings, including a printed piece of ephemera that implied "S.K.M." was in fact an artist. I needed a clear case, not circumstantial evidence, and so far I hadn't found any documents that stated "S.K.M." was the standard abbreviation used for the museum. Furthermore, this sketchbook dated from the early 20th century, *after* the name change.

In search of direct proof, I pulled up a 19th-century catalogue of the holdings of the Victoria & Albert Museum. I looked up items in the sketchbook labeled "S.K.M." The Chimney of Tattershall Castle? Not in Tattershall. The "Adoration of the Magi" stained-glass window from the cathedral at Cortona? Not in Cortona. The "The Framework of a window in oak / From an old house / at Delft Holland / Dutch 1537 / S.K.M. / 5 Dec. 04?" Not in Delft. All at the Victoria & Albert.

Is it obvious now? With only the straight line of narrative describing the relevant details, you see it clearly and quickly, just as one does reading a summary of a Sherlock Holmes story. But at the time I had a sketchbook with more questions than answers, and no easy leads. With so many different possibilities, it wasn't so obvious: not to the owners and scholars who came before me, and not immediately to me. I had to track down the truth by chasing seemingly irrelevant facts.

Yet with the connections we were able to draw to one of the most important museums in England, in the end we were rightfully able to ask much, much more than we paid for it. This is how a rare book dealer Sherlocks a book in order to make a living.

As a Sherlockian, any time I search for the hidden narrative, the truth behind the mystery, I think about how Sherlock Holmes solved crimes. We collect the data that others overlook, then we present it in a way that allows them to be part of the discovery too. Yes, all rare book dealers are, each in our own way, Sherlockians.

Rebecca Romney (Philadelphia, Pennsylvania) is a rare book dealer at Honey & Wax Booksellers, the author (with JP Romney) of *Printer's Error: Irreverent Stories from Book History*, and the rare book specialist on the History Channel's television show *Pawn Stars*.

THE ADVENTURE OF
THE GASLIGHT CLASSICS

MICHAEL DIRDA

As readers of my book *On Conan Doyle* know, I first encountered Sherlock Holmes in a paperback copy of *The Hound of the Baskervilles,* purchased from the TAB Book Club in the late 1950s. Back then the club's newsprint sale catalogues were distributed to the older kids in elementary school, and I always zeroed in on any title that promised thrills and adventure. In fourth grade I had devoured *Mystery of the Piper's Ghost, The Spanish Cave Mystery, Treasure at First Base,* and many others, but none of them had ever featured a hero like Sherlock Holmes. Having bought *The Hound* at the beginning of fifth grade, I raced through Holmes and Watson's exploits in Dartmoor, then checked out the Christopher Morley-prefaced complete adventures from the local branch library. Only after I'd finished the 60 canonical cases did I raise my head to look around. Might there be other detective stories anywhere near as good?

As it turned out, there were—sort of. For instance, a few months later I noticed that the TAB Book Club was offering a paperback entitled *The Thinking Machine: Adventures of a Mastermind,* by Jacques Futrelle. According to the accompanying write-up, Professor S.F.X. Van Dusen declared that he could escape from any maximum security cell inside a week. Could he possibly do it? And how? A month later, I sat down to read "The Problem of Cell Thirteen," which to this day remains one of my favorite mystery stories. I especially love the end, in which Van Dusen reveals that, besides the method he actually employed, there were two other ways he could have escaped.

Alas, the other "Thinking Machine" stories weren't quite so good as that masterpiece, but I soon found another detective, quite different in character, who nearly did rival Holmes. I was sitting in catechism class, feeling rather bored as usual, when I picked up the latest issue of a Catholic youth magazine. Its cover featured what I initially thought must be a tedious religious article, but—miraculously, so to speak—"The Blue Cross" turned out to be something quite different. I devoured this first of G.K. Chesterton's Father Brown stories, then borrowed from the public library downtown an omnibus of all the cases solved by this innocuous yet utterly brilliant little cleric.

Surprisingly, even my tiny school library helped fan my growing passion for golden-age whodunits. On its otherwise rather Spartan shelves I happened upon Howard Haycraft's *The Boy's Book of Detective Stories* and several of those oversized Alfred Hitchcock anthologies for young people with titles like *Spellbinders in Suspense*. All provided good reading, but only the blind but debonair Max Carrados, created by Ernest Bramah, came close to Holmes, The Thinking Machine, or Father Brown.

As was my practice in those idyllic days, I regularly visited Whalen's Drug Store to scan its racks of comics, magazines, and paperbacks, then treat myself to a nickel Coke at the soda fountain. One Saturday evening I was spinning the paperback rack when I noticed a cover depicting a hunter fending off a tyrannosaur with the butt end of a rifle. When I looked more closely at *The Lost World* I saw that its author was Sir Arthur Conan Doyle.

Professor George Edward Challenger's expedition into the jungles of South America proved just as thrilling as what were then my two favorite adventure novels, H. Rider Haggard's *King Solomon's Mines* and Jules Verne's *Journey to the Center of the Earth*. There was clearly something about these books, and others like them from the late 19th and early 20th centuries, that deeply appealed to me. But what?

I forgot about that question for the next 40 years. But after I was invested into the Baker Street Irregulars I began to think again about the allure of fiction from this gaslight era. At one of my first BSI banquets I met Barbara and Christopher Roden, who were the driving force behind the Arthur Conan Doyle Society, its mission being to promote the whole range of writing by "the greatest natural-born storyteller of the age." Through the Rodens I learned about the comic and wistful stories of Brigadier Gerard, enjoyed a surprisingly entertaining novel about female emancipation called *Beyond the City*, and acquired copies of Conan Doyle's autobiographical *Memories and Adventures* and his celebration of reading, *Through the Magic Door*.

As it happened, the Rodens were also the publishers of Ash-Tree Press, which specialized in producing handsome, well-made volumes of classic ghost stories. Among my most treasured volumes is Ash-Tree's *A Pleasing Terror: The Complete Supernatural Writings of M.R. James*, with a warm inscription from the publishers. I soon recognized that what the Sherlock Holmes cases are to detective fiction, M.R. James's unsettling "ghost stories of an antiquary" are to supernatural literature—the gold standard.

Through *All-Hallows: The Journal of the Ghost Story Society*—a periodical edited by the industrious Rodens—I also grew aware of several other small presses that focused on mysteries, adventure novels, and weird tales. Night Shade Books brought out the complete Joseph Jorkens "club stories" of Lord Dunsany, as well as a six-volume edition of the poetic fantasies and science fiction of Clark Ashton Smith. Tartarus Press ranged widely but never too far from Arthur Machen and the English tradition of the "strange story," as represented by Algernon Blackwood, Walter de la Mare, L. P. Hartley, Sarban, Robert Aickman, Reggie Oliver, and Mark Valentine. Hippocampus issued new editions of H.P. Lovecraft and the authors who had influenced him as well as the *Weird Tales* stalwarts he corresponded with. I was soon reading related scholarship and criticism too, so much so that my copies of E.F. Bleiler's *Guide to Supernatural Fiction* and Jacques Barzun and Wendell Taylor's *A Catalogue of Crime* are now held together with duct tape.

More and more, I realized that the heyday of the Holmes stories was also the period when our modern genre literatures were born. Science fiction, detective stories, modern children literature, classic swashbucklers, eerie tales of all kinds—they all emerged during the lifetime of Arthur Conan Doyle (1859-1930), who, not incidentally, contributed to every one of these areas of popular literary entertainment. But he was only *primus inter pares*, the first among equals.

Over the last half-dozen years, I've been reading the work of these storytellers in earnest, though "earnest" seems the wrong word for books that deliver so much pleasure. I've devoured Guy Boothby's novels about the mysterious Dr. Nikola and his search for the elixir of immortality, the witty children's fantasies of E. Nesbit, and such early spy thrillers as Erskine Childers's *The Riddle of the Sands*, John Buchan's *The Power-House*, and E. Phillips Oppenheim's *The Great Impersonation*. I've shivered at the supernatural tales of Vernon Lee, Arthur Machen, and E.F. Benson, explored the lesser-known novels of Rider Haggard, thrilled to Anthony Hope's *The Prisoner of Zenda* and Stanley Weyman's *Under the Red Robe*, and reveled in Baroness Orczy's adventures of the Scarlet Pimpernel and Rafael Sabatini's Captain Blood. I've even grown fond of those gentleman-thieves, Grant Allen's Colonel Clay, E.W. Hornung's Raffles, and—looking across the Channel—Maurice Leblanc's Arsène Lupin. After rereading Bram Stoker's *Dracula* I found myself equally impressed by the other chilling masterpiece of 1897, Richard Marsh's *The Beetle*. I laughed, as who could not, over Jerome K. Jerome's *Three Men in a Boat* and the early stories of Conan Doyle's most gifted disciple, P.G. Wodehouse. I learned that Robert Louis Stevenson and Lloyd Osbourne's *The Wrong Box* was a comic masterpiece and that J.M. Barrie produced other fantasies—"Mary Rose," "Dear Brutus," *Farewell, Miss Julie Logan*—almost as haunting as "Peter Pan." H.G. Wells certainly rivaled Kipling in storytelling power, and I explored other writers of scientific romance, including George Griffith, J.D. Beresford, S. Fowler Wright, and Olaf Stapledon. To my mind, R. Austin Freeman's Dr. Thorndyke wasn't just a scientific detective, he was far more entertaining than that faint praise would suggest, as was, for that matter, Edgar Wallace, at least in such books as *The Four Just Men* and *The Green Archer*. Even largely forgotten writers, I realized, could produce masterpieces—consider C.J. Cutcliffe Hyne's *The Lost Continent* or any of John Meade Falkner's three novels, each in a different genre: *Moonfleet*, *The Lost Stradivarius*, and *The Nebuly Coat*.

All this pleasure and reading excitement, I ultimately owe to Holmes and Watson. Becoming a Sherlockian opened up the entire world of late Victorian and Edwardian popular fiction for me. Had I not discovered the great detective when I was a boy and, years later, been invested into the Baker Street Irregulars, I don't know that I would have ever filled my house with all these wonderful books. And they are wonderful. As I can affirm, if you're looking for classic adventure, mystery, and romance it should always be, give or take a couple of decades, 1895.

Michael Dirda (Washington, DC) is a Baker Street Irregular and a Pulitzer Prize-winning literary journalist. He is the author of the memoir *An Open Book*, of *On Conan Doyle*, which received a 2012 Edgar Award, and of four collections of essays. He contributed the introduction to the Penguin Classics Deluxe Edition of the four Sherlock Holmes novels.

THE ADVENTURE OF
THE GUILTY PLEASURE

TATYANA DYBINA

One lovely morning I was sitting in my armchair reading *The Memoirs of Sherlock Holmes*—although after writing that sentence I instantly recall that the morning wasn't lovely at all and, in fact, was a stormy night. All the same, what matters is that I was reading *The Memoirs*.

By no means was it my first acquaintance with these stories. That happy moment took place some 30 years ago (and the only thing in this world that doesn't let me write "40" is vanity). However, these stories were being read from the beginning to the end, then from the end to the beginning, and even from the middle to some point of the narrative at which I was told it was time for dinner. Such a deep and continuous plunge left me somewhat disoriented and dizzy, but I definitely knew better than to contemplate the mystery of a once married and then unmarried character. Some whim of those inscrutable adults, that was my verdict.

There was more than that in these stories. There were spies, cyphers, and coded messages. There were quite informative mud stains, footprints, broken twigs, hemoglobin precipitation and other delightful stuff of the sort that brings a primary school girl into a state of euphoria. Cyphers were waiting to be used just for the sake of sheer pleasure of secrecy, footprints needed to be studied (with the help of a magnifying glass, preferably), soil samples were waiting to be collected and examined. History and literature classes were filled with writing coded messages in some recently invented cypher, passing them to another victim of the madness, and deciphering an answer.

My parents did not go so far as to scribble a list of curious facts about me back then, but I'm quite sure it would have included nil at history, profound knowledge of anything that burns or explodes (alas, poor carpet in my friend's room), and the same thing with poisonous plants.

Yet this story doesn't end there.

Even back then, at the end of the last century, there was television, which means there were Sherlock Holmes stories on screen. They were adaptations with Vasily Livanov mostly—a solidly built production of the Soviet filmmaking industry. Originally conceived as a story of two equal characters (Watson in this adaptation had his fair share of the screenwriter's attention, which was almost unheard of before the Granada series hit the screens), these episodes amused their audience with Watson practicing his own investigating skills (the good doctor suspected Holmes of being a criminal), Watson disguised as a clergyman in the name of a case, Watson getting arrested right before the Great Detective's timely return from the murky depths of the Reichenbach Falls. After having met in "A Study in Scarlet", the characters walked hand in hand through adventures, barely escaped the danger of being collared, made the audience sob in "The Final Problem" and again in "The Empty House", played hide-and-seek, and finally made the long-suffering viewers cry into their drinks as Watson left his friend for a wife in "The Sign of the Four". This mini-series directed by Igor Maslennikov had an enormous impact on the audience: a significant number of Russian-speaking TV viewers still consider Vasily Livanov and Vitaly Solomin to be the definitive Holmes and Watson. And I haven't yet mentioned all the jokes about Holmes and Watson that became popular after the series premiere, most of them indecent.

Besides Livanov, I spotted Basil Rathbone on screen once or twice and was deeply shocked by the absence of a Victorian entourage and by the involvement of Nazis instead of good old respectable criminals. These films were aired with insufferably long pauses between episodes, so the hiatus effect was my constant companion. To fill these exhausting intervals with a tolerable substitute, I started to read the Holmes stories anew. To my utmost surprise, the main character of these stories was not the same Great Detective of the movies. After brief consideration, I saw that the difference was not bad at all. Then came the new, previously undiscovered pleasure of getting more Holmes for the holidays…sorry, that's a pastiche collection title.

And then came the year 1986 when, rather unexpectedly, the 20th century approached. That wasn't an ordinary chronological perversion, not at all. That was just the last part of Maslennikov's series, aired under the title "The Twentieth Century Approaches". The final part of the story was long awaited by an enthusiastic audience who had not been satisfied either with Watson leaving his friend for a wife, nor with the director leaving his characters just like that. It sends a viewer to those times when Holmes unsuccessfully pretended to be retired, wore a goatee beard, and caught German spies. Although screenwriters made a neat job weaving together "His Last Bow" with multiple other stories, it wasn't 1895 any more, which was regrettable. 221B filled with furniture in dusty covers looked like the scene of a nightmare. Needless to say, I grabbed the book of Holmes stories again right after the movie ended. At least there still were these ghostly gas lamps that fail at 20 feet, a lonely hansom, and other good old Victorian paraphernalia.

Some years later (more than 20, actually, after I had had a rather unpleasant experience of losing a job and searching for a new one), I was commuting from home to office translating Vincent Starrett's "221B" and rereading Holmes stories to get some inspiration. It is not that both processes ran smoothly at the same time. While standing at a bus stop or train station I was trying to make legendary images fit the strict metric pattern. They weren't too cooperative, by the way, so after I boarded the bus my attention turned back to the book where the legendary images weren't so legendary. With unfettered delight I realized that these characters chuckled, wriggled in their chairs, definitely enjoyed mutual teasing, pretended to be smart and so forth. These small yet delightful moments became one more pleasure of reading Holmes stories.

Once again I found myself reading that mysteriously migrating scene from "The Cardboard Box". Neither story nor scene was among my favorites so far. While Holmes was channeling Dupin to Watson's amusement, I wondered whether the scene had been written just to build up the necessary word length. To my exasperation, the weather beyond my window had nothing in common with the sunlight in the text. And then, quite suddenly, it occurred to me that I knew precisely what that scene was about. It wasn't about Dupin, deduction, an unframed portrait, or Holmes's usual boasting. It was about being comfortable with one another's company, waiting behind half-drawn blinds for the summer heat to subside, talking about everything and anything, relishing the last lazy minutes before the next case. All in all, it was about friendship.

Then I found myself thinking about a remarkably curious instance of the observer effect. It is not that the mere act of reading alters the text in this case. Yet it looks like these stories, after being polished by eyes of several generations of readers, after enduring the enthusiastic if tiresome attention of assorted artists across the world, have become a sort of magic mirror that reflects whatever the observer wants. Beautiful things and curious events, a place of safety and something worth studying, a playground full of wonders, all emerge in their depth. And when all other reflections melt away, there will be the observer. This is exactly what a respectable mirror is meant to do, after all.

Thus the act of reading turns into a magic journey akin to introspection. By no means is it a once-in-a-lifetime experience, for although the mirror does not change, the observer does. It's one of the most curious things about reading Sherlock Holmes stories, as well as one of the simplest pleasures. Perhaps it's a guilty one as well. But aren't the most vivid human pleasures of the same sort?

Tatyana Dybina (Moscow, Russian Federation) is a freelance photographer and a writer. She is also a proud member of several assorted Sherlockian Facebook communities, but claims that she has done nothing remarkable yet.

CPSIA information can be obtained
at www.ICGtesting.com
Printed in the USA
BVHW081956040319
541770BV00001B/117/P

9 781479 435753